Who Will Hold the Ladder?

Katherine King

Who Will Hold the Ladder?

© Katherine King 2018

This book is a work of fiction. Named locations are used fictitiously, and characters and incidents are the product of the author's imagination. Any resemblance to actual events or places or persons, living or dead, is entirely coincidental.

Published by
Lighthouse Christian Publishing
SAN 257-4330
5531 Dufferin Drive
Savage, Minnesota, 55378
United States of America

www.lighthousechristianpublishing.com

Acknowledgements:

Many people deserve recognition for their kindness, encouragement and faith in me that I could do this.   There is no possible way "<u>Who Will Hold the Ladder?</u>," would have been written if I had not endured the hardships of life, the patience and support of my friends and family and the joy of making memories. To Phyllis Moore, who agreed to "go on this journey" with me as I sought her out unbelievably, through grief counseling at a local funeral home. I was grieving a loss. A loss of me.   I had been traumatized, a victim of domestic violence for over five years. Though this was a different kind of grief counseling for Phyllis, when I briefly summarized those years, she introduced me to "lament," the verbal definition of lament is to grieve audibly; wail, to express sorrow or regret. The noun definition: a feeling or an expression of grief; a lamentation, a song or poem expressing deep grief or mourning. She presented me with many verses of the Psalms that I had read before, but now had new meaning and deep healing for me.

To my children, Amber, Matt and Evan, whom I love dearly, and am proud of each of them.

Most importantly, I want to acknowledge the perseverance of God. My partner in writing this book. A wonderful, merciful, gracious God who chose me when my life was certainly doomed from the beginning, yet, amazingly, He chose me.

Introduction:

Eventually life takes us on a journey from comfort to suffering. Circumstances spin out of our control and we find ourselves in situations we never intended to be. A journey we have to take. One that we may not choose, one that will test our faith and change our lives forever. One that will cause us to stumble or one that will make us climb higher up the ladder towards God.

As I began this journey, I can tell you that many times I questioned myself on what I could I have done different even though deep down inside I know I did my best. At times, through the bruises and emotional scars, I had no say or choice, only fearful moments to endure. Now, there are huge pieces of me scarred and missing.

I would also have to admit that as I went through all the files in preparation for this book, records from doctors, hospitals, counselors, the Department of Social Services (DSS), even my own fragmented journals over a five-year period, painful memories of truth flooded my heart and mind causing me great distress and shedding of many tears. Nevertheless, forcing me to realize what my domestic violence counselor said repeatedly, "When love and pain meet, then the healing begins," slowly I began to realize that we live our lives where the facts hit the feelings and the fact is it had been five years of domestic violence abuse and a new walk had to begin for me, in order to heal those traumatic episodes.

Thousands of people are out there with memories and life experiences far worse than mine, but then there are some very similar to mine. There were moments when I doubted that I would emotionally be able to journey on with the writing of this book. However, driven by the grace of God I surged on towards His leading. "Who Will Hold the Ladder?," is a story of strength, perseverance and the amazing love God had for a little girl whose future held no hope from the beginning of her existence. A story of how God can turn around a genetic generation full of abuse and ugliness to make something good. Many times throughout my life, I have heard people say, "That's just the way my family was, therefore I am," Nevertheless, I am living proof that does not have to be true.

In writing, "Who Will Hold the Ladder?," I learned that the moment God calls ordinary people such as me to do extraordinary things then comes our part as to whether we answer "yes" or "no," Stepping out of the norm literally scared the living daylights out of me once I began to consolidate all of this into a book. Yet, God assured me all the way that He would be with me and give me the words to write. I learned and have grown since the moment I said "yes" to this journey, realizing that being still is sometimes not an option for a Christian.

Chapter One: Out of Fear and into Hope

"It's time, Kathy. We have to take advantage of the weather and daylight," Cindy urged. I knew she was right, but I was scared. The dreaded moment had come. It had been a week since I had filed charges against Daniel. I had put off going to the mountain cabin out of fear. Fear of the memories; fear of what I might find there, a fear so overwhelming it made my heart race. My breathing coming faster as my chest heaved up and down frantically trying to keep up with my racing heartbeat.

Cindy, Gary and I had been friends for many years. This was a second marriage for both of them. Except for the normal struggles of blending families', they fit together like hand and glove. Cindy was petite with curly red hair that fit her quick spirit. Gary was a tall, good 'ol country boy, with a short temper when it came to defending right and wrong. Both were housekeepers at the college where I worked. They shared more than just common careers; they were kindred spirits. Something I had yet to find in a lifelong mate. They were at my wedding to Daniel, and until this past week, I had never confided in them about the abuse. Now, they were here, to take me to the cabin, to check on the unfinished work on the roof, and prepare the cabin for storage of my personal things. The children and my attorney felt the cabin was the most practical place once the arrangements were finalized to remove all my belongings from Daniel's house. Each day I went to work as if nothing had happened, confiding only in Cindy and Gary about the abuse and failure of my marriage.

"Kathy, please we have to leave," Again Cindy pleaded with urgency, her hand on my shoulder. A final glance in the motel mirror showed a shell of a woman I wanted so badly not to be me. My face was pale and thinner, my dark brown eyes empty and expressionless. Absentmindedly, I tucked a strand of my long dark brown hair behind my ear. I felt numb, emotionally drained, fearful about what the future would hold.

Reluctantly, I grabbed the small duffel bag containing the only possessions I had, a few pieces of clothing along with personal items given to me by the motel and hospital.

"I'm ready," I whispered softly, glancing around the motel room, inwardly saying goodbye to what had been my safe haven for the past week. Once we were finished at the cabin, Cindy and Gary would be taking me to my new "home", a small cottage in a town about 30 minutes away. Everyone felt sure Daniel wouldn't be able to find me there. The past five days, family members, friends and my attorney made most of the decisions for me. People who realized I was fragile, barely able to keep working much less make a rational decision.

Fear was my constant companion during the day hours. Fear crept into my dreams every night.

Walking down the long motel corridor to the elevator, I thought of the strength God had given me to courageously stand steadfast when Daniel would call. Phone calls that consisted mostly of accusations and threats, which would abruptly end with me hanging up the receiver. There was no way I could screen my incoming calls at work. Sometimes Daniel called the main line; sometimes he called the second line. I refused to answer the incoming call for fear it was him, allowing it to roll over into my voice mail. If it was him there was either a slam of a receiver or a directive from Daniel to call immediately. As a born again Christian, I was holding on to my faith and God's promises to me.

With dark clouds hovering above us, Cindy gently helped me into the backseat of their car while Gary completed the paperwork for my checkout at the front desk. The air held a dampness that made me shiver. I wondered if I was reacting to the dampness or physical pain. My leg was still sore and tender from the contusion. Absent-mindedly, I fastened the seat belt while glancing across the parking lot. A local family owned tree farm and was setting up a tent and rope fence for their annual Christmas tree sale. Christmas. The Christmas gifts for my children, our decorations from years past, were all being held hostage at Daniel's house. How could I begin to put closure to the past, when Daniel was in possession of both my past and present? Resting my head against the soft, velvety cloth of the backseat headrest, I stared blankly out the window.

A week had passed, since the day I awoke in the wee hours of the morning in a strange motel room with an instant awareness of unbelievable stiffness throughout my body. Almost immediately I felt a sharp pain race like fire down my left leg. The day I painfully struggled into the bathroom and began removing my clothes, the same clothing I had worn since Thanksgiving Day three days prior.

Painstakingly slow, I removed the layers, gasping in pain with every movement. I was like a zombie portrayed in a slow motion horror film. I was alert, I was alive and I could feel.

I was gripped with pain, weak and shaking uncontrollably, having to stop occasionally to breathe. A glance in the bathroom mirror was a sight that made me jump. I hardly recognized myself. A ghostly, pale white face with dried, chapped lips.   My fingers reached up to push the mangled hair from my face, only to stop over a raised bluish-yellow knot on my left forehead. Further investigation through my hair found a hard, tender lump at the back of my head.

Everything was a blur, as I slowly shook my head, trying unsuccessfully to clear the fog that surrounded my brain. Backing away from the mirror, I lowered myself to sit on the side of the bathtub while slowly removing my shoes. Every muscle in my body seemed to fight against any kind of movement. I had no strength as I struggled to remove each shoe. Sitting back upright, to catch my breath, an urge to crawl back into bed overwhelmed me. Yet somehow I knew I had to wake up, I had to move forward.

Each item of clothing removed revealed more bruising. The drop of my shirt illuminated Daniel's fingerprint bruises on both my upper arms.

"Why?," Tears slowly began to stream down my face. "What did I do that was so bad to deserve this?," I was afraid to look at the face in the mirror and hear her response.

Stiffly attempting to stand up, I awkwardly began to remove my pants. Lifting my left leg was the most painful of movements and soon came the revelation it was my body part that took the worst of the abuse.

The sharp leg pain and the bruising, somehow the realization came to me that I would have to have the leg medically examined.

Stepping into the shower, the warm, clean water from the shower head flowed over my abused body yet did little to jar me into awareness as my mind searched for clues of the past three days. A search ending with a fragmented memory of Thanksgiving Day and the days that followed.

Exhausted from bathing, I stepped slowly out of the shower feeling helpless, then embarrassed to realize all that effort only to accomplish putting the same clothes back on.

An hour later, curled up tightly in a fetal position on the examining table, drifting in and out of an exhausting, disturbing sleep, is how the doctor found me as she entered the examination room. I could barely lift my head in acknowledgement of her soft greeting. The walk to the car, the drive to the hospital had taken every ounce of strength left in my body. All I wanted to do was sleep.

"Thank God it's a woman," Was my first drowsy thought as I tried to pull myself somewhat together and focus. The doctor was small in frame, her skin flushed out hospital-white, with her hair pulled back in a long, blond ponytail. Her head was bent down, as she walked by memory towards the small black stool beside the examining table, absorbed in reading the notes entered into the laptop computer by the nurse at intake. Her voice was somewhat mechanical as she began to question me on what happened. Weak, barely audible even to my own ears, my voice sounded strained, like someone else was speaking as I tried to answer. My responses to her questions seemed to ramble, jumbled together, making absolutely no sense even to me. So many, many voids in my memory.

"I didn't push you. You know I didn't push you. You fell on your own. Damn it! Admit it!," Daniel's words resonating in my head, words he had said so many times before. His deep baritone voice, strong and persuasive. I was trapped, pinned in the corner of our bedroom, his fingers digging deep into my upper arms as he violently shook me. His grip so tight I knew bruises would reveal themselves once again. But then, according to Daniel, I bruise easily. His yelling and cursing with his finger just inches from my face.

"You're twisting what happened. You're always twisting everything Janelle and I say and do. Fuck you! You call yourself a Christian. Just look at yourself! All of this is your own damn fault. You make me so mad I could kill you!,"

Confused, I shook my still damp hair, attempting to eliminate the fog.

"Focus, Kathy, focus," I said to myself. Yet, everything was so vague and scrambled.

I know it happened. I felt it, no matter what Daniel said. I told myself as I lay on the white sheets under the heated warm blanket. Tears began to roll out of the corner of my eyes.

Rolling her stool closer to the examining table, the doctor began the physical examine.

"Domestic violence is real," her voice sounded caring, yet firm as she examined my arms, back, legs and neck, her fingers gently gliding as she paused to look closer at each at each swollen bump and bruise.

"It doesn't matter whether he pushed you or not, self-defense is backing away from someone or something that is life threatening to you. You were in danger. The next time," she turned to reach for the lighted scope.

"The next time you may not live," she said sternly as she completed her visual examination.

The wheels from the stool she was sitting on made a loud noise causing me to jump in fear at the sharp, squeaky sound. Everything seemed to make me jump lately.

I watched her movements as she stood at the small counter sink washing her hands. Grabbing a few paper towels from the dispenser, she turned back, and sat down once again on the stool, quietly reading through my medical records on her laptop computer. Medical records that slowly uncovered my life of the past five years.
"You have a rather extensive record of domestic abuse," she broke the silence as she looked up at me.

Looking over her small height, I avoided her eyes, starring at the white sterile wall behind her as tears continued to stream down my cheeks. Then I felt her hand softly stroking my arm, her words firm, yet gentle and kind. "Whether he admits to pushing you or not, is irrelevant; his threatening behavior placed you in fear, causing you to go backwards instinctively. Your back hit the metal stand and you fell. He's the cause of this. Not you,"

I opened my mouth to respond, only to quickly close it, realizing she would never understand what I was feeling or what I had lived through. No one would understand.

Seeing my discomfort and unwillingness to respond, the doctor abruptly turned as if admitting defeat. Leaving me alone once again in the silence of the sterile, white hospital room. Closing my eyes, once again I drifted into sleep.

"Knock, knock," I jumped as the technician came into the room. "I'm here to take you down for x-rays," mechanically he unlocked the wheels, positioned and locked the IV onto the side of the bed. We were in the hallway in what seemed like seconds.

Rolling myself feebly off the table onto the x-ray table caused me to gasp in pain. Every inch of my body stiff and sore. My small, 5'0, 110 lb. frame seemed as if to weigh 200 lbs. as my breathing came heavy and quick from the effort. Holding my breath as a reflex to the pain only hurt worse when I had to exhale. Silently I lay, helpless, obeying the commands from the technician, while listening to each photograph click images of my sore, bruised, abused body.

Viewing my x-rays on the lighted box, the doctor released an audible sigh as she turned to help me sit up. "It was real; it did happen," she said forcing me to sit up and look at the contusion on my leg, then pointing to various sections of the four x-rays. "You have been in shock and disbelief for the past several days, suffering severely from Post-Traumatic Stress Disorder. Again," giving a strong emphasis on the word "AGAIN,"

"Did it ever occur to you that when he abuses you other people are also victimized? Your family, friends, children?," she asked.

"You have been traumatized for the last five years, and this is just another diagnosis in your file: 'extreme control, possessiveness and domestic violence.'" Closing her laptop, she left the room to prepare my instructions for discharge.

"I didn't use to be like this," I thought. "I use to be strong and confident,"

I wanted to reclaim the life I had once upon a time and my identity, but I was scared. Scared for myself, scared for my children.

"You're a fuckin' liar, a damn failure!," Daniel's last words sank deep into my heart. Slowly I sat up on the side of the bed. Then looked down at my leg. "I can never go back," I said to the hospital walls.

"Never. It's over Daniel. Over," not knowing what the future would hold, only knowing this time would be the last time.

Fully dressed, my head held low, I sat on the edge of the examining table, waiting for the discharge papers. Tears came again, this time falling onto the white-speckled floor. Puddles of water. More physical, visible evidence of my pain.

"I'm really sorry, Mrs. Thomas," apologetically, the doctor said as she came through the door and handed me my discharge papers.

"No one can imagine what you've lived through or what you're going through now. Nevertheless, for sure, you are in danger and somehow, someway, you're going to have to escape from this man. Are you sure you're safe? Are you sure you'll be okay? Do you have a place to go?," Her voice full of questions and concern.

She reached out to assist me off the examining table. My head throbbed, as a sharp pain shot up my leg. Taking deep, shaky breaths, I mustered up my best, weak smile, welcoming her assistance as my feet touched the floor.

"I'll be fine," I tried to reassure her, even though, deep down inside, I wondered. "No more, Daniel, no more!," I closed my eyes and sternly told myself. "It's over!"

The discharge papers from the hospital read: "You have a deep contusion. A result of trauma and bleeding in the lower left leg area," Second diagnosis: "Domestic Abuse. Your doctor wants you to seek shelter and counseling. The facts must be faced and the situation changed. Please contact a counselor who works with abused women." Additional Instructions: "Go to local Police Department now."

Arriving back at the motel, I called my daughter, Amber. "Can you come?," Defeated I pleaded after briefly explaining where I was and what had happened. I hated for Amber to see me in such a vulnerable state. I was her mother. I was supposed to be strong, maternal, protecting her, not her protecting me.

A brief short time later, Amber's soft knock on the door awoke me from another fitful sleep. Looking around the motel room, then settling onto my tear stained face, Amber gently took me in her arms as I sobbed uncontrollably into her shoulder. Amber had my brown hair and dark brown eyes, yet she carried her father's height and heftiness. At the age of almost thirty, she was the mother of my beautiful granddaughter, Stephanie. Yet, at that moment, I wasn't the mother. I was a victim, needing support and love. Our roles awkwardly reversed.

From the motel, Amber drove me to the police department where we were directed down a long, dimly lit hallway to the magistrate's office. Ashamed, my head down, tears making a trail down my already tear-stained cheeks, I handed the hospital papers to a short, round-belly, straight-to-the point, no nonsense type of man. Occasionally, he looked up at us over his black-rimmed bi-focal, as he read over the reports, grunting and making brief notes on a form.

"He needs to be locked up," Was his first initial, deep baritone response as he finished reading.

Shamefully embarrassed, I avoided looking directly into his face and eyes. Avoidance. I had learned that trick from Daniel. Avoiding the truth, avoiding confrontation, avoiding him.

"Domestic violence of this nature is an automatic 48-hours incarceration," he informed us and for the next ten minutes both Amber and the magistrate tried unsuccessfully to convince me to have Daniel arrested. I was afraid for my children and myself. No one knew the depth of Daniel's rage and I knew that once Daniel was released from jail, his revenge would be deadly.

"Having it on record is good enough for me," I firmly stated. That was the only thing I was sure of at that point and no one was going to convince me otherwise.

Amber and I left the magistrate's office with a copy of the report filed against Daniel that read "assault charges against a female,"

Safely back within the walls of the motel, Amber retreated into the straight, plaid, winged-back chair next to the window and watched as I slowly, painfully crawled between the covers on the bed, overcome with exhaustion. Afraid to sleep, afraid of the nightmares, confused and disoriented. I was so tired. The sun began to set as Amber kept watch and I drifted off into more fitful dreams.

Chapter Two: Mr. Draper's Farm

Many would say that my life was doomed from birth. Born as the third and youngest to a "not so very nice," woman and a verbally, as well as physically abusive father. My biological parents gave birth to the oldest, my brother, Randy, when my mother was 15 and my father was 16. A little under 2 years later, my sister Cindy was born, and then there was me, born prematurely 22 months later. My real mother disappeared shortly after my birth. She married and remarried so many times that it is unclear exactly how many siblings I actually have, with some whom I hear were scattered and abandoned just like the three of us. The facts of my real mother and her life have always been a mystery. Rumors and tales were that my biological mother left with only my brother and me when I was less than a year old and lived a somewhat "questionable" lifestyle. My sister was living with an aunt. Months later, when my brother and I resurfaced with my mother. She had either run out of money or returned to her parents, or we just appeared; no one was ever clear. Some even rumored that my brother, who was around four at the time, and I had been living out of cars and various shady hotels. None of these events are in my memory, only my brother's.

My father remarried when I was two, to a woman that always said she never wanted us children. My father quickly sought out the courts for adoption by my stepmother.

Our new mother was not an affectionate person. I have no memories of her holding, hugging, or telling me, she loved me. She was a very cold individual frequently referring to us as "his kids," making sure we knew that we were not hers, we just came as a "package deal" through her marriage to my father.

My father left deep scars of abuse. When he was angry with us for doing something wrong or he was in "one of those moods," we paid the price with severe beatings and verbal abuse. I became aware of the violence at a very early age with horrible remembrance of screams, scenes of children being thrown against the wall or down onto the floor or ground. Choking and beatings with hands, belts, and sticks, whatever was convenient at the time for my father to grab and administer the abuse. Most of the time, my father would be so carried away in the abusive moment that he didn't seem to know when to stop.

During our abuses, my stepmother stood by and watched, doing nothing to help us. But then, why should she? We were his kids. Some of the abuses she instigated, and my father obliged her wishes creating a home environment where we were physically abused by our father and emotionally abused by our stepmother.

At the age of nine, we moved from a subdivision in the city to a run down, old farmhouse in the country about 30 minutes outside of town. We literally moved from bad to worse not just in physical living conditions, but deeper into a dysfunctional, abusive home life. To this day, I can truly confess before God, that other than the greatness of His creation, a horse named Black Jack, a collie dog named Lady Cheltenham of Pine Burr, and Mr. Draper's farm, there were no traditions or special memories from my childhood, divine amnesia. Nevertheless, God was always there. Always.

From the moment we moved to the farm, I learned to cope with our abusive life by running. On that 11 acres, just like Black Jack's free spirit of breaking into a wild, smooth, gallop through our open pasture, I was able to run with the wind blowing through my long hair breaking loose from the abusive environment within the old tongue-in-groove walls. If I knew a beating was about to take place, I would run as fast as I could, hands covering my ears, through our yard, scrambling underneath the barbed wire fence that access to our open pasture. Running past horses and cows, stepping through the next set of barbed wire fence escaping deep into the woods. Stopping only when I had reached the edge of Mr. Draper's cow pasture. There beside the soothing sound of Polecat Creek, lying on a cool, soft bed of moss that served as a comforting blanket, I would collapse, panting out of breath. Far from witnessing or safe from hearing the screams and cries of a child being beaten. I was so very young, when I learned this coping skill. Mr. Draper's creek and pasture became my secret hiding place. There I found God, and there I found me. Young, yet mature and aware enough to feel God's presence and protection.

Mr. Draper raised cattle. I never ventured to his house, but from the road, it looked to be a pleasant, warm home, crisp and white with beautiful shade trees and green grass. Our house was far from visible from where I laid alongside Polecat Creek, at the woods edge of Mr. Draper's cow pasture. There I learned to talk with God and began my lessons in what we Quakers call "centering-down". Many conversations, tears, and frightened moments were spent in my secret hiding place, and Mr. Draper never knew I was there. Only God knew. There I learned to be content to wait for that inner light and inward peace that could only be given by God.

Beside the creek was an old, weathered tree stump where two tiny eyes burrowed deep inside would sometimes peer out at me. I use to pretend the eyes belonged to God, and He was there watching, comforting and protecting me.

My friend, Lyla, and I camped out alongside Mr. Draper's creek many times during our summer vacations. Lyla was a complete opposite contrast to me in appearance with her blond hair, blue eyes and tall lanky figure.

Today I am in awe at those two brave little girls, alone in the woods, camping out in a makeshift tent of two blankets, a large center stick and rocks to hold the edges down. We pitched our tent on the edge of where the woods met Mr. Draper's open pasture. Close enough for us to walk to the creek, yet comforting enough that we were visible in case we ever needed to be seen by Mr. Draper. Our supplies that needed to be kept cold, we placed in the creek, tied tightly in a plastic bag and secured with a rock so it wouldn't float down stream. There were occasional mornings when we would find our supplies had been rummaged through by cows or night creatures, but it never dampened our spirits. We were at peace with nature and dreaded our night's camping experience to end, but daily chores on the farm still needed to be done. I used to think I could have stayed there every night throughout the summer and been content.

Lyla and I felt happy and rich with the splendor of our independence. Many times, we awoke to one of Mr. Draper's cows poking their heads inside our tent. I was always amazed how quietly such a big animal could creep up without us hearing. I believe the cows were curious of those two young girls invading their territory, and I'm sure the makeshift tent challenged their understanding and vision.

Snakes were always a fear for both of us. We surrounded our tent with a long rope because we once heard a snake would mistake it for another snake and not bother us. It must have worked because I never remember seeing a snake around our campsite. Cows and night creatures were the only living things aware of our existence on Mr. Draper's farm.

My father had some strange theories about snakes and I never realized that until I was much older. My first exposure to a real snake was when I was around ten years old, and I was completely terrified. My father's explanation of a snake was that a snake was just as afraid of you as you were of it. Of course, that was his theory about bees, spiders, raccoons, possums or any other creature I was afraid of.

Psychologically, I guess part of my fear could be explained from the tales of the devil being a serpent and my father showing us a picture out of a book depicting what hell would look like. The picture was in black and white of a huge serpent, the devil, surrounded in flames of fire. A grotesque demon torturing people. The picture terrified me. My father at times would show us the picture with a lesson of, "this is where you will go if you are bad."

The appearance of the serpent as a snake was the same in my mind as a child. If the devil was indeed a snake, I wanted nothing to do with either.

A snake and I were never going to get used to each other's existence or meet halfway through my fear. It was an unworkable relationship that remains to this day. Killing a snake was another theory with my father.

"Snakes can grow back together," he explained. I knew this had to be true because I watched it with my own eyes. My father would chop the snake into two separate pieces with a hoe. I fearfully watched my father as he strategically placed one piece of the snake at one end of our clothesline and one at the opposite end. Each morning I would run outside to check the snake and watched horrified as overnight the pieces had moved ever so slowly towards each other. Then came that fateful morning when the snake was gone.

Rationalizing too that it had to be true because once I read in a book that your liver could grow back together and a lizard could grow back its tail. I was convinced that a snake was made out of the same material as a liver and lizard. My father still stands by his theory that a snake can grow back together, and I have no desire to disprove his theory.

At times, my father had mercy on his daughter and would grab his shotgun, explaining that the only true way to get rid of a snake was to "blow it to pieces," That way it would be virtually impossible for all the pieces to grow back together. I liked that theory much better. I was raised in the Quaker faith and this was the only time in my Quaker belief when I truly believed in the "taking up of arms", justifying that we were going against the devil and in God's book that was okay.

To this day, I still find a Mr. Draper's place as often as I can. I call them my "hiding places," there I spend hours at a time praying, talking and crying to the One who loves me and always listens. I don't know the exact moment when I first found Him and accepted Him as my Lord and Savior. I am not one of those who had a magnificent moment when I was "struck" by lightening in the hour of my lowest means and found "the Lord!," For as long as I can remember, He has always been there for me. Why He chose me, I will never understand, but He did and I know He must have considered me special or He wouldn't have trained my dependence on Him.

At times, I wonder if God rewards those for deeds unbeknownst by them. Mr. Draper was a part of my past. I never met him and he never knew me. I was the little girl that used his farm to escape from the fears of reality.

My father and stepmother divorced when I was 18. Then I was officially "unadopted" from the woman who never really wanted "his kids" and she moved on to another life. My father disappeared shortly thereafter for over 20 years. My children never met their grandfather until they were in their late teens. Though I may not have had the perfect family, I have the perfect Heavenly Father.

Very seldom do my brother or I talk about our childhood, yet on those rare occasions when we venture close to discussing a part of our past, my brother frequently puts an abrupt stop to it by saying, "Let's just face it, Kathy; we came from a very dysfunctional family,"

Chapter Three: A Family of My Own

I once heard that it takes several generations to undo certain bad elements like alcoholism or abuse patterned and handed down generation after generation. I was determined that my life and the family I created would be the first generation to break that cycle. I married Richard when I was 18. Richard was 5 years older than I was. He wanted a good Christian, innocent girl, and he got her. He was tall, handsome with blond hair and blue eyes. Our marriage, at times, was a struggle. We came from very different family backgrounds.

After two and half years of marriage, a family of my own became a reality with the birth of Amber. I fell in love with her the moment I saw her. What a blessing! When we first brought her home from the hospital, I laid her in a bassinet beside our bed. Day and night, what seemed to be like every few minutes, I was peeking down at her. She was so beautiful! It didn't take Richard long to realize that I wasn't going to stop peeking into the bassinet in awe and adoration of our little baby girl, and he finally made the decision she had to go into her own room. It broke my heart. Mornings after Richard would leave for work, I would quietly sneak into Amber's room and softly say, "Good Morning Sunshine," while she smiled in response, without opening her eyes. Then gently I would sweep her up into my arms and carry her back to bed with me where we would cuddle and play. She was truly my little blessing from God.

I thought I could never love any child more than I loved Amber, but then Matt and Evan came along, and there was even more love to share. Their tiny hands, reaching up to grab my fingers as I fed them, the warmth, comfort and security. They were mine. I was complete and happy.

Richard was the disciplinarian in our household since I was still running from the pain and violence of my childhood. I was afraid of myself, never wanting to be like my father. When a child needed a "behavior adjustment," I would wait for Richard to come home and just like that little girl of years past; I would run deep into the woods behind our house to hide from the sounds.

My love for my children as well as other's children grew and grew. Our doors were always open, phone always ringing; the sound of our children's laughter and many other children's laughter are still my fondest memories.

I was determined to do things the right way, God's way, and have a home full of love, fun and laughter. A family where we created memories and lived out adventures. A home with family traditions. I had always envied children at church or school who told of their family traditions for the holidays. It lay a deep longing in me for that kind of family life not just for me, but someday for my children as well. Early on, I searched out ways, listened to numerous families, read magazines, seeking and learning about traditions. Only to realize it was up to my own creativity to the make memories and traditions unique to our family. One of my biggest blessings is to know that I was successful. Each year around the holidays, I smile and thoughtfully reminisce as my children tell their children of their fondest childhood memories. To this day, we continue to carry out those same traditions.

When Amber was five years old and Matt was about two, we were able to purchase a new refrigerator from Sears. It was around Easter. Richard and I decided to save the box and make a house out of it. The night before Easter Sunday, we spent hours cutting out windows and doors, drawing, coloring flowers and trees making a huge "Easter Bunny House," Inside the cardboard house, we set up their Easter baskets. We took baby powder and made Easter bunny footprints through the house, out the door and across the yard. Amber and Matt played in that cardboard house from Easter until winter.

By the time the first real snow fell, the cardboard house had deteriorated so much that we were about to burn it, when we decided to fold, tape it up and make a sled for the children. It made a few good runs down the slope across the street before it finally collapsed into a mush of soppy wet cardboard.

All our Easter baskets were homemade, including Richard's and mine. The children never seemed to want store bought ones, especially when they were old enough to realize that Mom's homemade baskets had more candy and fun stuff inside. Even still, our Easters are celebrated with lunch, a chocolate bunny and reliving our memories.

My children tell Halloween stories of the ridiculous costumes I made and still have. Amber's favorite was to dress up like a clown or princess; Matt a cowboy or pirate, and Evan a Ninja Turtle or Power Ranger. Other ridiculous accumulations of capes, glasses, masks, dresses, shredded old pants, jackets, and hats, are all packed in a large wooden crate loaded with memories.

One year we had no trick or treat children come to our home. Our house was set back quite a ways off the road, and it was spooky to walk up the long driveway in the dark. Living with us at the time was one of many "stray" children, Roland. His home life was difficult, and one day he appeared and never left. What difference did it make to have one more mouth to feed? I loved it! When Roland first arrived, he wouldn't eat at the kitchen table or in front of anyone. He didn't know how to act at mealtime or how to sit down at a table as a family. Mealtimes were my favorite time of sharing with the children. Roland would bashfully get a plate of food, retreat to the downstairs den and eat alone. It took months to break him of this habit, to teach him table manners, how to set a table, and to be more comfortable eating as a family.

On this particular Halloween, our house was loaded with teenagers, which was the norm, all camped out in our downstairs den, eating junk food and watching horror shows. However, to me it didn't feel like Halloween because we hadn't been visited by a single trick or treat child. Quietly I snuck upstairs, put on Roland's brogans, Matt's tube socks, and an old housecoat, blacked out my teeth, put green mud mask on my face, and placed big rollers in my hair. Then I crept down the stairs, through the kitchen and out the back door. Once outside, I broke into a run around the house to the front door and rang the doorbell. I stood there impatiently waiting for one of the children to open the door. No one answered. Again, I rang the doorbell. Still no answer. I ended up ringing the doorbell at least a half a dozen times before anyone heard it above the TV and conversations.

"Someone's at the door!," I finally heard someone shout, with the sound of footsteps running up the staircase and across the front foyer ceramic floor. I stood there and watched as they peeked through the side glass, eight faces, over, under and around each other. Yet once they realized it was I, they refused to open the door and retreated down into the den, leaving me standing on the front stoop, ringing the doorbell. Defeated, I finally gave up, went inside, and down into the den where they were all rolling on the floor with laughter talking about how ridiculous I looked.

"You looked so stupid and crazy!," They all agreed. Nevertheless, that was okay. It made them laugh and we made another memory to talk about in years to come.

A Thanksgiving tradition was even more challenging to find. I always mourned the fact that I had no "real" grandparents to offer my children even though they never questioned or seemed to mind. I settled on a traditional "Thanksgiving brunch" learning to do this to help with scheduling around Richard's "family" events, while also realizing that someday when the children were older and had families of their own, it would be difficult to work around everyone's schedule.

Brunch consisted of sausage and cheese balls, ham and Swiss rolls, chip beef and gravy, biscuits, eggs, rice Krispy treats, fudge, pumpkin pie, pecan pie, grits, and whatever else I could come up with. This was our established, traditional menu. This tradition has remained sacred within our family and if anyone on the "in-law" side even hints at wanting to steal our tradition, my children and brother are protective of it. At each brunch, we hold hands in a circle and give grace, concluding with a hand squeeze to "pass the love," By carrying out the will of God, the traditions gave my children and me the stability of home and family.

Immediately after brunch on Thanksgiving Day, I created another "so-called" tradition. A search for the perfect Christmas tree. Each search was an adventure. It went on for more years than I can remember. Through their childhood, we lived in several different homes and neighborhoods, but regardless of where we lived, after Thanksgiving brunch we would have a place somewhere, in our back yard, either across the street or down the road to search for that one perfect tree. God always seemed to provide a place for us to live out this adventure. Many years came and went, we searched high and low, and through this "tradition", we never found that one perfect tree. Bundled up in coats, boots, scarves and gloves with a trip to the utility room or shed to get the sled and an ax, adventurously our family (and sometimes friends) would trump through some stranger's woods in our search. Every potential tree was examined closely, inspecting for height, fullness and color, specs for our one perfect tree.

One such memory was a Thanksgiving Day when my daughter Amber, who was eighteen at the time, was dating a boy named Kevin. Around mid-afternoon on this particular Thanksgiving I made the announcement, it was time. The children all moaned and groaned, lazily, half-asleep watching TV in front of the woodstove, cozy, comfortable and warm. "Nope, everyone up, daylight is wasting and we need to find the tree," I commanded sternly. The moans and sighs continued with "not again, we've never found a tree yet!" Nevertheless, the children humored me, dressed in their usual "hunting" garb, and we loaded the ax onto the sled, through the backyard, under the fence, and into the woods, we went.

We searched high and low only to find scrawny looking cedar trees, or tiny pine trees that reminded me of a "Charlie Brown Christmas Tree." Once again, another year to pass with no tree that met our description of the perfect tree. We continued deeper into the woods, crossing a creek, crawling under a barbwire fence, ending up on the side of a road. Slowly we began to retrace our steps back home when all of a sudden a glistening treasure caught our eyes. Kevin spotted it first. Bending down, he began digging into the dirt with his bare hands. Soon the others joined in and they uncovered the so-called "treasure" with all the boys "ooohhing" and "ahhhing" over a stupid old hubcap. Our trip back to the house was full of laughter and crazy ideas of decorating our Christmas hubcap.

"This special hubcap will adorn our perfect Christmas tree!," we loudly proclaimed as we trampled through the woods. That is, if we ever found a tree.

The old sled and ax are still in our family as well as the memories. The hubcap we allowed Kevin to keep, since he was the rightful owner of the find. Occasionally Amber sees Kevin who reminds her he still has the old hubcap and I believe someone described that day as us having a true "redneck" Thanksgiving tradition.

Though the children are grown and on their own, occasionally I mention at our Thanksgiving Brunch that we need to go and search for the perfect tree. We reminisce about our searches and recently, it was Matt who discovered that it wasn't about finding that "one perfect tree," but it was all about the time we spent together, walking, laughing, and talking, the making of wonderful memories all bundled up into a search for a tree.

At Christmas, I made sure I made extra stockings for those strays that always appeared and like Thanksgiving, we prepared a traditional brunch. Coffee and cookies were left out for Santa. Our Santa preferred coffee to milk.

Stockings were always overstuffed. When they were younger, Matt and Amber created their own tradition for Christmas. They would go to bed as soon as Santa was about to arrive and then get up after dad and mom went to bed. They opened their stockings, played cards and board games all night in front of the Christmas tree until they fell asleep on the floor that was covered with their pillows and blankets. At the break of daylight, they would wake up Evan and come pounding into our bed gleefully screaming, "Get up! It's Christmas!," their excitement could be contained no longer.

I truly believe we were successful in creating traditions and great memories for many generations to come. These traditions and memories gave me a sense of comfort, love, acceptance and security. Things I yearned for as a child. Throughout the years, I strove to create a warm, normal, loving family bound together in love in hopes my children would someday be able to build on our traditions and memories within their own families.

Like the hands on a clock, the years of our marriage clicked by, and Richard and I soon began to drift further and further apart. Richard was an individual who was cold and distant emotionally. He displayed or offered very little affection. Meanwhile, I yearned for the warmth of love, security of strong-arms holding me with soothing words of endearment. Emotions and feelings that were withheld from me as a child. That was not Richard's personality or being. Therefore, I went from my childhood, into adulthood being emotionally abandoned. To cope, I threw myself more and more into the lives of our children. Basketball, soccer, youth groups, sleepovers, parties, all about the children while my marriage starved for time and attention. The children were my primary focus, a coping skill, centering my life around them, choosing to avoid the issues of my needs, while Richard centered his life on his job and career goals. Soon, we became just roommates with only one common thread holding us together, the children.

Chapter Four: Father's Day

Gary and Cindy spoke very little during the drive, leaving me to my own private thoughts, for which I was thankful. Closing my eyes with my head leaned against the glass, I needed the long distance drive and time to muster up the strength and courage to see the cabin again.   So many decisions to make, fear constantly knocked at my heart's door. All week, I worried Daniel would just "show up" at the college or follow me when I left work to go back to the motel. I was afraid to answer the phone for fear it would be another phone call from him, trying to convince me that the abuse of the past five years never happened. He demanded to know whom I talked with and what I told them. Sleepless nights were full of horrible nightmares.   Fear, guilt, regrets all haunted me.

During my childhood, Mother's Day and Father's Day were filled with deep regret and sadness. As a young child, I wanted to crawl under the pew and hide from being surrounded in church by people discussing how great their fathers and mothers were.   It was like a bragging competition on who had the godliest of mothers and the most honorable of fathers. It didn't seem fair. In my mind, I knew there had to be someone like me somewhere, but it didn't make it any easier sitting there and listening. Where were my godly parents? They were there, sitting next to me in church, yet they led a much different life as parents within the walls of our home.

My parents' inconsistency was confusing for me as I questioned how they could be ideal role models in church and in front of other people, yet towards their children, they were verbally, emotionally and physically abusive. There were times I hated them for the mask they wore in public and fought the urge to yell out, "That's not who you really are!" The protective, more sensible side of me knew, no one would ever believe me. Besides, the physical abuse I would suffer afterwards would force me to remain quiet and suffer through their charade.

The dread of Mother's Day and Father's Day continued into my adulthood. Going to church for those honors only surfaced painful memories. Rarely did I not leave drenched from crying. Soon it was just easier to skip church on Mother's Day and Father's Days to hide from the truth and pain of the past.

The reality that there were others like me surfaced about fifteen years ago on Father's Day. I dreaded that day with a passion and debated on whether or not to go to church. My mind played childlike game of excuses. Certainly, God would understand. He knew my pain and would forgive me. I had children of my own now who would not understand. Of all days, their mother would most certainly live by her Christian example and not skip church, allowing them to honor their Dad. How would I explain? I never divulged my childhood secrets to my children. All they knew was that I was an "orphan" whose mother and father existed, but did not exist in our lives.

This particular Sunday morning, while the children were in their respective Sunday school classes, excited about the gifts they were making to honor their father, I was in my adult Sunday school class miserable. To make matters worse, my worst nightmare was taking place. The teacher began class by asking everyone to share their fondest stories, memories, or teachings of their fathers. Instantly I felt a sting of fear and pain. A thousand things were running through my mind. I thought of making up a glamorous story. That would be a lie; my conscience convinced me otherwise, I was 35 years old, too old to be making up lies, even if God did understand. I had a secret, and it was too personal to share. Afraid when it was my turn I would just sit and cry, making an absolute fool of myself. My friend Teri would say I was weeping for that little lost child inside of me. Frantically I searched my memory. Surely, I was being ridiculous. There just had to be one good memory somewhere during my childhood years with my father.

"Be honest with yourself, Kathy," I sternly chastised myself. "There has to be something?," thoroughly and hopelessly, I searched within my heart; I searched my memory, somewhere there had to be something. "Please, God," I pleaded in desperation. "Give me one truthful, good memory to share." Nevertheless, there was nothing.

What I thought had been minutes had only been a few brief seconds, as the Sunday school teacher had only paused during her instructions. Miraculously her next words gave me amazing grace. "But if you wish not talk about your father, just say, "Pass".

One simple word, "Pass," Again, frantically I prayed, "God, please don't let me be the only one to say, "Pass,"" I watched and listened as we went around the room. No "passes," just beautiful stories and memories being shared of wonderful fathers. From the direction the room was going, I would be the last person in the room to share. "Please, please dear God," I closed my eyes while silently, fervently praying. "Please don't let me be the only one to say pass," there was still enough time to think up a glamorous story, maybe something I had read or heard. I could pretend it was my father. "Please God just let there be one 'Pass.'" I knew if there could be just one, it would give me the strength I needed to say, "Pass," I looked around at the remaining faces. Faces that revealed no sign of pain or a broken childhood.

By now, there was only one person left sitting next to me. His name was Kevin. He was a young, respectable man with a loving wife and three children. He could speak and pray in such a godly spirit that it would truly touch your inner soul. I remembered his mother had visited our church not too long ago. I was doomed as I felt tears begin to well up in my eyes. My heart felt as if it was beating a thousand beats per minute. A lump began to form in my throat. One final silent prayer of mercy, I prayed, "God please just one good memory to share."

Then to my amazement Kevin simply said, "Pass," his head held low, his voice soft, with a slight shake.

"He just said, "Pass,"" I repeated within. "He really did say, 'Pass.'" The room held only a brief pause. Then all eyes were now on me. With newfound courage and strength, a pool of tears in my eyes, I too said, "Pass," As years of a tremendous weight lifted off my shoulders.

A scripture verse most quoted in church on Father's Day is, **"Besides this, we have had earthly fathers to discipline us and we respected them,"** I can't help but hope someday I will be able to forgive and forget the past. That someday I will accept what happened to me as a child, realizing that my father may not have been what he should have been or even what I wanted him to be. Yet, as a Christian, I cannot begin to believe I will be received in my Heavenly Father's house unless I forgive my earthly father.

Where is that godly woman who is a priceless treasure to her family, her church, and her God? The one whose price is far above rubies? I hope she will be within me. I pray that she will be within me. Doors of freedom opened for me that Sunday. Freedom from the past and acceptance of the future. There would be more Mother's Days and Father's Days but I need not fear. I could go to church and be not afraid. For the first time in my life, on that fateful Sunday, I found someone who shared my pain.

My spiritual side tells me that we are never alone once we accept Christ as our Savior, yet the human side of me says that even in church, God's house, a place where we should not feel alone, that human side can cause us pressure, pain and inflict feelings of being alone.

No one ever questioned me that day about my response, and I've never felt compelled to share that secret part of my life within my church family or friends. Yet, from that moment on, never again was I intimidated by my past. Hearing the others share that day made me laugh and made me cry. I accepted them and they accepted me. A simple word, 'Pass' had set me free.

Chapter Five: Who Will Hold the Ladder?

In July of 1996, I ventured out into the mission fields of rural Jamaica. Amber, Matt and Evan were old enough and I felt a personal calling from God. From the first video, I saw of the work of the Quakers in Jamaica, the faces and needs of those children, I knew that one day, if God would call me to do His work, I wanted to go. Earlier that year I received a phone call asking me if I would like to go and help teach VBS to 500 children in Port Antonio, Jamaica. I was elated! From January until June, I wrote bible lessons, created activity sheets, sought out craft ideas, picked songs and was so organized for my first trip that even the team leader made fun of me being "too organized," Yet, I wanted to do my best for God and the children. One small payment for all He had done for me. My hands were being used as God's hands in poverty-stricken, rural Jamaica.

We flew out on an early Friday morning in July and were gone ten days. The Sunday evening I returned, Richard was waiting for me at the airport. It was the way he was standing, the look in his eyes; his back leaned against the wall with his arms crossed. It certainly wasn't a warm, "I missed you" welcome and at that moment I knew our marriage was over. It wasn't as if I didn't know this day was coming. Our lives had been going in different directions and many times my faith got in the way. Richard was not as religious as I and even though he allowed me to raise our children in the Quaker faith, Richard was restless and felt sometimes it was embarrassing for me to be a Christian amongst his family and friends. He spoke often of how my faith hindered him from being invited to certain social events, which was something he missed. His family and friends weren't comfortable drinking and telling jokes around me. Now that I was venturing into mission work, it was making it even more difficult and uncomfortable for him.

Richard left us the Friday after my return from Jamaica. Our marital separation was as amicable as a separation could be, even though I do not think either one of us believed in divorce, we both agreed we did not see a future for the two of us. Our twenty-one year marriage was over. Amber was eighteen, Matt fourteen, and Evan eight. I will always be thankful to Richard and his family for our marriage, the creation of our three children, and the memories made not just for my children, but for me as well.

Soon after Richard left, I began to notice more and more stray teenagers coming to our home, especially around Easter, Thanksgiving and Christmas. Most were teenagers that my children knew from school and friends of friends. There were the Baker boys, who drove loud, redneck trucks, along with their cousins from Mount Airy, then some person whose name started with a "T", a boy named Charlie, and I never knew who the rest were. When Charlie got a job at the BP station for his last two years of high school, he would call and ask for his "brunch plate" to be delivered to him at work with his favorite brownies, sausage and cheese balls and rice Krispy treats. I truly believe all those "extra" children were children who were an image of me during my childhood, looking for a "traditional" family home to feel the spirit of love, warmth and acceptance during the holiday season.

I never felt threatened or scared by the strange kids that came and went. They were all loved and welcomed. Most would grab a plate of food off the bar and retreat downstairs into the den where they sat in front of the old woodstove, ate, laughed, watched TV, rode the go-cart in circles outside, and just had fun. It was a wonderful warm, fuzzy feeling for me, making me ever so grateful and thankful to God. Now I had a really big family, and I believe God knew I needed to be surrounded by these children for healing, growth, and renewal of spirit.

I was fragile and shaky with the responsibility of raising our three children plus one, Roland, age sixteen. Yet I drew my strength from God. God saw my wounds, scars and sins, loving me and transforming me into His creation, giving me even more purpose for my life. I branched out even further in my faith, continuing my work in Jamaica and assuming the role as director of the North Carolina Friends Junior Yearly Meeting. Writing Christian lessons and planning programs for the next five years was a great source of healing, throwing me even further into God's work and knowledge of the Bible. Amber, Matt and Roland were a huge help in supporting me in my work and assisting with the raising of Evan.

The last house Richard and I had bought was 2½ stories, around 2,500 square feet and sat on a little over an acre of land. With Richard gone, it took me all day just to clean the house, and another whole day in the summer to complete all the mowing and trimming. It was a huge responsibility for me to tend to. Amber and Matt were both in school and worked part-time jobs.

Nevertheless, our family was less a father. We continued to keep our sense of humor and laughter, live out memories and adventures. That first fall after Richard left, the toilet in the downstairs basement broke.

We blamed it on Roland because every time he used that bathroom something happened. Regardless, I learned how to replace a toilet, snake out the drain, set in a new toilet, seal and all. For a prank on the children, I placed a stuffed made-up man in Roland's old work clothes and boots, topped with a hat and fake arms, sitting on the old toilet, reading a newspaper in the front yard. The neighbors never complained but the boys sure were mad. I left it there for a few days, and then it mysteriously "disappeared," probably to one of the Baker boy's junk yards or as a prank in someone else's yard.

The following summer, Matt began driving and the task of selecting a vehicle for Matt's first car was a challenge. I wanted it to be safe, durable, not too fast, and inexpensive. Being a single parent, raising a soon-to-be driver, laid a heavy, frightening burden on my shoulders. I spent weeks searching newspaper ads, with not the slightest idea of what to buy. Of course, Matt's wishes were different, sporty, fast, and red.

One day an ad in the local newspaper caught my eye: "Red Ford Ranger Pick-Up, one owner, low miles, automatic," At least it met one of Matt's requirements — it was red. Matt wasn't keen on a pick-up truck for his first vehicle, but he went along and agreed to look at it. With his father gone and some insight into our financial struggles, Matt probably figured at that point he was lucky to get anything.

Matt worked hard that summer saving the money he earned at a little café not far from the house and soon, a red Ford ranger, with low miles, bought at a good price, became Matt's first "set of wheels" at age sixteen. That old Ford truck stayed in our family for four years going through a beating with an inexperienced teenage boy behind the wheel. Matt and I together learned how to change the oil, spark plugs, and even the transmission fluid, with the help of a Chilton's book, checked out from the local public library. Soon the truck developed problems with the transmission linkage cable, stranding us in traffic numerous times forcing us to get out, raise the hood, and "jiggle" the cable to get the transmission to slip back into gear.

Late one Friday evening I heard Matt and Roland come in from work. Both boys always came into my room at night and would lie at the foot of my bed telling me the events of their day. It was a special moment that I cherished and looked forward to each evening. This particular Friday evening, the boys had finished their nightly talk with me, when I heard a lot of commotion downstairs. I wasn't too alarmed since they were always cooking and moving around late at night. The next morning I awoke, noticing that Mitzi, our family dog, was missing. Mitzi was a small mixed breed of Lhasa Asa and Pomeranian. She slept with me every night, but on this particular morning, Mitzi was missing. I went down the stairs, searching throughout the house, but there was no Mitzi, Matt, or Roland to be found. I walked across the kitchen floor and looked out the window. My car had been removed from the carport and in its place was the old red Ford Ranger pick-up truck backed in with Roland and Matt, in the back truck bed loaded down with their stereo, pillows, blankets and Mitzi, in between them, all sound asleep. Another memory, another adventure, one that gave me a warm fuzzy feeling my "boys" were there, safe and warm, exactly where they wanted to be, unlike most 16 and 17-year-old boys who wanted to be away from home, out at all hours of the night, or far away from home and their mother as they could get. That moment warranted the purchase of a sign placed at the corner of the driveway, "Redneck Parking Only."

Amber moved out the following summer, it was Matt's last year in high school and Evan's last year in elementary school. We all agreed that once the school year was over, I would sell the house. With Matt leaving for college, the house and yard were too much for me to maintain alone and financially difficult to make ends meet. Moreover, the school district was not the best, and I wanted something better, more challenging for Evan.

I learned a lot about my capabilities as a single-mom that final year we lived in our last "real home place," I worked getting the house prepared to be sold by checking out library books and purchasing instructional guides from Lowe's Hardware store. I pulled up the carpet upstairs and found beautiful hardwood floors. In fact, they were so beautiful, all I had to do was put a clear polyurethane protective sealant on them. I learned to tile the kitchen and dining room floors; painted rooms, and by spring, the house was ready to be put on the market.

The day before our first "Open House", I went into the master bath to open the window for fresh air while I was cleaning only to find that with all the painting I had done, the window was stuck. I tried everything to get it open; I ran a knife around the sides and top, but the window wouldn't budge. Soon my efforts resulted in breaking the lower glass with my hand going completely through the broken window. A few minor scratches on my hand were the least of my worries. The window was shattered. With "Open House" in less than twenty-four hours, I was going to have to learn how to install window glass. Measuring the empty frame, it was off to Lowe's, once again, for instructions and a piece of glass.

Purchasing the glass and obtaining a brochure of installation was the easiest part. Installing the new glass created a major problem. The bathroom was on the third floor and I desperately needed Matt and Evan's help, but Matt is terrified of heights. Since I had to work from inside the bathroom, I needed Matt on the outside, to stand on the ladder and hold the glass in place. I stood the ladder firmly into place, shaking it for stability, allowing Matt to see how steady and sturdy it was, but it was to no avail. Matt, really, really has a phobia of heights and nothing I could say or do was very convincing to coerce Matt to climb up the ladder. My speech about this being "another adventure;" a "making of memories" was running weak. Matt's face and hands were as white as the caulking I was about to use on the glass. Evan stood at the bottom holding the ladder as Matt, ever so slowly, inched his way up the ladder, one fearful step at a time. The metal ladder rattling loudly from Matt's shaky hands and unwilling feet. All the while I stood up at the top with my head hanging out the bathroom window, trying my best to give Matt motherly words of encouragement and wisdom, telling both Evan and him, "This is a valuable learning experience for us all. Someday the two of will have to do this for your own homes. Look at the level of skills you're learning!," I triumphantly explained.

Matt just glared at me with the same identical color of eyes as mine, yet eyes huge with fear as his fingers appeared frozen on the rungs.

Evan, my youngest and wisest yelled up, "Yeah Mom? But who will hold the ladder for us?"

That question has been implanted deep within my heart and mind all these years. In life's challenges and moments of weakness, many times I was the one repeating Evan's question asking, "Yeah God? Who's Holding the Ladder?" The Christian and practical side of me knew God was there holding the ladder, His still small voice and scripture giving me encouragement to move up, higher towards His kingdom. Life to me is like those steps, each step representing a year or rite of passage, as I grow older. At times, my legs are shaky just as Matt's were that day. My spirit fragile and discouragement makes it difficult for me to climb up each step to the next level of my life. Yet, when my feet are planted firmly in the middle of each rung, God's steady hands are holding the ladder firmly in place, keeping me from falling out of my relationship with Him. Guiding me on the right path for spiritual growth and healing from the past or my mistakes. Each step, a step of faith as I hear God's voice saying, "Keep climbing, you can make it, I am here. I am the one holding the ladder." In the most difficult moments, I would have to stop and catch my breath, resting in Him, soaking up what He would have me to learn from the experience of each step. Knowing when I reach the top step of the ladder, God will be there, smiling down at me and I will be ever so grateful to see Him. That final step, my ascension into His kingdom, the journey I've climbed each step to achieve.

The house sold quicker than we anticipated, and we contracted with the new buyers to stay until Evan and Matt finished out the school year. It was painful to leave our home. This was the only house any of us ever felt was our real home. Many children had passed through those doors, and that was our heritage. All we had now were our memories.

Chapter Six: The Little White House

"Are you asleep?," Gary asked from the front seat of the car.

"Just resting," I responded. We were halfway to the cabin. The skies were a wintry gray. The small towns we went through revealed store windows beautifully decorated for the fast approaching Christmas holiday. Streets lined with utility poles, adorned with Christmas wreaths. Cheery red, green and white lights edged rooflines of houses. By now, you could make out the shape of mountains against the skyline ahead.

I was tired, yet afraid to sleep. Afraid of the nightmares. Leaning my head once again on the back seat headrest, the side window felt cool against my forehead. Even with Gary and Cindy in the front seat of the car, I felt alone. The past week had been filled with a flurry of activities. Daily calls from Dr. Smith, my attorney, and the domestic violence counselor. Campus police at work were notified immediately of the situation and were positioned during my working hours at various places in the upper and lower parking lots near my building. Each morning and sometime during the afternoon an officer would come by my office to check on me. Amazingly, I was able to work completing the end of the semester paperwork and in preparation for the Christmas holiday break.

At night, Matt, Evan or Amber would come and spend time with me at the motel. Arrangements were quickly falling into place on a more permanent, hidden place for me to live.

In the summer of 1999, Amber, who had been living on her own for about a year, was struggling financially with working two jobs while attending college part-time. She just recently rented a small white house in the school district we wanted for Evan. The realtor hadn't found a house within my price range, so we made the decision for Matt, who was entering college in the fall, Evan and I to move in temporarily with Amber. All four of us in a two-bedroom, one bath, white frame house, built sometime in the early 1900's.

The little white house for me was another adventure, a new journey of making more memories. I was looking forward to wintertime in that little white house, cozy and warm with Amber, Matt, Evan and me. Little did I know that we would literally freeze our butts off. We soon found out that the reason the rent on the house was so cheap was the antique oil furnace didn't work. To top it off, the winter of 2000 in North Carolina was one of our worse winters for snow and ice. We weren't able to run electric heaters because they would overload the circuit and blow fuses, leaving our sole source of heat a kerosene heater that ran exactly thirteen hours on one tank of fuel. I quickly learned how to change a wick, certain brands of kerosene burned cleaner and longer than others did. Once again, the little red pick-up truck became a valuable addition to our family, but loading a 5-gallon plastic jug of kerosene in the back of that old red pick-up truck grew frustrating and old fast.

The thin vinyl kitchen floor sloped downhill due to settling, while the windows and doors leaked in bitter cold, winter air. We all took turns dressing in front of the kerosene heater each day, laying our clothes on the floor in front of the heater the night before so they would be warm the next morning.

The holidays were soon approaching and I knew this year would be different because the "old gang" of teenagers didn't know where we lived. I tried talking my brother into doing Thanksgiving and Christmas brunch at his house, but the children and he wouldn't hear of it. They wanted the holidays celebrated the same way it had always been, brunch at my house. Thanksgiving found us gathered around the small kitchen, sloping downhill, holding hands and giving thanks to God.

In the midst of our prayer came the loud noise of mufflers from outside. Finishing our prayers and gathering our plates, the sound of a firm knock, a slam of the old screen door and in walked the Baker Boys with their cousins from Mt. Airy, some guy whose name started with a "T" and a few more strays. The gang of teenagers had found us. Our holiday was complete.

January came with more bitter cold weather, blizzard-like snows, and ice storms. Storms so bad that the college where I worked closed for almost two weeks straight. I was about to go crazy cooped up in the little white house, with weekly runs of all three of us crammed in the front seat of the old red truck to the closest service station for kerosene. Storms kept hitting. It was miserable. Finally, trying to lift our spirits, knowing it was too bad to drive with the driveway nothing more than glazed over snow and ice. I got the wild notion for us to walk up the main road, visiting what few stores were open. Amber was game, yet, Evan was apprehensive.

Bundled up in boots, hats, scarves, gloves and heavy coats, we took off on our adventure. Our first destination, Eckerd's Drugstore, only a block away.

Through the cold wind, snow and ice, we made it. "Wow, since we did this without too much trouble, why don't we walk to K-Mart? It's only about ½ mile up the road?," I asked. Amber was game but Evan refused. I had just about humiliated him enough in our outlandish outfits. Evan returned home while Amber and I headed towards K-Mart. That was the longest cold walk of our lives. Walking into the wind made it worse. Yet, stubborn pride and a bit of "Rocky II" visions in my mind, we forged on towards our destination. We joked about the little red caboose, "I think I can, I think I can," the further we walked, the more we realized this was not the brightest of ideas, especially since we were going to have to walk the same distance back. Very few cars were on the road and the ones that were honked, waved and threw slush all over us. We were afraid our faces would suffer frostbite. Amber complained that even her teeth hurt, and I told her not to worry, we would replace them with Chiclets gum. We laughed so hard that it made things worse because our tears and nose drippings were freezing to our face.

Finally, we made it to K-Mart. It took us over forty-five minutes to walk the short distance. Calling Evan from the payphone in the lobby, he was worried that it took us so long, we were worried about getting back. We asked if maybe Evan would consider driving the go-cart to pick us up, pulling the sled hooked on the back, but that wasn't an option. The go-cart had a blown engine. Laughing and a hilarious mess, we hung up the phone with hopes of seeing Evan sometime in the near future.

Once we entered the store, our first stop we knew had to be the bathroom. Making our way to the back of the store the restroom area greeted us with a handwritten note, "Closed due to frozen pipes." Looking like two homeless people, security began following us around the store. As soon as we somewhat "thawed out" footprints leaving puddles of water on the floor, we braved the journey back. We talked of death and what it would feel like to freeze to death. How Evan was the youngest, yet the smartest of the both of us.

"Mom, this is the dumbest idea you've come up with yet," Amber complained.

"But Amber, it's an adventure, we're making memories!," I triumphantly declared. That got me hit with the biggest snowball she could make.

"Never again, Mom," she retorted. "I should have known by now of your hare-brain adventures." Nevertheless, I'm glad we did it. Amber and I have another special memory with a new tradition every year at Christmas Amber gets a box of Chiclets in her stocking!

Evan enrolled in his new middle school. He adjusted well, made new friends, was on the soccer team and played drums in the school band. A friend of mine from work, Brenda, had a niece, Janelle that she pretty much had been raising since birth and who attended the same school as Evan. Janelle was in band as well. I felt sorry for both Brenda and her niece because Janelle's mother was dying from a brain tumor, and Brenda was going through a difficult break-up with her boyfriend, all at the same time. Brenda called daily discussing problems with her break-up, the behavior problems she was experiencing with Janelle, and Janelle's mother, Cheryl, pending death. Cheryl suffered a mild stroke while Daniel, her husband, was at a film convention in July. When Daniel returned from his trip, he could tell she had suffered a stroke by the droopy left side of her face and slurred speech. Shortly thereafter, the bad news came. It was an inoperable brain tumor.

Brenda and I had worked together for over a year in the same department and after I was transferred into another department, we continued our friendship, at times more frequently than others but during this particular time, more frequent due to the severity of the problems within Brenda's life.

Evan came home from school one afternoon and showed me a note he had received from a girl named Janelle. The note, somewhat elementary for the 6th grade, had the usual, "I think you're cute, would you be my boyfriend? Check yes or no," type of message. Evan felt sorry for the girl. She had written notes to almost every boy in the 6th grade, asking them to be her boyfriend, Evan explained, and she was grossly overweight. I instructed Evan be polite to her, and not reference or acknowledge the note from Janelle to anyone in his class for fear of making her problems worse. Later that evening I put "two and two" together, realizing the Janelle in Evan's class was Brenda's niece. Conversations with Brenda the next day confirmed the same.

"Janelle's been desperate for a boyfriend for as long as I can remember," Brenda explained. "It's almost as if she's obsessed with it," Brenda was struggling with Janelle's bad grades and behavior. I knew Brenda was raising Janelle and had been since Janelle's birth but never understood why. In fact, I honestly thought that Janelle's parents just didn't want her or have time for her, turning her over to Brenda.

The end of November, Brenda and I met at the middle school to watch Evan and Janelle perform in their middle school holiday band concert. That was the first time I met Janelle and my first impression of her was sadness. She was one of the tallest in her class and grossly overweight. She wore a lot of make-up and dressed outlandishly, somewhat provocatively. Her relationship with Brenda was very close, and you would not have guessed they were any different from mother and daughter. No other members of Janelle's family attended the concert due to Cheryl's illness being at the ending critical stages of her life.

Cheryl passed away on January 3, 2000, six months after her diagnosis. I went to the funeral home to support Brenda and pay my respects to the family, speaking with Brenda, Janelle and briefly meeting and expressing my condolences to Janelle's father. Janelle appeared to be doing very well, exhibiting very little grief at the loss of her mother, making it even more apparent to me that Janelle's relationship with her aunt Brenda was closer and more connected than it had been with her own mother. There seemed to be no sorrow, tears or evidence of pain in Janelle's actions and words. She just seemed to belong with Brenda and Cheryl seemed to be someone else not closely related to her.

In the spring of 2000, somewhere around the middle of May, the school had their end-of-the year band concert. Brenda and I made our usual plans, Brenda was to pick Janelle up from daycare, and I would save her a seat. Late, as usual, Brenda rushed in and slid into the seat beside me, accompanied by her brother, the man I had met at the funeral home five months prior. I vaguely remembered him. From a sideways glance, I noticed he was a small man in stature and weight, gray hair combed straight back, a neatly trimmed beard and mustache, and brown eyes behind silver-rimmed glasses. A man I guessed to be around fifty years old. Our introduction quickly whispered and brief, as the concert had already begun. After the concert, our conversations were chaotic and superficial above the noise of the crowd and excited students. Daniel seemed preoccupied and out-of-place in the setting as he glanced down mostly at his shuffling feet. Soon we said our goodbyes and went our separate ways.

A week later, the school had an outside concert on Saturday afternoon. I went with some friends of Evan and their parents. There I saw Brenda's brother, Daniel, standing alone. His facial expression revealed him miles away in some distant thought. He was isolated from everyone else, which seemed to be on purpose, giving me the impression he was one who preferred to be alone with little tolerance of people and small conversation. It was a hot, clear day and the children performed well considering the blistering heat. With a little hesitance, yet feeling somewhat sorry for Brenda's brother, I took in a deep breath and walked towards him. A slight smile of recognition appeared across his face, coming out of his private world of thought as I drew near. We acknowledged each other briefly, reacquainting ourselves from the previous concert. Our conversation was idle chitchat about a movie I had seen the night before. Our meeting was brief and casual as I was with other people and felt guilty staying away from them too long. We parted with the usual common courtesy.

The following Monday, Brenda called upset, unloading on me her struggles with Janelle's defiance, lying, and stealing. Janelle had snuck out of the house with an inappropriate outfit she knew better than to wear, but had hidden it under another shirt. The school had called complaining. Brenda felt hopeless, not knowing what to do. In addition, Janelle called Brenda almost daily from school complaining of not feeling well, headaches or stomachaches.

"I'm at my wits end with her," Brenda complained. "Daniel works two part-time jobs, one in Burlington, over an hour away and one at a local hardware store. He can't just drop what he's doing and drive home to pick her up from school and I can't keep missing work," I was Brenda's sounding board.

"Brenda, I don't work on Fridays, and since I've already met Janelle and Daniel, if you ever need me to run to the school and pick-up Janelle and drop her off at your house, I'd be happy to," I offered, feeling concern for all of them, especially Janelle.

The following week I received a phone call from Daniel transferred to me from Brenda's extension at work.   At first, I thought he was calling because something was wrong with Janelle, and he was going to ask me to pick her up. Instead, he was calling to see if I would like to go and see a movie with him on Friday since we both had Fridays off from work. I agreed to meet him where I worked and go to the movies from there.

Our first date was on Friday, May 26th, the weekend of Memorial Day. The night before a terrible storm hit our community and there were numerous power outages throughout the city. Most movie theatres were closed, as we drove all over the city trying to find a theatre that was open. Finally, we found one. After the movie, we went to High Point City Lake for a walk, sat on a park bench, and talked. Most of the conversation centered on the difficulty of Cheryl's death and Janelle. Daniel was concerned about Janelle's health, and her medical doctor was frustrated with her weight and behavior, recommending sending Janelle to a psychiatrist and nutritionist. Janelle had just turned twelve and weighed well over 200 lbs. There were so many problems. I sat on the park bench and listened, feeling a lot of sympathy for Daniel and what he must have gone through with his wife's difficult death and now the struggles of his teenage daughter. With Evan soon to arrive home from school, Daniel dropped me off at my car and we parted ways.

The following Monday evening, Daniel called and asked if I would like to attend Janelle's dance recital on Saturday. I was a little apprehensive because I didn't want things to move too quickly. I hadn't really dated much since Richard had left, so I didn't give him an answer right away. Later he told me that Brenda had warned him he would scare me off if he moved too quickly. As the week went on and we talked more on the phone, I became a little more comfortable and agreed to meet Daniel and Janelle at the recital.

Daniel and Janelle were standing by a black pick-up truck in the parking lot when I arrived at the recital. As we were walking from the parking lot towards the building, I noticed Janelle was having difficulty walking.

"Janelle, what's wrong," I stopped and asked, looking down at her feet. First glance showed that her feet were too big for her dancing shoes and she wore no tights.

"Let me see," I asked her as we paused in the parking lot. Janelle removed her shoes for me to look closer. Her heals were red and blistered.

"Let's go back to my car," I quickly said. "I think we can make this a little better. At least enough to get you through the concert," we turned and walked back to the trunk of my car. Pulling out a first aid kit, I went to work with an antibiotic cream, gauze and band aids. With Janelle's heals taped up in an effort to relieve some of the pain, we were soon back on our way to the building for the concert.

Waiting for the recital to begin, Daniel thanked me for assisting Janelle and our conversation soon went back to the same things we had talked about on our first date. Daniel seemed eager and relieved to have someone he could talk freely with about his wife's illness and Janelle. The information he shared wasn't much different from my conversations with Brenda. I could feel the exhaustion, stress, and hardships Daniel was experiencing.

Soon the lights dimmed and the recital began. The first thing I noticed was that Janelle was the biggest girl in the dance recital. She seemed to be somewhat clumsy at times, not because of not knowing the steps, she appeared to be well versed in the routine, but primarily due to her weight. I couldn't help but feel sorry for her as she awkwardly attempted the routine of steps and balance, trying desperately to keep up with the dance team. Out of breath at moments, her weight inhibited her in so many ways.

After the recital, we said our pleasantries, a quick hug from Janelle with a sincere "thank you" whispered in my ear, and we went our separate ways. Alone that night in bed, my eyes staring up at the dark, unseen ceiling, I realized how exhausted I was from the worries of Daniel and Janelle's life. I could not imagine how they both could even function from day to day. Slowly I began to drift off to sleep; taking comfort in knowing that at least Daniel had Brenda who upheld the "mother image" in Janelle's life.

The following week Daniel called several times and so did Brenda. In one particular phone call from Brenda, she asked if she had ever told me Daniel had a right leg prosthesis. I told her no, but I noticed a slight limp while he was walking.

"He lost his leg below the knee in an automobile accident when he was six years old," Brenda explained. "Do you think it would make a difference if he wants to keep seeing you?," she asked.

"Why would it matter?," I asked, somewhat confused.

"I don't know," she continued. "Daniel just asked if I had ever told you and I couldn't remember,"

Chapter Seven: Learning Each Other

"Are you going to be okay with this?," Cindy asked as we walked inside the quaint mountain store while Gary pumped gas.

"I think so," I replied, "just nervous." If Cindy only knew. Finding peace and comfort seemed so far out of reach at this moment.

With no "bathroom" at the cabin, this was our last chance of using proper "facilities," the imminent future held using the "Johnny house" or the woods. Cindy wasn't looking forward to either option. A quick run to the bathroom, the purchase of snacks and soda had us soon back on our way again with me tucked once again in the backseat.

I dreaded seeing the cabin. I hated the memories it stirred inside of me. Somehow, someway, I had to make this work. I had to move on. As I looked out the window from the backseat, I watched the clouds rolling in, darker now, threatening rain. A sky that mirrored my heart, gray and dreary.

The relationship between Daniel and Janelle was broken, at least that was the way I sensed it immediately from the beginning. Their brokenness caused a lot of struggles during our dating hindering the normal process of learning each other and blending of the two families. On Sundays, Daniel and Janelle came to the little white house to go to church with Evan and me. Numerous times upon entrance, Janelle would go straight to the bathroom without speaking, Daniel would come in angry. They had quarreled all the way to my house over Janelle's excessive make-up and outlandish choice of outfits. I would have to admit, Janelle could really make herself stand out in a negative, provocative way. I could say little, only tried to support Janelle by telling her she had a pretty face without all the make-up and skimpy tight clothes, but it was to no avail. Brenda had tried to work with Janelle in the past, and said her mother had tried as well but no one could seem to get through to Janelle. Arguments between Daniel and Janelle consisted of yelling, cursing and slamming of doors. Vulgar cursing had never been a part of my life. I remember when I entered the public work force at the age of sixteen came my first real exposure to vulgar language and I prayed that God would never let my heart or ears become accustomed to those types of words or an acceptance of them. Praying they would always "sting" when I heard them, never, ever wanting to get accustomed to hearing them.

Daniel and Janelle used profanity as if it was everyday language, though Daniel seldom used profanity around Evan or me, knowing I was a Christian and not accustomed to that type of language nor did I accept it. I flinched each time one of those nasty words was flung out. The profanity seemed contained within the arguments between Janelle and Daniel with an occasional "slip up" every now and then by Daniel and a quick apology of, "I'm sorry" afterwards.

Daniel and Brenda were right. Nothing seemed to work. Immediately I too learned that no one could tell

Janelle what to do as Janelle continued to pour on the make-up and create "interesting" outfits to wear. Finally, I suggested to Daniel that the next time they visited Cheryl's niece, Shelia; maybe she could talk to Janelle about applying the right amount of make-up. Shelia was a beautician and could maybe introduce her to some different "hip" styles.

"Shelia's tried in the past when she came up to help with Cheryl," Daniel responded. "Shelia gave up. We all gave up."

"Then just throw the make-up away," exasperated, I suggested. Anything to stop the cursing arguments. "Every time you find make-up, throw it away."

Throwing away the make-up seemed to work at first until Janelle figured out she could use colored pencils or crayons to color her eyelids, lips and cheeks. Then it was like starting all over again.

I tried different ways to help but I was a failure from the beginning. I kept repeating Ephesians 6:1-4 in my mind, "Children, obey your parents in the Lord for this is right. Honor your father and mother," the first commandment accompanied by a promise, namely, so that all may go well with you and that you will live [a] long time on the earth. "Fathers, do not provoke your children to anger, but raise them up in the discipline and instruction of the Lord," This teenager, Janelle, was not raised in a Christian home, seldom did they attend church, and this was a "foreign" mission field for me. I'm not making excuses for myself; only admitting I literally failed stepping into the life of this teenager, who had already reached the age of "accountability according to God." Trying to re-train or re-route the past twelve years of her life, was virtually impossible.

Meeting both Daniel and Cheryl's family revealed much of the same information Brenda and Daniel had shared with me, concerning challenges in raising Janelle.

One cousin stated Janelle was a spoiled brat, and her treatment of her mother, during her final days was cruel. The worst I heard was that Cheryl, who was bedridden, an invalid, asked Janelle for a glass of water. Janelle refused.

"If I could get up off this couch, I would beat your ass!," Cheryl fired at her.

It was also during this time that Janelle took full advantage of her mother's illness to get what she wanted. She asked for a third hole pierced in her ears. Her dad said "no," her mother said "no", but Janelle managed to convince a cousin to take her to the mall and have it done anyway.

Then came the day Janelle, age eleven, asked to have her navel pierced. Both parents once again said "no." Nevertheless, Janelle took an ice cube and ice pick, went to the bathroom and pierced her navel. A few days afterwards, a severe infection erupted and Janelle became scared. She was then forced to reveal her actions and the new navel piercing.

Two months after my first date with Daniel, I left on a mission trip to Jamaica. This particular year I was assigned to a new site in the Blue Mountains of Jamaica, a place called Cascade. There were no phones except for a cell phone that belonged to the woman we stayed with. In order to get a signal, we had to go to the top of a mountain and literally stand on one foot. From that spot, I managed enough of a signal to place a brief phone call to Daniel letting him know we were trying to find a place clearer to make a call and to keep waiting. We traveled further up the mountain to a military base where I was able to use a pay phone. Daniel was clearly relieved to finally hear from me even though I had warned him before I left that I might not be able to call him until we arrived in Kingston, the day before our flight back home.

"I'm more than ready for you to come home," Daniel stated. "I miss you and Janelle....well, she's being her usual challenging self. Her medical doctor wants her to see a nutritionist and a psychiatrist. I don't know what to do with her. Brenda's upset with her most of the time too," Daniel complained. "Work is hard. The heat index is well over 100 degrees and there's no air conditioning at the plant, just a fan. It's miserable."

This was the first time in all my years of mission work that I had ever had someone meet me at the airport after an exhausting ten days with a warm hug and kiss. It felt so good! For years it was a "family event" of the children meeting me at the airport. At times, it was just Matt and Roland with a rose or a carnation and hugs. This was so much better. I had longed to have this kind of "welcome home" since I had begun my work in Jamaica. Everyone had a loved one there anxious to see them, and I was envious. Still, Jamaica gave meaning to my life, a sense of fulfillment and joy. I loved serving God, yet, the human feelings of coming home caused pain. To see a face smiling and excited to see me was wonderful. I couldn't wait to be held, to feel Daniel's arms engulf me. Just as I had seen others experience in years past.

The moment Daniel and I retrieved my luggage and settled into the car for our journey home, Daniel paused, turned, took me in his arms, and gave me another warm hug and long kiss. Then he reached into his pocket and handed me a small box.

"I'm not expecting an answer just yet," he began. "And I hope this doesn't frighten you," he stumbled with his words. "This being so soon in our relationship and all," he paused. "You can just maybe consider it the next step of our commitment to each other. A deepening of my feelings for you?" It was more like a question than a statement.

I opened the small blue box and gasped in shock. It was an engagement ring. A small pear-shaped diamond set in yellow gold surrounded by rows of small, round baguettes. It was beautiful.

"I hope that someday you will marry me," Daniel sheepishly said.

"Yes," I responded in shock. "Yes, someday I hope we will," was all I could say. I was so touched. I missed Daniel and I realized at that moment I had fallen in love with him. In addition, the "someday" didn't feel like pressure, it was just left as "someday."

We left the airport to meet up with all the children at a local restaurant. I showed them the ring, but we didn't discuss when the marriage would be.

Within a week, Daniel began suggesting a possible Christmas wedding. That was our very first disagreement.

"No Daniel," I softly pleaded. "It's too soon,"

"I've always wanted a Christmas wedding," was Daniel's argument.

"Christmas is only a five short months away. What happened to someday?," I questioned him.

"You don't want to marry me. Do you?," Daniel was beginning to show signs of anger and insecurity.

"Yes, I want to marry you. But a Christmas wedding is too soon," I feebly did my best to explain. "What about Cheryl? Out of honor of her, shouldn't we at least wait for the one year anniversary of her death?" It was a difficult discussion.

After several days, finally Daniel conceded and agreed to set a date of April 28, 2001 for our wedding. The one-year anniversary of Cheryl's death was January 3, 2001.

Janelle, on the other hand was still struggling even though I saw little of her since she was living at Brenda's most of the time. Janelle's medical doctor continued to express concerns with his inability to handle Janelle's emotional and behavioral problems as well as her weight, which continued to rise. Janelle was in what he called "the red zone." At risk of a heart attack, diabetes as well as other serious medical problems.

"It seems like even Janelle's doctor is frustrated and giving upon her," Daniel unloaded.

Daniel set up appointments with a nutritionist for Janelle. The sessions were a complete disaster. Janelle gained weight instead of losing by manipulating everything the nutritionist said. Sessions that only revealed what I already knew and had heard, for the past twelve years this child had spent glued to her bedroom TV, munching endlessly on Doritos, cookies and guzzling down 2-liter Mountain Dews. It was the only life she knew. The nutritionist soon admitted defeat, forcing Daniel to proceed with the medical doctor's next suggestion, seek out a psychiatrist.

Daniel settled on a psychiatrist by the name of Dr. Westlake who specialized in adolescent counseling. Dr. Westlake had children of his own who were around the same age as Janelle. He would alternate twenty-five minute sessions with Janelle and twenty-five minutes with Daniel and me, the remaining five minutes with all of us together. Dr. Westlake began trying to understand Janelle's mental problems while I took over working with her on her weight. This was the first of many counselors for Janelle over the next five years. Too many for me to remember.

The blending of our families was difficult. One reason was I had full custody of Evan. Richard had begun a new life and was rarely in the picture. Brenda had custody of Janelle, Thursday through Sunday of each week, and sometimes more. At times, I felt guilty because I had the responsibility of raising Evan with limited freedom while Daniel was "free" with Brenda was raising his daughter. Evan was actively involved in sports, band, youth group at church, and his friends. I fit in the category of an average "carpool" mom. I enjoyed being a part of these special years with Evan, just as I had with Amber and Matt.

During Daniel and Janelle's visits to our house, I soon ran into the same problems Daniel, Brenda and everyone else had, Janelle's stealing and lying. Janelle stole things from just about every home she visited, the daycare, the youth meetings at church, wherever, whenever she had the opportunity. If she wanted it, she just took it. I had never dealt with issues of stealing in our home, except on one occasion with Matt, and the penalty was harsh enough that he never did it again.

Evan and I learned quickly that we had to change our lifestyle. I used to have a basket of snack foods for the children and anyone else on the kitchen counter, but the basket had to be moved to Evan's room due to Janelle's weight and stealing problem. That didn't work. Janelle found a way to sneak into Evan's room and steal not only food but other items as well. It was difficult and uncomfortable for me to address this with Daniel, knowing all the problems he and Brenda were already struggling with and feeling this would only put a strain on our relationship. Finally, the stealing became so bad, I had no other choice but to address it with Daniel in the presence of Dr. Westlake. Daniel revealed Janelle's history of stealing money from her mom's pocketbook, a book from the book fair at school, items from daycare. In conclusion, it was a lifelong behavioral pattern for Janelle. Nothing seemed to be learned from any of Janelle's misbehaviors and it was exasperating for us all, including Dr. Westlake.

As the weeks of counseling continued, Dr. Westlake found a lot of confusion with Janelle being raised by two mothers, Cheryl and Brenda. Daniel stated it was a mistake to allow Brenda to raise Janelle and that she was not a good "role model". It was during these counseling sessions with Dr. Westlake that Daniel stated it was a mutual agreement amongst Daniel, Cheryl and Brenda to raise Janelle between all of them. Daniel explained that Cheryl and Janelle were constantly arguing. Cheryl would become so frustrated, she would quarrel with Daniel yelling at him, "Why don't you try raising her?,"

Janelle told Dr. Westlake she loved Brenda more than she loved her mother, with Daniel reaffirming that Janelle never shed a tear at her mother's funeral. Janelle conveyed to Dr. Westlake that it would have been far worse on her if Brenda had died.

The most surprising information revealed in Dr. Westlake's counseling sessions was when Janelle and Daniel began elaborating on the male relationships in Brenda's life. Janelle was jealous of Brenda's current boyfriend. Brenda openly discussed intimate details of her relationships with Janelle. I sat in shock as Brenda's life began to unfold. Even though I had known Brenda for years, we had never discussed her past or anything of a personal, intimate nature. Daniel and Janelle surrendered information of Brenda's life that was bad from the past to the present. I was hearing and learning things for the first time about a friend whom I had known for years, and the picture they painted of her was very ugly. Descriptive details that reminded me of the story in the bible of the harlot, yet far worse.

The sessions went on for over a month focusing on the ill repute of Brenda's relationships with men and their behaviors with certain acts in the presence of Janelle. Daniel gave historical details prior to Janelle's birth adding validity to Janelle's current personal experiences with Brenda. Finally, with the shocking and nasty details laid out on the table, Dr. Westlake made his first counseling suggestion, stating Brenda played a significant part in Janelle's behavioral problems with the inappropriate relationships she was exposing to Janelle.

"The raising of Janelle between the two homes has to be confusing for a twelve year old," Dr. Westlake stated. "If all of this information is true, than Janelle's relationship with Brenda needs to stop immediately," he continued, "it should have never been agreed upon in the first place," he positioned his eyes on Daniel.

"Janelle was and is difficult for all of us to raise," Daniel defensively stated. "We all needed a break from Janelle. Besides, Janelle and her mother didn't get along."

"Daniel, this is your responsibility. Cheryl's gone and Brenda isn't the parent. You are," Dr. Westlake instructed. "Ending this unhealthy relationship and taking Janelle out of this type of environment of living with her aunt has to seize immediately and it has to be done by you," he continued. "Brenda's relationship with Janelle at times is either hot or cold. When there is a man in Brenda's life who has kids, Brenda uses Janelle to portray herself as a motherly image. When there's not a man in Brenda's life, she uses Janelle for companionship and help with the house and yard work. The current man in Brenda's life does not have kids, therefore, she is neglecting Janelle. She's "pushing her away" and it's confusing for Janelle. Janelle is jealous and is acting out negatively."

"Janelle in reality has had two mothers in her life for the past twelve years. One is her aunt who has a "hot or cold" relationship with her. The other, her deceased mother whom she had a lukewarm or cool relationship with. Not a natural bonding between a maternal mother and child. Wouldn't you agree?," Dr. Westlake questioned Daniel.

Meekly Daniel agreed and with Dr. Westlake's instructions, Daniel and I left that evening knowing the situation with Brenda and Janelle would have to be dealt with immediately.

The next day Daniel called Brenda and scheduled a meeting for Saturday. At Brenda's house, I waited in the car as Daniel and Brenda stood out on the front stoop. I could hear and see the defensive pleading in Daniel's face and body language. I watched as Barbara's facial expression changed from confusion to rage. Then I watched as Brenda's fists tightly clinched at her side then she glanced at me sitting in the car.

"Here we go," I said aloud to the interior of the car.

"I don't understand," Brenda yelled at me. Then she turned to Daniel, her voice angry and loud. "What did you and Janelle say to the counselor? Why would he make such a decision?," Brenda was completely in the dark that her life had been revealed like an opened book to Dr. Westlake and I.

Daniel's response was now loud enough for me to make out, "Adult conversations and situations unsuitable for Janelle."

"Janelle's just jealous," Brenda shouted in Daniel's face. "Why in hell did you allow me to raise her for the past twelve years if you were going to take her away from me?," Brenda began to cry.

Brenda and Daniel were now yelling accusations at each other. Brenda was relentless, her voice hard and mean, her cheeks rosy with anger, but then, so were Daniel's. She was obsessed in trying to find out what was said to Dr. Westlake by Janelle and Daniel. Yet Daniel refused to the point of storming away from Brenda, leaving her standing on the steps. A cold hard, look from her dark brown eyes piercing into mine.

"She blames me," was my immediate thought. "Oh, no, she blames me."

Silence filled the car as we drove back to Daniel's house. The days and weeks that followed only confirmed my final thought as we drove out of Brenda's driveway. With Dr. Westlake and I being new in the picture, we took the brunt of Brenda's anger. As a mother, I could understand why Brenda fought so hard to keep Janelle. She had joint custody of Janelle since her birth. There was a maternal bond established. The way it looked to her now was this would have never happened if Dr. Westlake or I hadn't come into their lives.

Daniel and Janelle never realized how it changed my life knowing the friend I once knew was not what she portrayed herself to be. Daniel and Janelle made me promise to never reveal the secrets of Brenda's behavior spoken of in those sessions with Dr. Westlake. It was to always remain a secret. We would invite Brenda to our family events. If she came, she treated me like I was invisible or she would be cold and openly sarcastic; leaving me upset over her direct insults or rudeness. Yet, I never revealed "the secrets" no matter how much Brenda mistreated me. I lost a friend even though it was Daniel and Janelle who painted the vulgar picture of Brenda. I was bound to my promise of secrecy. A secret that loomed over our relationship. The guilt seemed almost unbearable for both Daniel and Janelle.

Chapter Eight: Seeking the Truth

Six months before Daniel and I married, I finally found a house. Amber, Evan and I were moving away from the adventures and memories of the little white house. Amber moved into an apartment a short distance from our new home and all was looking well. I knew I wouldn't get to live in my new home very long before my marriage to Daniel, but it was the accomplishment of owning my very own home that I cherished the most. The house was in a quiet cul-de-sac not far from the little white house. It was a three-bedroom brick ranch with two baths, a den, living room and a two-car carport. Unpacking and seeing things I had not seen in almost two years was like Christmas.

Plans were in progress for our spring wedding and Daniel was in the process of selling his house. Daniel was to pay off bills incurred by Cheryl's medical and funeral expenses with the equity money from the sale and whatever money was left over he would re-invest in a house closer to town. My house would be rental property used for income.

Daniel's house sold quickly and Janelle and he moved in with us for three months while he searched for another home. Living with Daniel and Janelle was a learning experience, one I look back on and find a deep revelation into the depth of Janelle's problems.

After Christmas, Janelle's weight began to decrease as she and I worked on dieting and exercise. It was easier to work with Janelle now that we had full custody of her. By now, Janelle was well over 235 lbs. and walking seemed to be the best form of exercise. Janelle's weight made it too difficult for her to ride her bike. Our walks were working and I enjoyed the time with Janelle, enabling us to "bond."

Janelle struggled academically in school and Amber offered to help her with her schoolwork. Amber was tutoring developmental courses part-time at the community college, which gave her materials to enhance Janelle's studies. Soon it became blatantly obvious Janelle didn't like school and didn't like to study. An "attitude arose," making it difficult for Amber to work with Janelle. Eventually Janelle became uncooperative to the point that if Janelle walked into the room and saw Amber, she would immediately turn and walk out of the room, letting us know there would be no studying or tutoring that evening. If Amber were in the living room with Evan and me, Janelle would eavesdrop on our conversations by standing in the hallway. At times, we could see her shadow and we would make up stories just to be ridiculous at her silliness. Needless to say, the tutoring stopped long before it really began.

Janelle had absolutely no respect for rules or authority. One of the worst things was her morning showers. I supported Daniel and Janelle during the three months they lived with us, never asking for financial assistance towards the utilities and food. Daniel left for work around 4:00 each morning and it was my responsibility to get Evan and Janelle to school. Janelle was a challenge to get up and she would take 30 to 45 minute morning showers. She would stand in the shower, sleeping, until all the hot water ran out. I tried to discuss the problem with Daniel, but it was to no avail. Daniel stated Cheryl had the same problem with Janelle, but he would talk to her. When I mentioned it again to Daniel, he erupted in defense and anger directed at me, then cursing and yelling at Janelle. Evan and I were forced to switch our showers to evenings in order to avoid another volcanic eruption.

Then came my first water bill since Daniel and Janelle had moved in. It was $150, when it was usually less than $30. The City sent a letter accompanying the bill suggesting I may have a leak due to the huge consumption of water and the history of the household's prior usage. The City had already checked the main water line and found no leakage. When I showed Daniel the letter, he searched all under the house looking for a leak, which he never found, refusing to believe that Janelle was still taking long showers. A dirty, muddy, Daniel came crawling out from under the house and gave Janelle his usual yelling and cursing speech, which never seemed to accomplish or solve anything. The next month, with a water bill of $155 in hand, I sought out advice from Dr. Westlake. Dr. Westlake's suggestion wasn't exactly what Daniel wanted to hear.

"Since you and Janelle's mother had this same problem in the past," he began. "I suggest you take Janelle's showering privileges away. I'm not all for this arguing, yelling and cursing. It's not getting anywhere with Janelle except teaching her the same behavior of yelling and cursing. Deal with the issue at hand, Daniel, enforce an action with a consequence related."

Daniel sat dumbfounded. Complete silence filled the room for what seemed like minutes.

"For how long?," Daniel finally asked.

"Just a month this first time," Dr. Westlake stated. "I think it'll work," he was hopeful. "Janelle's crying out for attention in a negative way from you. She can take baths for a month and Kathy can hopefully get caught up on the water bills."

We left the session with Daniel instructed to tell Janelle she would only be allowed take a bath at night and could wash her hair under the bath or sink faucet, along with an in depth discussion about action/consequences. Daniel was reluctant and disgruntled. He appeared to be afraid to discipline Janelle. His preference was yelling and cursing.

Once home, Daniel told Janelle of Dr. Westlake's suggestion.

"You can't do that!," Anger swept over Janelle's face as she glared at Daniel. Daniel fought back reminding Janelle of her mother's struggles with her and pointed out the letter from the City. Yet, no one was permitted to punish Janelle, and soon Janelle developed a plan. Over the next few days, Janelle exaggerated the consequences of a bath to her daycare worker at the afterschool program. By the end of the week, we received a call insinuating child abuse and negligence by the director who felt an investigation was needed by the daycare as well as Social Services. Daniel scheduled a meeting with the daycare worker and director. We explained the deviance of Janelle to obey rules, Evan and I having to take our showers at night, and the suggestion of action/consequence made under the direction of Janelle's psychiatrist. Janelle lost her case of child abuse against us, only drawing negative attention towards herself by the daycare worker and director. Bottom line, the director and daycare worker said if Janelle were their child, the punishment would have been far worse.

The thermostat was another controlled event by Janelle. She ruled. If she was cold, she turned it up, if she was hot, she turned it down. She was in control and could not be reasoned with. Her room would be literally roasting with heat. Routinely I had to check the thermostats, especially in her room, dealing now with another astronomical utility bill to pay. Once again frustrated, Dr. Westlake began steps towards boundaries and consequences of misbehavior, to be implemented by Daniel. When Daniel would try to discipline Janelle, she would defiantly say, "That's not fair," "You can't do that," or "You didn't tell me," she manipulated and controlled everything Dr. Westlake and Daniel tried to do. Daniel's punishments would end up with the usual arguing, yelling and cursing, with no positive results. I don't think that was what Dr. Westlake had in mind. Nevertheless, that was the way it had always been between Daniel, Cheryl and Janelle. Arguing, yelling and cursing, resulting in no behavioral changes. After these confrontations, Janelle would go to her room, isolate herself and pout.

Daniel and Janelle were not regular attendees of church. When they did attend, it was usually a Baptist church or occasionally a Methodist church, where Daniel's brother-in-law was an associate minister. Evan and I were members of a local Quaker meeting. Daniel and I decided that we would alternate Sundays and I would attend his church one Sunday and the next we would attend mine. Soon Daniel started gravitating towards my church. He liked the minister (he found that they both liked old western movies, Daniel's hobby) and the messages he said were clearer. Our church was an evangelical Quaker church, which meant it had a "little Baptist fire" in it. Daniel and Janelle had difficulty at first with "the moment of silence waiting on the Spirit" in the Quaker faith, but soon grew accustomed to it.

For youth services, Evan went to a different Quaker church. I was always sensitive to the religious needs of my children and Evan (as well as Matt) had grown fond of another Quaker church not far from the house because they liked their youth group and youth minister. Therefore, we went to one Quaker church for Sunday morning service and another one for Sunday evening. We let Janelle decide which youth group she wanted to attend and she chose the same as Evan.

At youth, Janelle had difficulty getting along with other children, and the leaders quickly noticed her "moods," frequently asking what they could do to help. At times Janelle would stand and kick at the dirt, hold her head down, poke out her lip in a facial pout. Then there would be times she would be in a good mood, acting somewhat normal. Janelle's need for attention was insatiable.

Two short months before our wedding came another shock. Just when I thought that I had enough with the "Brenda secrets", it got even worse. This time I was beginning to wonder if God wanted me to run up the ladder, or maybe superstition was right, I was under the ladder with a lot of bad luck. At the age of twelve, Janelle's sexual behavior was out of control and she was suffering with a severe vaginal infection. Janelle revealed to Dr. Westlake that since the age of nine she had been sexually active, performing gross and inappropriate acts to her body for personal pleasure. Red flags immediately went up with Dr. Westlake. At one session, Daniel was unable to attend and Dr. Westlake seized the opportunity with me to disclose this information asking me if I knew enough about Janelle to suspect she had been molested at an earlier age. Dr. Westlake felt, the age of nine was a little young to be experimenting vaginally with various types of objects and performing explicit sexual acts, which in turn were harmful to her body and causing infections. Dr. Westlake questioned me about Brenda's relationship with various men, Daniel, and other family members. There was nothing I knew that could help. All I knew was exactly what Janelle and Daniel had revealed in earlier counseling sessions, the same as what Dr. Westlake already knew.

I revealed to Dr. Westlake a situation with Janelle at a Halloween party the year before which concerned me but I just shrugged it off and had really forgotten about it. At the party, Janelle kept grabbing, hugging, and rubbing herself against one of her relatives who was a man in his mid-30's. I knew Janelle was starving for attention yet didn't really know the man or how close his relationship was with Janelle, only observing the desire she had for his attentions. The man became aggravated and embarrassed by her hanging on him. Finally he was able to disconnect Janelle's arms from around his neck and pushed her away, while ordering her to stop. At that point, Janelle threw herself on the couch, placed a pillow between her legs and began rubbing herself in masturbation, ignoring everyone while staring blankly at the TV.

At various times, Janelle revealed to us she had extensive knowledge of sex, and knew explicit terminology, often bragging of what she knew. It was awkward and embarrassing. Amber and I had to admit, Janelle was far more knowledgeable at her young age of twelve than we were as adults in the area of sex.

Janelle confided in Dr. Westlake that she had an infection. Dr. Westlake presumed it was just a yeast infection. Janelle told him usually her father and other various members of her family such as her aunt and cousins as well as her mother all knew about the infections and bought her creams to treat the infections whenever she needed them.

"Most of the time the creams never worked and the infections always come back," Janelle told Dr. Westlake.

Dr. Westlake instructed me to speak with Daniel that evening about the history of the infections for validity of Janelle's story.

"Go by the drugstore on your way home and purchase Monistat Cream," Dr. Westlake stated. "Maybe it is just a yeast infection, we'll see,"

When I spoke with Daniel that evening about the infections, he showed little concern. "She's had them since she was, I don't know, eight or nine," he shrugged off any concern. "We've all been treating her with over-the-counter vaginal creams," said Daniel validating Janelle's story.

The first time I loaded the Monistat cream into the plastic tube, it broke my heart. I literally struggled within as I watched an experienced twelve-year-old, who for years had been inserting tubes of medication into her vagina. I left Janelle's room tearful each night after giving her the tube of medication. Janelle seemed happy stating no one had ever treated the infections properly and it was clearing up. However, that was just temporary; soon the infections and the inappropriate outward sexual behavior began again. Daniel remained silent, leaving Dr. Westlake and I struggling with all of this.

Dr. Westlake questioned Daniel as to why his family participated in purchasing and treating these infections for years. Did no one ever care enough to try to help this child? However, Daniel was evasive, stating it was just "the norm" for Janelle. When Janelle would perform her inappropriate sexual behavior in front of family and friends, I would politely take the pillow away from her. At times I would ask her to sit differently or more properly on the couch or chair, or suggest maybe she would like to go to her room. Anything I could think of in a futile attempt to stop the act. It was embarrassing to walk past her bedroom and see her masturbating on her bed while watching TV.

Dr. Westlake tried counseling Janelle and Daniel about how it was normal to have these desires but abnormal to follow through with experimentation. Nevertheless, Janelle was good at manipulating and twisting words. She told us the opposite, stating Dr. Westlake told her that her sexual activities for pleasure were normal. You can imagine what the next meeting with Dr. Westlake was like. Janelle could lie so convincingly, she even had the experts fooled, just like the nutritionist.

"She's good," Dr. Westlake admitted. "In fact she is one of the best liars I have ever counseled," Once again, he started trying to get to the bottom of where and when this all began, how the family became so involved, trying his best to get her to stop. After two rounds of Monistat cream, another infection came. Janelle was miserable.

"Look," said Daniel obviously frustrated with both Dr. Westlake and I. "Janelle just has these infections. She's had them for years. Her mother had them too. She'll get over them eventually," this time Daniel and I met with Dr. Westlake privately for the entire fifty-five minute session, as Dr. Westlake forced Daniel's assistance with us on the infections.

"I'm concerned," Dr. Westlake stated sternly. "How do we know what's causing the infections? Janelle is very sexually active and the objects she's using for pleasure can cause damage and bacterial infection. Daniel, eight or nine is a little young for a girl to begin these activities and I have my concerns as to the root of all this. Most of all, the participation of the family in purchasing the cream," Dr. Westlake left that part wide open and unanswered. The infections had been a part of their lives since Janelle was eight or nine years old and no one ever thought this was strange or questioned the cause of Janelle's infections; it was just a family affair up to the purchasing of creams. Dr. Westlake left the decision for a way to stop the infections and a cure for prayer and consideration until the next session.

By now, it was a little over a month before our wedding. Janelle's infection was beyond a normal yeast infection, it was a full-blown bacterial infection with a pungent odor. I felt Dr. Westlake was feeling like me, we were both "way in over our heads,"

The next session with Dr. Westlake recommended Daniel exercise parental control over the situation, pointing out that Daniel had been uncooperative with discipline in the past. Dr. Westlake's suggestion was to have Daniel take Janelle's bedroom door off.

"Privacy is a privilege," Dr. Westlake stated. "Hopefully Janelle will realize that and this will stop her from performing these inappropriate sexual acts,"

He continued, "Set up an appointment with your family physician or a gynecologist," Dr. Westlake instructed me in front of Daniel. "Maybe she needs a more thorough exam since over-the-counter drugs don't seem to be a cure,"

I was to continue removing objects utilized for her sexual pleasure, to pay closer attention to her behavior in front of others, and try to discourage it. Dr. Westlake then dismissed us while he met with Janelle and discussed the removal of the door. Janelle was furious!

I would have tried anything to help stop the infections and keep Janelle from hurting herself. Janelle utilized everything imaginable for pleasure and experimentation. I was forced to hide my tapered candles, rubber gloves, anything that remotely resembled the shape and size of an exciting form of ecstasy for her, she used. When Daniel and I were alerted that Janelle was using a new item, that item would be taken away and hidden as well. What amazed me the most was that Janelle was never embarrassed or showed any signs of understanding the inappropriateness of her behavior. It became impossible for me to help Janelle. She just hungered and hungered for more.

The next day I placed a call to my doctor, explaining our counseling with Dr. Westlake and made an appointment for Janelle.

That weekend Daniel and Janelle moved into their new home.

The following week I took Janelle in for a complete physical exam.

"Janelle has a bacterial infection in both her vaginal area as well as in her urinary tract. That's why the over-the counter drugs wouldn't cure it," Dr. Smith called me after work the following evening.

"What caused this?," Confused, I asked.

"A number of things," Dr. Smith seemed hesitant to go on.

"Like?," I was confused.

"Well, Janelle is certainly sexually active," The conversation seemed awkward for some reason. "But, well, she also has another problem," she paused.

"What?," I was scared of the response.

"Has anyone ever taught Janelle how to clean herself after a bowel movement?," Dr. Smith uncomfortably asked.

"What?," I cautiously moved forward.

"A bacteria caused by human feces in the vaginal and urinary track. It's not uncommon when someone is not cleaning properly after each bowel movement," she awkwardly explained.

I could have thrown the phone into the wall. "No, No!," I felt myself screaming inside.

"I'll handle it," somewhat composed, was all I could say as I gave her the preferred pharmacy.

"I'm sorry," was Dr. Smith's last words in an attempt to comfort me.

Slamming down the receiver of the phone, I was furious. Here I had an almost thirteen-year-old teenager, overweight, sexually active and she didn't even know how to clean herself. "This is gross! Gross!," I screamed out in the woods behind my house. Stomping out my anger, throwing my fist into the air. "What next God?," I screamed into the voided air. "What next?"

The following evening I met with Daniel at his house. In the basement, amongst the piles of moving boxes, we privately discussed my conversation with Dr. Smith as I gave him the antibiotics and cream.

"Has anyone ever shown Janelle how to properly clean herself after a bowel movement?," I asked Daniel.

"Her mother taught her the way she was taught," was his response.

"Daniel, she's not cleaning herself and that's part of the reason for the urinary tract infection and a small part of the vaginal infections," I gently tried to explain, "That's why the creams have never completely cured Janelle. These are bacterial infections not yeast infections,"

It was apparent Daniel knew of these types of infection and wanted to avoid further discussion as I watched him move to open another box.

"That's the way Cheryl did it? That's the way Janelle was taught?," This is unbelievable I thought.

"Yeah," Daniel was becoming angry. "And Cheryl carried an infection most of the time we were married,"

"How in the world did you have sex with that smell?," was all I could say in shock.

"Cheryl always showered before we had sex," End of subject.

Driving home that evening, my fist pounded on the steering wheel. "I can't believe this!," I screamed into the car interior. "I just can't believe this. These people are crazy!"

The wedding was fast approaching, wedding invitations all mailed out, the caterer and church all lined up. Bouquets and boutonnières made, all in a shoebox in my living room. Two short weeks and now this. I was having doubts. Many doubts. It seemed as if Janelle's misbehavior and deviance was really that Janelle didn't want Daniel and me to marry. In addition, Janelle's problems were far more than I felt I could handle.

The next day I called Dr. Westlake and revealed Janelle's test results.

"I'm so sorry, Kathy," was his response. "I get the feeling Janelle is holding something over Daniel and I can't seem to get to the bottom of it," Dr. Westlake took our phone conversation to speak to me in privacy. "Daniel's afraid of Janelle, but why, I haven't been able to figure out."

"I don't think I can go through with the wedding," I began to cry.

"Let me meet with just Daniel and you at our next session. Leave Janelle at home," he tried to console me.

Little did I know that the following week, one week before our wedding, would be our last session with Dr. Westlake. We discussed my doubts and I asked Dr. Westlake if we should go ahead with our plans to get married. There was a lot of concern about Janelle's behavior, especially at the wedding.

"Don't let Janelle's actions control your lives," Dr. Westlake advised us. "Go forward with the wedding, but sit down and talk with her about actions/consequences. If she acts out or misbehaves, she'll be asked to leave and escorted from the wedding ceremony. It's as simple as that."

Chapter Nine: He Wore a Mask

We could not have planned a more perfect wedding. Daniel and Cheryl did not have a so-called wedding, just a quick Justice of the Peace ceremony in a courthouse; therefore, it was important to Daniel to have a real wedding with all the romance and "frills" of a traditional ceremony. Our wedding took place on a beautiful spring evening on April 28, 2001. Daniel was in a lot of pain with a slipped disk in his back and on prescription pain pills. During the wedding ceremony, he had to sit in a chair for part of our vows.

Prior to the wedding, Janelle and I worked hard on her weight and she had lost fifty pounds. She looked great. Janelle soaked in the compliments from family and friends on how good she looked. Compliments that boosted her self-esteem and her attitude was for the better as well.

"She's acting more like a lady," her mother's family commented.

The morning after the wedding, we left early for our flight to Switzerland. We had planned everything around what Daniel wanted. He wanted snow, trains, and quaint towns. Switzerland at that time of year provided it all. Just like in the movie <u>Trains, Planes and Automobiles</u>, we experienced all. We had a wonderful travel agent from California who planned our trip from the walk through Zurich Airport, to the lake launch, where we caught a boat ride to our first destination. Daniel was in a wheelchair throughout the airport travel but after the airport, we were on our own working with Daniel's prosthesis.

April is the "off season" in Switzerland and at our first motel we were the only ones in the entire motel. The motel was very old and mirrored the unique atmosphere of Switzerland. It had an old service elevator, plump white comforters, and soft goose down pillows. It was located beside a lake with a beautiful view of a small island. We stayed two nights at this motel.

Daniel had seen two different doctors the day before we were married. One had given him cortisone injections to hopefully last throughout the honeymoon. The other gave him quite a supply of high power pain and sleeping pills. Daniel's mood swings were up and down, making it difficult for him to function without taking pills every four to six hours. I use to dread seeing him take the pills, then dreaded it if he didn't. Daniel would be nice the first hour, then for the next three hours, he was in a "drug induced daze," Movement from place to place was difficult because Daniel was somewhat dysfunctional. When he began to "come down off the pain pills," he would get mean and nasty. At that moment, I knew he would soon be popping another pain pill.

My first taste of Daniel's true violent side came on the third day of our honeymoon. We traveled by train to our next destination which was another quaint Swiss town. Daniel was late taking his next pain pill and the walk from the train to the motel was mostly uphill. I felt like a packhorse in biblical days, trying to carry both my own load and part of Daniel's due to his discomfort in his back and with his prosthesis. By the time we reached the motel, Daniel was in a violent mood.

"You're so damn, fuckin' perfect," he raged as soon as the door closed behind us. It was as if he was a coffee pot brewing up until we had reached inside the room then he exploded. Standing by the bed, I had just dropped the backpacks and luggage. Turning to face him, his eyes were blazing red with anger. Kicking the furniture out of his way, Daniel came towards me cursing. Instinctively I wanted to flee from the room, yet Daniel stood solid between the door and me. His temper had taken me totally off guard. Quickly I glanced around the room.

"Maybe the bathroom," I thought. It was too late, Daniel was now just inches from me as he reached out and pushed me backwards onto the bed. With quick reflex and instinct, I rolled over on my right side and ducked under Daniel's reaching grasp. Finding myself in a standing position. Daniel held me hostage with vise-like grip on my arms. His strength unbelievable as pain shot up my right shoulder.

"He's going to kill me," I panicked as he slammed me against the wall.

"I could choke you," Daniel stretched out his right hand, relieving my arm from pain, while he demonstrated strangulation. His fingers pierced into my neck, his breath hot on my face. "It would be easy to kill you!," He seethed into my face.

"Daniel, please, I'm sorry you're upset. I'm sorry you feel this way," I pleaded with him.

"Sorry, Sorry? For what, that I'm a crazy nut case? Go ahead and say it. Say it! Daniel's a fuckin' crazy man?"

It was difficult for me to focus, and think of a plan to escape. "Focus, think, think!," I kept saying to myself. His flashing, mean, angry eyes glaring into my face. "He's going to kill me!"

All of a sudden, Daniel's grip loosened ever so slightly, yet I felt the pressure relax just enough for me to squirm out from under his strong hold. I ducked under his attempt to grab me again, frantically running towards the door.

"Get your ass out of here!," were the last words I heard as I slammed the door behind me.

Running through unfamiliar hallways, down an old staircase, opening and closing doors, frantically seeking out Exit signs, I made it out into the back, narrow alleyway of the motel. How I got there, I have no idea, but I was safe.

Into the cool, fresh air, I went for a walk in a foreign country, alone and frightened. It was hard for me to comprehend what had just happened. Nevertheless, I walked, unable to find a hiding place such as Mr. Draper's farm. Yearning for that place I once ran to as a child for strength and comfort. Far from the noise and rage of abuse. Through unfamiliar streets I walked, keeping sight of the motel at all times for direction back.

Dusk came upon me and I returned to the old inn, making the same entrance Daniel and I had made hours earlier. I sat on the hard hallway floor, not sure of what to do. It was late when I finally felt it might be safe to sneak back into the room. It was dark and I could hear Daniel's snoring from the bed. Without undressing, I slipped in between the down comforter, beside Daniel. With my head deep into the pillow, sore, bruised and exhausted, apprehensive about what the remainder of our honeymoon held, I softly cried.

I don't know what Daniel remembered of Switzerland, his state of mind different from mine. It was a one of a beautiful European country. Every town had its own uniqueness and even though my husband was dysfunctional and violently abusive at times, God traveled with me. He gave me incredible strength to carry the luggage, struggle with Daniel's "disabilities", and endure the pain pills and abuse. I clung to the beauty and sight of everything I saw. The simplicity of friendly people. A country full of magnificent mountains, farmlands, waterfalls.

Zermatt, the city of no cars, only battery operated ones, beholds a beautiful view of the Matterhorn. We rode a gondola, then a cogwheel train to the top of a mountain. Switzerland is a memory planted in my mind as another part of God's amazing handy work and lessons in strength and faith.

That was our honeymoon. A revelation of the man I had married and the depth of his illness both physical and mental.

With the wedding and honeymoon over, it was back to work and everyday reality. We never once spoke of the violence of Daniel's behavior in Switzerland. It was as if it had never happened.

During our first month of marriage, we were still fixing up Daniel's house and moving items from my home into his.

It was Saturday, Daniel was up early, he couldn't sleep the night before. By now, he was off all the pain and sleeping pills. Daniel began the day by working in the master bathroom. Soon thereafter, he left to go to the hardware store and when he returned, he slammed the front door behind him, went stomping up the stairs, pushing past me, not looking nor speaking, straight into the bathroom, dropping his tools down onto the floor with a loud "thud." Something was obviously wrong, but what I had no idea. Thirty minutes later, I went back into the bathroom.

"Hey," I cautiously greeted Daniel. His response was a nasty glare as he looked up from under the bathroom sink. The same look I experienced numerous times in Switzerland.

I watched Daniel kick and throw things in an angry fit around the bathroom, all the while cursing.

"I wished I was dead," Daniel finally began to reveal his mood. "Cheryl was the lucky one. Everyone is dead, my brothers are dead my two sisters are dead," he continued. "I want cancer," he turned and glared at me. "Maybe God will give me cancer and I can die!," once again, by the look on Daniel's face and his words, I knew I was in danger. The man I was looking at was a different one from the one I had spoken marriage vows to a month ago, yet the same man who went crazy on our honeymoon in Switzerland.

His mood was different this time. It wasn't drug related. This was the real Daniel. The one I had really married and we weren't alone in Switzerland; the children were still in their bedrooms. I left Daniel lying on the bathroom floor cursing, kicking and throwing tools around the bathroom. I checked on Evan and Janelle. Janelle was asleep, Evan was watching TV. Reassured they were safe, I started thinking of a plan to get out of the house before I got hurt.

"Daniel?," I interrupted his cursing rage, "I need to go by my house and finish collecting our things, check the mail and take the bags we had for charity and drop them off,"

Daniel never looked up at me or acknowledged what I had said. Quietly I retreated from the bathroom and left. Once I arrived at my house, checking the mailbox, I realized it was Memorial Day.

"Memorial Day," I thought. "Exactly one year since our first date,"

I loaded my car with what was left from the house, dropped the items off at the local Goodwill store then drove straight back to Daniel's house.

"Hey, I'm back," Daniel looked at me with that same nasty glare I left him with earlier with no response, continuing to work. I retreated to the kitchen and began unpacking boxes.

"It takes an hour for you to check your mail? You're a liar! Where have you been? Where did you go?," Daniel came in yelling a few minutes into my work, ceasing my unpacking he grabbed my arm. His face was red and full of anger. "Who did you meet?"

"I didn't meet anyone Daniel," Trying to keep my voice low for Evan and Janelle's sake. "I went to the house and the Goodwill store."

"You're a damn liar!," Daniel yelled into my face. "You probably went and met up with Dr. Westlake. I know the two of you are having an affair."

I countered, "Daniel, we haven't seen Dr. Westlake since before the wedding. I'm not having an affair with anyone. Here, look, here's the receipt from Goodwill?," I pulled the receipt from my blue jean pocket.

Daniel slapped the receipt out of my hand and onto the floor. "You call yourself a Christian. You're lying! Admit it, you're lying! And there's a place called hell for people like you!," Daniel said, too angry to reason with. His fingers digged deeper into my arm as he firmly held me in place. I struggled and managed somehow to break free. I ran down the hallway to get Evan. Daniel caught up with me, grabbed my arm and threw me against the wall outside Evan's room. Then he began pulling me towards the staircase, away from Evan and Janelle's rooms.

Evan, hearing Daniel yelling and the struggle, stepped out of his bedroom, into the hallway. "Mom?," I could hear him question.

"It's okay," Daniel shot over his shoulder at Evan as he pulled me down the staircase. I could see Evan lingered in the hallway as he watched Daniel pulled me into the garage and quickly closed the door.

"You never went to the house and you damn well know it," Daniel was unreasonable. "You're playing games with me and I don't play games!," at this point,

Daniel had released my arm, thinking I was secured under his control in the garage. Quickly, I turned and ran back up the stairs. Daniel caught up with me mid-way up the second flight of stairs as he grabbed my leg, pulling me down onto the stairs, he rolled me over to face him.

Hovering over me with his eyes glazed over in pure rage I pleaded, "Daniel, please I didn't do anything wrong, I loaded the car with the items and dropped them off at Goodwill. I promise."

Daniel refused to listen. "No you didn't, you're lying and you know it."

Defeated, Daniel's entire body pinning me down, I saw no hope in sight, only further abuse. "Okay, Daniel, you're right," I said looking up at him. "Whatever you say I must have done. I give up."

There was no way to rationalize with Daniel as he continued to call me a liar, accusing me of playing games. The carpet step and the position of Daniel's hold me bruising and uncomfortable. Then suddenly I realized what this was all about. This was the first time I had ever gone anywhere alone without Daniel since we had been married. Daniel went with me everywhere. I had never noticed it before; it had just become mechanical that that was the way it was to be. Daniel controlled all the grocery shopping, running of errands, everything. I hadn't been allowed to do anything alone.

Abruptly Daniel sat up, I scrambled up the stairs, intent to get to Evan.

"We need to talk about this," Daniel grabbed my arm, stopping me again. "Admit it!," Daniel sternly looked into my eyes. "Who in hell did you meet with? Your boyfriend?"

"We have to leave. I have to get to Evan," trying not to panic, I kept saying repeatedly in my mind. Daniel was too far-gone. Everything I thought I did, I thought I felt, I thought I experienced, didn't exist Only what Daniel said I did was reality. Daniel had grabbed me and turned me around so many times my arms and shoulders hurt terribly, and were beginning to show red marks, but I couldn't say a word. I was numb with shock and dizzy from the grabbing and abuse.

Jerking my arm out of his grasp with more strength than I realized I had, I scurried up the remaining stairs, down the hall and into Evan's room.

"Evan, get up, pack some clothes quickly," I told him.

"No! We all need to talk," Daniel yelled out behind me catching the slamming of Evan's door with his hand. Then he turned and went into Janelle's room, literally dragging a sleeping Janelle behind him and thrusting her into Evan's room.

Evan and Janelle were crying.

"Evan, did you hear your mother yelling at me?," Daniel asked.

"No, I heard you yelling at my mother," Evan shot back sarcastically.

Janelle, leaning against the doorframe, was pale. and remained quiet.

"Well," Daniel responded defeated. "Did you see me put my hands on your mother?"

I could see the tears and fear in Evan's eyes. Evan was afraid to answer even though I watched as his eyes traveled down my bare arms, revealing the redness of Daniel's fingerprints that had already surfaced.

"Did you see me lay a hand on your mother?," Daniel repeated directly to Evan.

"Yes, in the hallway," Evan bravely responded. "Yes, I did," I hated to see Evan treated this way. It was humiliating and embarrassing.

"This isn't real," I closed my eyes and said to myself. "This can't be happening."

I reached out and grabbed Evan's hand, slowly pulling him with me, past Daniel, past Janelle and into the hallway. Step by step, when finding a way to safety seemed impossible, God went before us as we made it to the bottom of the stairs with Daniel hot on our heels.

"Where are you going?," Daniel yelled. "Answer me! Where do you think you are going?"

With Evan already out the door, Daniel stopped me, grabbing me by the arm once again, trying to jerk me back inside the house. His grip forcing me around to face him.

"I mean it, are you sure you want to do this?," he growled. This time I felt the pain shoot up my arm and instinctively cried out while pulling away.

"What the hell?," Daniel roared.

"You're hurting me. My arms can't take the pain anymore," I pleaded. "Please, let us go. You're not rational."

My response to the pain only made Daniel angrier.

"I didn't hurt you. You're just sore from all the moving," he stated.

Evan was nervously pacing in the yard, afraid to go on without me.

"Show me; show Evan. Show us where I've hurt you," Daniel ordered. I took the opportunity Daniel gave me as he released my arm to move closer to Evan in pretense of showing Evan my arm. Close enough I mouthed the words "run." Simultaneously, Evan and I raced to the car.

Daniel, realizing what we were doing was quickly in pursuit, and caught the car door just before I was able to slam it shut.

"Is this it, are you really going to leave? If you leave this is it, I mean it. I'll blow my head off!," Daniel threatened, while releasing his hold on the door in an effort to slam his fist on the top of the car for emphasis. Taking advantage of the release, I jerked at the door handle, catching Daniel off guard and slammed the door, locking it immediately. Quickly I started the car and backed out, leaving Daniel standing in the driveway.

Evan and I drove to Quaker Lake, a conference center maintained and owned by the Quakers not far from Daniel's house. We walked amongst the soft pine trees and the trail around the lake, not speaking about what had just happened. I think both of us were still dealing from the shock, not knowing what to say. After several hours, we returned to the house, knowing Janelle was still there, and we were both worried for her.

The house was quiet when we entered. Daniel was a different person from the raging beast hours before. He was sitting in his recliner with the TV on mute, a Bible in his hands, staring blankly into space. He remained that way the rest of the afternoon while I unpacked boxes. Later that evening Daniel called us all into the living room.

"I'm sorry for the way I acted," he apologized to us all. "Evan, 'manhandling' a woman isn't right and I shouldn't have done it. I'm sorry for what you heard and what you saw."

Then Daniel left to go down into the basement. Janelle and I went for an evening walk and Evan returned to his bedroom. When we returned, Daniel was still in the basement. I went on to bed.

"Do you hate me that much?," Were the first words out of Daniel's mouth as I awoke the next morning.

"Please, Daniel what did I do?," I asked, still groggy from a restless night of sleep.

"Never mind!," Daniel huffed as he sat up and slammed his fist in the covers, then he slung the covers off both us. Sitting up on the side of the bed, he jerked on his prosthesis then stormed out of the bedroom, slamming the door as he left.

"Not again," I said as I laid my head back onto the pillow. After showering and getting ready for work, I went into the living room to kiss Daniel goodbye. Turning his head to avoid my kiss he asked, "Do you hate me so much that you wouldn't even let me hold you last night?," he continued to eat his cereal.

"Daniel, I barely remember you coming to bed," I searched my memory. "Wait a minute, I do remember," I said. "I remember being snuggled up against you, your arm was underneath me and I was facing you. Just the way you like me to be."

"That was at first," Daniel sarcastically replied. "But sometime during the night while you were asleep you rolled over, away from me," he continued, "In your subconscious mind," he philosophized. "You really hate me."

"Daniel, please, I was asleep. How can I know what I do in my sleep?," Daniel was beyond reasoning with, and seemed convinced even in my sleep I was doing things on purpose. I knew from the past month where this was going. This was the third time Daniel had accused me of not responding to him in my sleep. My sleep pattern bothered him, and he frequently chastised me for the way I slept. Daniel wanted me next to him facing him at all times during the night. Each night I started out in the position Daniel desired, directly next to him. When I turned over during the night, Daniel felt I was awake and didn't want to snuggle or cuddle or to have him touch me. Twice since our wedding day, I was awaken in the middle of the night with Daniel sitting on the edge of the bed pouting and angry, complaining that I didn't love him, or that my feelings had changed. Holding covers or a pillow when I rolled over was also prohibited; it infuriated Daniel. He felt I loved the pillow or covers more than him. Daniel was jealous of the pillow, bed sheets and blankets on our bed. From that moment on, for the duration of our marriage, I had to take measurements from the edge of the bed to the center of the bed. If I measured from the tip of my toes to the edge of the mattress, I would be in the exact spot where

Daniel wanted me to be. If I awoke during the night or early in the morning not in the right position, I would quickly measure and quietly slide back up next to him. Measuring and measuring all during the night. I was controlled as to when I could go to bed at night and when I could get out of bed in the mornings. All of these demands/commands remained for the duration of our marriage. Daniel, training me that he was the authority of my life. I complied with complete submission and obedience to him.

Chapter Ten: Nightmares and Fear

"Which way from here?," Gary asked, jolting me from my thoughts. Coming into focus, I realized we were at a stop sign where the road ended. The mountains surrounded us and we were a few miles from the cabin.

"To the left. Stay on Hwy 89 west," I replied. "We're about 10 minutes from the cabin. You'll see a road to the left called Dan River Shores," I concluded. My heart beat racing again in fear of the fast approaching scene of the cabin. Matt use to tell me he would go to happy land whenever he was in a situation that was uncomfortable for him. Especially a trip shopping with his mom in the lingerie section of a department store. "Happy Land", a place we escape to in our minds to avoid the uncomfortable moments we find ourselves in.

Cindy and Gary were in conversation about the upcoming holidays. It was difficult for both of them with children from previous marriages; the typical struggles of blending the two families. Cindy's children and family lived in upper state New York, while Gary's family and children all lived in North Carolina, close to where Gary grew up. Balancing out the holidays and visits was a strain at times on their relationship.

From the moment Daniel and I were married, Janelle became my daughter. I didn't refer to her as my stepdaughter or isolate her as "Daniel's daughter," knowing how much pain that inflicted upon me during my own childhood with my stepmother's references that we were "his kids," I wanted stability in my relationship with Janelle, or at least as much as I could provide.

During the first month of our marriage, Janelle and I were closer than ever. It seemed Janelle had resolved within herself that I was going to be a part of her life, regardless of her actions.

It was my birthday, the first one since we were married, but we didn't celebrate. Daniel was in another bad mood. Evan mowed the yard that day, Daniel did the trim. I worked inside the house cleaning, while Janelle stayed in her room and slept most of the day.

"Is Janelle going to sleep all day?," Daniel came in from the heat to get a glass of water. "If you were a better mother to her, you'd be able to help her with her problems. She sleeps and is depressed most of the time,"

That seemed to be the "norm" for Janelle, and had been since I had known them. Moreover, I had no idea the routine Janelle had when she lived with Brenda.

My silence only made matters worse. "Evan did a lousy job mowing," Daniel said as he pushed Mitzi with his foot out of his way. "Damn dog! You need to get rid of her. I hate dogs and you know it. But then, you love her more than me. Of course," he sarcastically said. "You even love your children and everyone else more than you love me,"

Lately everything Janelle, Evan and I did was wrong. For over an hour, Daniel stood in the kitchen where I was emptying the dishwasher, cleaning the floor, counters, and raged. "You still seeing Dr. Westlake?," he started up again.

"No Daniel," I said as I kept working, avoiding the obvious ugly look on his face. "I haven't seen him since you and I saw him before the wedding,"

"You've probably called him I bet," Daniel relented. "You know having an affair isn't the act of a Christian. Look it up in the Bible," he continued. "A wife should honor and be submissive only unto her husband. If you would read your Bible and pray more it might help you with all your lies," Happy with his statement, Daniel turned to go back outside and finish with the trim. "But maybe you'll get lucky," he said as he walked down the stairs. "Maybe I'll get cancer, or better yet, maybe I'll just blow my goddamn brains out and make everyone happy," the slamming of the front door gave a relief of silence within the house.

Daniel's deep, dark moods were coming more frequently and lasting a lot longer, leaving Evan, Janelle, and I frightened and upset most of the time.

That evening after supper, Janelle and I went for a walk.

Out of sight of the house, Janelle began to open up and cry, revealing that even though we thought she spent her time sleeping in her bedroom, she could hear her father's rages. "This is the way dad was with mom and me," she tearfully started. "It was scary at times, but I thought he had stopped once he met you,"

"Janelle, I'm sorry," I softly spoke to her, touching her arm. "I wish I knew what to do."

"Nobody knows what to do," Janelle began to weep uncontrollably. "One time he was in one of his "moods" sitting outside on the front porch of our house, saying he was going to take a gun and kill himself. Mom asked me to go outside and suggest I watch a movie with him in his theater. 'Maybe that would make him happy,' Mom said. It didn't. Dad kept holding his head in his hands saying he wanted to die, he wanted to blow his brains out or maybe God would kill him with cancer,"

Janelle stopped at that point, gasping for breath in between the burst of hard flowing tears and emotions.

"What did you and your mother do?," I asked.

"Nothing," Janelle stated. "There was nothing we could do. I went back into the house and told Mom what Dad was saying and that I was scared he would kill himself. Mom just laughed it off and said 'Oh, he's just making an ass out of himself.' But I was scared. Really scared."

For a moment I was speechless. Not sure what to say. "Maybe your Mom just felt helpless, like you did," I tried.

"I don't know," Janelle shrugged her shoulders as she wiped the tears from her wet cheeks. "Mom and Dad loved each other, they just didn't get along. It was hard to talk to Mom."

We walked in silence as Janelle tried to get control over her emotions.

"Twice on our way to daycare after Mom died, dad started yelling and cursing at me about my weight. He accused me of stealing his snack cakes, sodas and eating his potato chips that he bought for work. 'What are you trying to do, kill me?' He kept saying. Then he dropped me off at the daycare, telling me he was going to kill himself. I really thought he was going to kill himself and I would never see him again," Janelle was tormented.

"Oh, Janelle, I'm so sorry," we stopped within sight of the house. "Why didn't you tell someone?," I asked.

"No one would have believed me," she cried. "I went straight inside the daycare and locked myself in the bathroom. I was too scared to tell anyone and scared Dad would get mad at me if I did tell,"

I was at a loss for words. I hugged her until the rage of tears were wept out. With Janelle composed, we started back to the house. Daniel was once again sitting in his recliner staring blankly at the TV that was turned off, a Bible laid unopened on his lap.

It was late; we were all exhausted and scared. I sent Janelle to her room not wanting Daniel to upset her any more than she already was. None of us knew what to do. I snuck downstairs to the basement with the cordless phone and called Dr. Westlake, feeling like if he couldn't help, he could at least direct us to someone that could. After describing Daniel's mood and actions along with the threat of suicide, Dr. Westlake gave me the number for the local Family Services Crisis line. "Call them immediately," Dr. Westlake was concerned.

"Do you think he's serious about killing himself?," the young female voice on the crisis line asked.

"I don't know," I wearily replied. "I'm finding out things that I never knew about my husband. I really can't say. All I know is the children and I are scared."

"Does he have a gun?," was the next question.

"Yes."

"Find it and remove it as well as any other type of weapon he might use against himself," she advised. "Stay close to the children and keep safe for the night, even if it means locking yourselves in a room. Call us in the morning and we'll have a plan for you and the children. If you need us, no matter what time it is, call, but especially in the morning. "

Evan helped me find the gun and we hid it along with a baseball bat under Evan's bed. I stayed with Janelle in her room with the cordless phone by the bed.

Around 2:00 in the morning, we heard a loud "pop" noise resembling a gunshot. Instantly I jumped up and ran out of Janelle's room, almost colliding with Evan in the hallway. "Wait here," I held my hand up and said to Janelle and Evan. Then I ran down the hallway into the kitchen, terrified Daniel had shot himself. Visions flooded my mind of what I might find. Daniel, lying on the floor in a pool of blood or slumped over the bar with a bullet hole in the side of his head. Would he be dead or barely alive? What would I do? By now I was mortally terrified at what I was about to find.

The moment my feet touched the linoleum floor, I looked at the island bar. There sitting on a barstool, with a sick grin on his face, was Daniel. No blood, no bullet hole, nothing. Just Daniel, looking at me as he questioned "What?"

I honestly can't believe this was all I could think.

"What was that noise?," I asked.

"What noise?," Daniel knew perfectly well what I was talking about. In his hand was some kind of tool he had used to make the popping noise that resembled the sound of a gunshot. All to get our attention and make us think he had shot himself. In that moment, I realized just how sick the man I married really was. Without another word, I retreated into Janelle's bedroom to call the Crisis Line.

The same sweet female voice answered. Explaining what just happened, by now I was on the verge of hysteria.

"Call in the morning around 8:00," she said. "I'll have the report written and we will arrange for a place safe for you and the children."

The next morning, Evan, Janelle and I packed a few clothes and necessities. Daniel was sitting once again in his recliner with a Bible open in his hands, staring at a blank TV screen. Without saying goodbye, directions to the local women's shelter in hand, the three of us left.

At the shelter, each of us were taken into separate rooms and given a thorough screening/intake process in an attempt to gather as much information as possible. We were also given a profile test to complete on Daniel as well as instructed to give a brief statement regarding the events of the night before. The profile test results from each of us were identical in scores and our own, individual observations. Each one of us stated our belief that Daniel was suicidal.

Because Janelle wasn't my biological child, the shelter contacted the police department, informing them I had Janelle, and we were safe at the shelter, in case Daniel decided to file kidnapping charges. We were allowed visits by Evan and Janelle's youth pastor. Janelle requested a visit from Daniel's brother-in-law, who was a minister. After a late breakfast and much needed rest, we all attended a domestic violence session.

The following day Daniel's brother-in-law asked Evan, Janelle, and I to go to his home and speak with Daniel's sister, Penny, regarding the events that happened.

"Sounds a lot like their father, from what I've been told," he said. "He was a pretty violent man."

The visit with Penny went badly. "Janelle, are you sure you're telling the truth? You know you have a history of being a liar?," Penny was cruel. "If this is true, you're going to hurt a lot of people," Penny kept going back and forth in a back room talking on the phone to various family members, one of which we knew for sure was Daniel.

"They didn't believe us," Janelle cried on the way back to the shelter.

"I know, Janelle," I could see her in the rearview mirror, her face red and swollen from hard crying.

"I would have never guessed we were walking into an ambush," It was obvious to all of us that it was a mistake to have gone there. Daniel's family turned deaf ears and blind eyes to what was happening. There was no support, just complete denial. Janelle, Evan, and I were at a complete loss and on our own.

For the next few days, Evan and I allowed Janelle to do most of the talking to the counselors. Janelle knew more about her dad's history of suicide threats, his relationship with her mother and her own personal experiences with her dad. Janelle frequently described the relationship between her mother and father the same, "They loved each other, but they just didn't get along," there were suicide threats, depression while her mother was alive, depression and threats to Janelle after her mother's death. It was painful to hear these statements from Janelle, a man so very different from whom I thought I knew and loved.

On our fourth day at the shelter, the director called me into her office.

"You're going to have to seek advice from an attorney," she began. "We're afraid since Janelle isn't your biological daughter, Daniel could make trouble."

The following day we went to see an attorney. We waited in the waiting room while the attorney placed a phone call to Family Services.

"I'm sorry guy," the attorney started. "Family Services contacted the Department of Social Service. The bad news is we'll have to follow the rule book," she bent down in front of the three of us. "You have to return to Daniel's home for at least one night while DSS does an 'official' investigation."

"Oh, no," my composure began to melt. "The children. Please, I'll go back, but not the children," I pleaded.

"It's Janelle," she explained. "DSS has to do an investigation in order to officially make a report and remove Janelle. If not, Daniel can take Janelle away from you. I'm so sorry," she concluded.

All of us were crying once we reached the shelter. Before leaving, Janelle, Evan, and I were once again placed in separate rooms and given another psychological evaluation test of Daniel and his behavioral patterns. Again, all three of our answers scored identical in all areas, concluding Daniel was suicidal, suffering from depression and mental illness.

Afraid to go back into Daniel's house, yet we knew we could lose Janelle if we didn't follow procedure. In Daniel's house, Evan and Janelle waited behind their closed bedroom doors, while I waited in the basement for the DSS's visit. Each of us wanting as little contact as possible with Daniel who was in the same position as when we left, sitting in his recliner, staring blankly at the TV with an open Bible in his lap.

The investigative officer arrived around 5pm. She was a petite woman with short blond hair, a warm, friendly smile and was easy to talk to. Her interview began with each of us separately, then all of us together.

"My results will be given to the Lead Director of DSS in the morning," she spoke to us all together in the living room. Our fear and insecurities of being near Daniel had Janelle, Evan and I sitting on the couch close to each other. "You should hear from us within twenty-four hours."

Looking at the two disappointed faces staring at me, I knew Janelle and Evan felt the same as I; another terrifying night with Daniel was the last thing any of us wanted to do. Yet, we knew we would have to for Janelle's sake.

That night was another night of fear. Once again, I slept with Janelle, while Evan slept in his room with a baseball bat and the gun under his bed. This night was different from the one before. Daniel spent the entire night screaming out with nightmares awakening us numerous times during the night. At times, all three of us, Janelle, Evan and I, would be standing in the hallway listening to Daniel's raging and his screams of fears in his dreams.

The moment I arrived at work the next morning after dropping Evan and Janelle off at Amber's apartment, I received a frantic phone call from the investigator.

"Mrs. Thomas, tell me you're all safe," she was audibly upset. "That man's crazy. I've been worried about the three of you all night," she stated. "I was so upset when I left that I called the Lead Investigator immediately when I got home, filling him in on the situation. We've arranged for Janelle to see a counselor this afternoon at Family Services," she continued. "Since Daniel is her biological father, he'll have to consent to it of course. This also means he'll also have to be the one to take Janelle. I'm sorry," she apologized. "It's 'protocol'. We're concerned for your safety and this is the quickest way to get all of you out of Daniel's house legally through the DSS system," she explained.

I left work early that afternoon, to pick Janelle up from Amber's apartment. Janelle was in tears when I arrived. Daniel had called Janelle and told her he had invited his sister, Penny and her daughter, Lynn, to go with them to the counseling session. Janelle was still upset from our previous visit to Penny's home and was afraid of what they would say or do.

"Please, please Kathy," she cried. "I don't want to go. It'll just be like it was at Penny's house."

"You have to Janelle," I tried hard to explain without bursting into tears myself. "We have to follow the rules."

Daniel was waiting for us when we pulled into the driveway.

"I'll be in your room when you get back. It'll be okay," Knowing the words had to be said for Janelle's comfort and reassurance. "I love you," I said as we hugged 'goodbye,.'" I watched as Janelle's eyes never seemed to leave my face as she entered into Daniel's truck and they drove away.

"Lord, please, please be with her," I prayed. "Please protect her and give her strength."

The moment I saw Janelle's face when she returned home, the dried tearstains on her cheeks, her face pale and scared, I knew things didn't go well. I was sitting on her bed as she came in, slamming the door Janelle literally ran into my arms.

"It was all a joke," Throwing herself out of my arms and onto the bed, burying her head into the bed pillows she sobbed, "My dad, Aunt Penny, and Lee were all joking and making fun of the questions on the application," she choked and started coughing. "Where dad was supposed to check 'Sex, Male or Female' he was laughing and said 'Every chance I can get'. They were making fun of us all," by now, Janelle was almost hysterical and I could barely make sense of what she was saying. "It was horrible. I couldn't say all I wanted to say with Dad sitting there next to me, staring at me. I was so scared," Janelle seemed even more frightened now. "They all kept talking, telling the counselor I was a liar and bad things from my past. When the counselor asked me about that night you called the shelter, I told them I was scared dad would kill himself."

"I was just depressed; everybody gets depressed and says things they don't really mean. Even you do Janelle," Janelle mocked Daniel's deep baritone voice as she repeated what he said.

"It was horrible, just horrible!," Janelle cried even harder into her pillows. There was nothing I could do but rub her back as she unloaded her burdens and stress into the soft pillow.

After a few minutes, Janelle rolled over and looked up and grabbed onto me for comfort.

"It's going to be alright, Janelle. I promise," I told her once again. Yet, I wasn't sure. It seemed to be another ambush. Janelle was right, it was like it was at Penny's house the week before. The family once again ganging up against Janelle, Evan and I.

"Let's eat," the smell of French fries suddenly grabbing my attention and an attempt to change the subject and brighten Janelle's mood.

"I went to Ann's while you were gone. I'll get Evan. Spread out a blanket, put on some music, we'll have a picnic right here on the floor," I jumped up off the bed and pulled the blanket onto the floor while Janelle went next door to get Evan.

That evening Janelle, Evan and I stayed in Janelle's room until late. Then with Evan tucked away his room, I returned to stay with Janelle. Another fearful night.

The next morning a phone call from DSS revealed that the behavior and 'light-hearted jokes' Daniel and his family made at the counseling session with Family Services backfired on them. The counselor saw through Daniel and reported her findings immediately to DSS. Arrangements were made to have Daniel meet at the office of DSS that afternoon, while movers were contacted to remove as many items as possible from the house for Evan, Janelle, and I. We were to wait at Amber's apartment. The children and I were being removed from the home by DSS.

Even though the final report from DSS was only partially complete, Daniel was to relinquish custody of Janelle based upon the preliminary investigation. We knew from our meeting with Family Services and the attorney that this was a possibility. Janelle requested to not be placed with any of her father's family members due to the recent treatment of her by Penny and other family members. Janelle wanted to stay with Evan and me, but Daniel chose to send Janelle to live with her mom's niece, Shelia, in Boone, NC. Daniel's decision was vindictive and literally tore my heart out. He knew Janelle didn't want to be separated from Evan and me. Janelle tearfully told us the days we spent together in the shelter were the happiest days of her life. How could five days in a women's shelter be fun? Evan and I were the closest Janelle had ever come to having a real family.

While Janelle was living in Boone, Evan and I moved in with my brother, Randy briefly and then into a basement apartment that belonged to a friend of mine.

The final investigation report from DSS arrived and read: "There was sufficient evidence to substantiate abuse, neglect, or dependency by Daniel Thomas. Suicide threats in front of children."

Social Services assigned caseworkers for Janelle in Boone as well as for Evan and I. Daniel was ordered into an anger management treatment program. We were requested to receive marriage counseling. I was to continue in domestic violence counseling. Dr. Bryant was assigned to Daniel for anger management treatment, and Daniel chose Dr. Leighman as our marriage counselor. A young woman named Elizabeth was assigned to Evan and me as our caseworker from DSS.

Chapter Eleven: Games

"Right around this curve," I directed Gary. While taking in a deep breath for strength and to clear my head. Bracing for what might lay ahead of us at the cabin. During the past week, my nights were filled with confusing dreams and nightmares. During the day, my mind was sluggish, pre-occupied with thoughts and fears. I lived in constant fear. I was exhausted and weak, but I was free. My life belonged to me now.

As we pulled into the driveway, my eyes frantically searched for any evidence of Daniel. The cabin looked empty, cold and dark. It was a rustic mountain cabin with one bedroom, a small living space, kitchen and partially finished bathroom. Instead of facing the road, the cabin was situated sideways. A deck, high off the ground surrendered to an up close and personal view of the magnificent mountains A small, white shed and a "still functional" weathered out-house laid further down a narrow path leading from the cabin, into the woods.

Gary came around the car to open my door, gently lifting me from out of the backseat. I felt as if I was walking in a fog, groping for stability and reality. Cindy cupped my elbow as I slowly climbed the up the wooden steps. Each step I climbed, a piercing pain shot up my leg. Pausing at the top to catch my breath, leaning against the railing, my eyes frantically searching in fear of any evidence Daniel may have been there. Always fear. "Will I ever feel safe again?," I wondered. My hands shook as I fumbled for the key.

Inside the cabin was empty except for panels of metal roofing on the floor fitting just barely inside the doorway. Next to the roofing was a blanket in front of a kerosene heater. Evidence of where I had slept for days only a week and half prior with no electricity, food or water. The day I escaped from Daniel's final abuse. No one knew how I made it to the cabin.

Tears streamed down my cheek as I dissolved into uncontrollable sobs. Cindy grabbed me into a hug, trying to console me. "Who was I? How did I get here? How did I survive? It's freezing up here!," erratically questions poured from my lips. Questions no one could answer because I had a deep, dark void in my life. Cindy tried to assure me I was safe, that everything would be okay. Gary, big-strong, Gary, looming outside the door. At any other time, Gary would have been outspoken and furious at what Daniel had done. Now, wringing his hands, pacing on the porch, Gary was at a loss for words. Both had worried looks on their faces and I knew they were questioning whether this had been the right thing to do. Gently pushing away from Cindy, I wiped at my tears with the back of my hand.

"Give me a few minutes," I exited the cabin, leaning onto the deck railing for support, breathing in the crisp, cool air. Somehow, I had to pull myself together.

"How do you when your entire life is held in a vise-grip of fear? A fear so horrible that it haunts your every thought and movement, every minute both day and night," I thought.

Looking back at the cabin, I could see it was suffering both inside and out from the elements of the winter weather. The roof was only partially tinned with the new roof, furring strips were spaced in anticipation of the remaining sheet metal panels to be put into place.

The roof was still leaking as the ceiling in the living room revealed a large circular water stain. Most of me wished I hadn't come. At that moment, it seemed like a mistake, yet, time was of the essence to stop further deterioration to the cabin and door locks needed to be changed.

As I walked around the cabin, a lone hawk circled above my head, squawking at my interruption of his peace there on the mountain. I was the intruder, this was his space.

"Is there really anyplace for me in this world?," I asked the soaring hawk. "Have I really ever 'fit in' with the world?," silently I wandered away from the cabin, allowing Gary to begin changing out the door locks. My feet blindly followed the narrow path that led to the gentle, soothing sound of water trickling across rocks, fallen leaves and branches.

"My 'Mr. Draper's place'," the thought brought a brief smile. "Somewhere, somehow, it seems like when I most need it, God, you take me to that place."

It seemed like only yesterday I was standing in a church, dimly lit, exchanging wedding vows with Daniel. A bitter cold numbness spread through my body as I looked up over the treetops to the strength of mountains.

Evan and I lived separate from Daniel for approximately three months after DSS removed us. During that time, Daniel and I saw each other frequently and attended marriage counseling with Dr. Leighman weekly, as requested by DSS. Daniel refused to take responsibility for his actions, acknowledge charges of domestic violence or the removal of Evan, Janelle, and I. Members of Daniel's family were outspoken and critical of us, stating what Janelle, Evan and I did was wrong. Asking why we would leave Daniel if he were really contemplating suicide, concluding we should have never gone to the shelter but instead to them.

During the marriage counseling sessions, Daniel brought up ridiculous things, making a fool of himself. He complained there were times when I was cooking dinner that I didn't greet him at the door with a warm hug or kiss or the kiss was not long or passionate enough. The pressure of my hand in his while we were holding hands was not firm enough, or sometimes I would forget to hold his hand. The way I slept, the pillows, the covers, Mitzi. Daniel was jealous of everything and everyone. Daniel controlled whom I could see and whom I could not see, including my own children as well as where I went, whom I spoke to, every aspect of my life. Daniel, validating all his insecurities and control over me to Dr. Leighman.

One entire session, Dr. Leighman spent trying to persuade Daniel to let me go on an occasional Friday morning to the beauty parlor to get my hair done. It was a session of me begging and Dr. Leighman trying to understand why Daniel wouldn't let me go. Finally, we reached a compromise where Daniel would take me and either wait for me or pick me up a few hours later. The same control issues spilled over into our sessions with Elizabeth from DSS.

On one particular trip to the beauty parlor, I had my hair cut shorter and styled differently.

"Someone must have told you your hair would look good short, and you got it cut for him," Daniel accused. "Did you ask me if you could get your hair cut?," he chastised me as if I were a child.

"No," meekly I responded, realizing this was just another thing I needed permission before doing.

"Well if you had, the answer would have been 'no'," he retorted.

Daniel took the same accusations of my haircut to Dr. Leighman and Elizabeth. Dr. Leighman was dumbfounded, offering no opinion or response.

"I think the haircut and style is cute on Kathy. What difference does it make anyway? It's her hair," Elizabeth was more outspoken and less intimidated by Daniel. "Is there anything you don't try and control?," She directly asked Daniel. Leaving Daniel at a loss for words.

Daniel continued making a fool of himself to all the counselors. All I could do was sit quietly and let him hang himself, watching and listening as they tried to understand and deal with Daniel's manipulation, control, and jealousy.

While waiting in the waiting room for another session in late July, Daniel told me he had been to the doctor, and they thought he had rectal cancer.

Immediately, I was concerned, an instant thought, "Oh no, you wished it, and now God is allowing it to come true," with sympathy, I consoled Daniel and asked him to keep me informed. When the forms came through my office at work, it was only a hemorrhoid; no indication or reference to cancer.

Soon Daniel began telling the counselors that he felt I was suffering from menopause.

"That's why Kathy overreacted the night they went to the shelter," Daniel, still in denial and avoidance. "She needs to be tested," he was insistent.

Where this latest "revolutionary idea" came from, we never knew. I wasn't old enough to be going through menopause, and my body seemed to be functioning well, but to put this latest theory out of Daniel's mind, Dr. Leighman and Elizabeth recommended I be tested.

"Let's just deal with one accusation at a time and put this latest theory of Daniel's to rest," Dr. Leighman concluded.

Embarrassingly, I asked my doctor to perform the test, even though he didn't understand. The results showed no sign or symptoms of menopause or pre-menopausal condition.

Daniel continued questioning, trying to find reasons, not letting up, constantly saying, "If you love me, why did you go to the shelter?," or "You need to admit you made a mistake. You panicked," obsessed with trying to force the children and me to admit the events of that evening and the abuse we endured never happened.

At first, Janelle and I communicated frequently by e-mails and phone calls. The e-mails and phone calls slowed down a bit as Janelle became settled and adjusted to living with Shelia in Boone.

Once every two to three weeks Daniel would go visit with Janelle. I didn't go because I felt they needed this time alone. Besides, I was busy with Evan's soccer games, marching band practice, and the upcoming school year. In the beginning, Janelle avoided visits from her dad. When she was forced to see Daniel, she described their meetings to Shelia and I as awkward. She didn't want to be alone with Daniel, insisting someone be with her. As time went on, Janelle confided in me that she wanted to stay longer than August. She wanted to stay indefinitely. She had met a new friend and was being "reacquainted with her mom's family," Janelle was the happiest I had ever seen her. She was being exposed to a an environment of a family unit with no yelling, cursing and threats. She was actually living a somewhat normal teenage, thirteen-year old life.

The first of August, Daniel called me at work upset. He had been to see Janelle, and she told him what I already knew; she was not homesick or ready to come home. She wanted to stay in Boone for the upcoming school year, and her DSS counselor agreed.

Janelle was now scheduled to come home the end of December, but from her e-mails to me, that was too soon as well. She wanted to finish out the school year in Boone. Daniel's phone calls to Janelle left him upset as he sensed Janelle's hesitance and dread to meet or talk with him. Janelle had entered her new school, and she liked it. Her life was moving forward with Shelia, her husband, Jim and their daughter Melissa. Janelle liked Jim, who appeared to be what a "real" father was like. Whenever Janelle mentioned what Jim said or what they had done, it made Daniel angry and jealous.

The weekend after Janelle started in her new school, Daniel left on Saturday morning for a visit with her. Shelia was out-of-town visiting a friend and this was the first visit Daniel had with Janelle completely alone. Upon Daniel's return on Sunday evening, he called and asked me to meet him at Ann's stating he had something very important to tell me. When I arrived, Daniel wasted no time telling me his shocking news.

"Janelle's story to DSS has changed," Daniel seemed boastful and triumphant. "She's going to report to DSS that you abused her."

"What?," I was dumbfounded, not believing what I was hearing.

"Yep," Daniel was exuberant. "Janelle says you abused her when you took the door off her bedroom and took away her shower privileges for a month."

All I could do was sit there with my mouth hung open in disbelief.

"This can't be happening," I kept saying over and over to myself. "It was Daniel and Dr. Westlake who removed the door and took shower privileges away."

"I've talked this over with Penny and her husband and they both agree it sounds like abuse to them as well." Daniel seemed cocky.

"I can't believe this," was all I could say as I turned and reached for the door handle of Daniel's car to retreat to my car.

"You realize this will release me from the charges made by DSS," Daniel grabbed my arm to stop me. "You, instead of me, will be charged."

Jerking my arm out of his grasp, without a response, I got out of his truck, into my car and drove away. All the way home thinking of how Daniel's manipulation of Janelle would only serve to hurt Janelle and him even more once the details behind Dr. Westlake's decision were revealed. That is, if what Daniel was saying was true.

"Why would Daniel want people to know about Janelle's sexual disorders or about the showers? Were they not thinking straight?," I shook my head in disbelief as I walked into my basement apartment and dropped my keys onto the counter. "Daniel's got to be crazy to think this new scheme of his was going to work in his favor. It's only going to make things worse maybe not as much for him, but for Janelle. Now even more negative "stuff" was going to be revealed."

Reaching for the phone, I sat down on the couch to call Shelia.

"Shelia," I started immediately. "What's going on?"

"I don't know," Shelia replied. "I was out of town visiting a sick friend, so I don't know exactly what was discussed between Janelle and Daniel. All I know is when I arrived home a couple of hours ago Janelle said you abused her by removing her bedroom door and not allowing her to take a shower for a month," Shelia said. "I'll call Janelle's DSS counselor in the morning. Hopefully we'll find out something soon."

The next morning, promptly at 9:00 a.m., I received a phone call from Elizabeth.

"Are you ready for this?," she asked.

"I already know," I told her of Daniel's conversation with me the evening before.

"Well, it's true," Elizabeth summed it up briefly. "It appears Janelle has changed her story after a visit alone with Daniel. She's now accusing you of child abuse."

"Shelia told me she was out of town and Daniel spent Saturday and part of Sunday alone with Janelle. This is going to be bad for Janelle, Elizabeth," I tried to explain. "This is really embarrassing, personal stuff about Janelle. I really don't think these personal things should be exposed or discussed by a lot of people."

"Oh, it's quite obvious it's another game by Daniel to get the heat off him," Elizabeth stated emphatically. "Just like the menopause and everything else. Nevertheless, we'll play along. We have to, especially now since Janelle has reported this to her DSS counselor in Boone," she continued. "Kathy, a thorough investigation, based upon Janelle's allegations will have to be done. It'll be okay. I promise."

Later that afternoon Elizabeth called me and stated the Lead Investigative Director personally requested to conduct the investigation himself since it appeared to be out of spite and vengeance on Daniel's part. The following morning, I met with Elizabeth and the Director to sign the appropriate paperwork referencing the allocations. I had to list names and addresses of my children, all "stray" children that lived in my home in the past and friends that had children I was exposed to. The safety of all children in my care or those whom I was associated with would be investigated. The Director would also contact Dr. Westlake to clarify the circumstances surrounding the accusations I was being accused of. Information from the shelter and counselors would be obtained and reviewed as well. I left DSS being informed an intense and thorough investigation would take approximately a week to ten days.

The days that followed were full of phone calls and e-mails from family and friends as the investigation moved forward. Communication with Janelle had come to an abrupt stop and I was advised by DSS not to pursue contact with Janelle until the investigation was complete. The investigation took a little over a week.

"Mrs. Thomas the report and findings of our office on the alleged charges against you have only made matters worse," The following Wednesday I received a phone call from the Lead Investigator. "Did you realize Dr. Westlake was suspicious of child molestation with regards to Janelle's sexual behavior since the age of nine and that her deviance and lack of discipline by her father sent up red flags of suspicion as well?"

"Yes, I was aware," I replied. "Am I cleared of the charges?"

"Dr. Westlake gave us a statement that 'Showers were removed due to deviance, excessive water consumption of 30-45 minute showers and a letter from the City of Greensboro voicing concern of water usage increase and a possible leak. Janelle was not denied a bath, just a shower;' and 'Mr. Thomas administered all punishments under Dr. Westlake's supervision due to a lack of discipline and deviant behavior.' You're clear," he said.

"Is that all?," I asked.

"That's pretty much it on our end," he continued. "We'll send a copy of the report to you, Mr. Thomas and all parties involved in Boone by the end of the week. I'm sorry, Mrs. Thomas. I know none of this has been easy on you, but we all needed to play along with Mr. Thomas's games. Now we have more than enough information to look more closely at Janelle's issues and their origin"

A few days later I received a letter from the DSS stating: 'There was no sufficient evidence to substantiate abuse, neglect, or dependency. Your case file is closed.'

The day after the letter came from DSS, Elizabeth called and scheduled an appointment to meet with Daniel and I.

"Mr. Thomas, all charges against you are still active, and I will not allow any more insinuations that Mrs. Thomas is the 'wicked stepmother.' What happened, happened. The neglect was on your part," Elizabeth was firm and controlled. "It is my opinion as well as the opinion of the Lead Director, that this is all games and manipulation by you to transfer the neglect onto someone other than yourself. Janelle will be staying in Boone until all of this mess is resolved," she paused for a moment. "Mr. Thomas, you need to continue in anger management and take some responsibility for your actions that has caused the majority of this."

Once the findings from the DSS investigation were released to Janelle and Shelia, my relationship with Janelle spiraled downhill. What Janelle and I had built those first three months of my marriage to Daniel had completely fallen apart.

Chapter Twelve: Never Say "No"

Evan and I moved back in with Daniel the first week of August in 2001. Daniel was to begin having a series of epidural injections in his back in hopes to avoid surgery on a slipped disk. The injections didn't help and surgery was scheduled for after Labor Day. Daniel needed me at home for both the injections and surgery. Meanwhile, Evan wanted to continue in the same school. If it hadn't been for the pressure of Evan returning to school and Daniel's injections and surgery, I knew deep down inside it would have been best for Evan and I to stay put in the basement apartment. Yet, I was still Daniel's wife and I didn't want another family interference of me not tending to my husband and being sympathetic to his medical conditions.

During the years, we were together; I never saw where Daniel worked at his manufacturing job. All I knew was the company was a small family owned operation and flexible with Daniel's work hours. He left at 3:15 a.m. Monday through Wednesday working 33-36 hours over the course of three days. There were only six employees in the company, which included the owner and his wife, their son, the wife's sister, a man called George and Daniel. The company offered no retirement, sick leave, health insurance or any other benefits, leaving the health insurance and retirement benefits upon me. On Thursdays, Daniel worked eight hours at a local hardware store. He hated the owner of the hardware store, always labeling him the "village idiot," frequently complaining the owner was lazy, ignorant, typical spoiled rich kid who never experienced a hard day of work in his life.

The manufacturing company closed down for vacation the second week of August. This particular year Daniel worked a few days at the hardware store to earn extra money. Money was tight with all the counseling and medical expenses. The remaining vacation week we spent in Gatlinburg, Tennessee. On our second night in Gatlinburg, Daniel wanted to have sex in the motel room, despite the fact Evan was in the room, awake, watching TV in the bed next to us. Daniel wanted to the day before immediately after we checked in and I managed to send Evan on an errand to get brochures. Now, Daniel was angry because I wouldn't consent to the act right then with Evan in the room. Slamming the covers with his fist, cursing, he literally threw a temper tantrum resembling that of a two-year-old. He pouted and stayed mad the rest of the evening. I couldn't believe Daniel would even think of committing such an act with Evan in the room. This was just another shock and it seemed since our marriage there had been one shock after another.

"Cheryl didn't like sex," he whined. "While we were dating, Daniel made me promise to never say "no" to sex. "There wasn't anything wrong with her, she just didn't like it. Promise me you'll never be like that. Promise."

The next morning, on our trip home, Daniel was still angry from the night before, informing me I was a liar because I had made a promise to never say "no".

"Daniel, please," I said softly so Evan, who was asleep in the backseat, wouldn't hear. "What can I do or say to stop this argument? I didn't want to have sex with Evan in the same room."

"You can be honest for once in your life!," Daniel whispered sternly. "Just tell the truth. You don't want me, you don't love me and you lied to me about never saying no."

It was useless trying to rationalize with Daniel and for the next five-hour drive, Daniel was angry. At the gas stop and restaurant, Daniel slammed the car door when he got out and slammed the door when he got in.

By the time we arrived home, it was late and I was emotionally exhausted from Daniel's ugliness during the drive. After unpacking, starting a load of laundry, I began getting things ready for work the next day while Daniel called Janelle.

After placing the first finished load of washed clothes in the dryer, and starting the next to wash, I went upstairs to the bedroom and began getting ready for bed.

"We've for sure lost Janelle now," Daniel came in complaining about his phone call with Janelle. "She's happy there. All she talked about was Jim, Shelia, and her new friends she met in school. Now, they're planning a family beach trip," his temper began to rise. "It's all your fuckin' fault. You never wanted her in the first place. You're the reason DSS removed her," deep in my heart, I knew the truth. I never wanted to loose Janelle. I tried everything possible to keep her with Evan and me. It was Daniel, who out of vindictiveness, made the decision to separate us. Now Daniel was paying the consequences of his actions.

Then Daniel reminded me that Elizabeth was scheduled to meet with us on Friday. "I'm sure she knows by now Janelle never wants to come home," he started. Then he stepped forward and grabbed me by the arm. "If you or Evan tell her what happened in Gatlinburg, you know what will happen," he threatened. "She'll take Evan away too." Suddenly an unimaginable, forceful fear gripped at me and settled as a sharp pain in the bottom of my stomach. I couldn't lose Evan. Not the same way I lost Janelle. The only true thing left in my life, the only thing that kept me going was Evan. Daniel had already isolated me from Amber, Matt, the rest of my family and my friends. Evan was all I had.

Elizabeth knew we had moved back in with Daniel due to his upcoming surgery and Evan's school. Elizabeth sympathized with me as I agonized over the decision to move back in with Daniel, but what other choice did I have? It was apparent Daniel's anger treatment sessions weren't working. It seemed as if Daniel was getting worse.

"You'll lose Evan, so you better talk to him," seeing the fear in my face, Daniel warned me again as he dropped my arm and stormed out of the bedroom.

Exhausted, I climbed into bed for the night, knowing I didn't have Daniel's permission to go to bed just yet, but I was too tired to care.

"Why are you in the bed? Are you asleep?," Daniel came into the bedroom an hour later and switched on the overhead light, startling and blinding me with the brightness. Making it clear, Daniel controlled when I was allowed to go to bed at night, when I was allowed to get up in the mornings and when I was allowed to sleep.

"I'm sorry, Daniel, I'm just tired," Angry at my response, Daniel turned and left the room, slamming the door. "Let what happens, happens," I thought. "I give up," A few minutes later, Daniel came back into the bedroom and crawled into bed.

"I wish you would quit lying to me," he started. "Admit it. You're a liar. You don't want to ever have sex with me do you?"

"Daniel, please," I was so tired. "Please. It was only because Evan was in the room with us. That's the only reason. I promise I'll never say 'no' to you again."

"Fuck you!," it was useless, Daniel was too far into a violent rage. "You made that same promise before. You love your kids more than you love me and this just proves it," Daniel was now up on one elbow, his face inches of mine. Grabbing my chin, jerking my face closer to his, I could see the angry blood vessels bulging upon his forehead, realizing Daniel wasn't going to stop. Things were only to get worse. "You want me to move out so your kids can move in with you? Is that what you want? Answer me, is that what you want?," the pressure of his finger digging deeper into my chin.

I sat up and tried to get out of bed, knowing I had no other choice but to get Evan and leave.

"You're not going anywhere," Daniel pinned me down onto the bed. I had never seen such hatred in a person's eyes. When I tried to speak, Daniel put his hand over my mouth and his arm across my neck, choking, pinning me down deeper and deeper into the mattress. "Shut the fuck up!," he whispered threatening in my ear, while making a tight fist with his other hand punching it into the mattress next to my body. The entire weight of his body against me.

I could hear Evan pacing in and out of his room, up and down the hallway. Daniel's tone and force was cruel and brutal. His voice loud enough for Evan to hear, giving Evan a sense I was in danger.

"If you tell anyone, Dr. Leighman, Elizabeth, Amber, anyone, about this past week in Gatlinburg, I'll never speak or have anything to do with you again. Do you hear me?," Grabbing my hair with his free hand Daniel forcibly jerked my head and neck down further into the pillow.

"Look at me!," he ordered. "Do you understand me?," I could barely speak above a whisper "yes" with Daniel's arm choking down upon my throat. "If you go tell any of this...," suddenly the bedroom door opened as Evan entered the room, "Mom, are you alright?"

Immediately Daniel loosened his hold and rolled off me as he turned to Evan.

"We're okay; we're just having a discussion," Daniel calmly responded as he lay back on his pillow, while fluffing the covers around him. Satisfied with the placement of the covers, Daniel folded his hands across his chest and looked directly at Evan, waiting for Evan's response.

Evan searched my face for answers, but all I could do was force myself to lie still, trying to avoid the look on Evan's face. Slowly, hesitantly, Evan turned and left the room, closing the door behind him. Immediately, Daniel jumped out of bed and without using his prosthesis, hopped over to the bedroom door and locked it. From that moment on, Daniel never left the door to our bedroom unlocked for the duration of our marriage.

The argument went on for over an hour. If I raised my voice slightly or a tone higher, Daniel would put his hand over my mouth and order, "Shhhh....be quiet!," If I tried to get up from the bed, Daniel would roughly force me back onto the bed. Begging him to stop was useless. All I could do was listen and take the abuse, knowing somehow, someway the next morning I would leave with Evan. Then abruptly, without any way to stop it or defend myself, Daniel threw himself on top of me, raping me. There was no way to fight him off only to endure the pain and humiliation. Slowly I found myself escaping to that peaceful, quiet place beside Mr. Draper's creek, with the sounds of the running water spilling gently over the rocks. The warmth and comfort of the tree branches engulfing me in their safe haven. "Hold me, God. Help me through this," I spoke to God as I did so long ago. Once again running far, far away from the abuse.

Satisfied, Daniel rolled over onto his right side, slamming and jerking the covers tightly around him, using them as a shield to prevent any human body contact between us. Quietly I lay beside him, not moving as my body welcomed the relief of Daniel's body weight off me, the cool night breeze swept over his sweat on my body. For the past two days, I had endured Daniel's verbal abuse, all for the word "no" out of morals and protection of Evan. Daniel made sure I was to learn my lesson and never say "no" again.

Morning found me nauseated, sore and ashamed at the rape. A deep numbness and sense of defeat flowed through my body. Sitting on the side of the bed, I began to cry quietly into the palms of my hand. The sounds of Daniel shaving and preparing for his morning shower came from the bathroom door. The moment the sound ceased was my cue for escape, and quickly I scurried across the bedroom to the dresser, throwing on a pair of jeans and t-shirt. Then I rushed into Evan's room.

"Evan, Evan, wake up. We're leaving," I shook Evan's sleeping body awake. Searching out a small duffle bag from Evan's closet I randomly threw clothes into the bag. Running back into my bedroom to grab my tennis shoes from the closet, not wasting time to put them on, I made it to the bedroom door, only to have Daniel exit the bathroom just in time to catch me with the duffle bag and shoes in one hand and the doorknob in the other. My heart sank in fear and despair.

"Where do you think you're going?," Daniel eyes raking across my body, seeing me dressed in jeans with the duffle bag and shoes in my hand.

"I'm leaving," my voice shaky. "I can't do this anymore, Daniel. "I can't put Evan or myself through this. It's over. What Evan saw last night..." Shaking my head, trying to erase the memory, tears began spilling down my cheeks. The thoughts were more than I could bear. Oh, how I wished Evan had never witnessed Daniel's abuse. Any of Daniel's abuses.

Daniel sunk as if defeated, down on the side of the bed in front of his prosthesis. He began to cry.

"I need help," he blurted out. "I know I need help." A combination of a statement and a plea. "Elizabeth is supposed to call me tomorrow and I'm going to tell her the anger treatment sessions aren't working. She has to find someone else. I'm wasting time and money on someone who doesn't give a damn about me," his voice, unlike the ugly, harsh, cruel, voice from the night before was full of anguish and remorse.

"Please," Daniel begged as his hand reached out to grab me, instinctively I backed away. Daniel's hand dropped quickly into his lap.

"I'm sorry I ruined our vacation. I'm sorry I've ruined your life. Kathy, I'll do whatever it takes to make it up to you and Evan. Whatever it takes. I promise," he continued to plead. "I know I can do better, it's just that...," then Daniel's eyes left the present and walked into his childhood past as his voice drifted into another place and time.

"I'm just like my father," he began. "My dad was a mean, violent person who could never forgive or forget anything. I witnessed a childhood full of alcohol and beatings," crying into his hands, shaking his head.

"Please, Kathy," Daniel looked up. "Please. I need help. I know I need help and I promise, I'll get that help, even if it takes being committed into a mental hospital. I've lost Janelle," he continued, "She never wants to come home. I can't lose you and Evan, too. Please, stay, I promise I'll do whatever it takes."

I stood and watched Daniel's emotions, apprehensive of Daniel's new change of mood and attitude. It was a standoff with me at the bedroom door and Daniel on the side of the bed. Silence filled the room as I struggled within on what to do. It wasn't that I was uncaring about Daniel and his past. This turn around moods of forgiveness never lasted long and I knew it. Yet in those moments, I was exhausted.

"I love you, Kathy. You're the best thing that has ever happened to me. I'm so sorry," I wanted to believe that maybe, just maybe, this time, Daniel really would seek out the right help, that somewhere there was someone who could help him.

"I need you. There's no one who will be there for me and help me through," Daniel's reminder of his upcoming surgery in less than two weeks forced me to stay. Once again, I allowed Daniel's tears and words of remorse suck me back into staying.

For the next several days, Daniel was preoccupied with building a theatre in the basement that supported his hobby of collecting 16mm western films. He had one similar in the house he shared with Cheryl.

Chapter Thirteen: Looking In From the Outside through Broken Blinds

"Kathy, Gary's finished. We need to get going," Cindy's voice startled me. Visions of the past vanishing for the moment, forcing me back to the present, harsh reality. "I'm alright," I said. Traces of the pain revealing on my pale, thin face. Shaking off thoughts of the last visit Daniel and I made to the cabin, remembering the abuse that began there and escalated during the week afterwards. A sudden gust of cold wind, making me more aware of my surroundings. Quietly I turned, laying my head on Cindy's shoulder, as she slowly led me up the path, back to the cabin.

"Here are the new keys," Gary was waiting for us. "And the list of tools and materials we need to complete the roof," One final check on all the windows and door locks, once again, I was tucked in the backseat, and we were on our way back to the motel to retrieve my car, then to my new place and life. The drizzle of rain had now turned into a downpour. Loud raindrops smacked sideways against the windows. I was so deep into my thoughts and memories while standing by the creek; I never realized the rain had started.   A walk, talk, prayerful moment and view of God's magnificent creation. Giving me strength in a time of trouble.

Backing out of the driveway, I shivered from the wet cold as I took one final look of the cabin and mountains. That's what sold me on the cabin just a few short months prior. God's beauty and the breathtaking view of the mountains.

Daniel's house was always covered in complete darkness. We lived with the blinds closed and curtains drawn tight. Doors to the outside were always closed and locked. Windows were shut and locked. Daylight was kept from entering into our home and the music from the night sounds were never let in to sing me to sleep. Daniel said it was for our protection, to keep people from seeing inside. I often thought of what could be seen from the outside of our home. A house with cruel words and physical abuse, a life within, that through the bent and broken slats of vinyl window blinds, was the presence of God, a stranger to one, but a friend and Savior to another. God, peeping through the blinds, seeing the abuse administered by a violent, emotionally tortured man.

By now, Daniel's abuse was almost a weekly event resulting in verbal, mental and at times physical abuse. Threats of suicide, by "taking a gun and blowing my head off" or more "I wished I would get cancer" was weekly language and conversation. Daniel became more possessive, controlling and jealous. If I spoke to someone at church, he would say, "Don't speak to that usher at church, I think he likes you" or "I see the way he looks at you, stay away from him." Every male counselor he or Janelle saw that I had contact with through the sessions; he accused me of having an affair with.

In the grocery store, I had to stay directly next to Daniel and the shopping cart, with my hand in his or under his on the cart hand rest. That was the rule. If I wondered off in the store looking for something, no matter where or what we were doing, he would chastise me saying, "I guess you don't want me," or "You don't want to be seen with me."

On one occasion, I was looking at something in the grocery store and Daniel went ahead, not realizing I wasn't with him attached to the buggy. I ran to catch up, and watched as Daniel spun around, his expression ready for war. He remained angry throughout the rest of the grocery shopping.

"You don't want me and you know it!," Daniel began as we were unloading the groceries at home.

"Daniel, I'm sorry, I wasn't paying attention," I apologized.

"You're a liar!," He yelled. At that point, Evan came rushing out of his room into the kitchen, only to quickly retreat. For fear of more bruises and violence, as Daniel began to approach me, I ran down the stairs, into the small basement closet beneath the staircase, as I learned numerous times before that with Daniel's prosthesis he wouldn't be able to grab and pull me out.

Deep into closet, as far from Daniel's pending abuse, on the cold cement floor next to the hot water heater became one of my many hiding places; especially when Evan was at home and I didn't feel it safe to leave him alone with Daniel. Cramped, surrounded by luggage, boxes, Jamaica supplies, within that tiny space, I would lay, praying, softly singing hymns and resting in the arms of God.

Constantly Daniel would come in and out of the closet doorway mocking me, saying, "You need to read your bible, you need to pray more, just look at yourself, you're not a Christian, you're a damn failure, a fuckin' liar," the moment Daniel would leave, I would pull the small chain light on and read the Bible I had hidden amongst the boxes beneath a blanket. Just a small space, hidden in a tiny corner, underneath the staircase, a space full of God's love and comfort.

Later that evening Daniel came to the closet door, bending over to look deep into the back of the closet. "You think I'm the devil. Don't you? Well come on out and watch this 'devil' jump out of the window!," He slammed his fist into the doorframe. "You're the cause of my anger. I can't do anything to please you. You're the crazy one," he stopped and laughed, "You're the one who needs all this counseling and mental help," The door slammed shut once again and the sound of Daniel stomping up the staircase permeated the walls within the closet. All of this because I didn't stay with the buggy. Apologizing was useless, so for the next several hours I endured Daniel's cursing and yelling consistently stating I was a failure as a Christian, a wife and a mother to Janelle, back and forth, outside the closet door, he paced and cursed, slamming the door after each explosive episode. Over and over I rocked on my heals, bent over in that tiny space saying the serenity prayer: "God grant me the serenity to accept the things I cannot change, courage to change the things I can, and wisdom to know the difference. Please God help me, please!," Daniel's final entry to the closet was of him letting Mitzi in, who had been whimpering outside the closet door the entire time. "Here's your fuckin' dog!," he said, "You love her more than me anyway," with his foot, Daniel kicked Mitzi inside the closet only to have her come racing into my arms as Daniel slammed the door shut, throwing us both into darkness. In the tiny basement closet, Mitzi and I stayed for the next five hours until I was sure Daniel was asleep in the bed. I snuck into the bedroom, undressed and crawled into bed, measured the distance to my proper place beside him. Silently I cried myself to sleep into the pillow while Mitzi lay on the floor beside the bed.

The next week Daniel phoned several times trying to talk to Janelle but since the findings of DSS, releasing me from any wrongdoing, Janelle wasn't responsive to Daniel's calls. Shelia told Daniel, Janelle didn't want to talk to him. She refused to even discuss her dad or plans to come home. Janelle was threatening if she were forced to come home and live with her dad she would run away. Shelia concluded she would talk to Janelle and try to persuade her to call. Finally, Janelle called.

"Janelle would barely talk to me," Daniel complained as he dropped down in his recliner. We sat in silence for a while, then all of a sudden, Daniel jumped up.

"Let's go. We'll go get something to eat." This was strange and out of character for Daniel. Normally he would have been raging war against me at his disappointment in Janelle.

"Maybe he's learning to handle these disappointments, and not take them out on me," I thought. "Maybe Dr. Bryant is getting through to him."

I was wrong. Dead wrong. Daniel just wanted to take me somewhere away from Evan's ears so he could rage. In Ann's, Daniel couldn't control his disappointment over Janelle's phone call any longer. He was like a teakettle boiling, steaming on high, ready to explode. Daniel wasn't yelling for the sake of being in a public place, but was curt and sharp with sarcasm. Once again, all of this was my fault, I was the reason Janelle didn't want to come home. On and on he quietly raged until I was afraid to leave with him.

"Let's go," Daniel stood up to grab my hand, pulling me out from the corner of the booth. Once inside his truck, he began beating the steering wheel with his fists, screeching tires as he drove out of the parking space and lot, driving recklessly.

"Bitch! You're the cause of all this. You make me so goddamn mad!," holding onto the door, I remained silent, terrified, taking Daniel's abuse. Slamming the truck door as he got out, coming over to my side, grabbing my hand and pulling me from the truck. His hand was firm over mine as he literally dragged me up to the front door. Once inside, I quickly escaped down the stairs back into the basement closet. I could hear Daniel cussing as he went up the stairs and down the hall.

The next day was Sunday. The alarm had just gone off and Daniel had hit the off button and went back to his gentle snoring. I was thirsty and needed to go to the bathroom. Quietly, slipped out of bed, tiptoed down the hallway and into the kitchen to get a glass of water, then into the hallway bathroom. When I snuck quietly back into the bedroom, softly closing the door, to my dismay, Daniel was awake, sitting up in bed, waiting for me. I was "busted," on Daniel's rule; I was not allowed to get out of bed until he did.

"I assumed you weren't coming back to bed," Daniel stated, glaring at me coldly. Before I could explain or make my way around the bed to crawl back in next to him, he flung the covers off.

"I guess not. With the way you slept last night, I guess you don't want me either!," he spatted out at me.

Somehow, during the night I must have slept the wrong way, again.

"Daniel, I'm sorry," I pleaded. "I measured the distance when I got in the bed, I don't remember moving, or holding the pillow or covers. What did I do wrong?"

"You moved away from me and were holding the pillow," he snapped. "You'd rather have a fuckin' pillow than me!"

Defeated, I sat on the side of the bed and waited for Daniel to finish his shower, then I showered and dressed in blue jeans, thinking there was no way Daniel was going to allow us to go to church.

"Where are you going? Don't you think we need to be in church today?," Daniel came into the bedroom and saw me in jeans. Jumping at the opportunity to go to church, I went to Evan's room to wake him up, but he was already awake from hearing Daniel. With Evan's questioning look, all I could quietly mouth was "I'm sorry" and "we're going to church." Evan dressed quickly, while I changed into church clothes.

Evan and I walked into the living room together and found Daniel eating his cereal and watching TV.

"We're ready," I told him.

"So?," Daniel turned back to eating his cereal.

"Are you going with us?," I asked.

"Church isn't a place for a devil like me. Besides, you don't want me there anyway. Just as you didn't want me but your pillow last night."

It was hopeless. Determined not to miss another opportunity to go to church, I took Evan's hand and we turned to leave.

"If you leave, you had better not come back home," Daniel shot out over his shoulder.

By now, I didn't care.

"Mom, it's okay, we need to get away for a while," Evan whispered in my ear as we walked down the stairs and out the door. Evan was right; we needed to be in church. Daniel controlled when we went to church and when we didn't go to church. Seizing the moment to go was all we could do.

"Did you and Evan have fun without me in church today?," Daniel was waiting for us at the top of the stairs when I opened the door. "Neither of you seemed to want me there with you. That was quite obvious," there was nothing Evan and I could say as we walked past him.

"Where did you sit? Did you speak to anyone?," Daniel asked.

"We sat where we always do," I told him.

"No, you didn't," Daniel's temper began to rise.

"We sat where we always sit," Evan turned and looked directly at Daniel.

"Daniel, we saved you a seat just in case you changed your mind," I told him.

"No, you didn't," Daniel grumped. "Who did you talk to?"

"No one spoke to us, except for Pastor Woods, who spoke only to Evan, asking how he was doing"

Evan retreated to his room. I sat on the couch and began looking through a magazine.

"You really like to read don't you?," Nothing I did seemed to please Daniel I thought as I gently closed the magazine and set it aside.

"I'm sorry; do you want to sit beside me?," Wearily I responded.

"No, I see now you prefer the couch pillows beside you than me," I honestly didn't know the pillows were beside me. They were just there.

"No Daniel, the couch pillows are not more important to me than you," some reason or another, I was beginning to get the feeling Daniel had some type of psychological problem with pillows.

Daniel plopped down into his recliner. Silence filled the room.

"You want this marriage to end?," Daniel broke the silence.

"The arguments have to stop and if that is the only way, 'yes,' Daniel. I think it might be best," I took the bait.

We sat in more silence.

"We'll discuss it with Dr. Leighman," Daniel stated in a matter-of-fact tone," he paused. "But when we meet with Dr. Leighman, there are certain things I will not allow you to discuss," Daniel abruptly stated.

"Daniel, what good is counseling going to accomplish if we can't be honest and talk to Dr. Leighman about the things that cause these arguments and our need to separate?," I asked.

"So, you want Leighman? Well, why the hell don't you just go and sleep with Dr. Leighman!," Daniel jumped up and yelled, then stormed out of the room, slamming the door his theatre.

I waited in the living room until time to take Evan to youth and then went to Quaker Lake until time to pick Evan up.

"I spoke with Dr. Leighman and Dr. Bryant this morning and they both think you have some serious mental problems," he began the following evening after work. "You need help and it might be best for us to separate until you get better," I stood there searching his eyes for the truth. Daniel looked away from me and began staring down at the kitchen floor.

"Daniel, I think they're both right," I didn't even pretend I was stunned at this latest story from Daniel. It didn't quite make sense, but then, lately, nothing Daniel said made sense.

I could see the surprise look on Daniel's face as shocked eyes looked straight into mine. I wasn't going to deny the solution of separation. Dr. Leighman, Dr. Bryant, and my feelings were mutual. If it was the truth. I'd long since been ready for Evan and I to leave and this was my chance with Dr. Leighman and Dr. Bryant's permission per Daniel.

"You're probably sleeping with Dr. Leighman and Dr. Bryant! Aren't you? Answer me, aren't you?," Daniel snapped, grabbing hold of my arm, jerking me close to him.

"I'm only agreeing with what you said," I stated, exasperated. "I've never even met Dr. Bryant so how could I possibly be having an affair with a man I haven't met?,"

"Dr. Leighman only said we needed to learn to communicate and work out our problems on our own, without involving counseling. He said nothing about us separating," By now, this entire conversation was irrational and didn't make sense. It was beginning to sound like another 'made-up scam' by Daniel. "Did they or did they not suggest we separate?," I thought, but was afraid to ask aloud for fear of more abusive damage.

"We need to leave the past in the past. That's what Dr. Leighman said," Daniel continued. "Including what happened in Gatlinburg and everything else,"

"But what about the advice from Dr. Bryant?," I asked.

"He doesn't know a damn thing about our relationship!," Daniel screamed.

Okay, now I really was confused. The conversation ended with Daniel storming down the stairs to the basement yelling he would have to think about separation.

The following week Daniel had surgery on his back. The surgeon said Daniel would notice an immediate improvement. Daniel stayed overnight in the hospital and was in a lot of pain. He was mean and hateful to the hospital staff. At one point, I had to go downstairs to get Daniel's prosthesis. When I returned I could hear him yelling obscenities all the way down the hall, demanding more morphine, telling them they were a shitty lousy hospital and what kind of fuckin' nurses were they? Rushing into his room, the poor, frustrated shift nurse pulled me out into the hallway.

"We're giving him the appropriate dosage of morphine, Mrs. Thomas," she was visibly upset. "But his profanity and yelling is completely unacceptable. It's upsetting everyone here on the floor."

"I'm sorry," I apologized to her. "I'll do my best to calm him down," For the next 24 hours, I laid beside Daniel, trying to soothe him through the pain, not leaving for fear of him going into one of his rages.

Once home, we were up and down during the next several nights with pain medication and nausea. Daniel wasn't able to use his prosthesis so we were using the wheelchair. Daniel slept in the living on the couch and I slept next to him on the small loveseat, rarely leaving his sight. A few days later, around 3:00 in the afternoon, I noticed Daniel was becoming irritable.

"Daniel, what's wrong?," I asked. "Is there anything you need? Can I do something for you?,"

"Why, are you avoiding me?," He stormed.

"Daniel, I've been right here the whole time,"

"No, you weren't, you're trying to find things to do to be away from me! Why?," Another rage brewing. "You don't want me," Daniel complained. On and on for almost an hour Daniel raged about how I wasn't any good at helping him, I was neglecting him and if he had known how I was going to treat him, he wouldn't have had the surgery. For three days I had been right there, giving him his daily bath, fixing his meals, bringing him everything he asked for, even setting up a make-shift screen in the living room and bringing up his projector and western films to watch, the more I tried to defend myself the angrier Daniel got. "Admit it," he said, "You don't want to be in the same room with me."

"What did she do this time?," hearing Daniel yelling, Evan came out of his room into the living room. Daniel looked up at the ceiling. Evan turned and went back into his bedroom. For the rest of the day Daniel pouted.

The following morning Daniel wouldn't let me help him in and out of his wheelchair, get dressed or fix his breakfast. "I don't need your shitty help!," he grumbled.

Sitting in the living room I watched as Daniel fumed and cussed, fumbling for his cereal and coffee.

"I need to learn how to fend for myself when you go back to work," Daniel was mumbling under his breath, how useless I was. He shouldn't have had the surgery, I was a lousy nurse; I didn't love him because I wouldn't lay on the couch or in the recliner with him.

"How about if I take you to the hardware store this afternoon?," I asked, trying to break his mood. "Janelle and Sheila will be by after Janelle's orthodontist appointment this morning. When they leave I'll load you and the wheel chair in the car, we'll stop by Ann's for a takeout and you can spend a few hours with your friends at the store."

"Why not, I'm sure you don't want to be with me the way you avoid me," Daniel sarcastically replied. His anger was hopeless and unrelinqishing.

Janelle and Shelia arrived in the midst of the argument. Daniel calmed down long enough to put on a good front for their visit. Daniel tried to hug Janelle, but she wouldn't respond, pretty much keeping her distance from him. Their stay was brief, stating they had a long drive and Janelle had homework.

Immediately after they left, Daniel started up again. No one wanted to be with him

"Even Janelle would hardly speak to me," he pouted. The trip to the hardware store I thought would at least pull him out of his mood, but the minute we returned home Daniel returned to his bad mood.

A week after Daniel's surgery I went back to work.   When I left that first morning, Daniel was depressed. When I came home at noon to check on him, he was crying, stating he was sorry for the way he treated me.   He didn't understand why or what made him constantly lash out at me. He felt hopeless, like a failure.

Daniel was in the same bad mood the next morning when I went to work. He called several times depressed. Finally I suggested he let me take him to the hardware store on my lunch hour. Maybe that would make him feel better.   Amber would pick him up two hours later and bring him home.

The hardware store excursion didn't seem to affect Daniel's frame of mind. I arrived home to another nasty mood.

"If you tell Dr. Leighman any of this, that'll be the end of it," he threatened. "And Amber, that damn daughter of yours, I offered her $5.00 for gas and she took it! You would have thought she would have refused it if she had any decency about her. She didn't have to take it."

Our first evening in our bed since Daniel's surgery. Two weeks of sleeping on the short, loveseat, I was looking forward to stretching out in the bed. Daniel came in from the bathroom, glanced at me on the bed.

" You don't want me near you do you?"

"I'm right where I'm supposed to be," Showing the measurement of my leg to the edge of the bed.

"You're a liar!," he slammed his fist into the bed and pillow.

"When was the last time you kissed me?"

"This morning. You were too mad at me when I came in from work,"

"That shouldn't have made a difference," he said. "If you really wanted to kiss me, you would have found an opportunity," At that point, I leaned over to kiss him but he and turned his head away from me.

I felt like a failure. Nothing I said or did was right.

"Hold me tight God, I need you!," I prayed as I finally drifted off to sleep.

"I'm tired of all this shit!," Daniel awoke in the same depressed mood. He glared at me with a cold, menacing look. "You think I'm a bad father, don't you. Well, nobody knows the hell Cheryl, Janelle and you put me through!"

I began the day downstairs trying to catch up on the laundry neglected during Daniel's recovery from surgery.

"DSS was wrong," Daniel yelled down into the laundry room from the top of the stairs. "You and Dr. Westlake abused Janelle with the showers, and removal of her bedroom door. And the $5.00 Amber took from me for gas, was pretty shitty of her!"

My lack of response seem to irritate him more.

"I bet you hate me, I know you hate me. I know your kids do. I wish you would kill me. Shoot me!, Choke me! Do something!"

"What are you doing to her?," Evan came out of his room, into the hallway, seeing Daniel yelling down the stairs at me. Neither Daniel nor I knew Evan had the phone hidden behind his back for Amber to hear.

"Go back to your room!," Daniel ordered Evan as he began to hop down the stairs, one by one. Out of breath, he rested one arm on the doorframe and with his other hand, grabbed me. Stable once again, he drug me into the garage and slammed the door behind us.

Daniel accused me of crying and talking too loud. He ordered me from that moment on to be quiet or go somewhere else to cry so Evan and no one else would hear me.

"Why don't you just take a gun and kill me! Maybe God will give me cancer and I'll die, yeah, I would love to get cancer. That would solve it all! Releasing me from all this hell! Everybody knows how mean and bad I am," For at least thirty minutes, Daniel stood there and raged. I couldn't speak, I couldn't cry, I couldn't let Evan see or hear me upset. All I could do was just stand there and take the abuse. Finally, exhausted, Daniel crawled up the stairs to retreat to his recliner. Into the basement I escaped, where no one would see or hear me, just God. As strange as it may have seemed, I was beginning to become accustomed to being in the closet.

Shortly thereafter, I heard the front door open and rapid footsteps on the stairs. It was Amber. She went first to Evan's room to check on him. Evan told her bits and pieces of what he heard and that I was in the closet.

"Mom, I'm so sorry," Amber was crying as she whispered into the darkness. "If I had known taking the $5.00 from Daniel would have caused all of this I would have never accepted it," she explained, "Evan called me, I heard it all. Please, Mom, what can I do?," she pleaded.

"Give him back the $5.00," was all I could wearily say. "Just give it back."

Thrusting me back into the darkness, I heard Amber's footsteps on the stairs, they stopped, then rapid footsteps down the stairs and a slam of the front door. Later I found out Amber confronted Daniel at the top of the stairs, literally throwing a $5.00 bill at his face, and abruptly leaving without a word.

I could feel the walls within the small closet shaking as Daniel once again hopped down the stairs. Jerking the door open, he yelled into the dark space "Just who do you think you are? You did that on purpose! Did you call Amber? Answer me! Did you call Amber?," Shaking with fear, I refused to answer, afraid for Evan. With his voice at a high pitch yell, "I'm going to divorce you for good this time," the door slammed.

Poor Mitzi. She tried so hard to protect me. I could hear her whimpering outside the closet door. I could see her shadow in the light seeping in under the door. I was too afraid to let her in knowing Daniel's jealousy of her. A whimper and an occasional paw scratch at the door. She wanted in so bad, yet she remained at the door for over two hours until Daniel got tired of pushing her out of his way with his foot each time he had a profound moment of new curse words and threats to throw at me. Angrily he jerked open the door and asked if I wanted Mitzi in the closet. I was afraid to answer, scared he would harm her. Daniel's foot roughly pushed Mitzi into the closet with his foot, thrusting us both into darkness. With soothing words, I cradled Mitzi in my arms. Whimpering she lifted her face and licked at the tears streaming down my face.

"You can come out now," It was past midnight, I had been in the closet for over fourteen hours. "I'm not going to yell or punish you anymore tonight."

I was tired and weak. My legs ached from being cramped in the tiny space on the cold concrete floor. I hadn't eaten since the night before. Once upstairs, Daniel didn't hold true to his promise. "You must hate me for the way I treat you," he started once again. "Now Amber hates me too. I know you love Mitzi and your children more than me," he continued. "And you need to choose. Mitzi or me. I'm not going to stand for you having that dog come between me and you," he concluded. "It's my house and I want Mitzi gone by tomorrow."

"She'll be gone tomorrow," I promised, tears spilling once again down my cheek. Exhausted, not wanting to argue anymore, all I could do was give in. Mitzi looked up from her pillow bead on the floor beside the bed. Her questioning brown eyes, trying to understand the words exchanged between Daniel and me. She could hear her name being said.

"I'll be gone tomorrow," Daniel threatened. "I'm going to put an end to everything. I won't be around to be a burden to any of you anymore," Once again, Daniel was threatening suicide. For the next hour he talked of how useless, he was and why didn't God take him instead of Cheryl, his brothers and sisters. "Why don't you just take a gun and shoot me!," were his final words as he left the bedroom. As it was months before, I was afraid to sleep. Listening to every sound. Daniel's outburst of anger were getting worse, sometimes lasting for hours, sometimes lasting for days. Occasionally, he would realize how far gone he had gone, and cry or be overly apologetic. It was those times, he would be so sincere, I believed him.

When I kissed Daniel goodbye before leaving for work the following morning, he began to cry.

"I guess you hate me, don't you?," he asked.

"How much more of this can I take?," I silently prayed to God.

"I love you Daniel," I reassured him, "I'll take care of Mitzi and I'll talk with Amber. Hopefully, you'll feel better about things by this afternoon."

"No, you'll feel better about things this afternoon. I'm taking matters into my own hands and you won't have to worry about me anymore," Daniel's depression had him deep into suicide threats. "I'll take care of things myself," he kept repeating as he cried into his hands.

"Daniel, I'm working through lunch and will be home around 3:00 so I can take you for your appointment with Dr. Bryant. Just wait," I pleaded with him gently. "Wait and talk all of this over with Dr. Bryant."

"I don't want to talk with anyone. I'm taking matters into my own hands," Daniel stated firmly. "Just leave, you'll be late for work. I won't be here when you get home," he threatened.

Placing his coffee on the table beside the recliner, I bent to kiss him goodbye. "Daniel, I'll be home a little after 3:00 to take you to Dr. Bryant's," was all I could say.

I called several times throughout the morning to check on Daniel, but he never answered the phone nor did he return my call after I left several messages. Driving home, I didn't know what to expect or what I would find. Daniel's threat of "blowing his head off" or "jumping out the window" were weekly threats. The house was quiet as I walked up the stairs. Daniel was just as I had left him that morning, sitting in his recliner, the TV on mute, a Bible in his hand.

The drive to Dr. Bryant's office was quiet. On the way home, Daniel said he spoke with Dr. Bryant about Amber, but didn't have much of a resolution about it. He said he also told him about Mitzi.

"Dr. Bryant said you need to get rid of her. He agreed that your relationship with her is causing too much stress to our marriage," he said.

"How in the world can a dog cause stress to a marriage?," I thought. I didn't believe Daniel. He seemed to manipulate to accomplish what he wanted.

That evening, Daniel, Evan and I took Mitzi to live with Amber. The separation and sacrifice of Mitzi caused Evan and I to grieve for weeks. She was more than a dog; she was unconditional love with a happy, wagging tail. We were comforted to know she was still in the family and we would at least get to see her occasionally. Each time we were able to visit Amber secretly, I could see in Mitzi's eyes questions of "Why? Why did you have to sacrifice me?," as she ran up to greet me; her tail wagging violently. When it was time for me the leave, she would jump at my legs, pacing back and forth to the door as if begging me to take her back home with me. It broke my heart.

Three weeks after Daniel's surgery, I met with Elizabeth on my lunch hour. Her visits to the home and with Evan privately were disturbing to her. She was concerned for our safety. Evan was revealing how violent the abuse towards me had become and the frequency. Elizabeth threatened to remove Evan if I stayed. I stated I was afraid of what would happen if we left. Fearing either Daniel would kill me or himself based upon his latest threats. Elizabeth went over the process of a 50B, challenged my choices and the potential of losing Evan. Daniel's surgery was over, he would soon be returning to work. Mitzi was gone, the children weren't coming around. I was totally his, striving to do everything perfect, yet things were getting worse, there was no denying.

Back during the summer, an elderly couple from church approached me while Evan, Janelle and I were at the shelter. They offered us a small loft cabin next to their house, saying we were welcome to use it if we ever needed to. The moment I left Elizabeth's office, I began the process of leaving, calling the elderly couple who were more than happy for Evan and I to come live with them.

Daniel was sitting on the back porch in a rocking chair with a Bible open in his lap, staring blankly across the yard when I arrived home.

"Hello, Daniel," I greeted him with a kiss on the forehead.

Slamming his hands down hard on the sides of the chair, the Bible tumbled to the porch deck. Daniel snapped as he abruptly stood up.

"You, everybody else, all of you think I'm a bastard! Don't you?," he began. "You. You're the nut case in this house. You're the one who needs help!," Daniel was irrational.

Gazing up at his raging red face. I remembered Elizabeth's words, "I'll remove Evan if you stay," everything was in place.

Without saying a word, I turned, went inside, told Evan to pack as much as he could. I did the same. Daniel, still sulking in the rocking chair on the back porch, was unaware of Evan and me leaving for safety to the small loft cabin.

Daniel had no way of finding us. The cabin was nestled in the woods beside a pond. The first thing we did was get Mitzi back. We had a weekly family night with the elderly couple at the main house having dinner and playing a card game called "Skippo," Guys against the girls. Evan and I were healing and doing well.

Daniel was constantly calling me on my cell phone and at work. After a couple of weeks, I agreed to meet him for dinner at a local restaurant. Daniel appeared to be taking his counseling more seriously and I could see small changes. DSS had granted Janelle's wishes to finish out her school year in Boone. She would be returning in May.

"How's he doing?," I asked Elizabeth.

"Small progress," Elizabeth was leery of Daniel's new change of character. It had now been a month since Evan and I had left. "I still think it will take a significant amount of time for changes to become permanent patterns with Daniel," she stated. "In the meantime, stay put and we'll all see."

As the weeks went on, Evan and I began seeing a little more of Daniel. He was more considerate and seemed to hold a lot of guilt for the way he treated us. He talked a lot about his father and his difficult childhood. Dr. Bryant was having him journal a lot of his emotions, the nightmares and memories. Daniel let me read some of the entries.

The next three months, small victories came out of Daniel's counseling sessions. He was more attentive to both Evan and I. He attended Evan's soccer games and band concerts. Elizabeth, Evan and I were all holding our breath, as we began to see changes in Daniel. Changes for the good. Daniel and I spent a long weekend together after the Christmas/New Year's holidays in the mountains of Asheville.

Daniel was scheduled to have more surgeries in January. This time on both hands for carpel tunnel, a hazard of his trade as an engraver. By the end of our first year of marriage, Daniel would have had seven surgical procedures. Evan and I began making plans to move back in with Daniel. Elizabeth was a little skeptical, but admitted Daniel appeared to be making improvements and knew Daniel would need assistance after the surgeries. During the three months we lived separate, Evan and I never saw the "old" Daniel. He was kind and considerate, lavishing us with dinners and gifts. He was even loving and playful with Mitzi. Giving us a glimmer of hope that the counseling was finally working for Daniel. Daniel even agreed to let Mitzi come back and live with us.

DSS's new plan of action was that Evan and I were to continue meeting with Elizabeth, sometimes at home and other times elsewhere. Yet, once we were back under Daniel's roof, the cycle of brutal domestic violence began again. This time far worse than before. Daniel used a combination of physical, sexual, emotional, and psychological methods to dominate and control me. The more I was abused, the more I withdrew within myself.

I tried staying away from the things I knew would cause Daniel to go into a rage, but nothing seem to work. His rages left me hiding in the closet sometimes for days, wrapped up in pieces of the children's snow clothing to stay warm, sneaking out only to go to the bathroom or to check on Evan. There were times, I went from Friday until Sunday without food or water, living in the same work clothes. I wasn't the only one being scarred with the emotional and physical effect of this, Evan was too.

Mitzi was there, whimpering at the closet door. Sometimes I would sneak her in, other times Daniel would open the door, shoving her inside with his foot, saying, "Here's your fuckin' dog. You love her more than me anyway," Daniel's vulgar profanity was degrading. No one had ever used such foul language around me and it made me whence in pain each time I heard those filthy words come from his mouth.

Mitzi, her unconditional love. The hopelessness she must have felt at her inability to protect me. I laid on the cold, concrete floor and held her in my arms. She nestled her body protectively next to mine in the darkness of the tiny, closet space. There was no one I could talk to, no one would understand how one minute Daniel could be a model husband and the next minute he was our worst nightmare. Only God knew the reality of what was happening as my life was slowly being taken away from me. No longer did I belong to my children or family. I belonged solely to Daniel and I felt completely powerless.

Chapter Fourteen: The Worse Case of Domestic Violence

"How are you feeling?," The nurse asked while she focused on the blood pressure cuff on my arm.

"Where am I?," I mumbled as I tried opening my eyes.

The nurse smiled down at me. "You're safe. You're in the hospital. Relax and rest. Your doctor will be in later," her voice sympathetic and kind.

I felt myself panic, realizing I had no memory of how or why I was in the hospital.

"Oh, no. What happened?," I tried to sit up, but was too weak and groggy. I laid back onto the white bed pillow. Glancing around the room, there were flowers and get-well cards on the table next to the bed.

"You're okay. You're safe," Seeing the fear in my eyes, she quickly assured me.

"Please.   What happened?," I pleaded for an answer.

"You've been 'asleep' for over thirty-six hours," she explained as she sat in the chair next to the bed. "Today's Thursday,"

"I don't understand," I began. "Was there an accident?"

A sad smile crossed her face. "I can't answer that," she stood and patted me gently on the shoulder. "Just rest," And she left the room.

She was right. I felt an overwhelming desire to sleep as I closed my heavy eyelids.

It was February, 2002. I awoke in a strange hospital room with no memory of how or why I was there.

Later that evening, a short, stocky, gray-hair man, with thick glasses, carrying a chart came into the room. He introduced himself as Dr. Jones. Checking my pulse and pupils, mashing my stomach and reading notes from my chart, finally he pulled the same chair the nurse has sat in earlier closer to my bed. "You arrived here two days ago by ambulance," he started. "Do you remember anything?"

"No," I shook my head.

"You were exhausted and dehydrated," he continued. "You had taken thirteen Zantacs over a 2 or 3 hour period of time for sleep. You were scheduled to have sinus surgery the next day."

I searched through my fragmented memory, but nothing was there.

"Did I have the surgery?," I questioned.

"No, you didn't make it that far," he replied. "We had to pump your stomach. You've been suffering from what we call PTSD, post-traumatic stress disorder," I couldn't believe what I was hearing. I was tired, so very tired. I felt myself slipping off to sleep again. The last words I remember hearing Dr. Jones say was, "It's okay, just sleep, that's the best thing for you right now."

Over the next few days, my life prior to my admittance began to unfold, not from my memory, but from nurses, doctors and counselors who had taken notes while I was semi-conscious. An ambulance had brought me to the hospital in the early hours of the morning. When I arrived at the hospital, I was unconscious.

At first, they believed it to have been a suicide attempt, but later determined it was PTSD from severe domestic violence. When I was semi-awake, I was begging to see my children, and pleading for God to hold me and give me strength. At other times I was confused and tearful, claiming, "I don't know who I am anymore."

The PTSD blackout period lasted over thirty-six hours. Whether it was from the Zantacs or sheer exhaustion, no one ever said. During those hours, throughout the day and night I was confused, tearful and afraid. From what I was told, doctors, Emergency Room personnel, the hospital counselors, and a representative from the County Domestic Violence Unit, were in and out of my hospital room sitting and asking questions, taking full advantage of my honest, uninhibited, "unconscious state," Pieces of my abusive marriage began to unfold as trained hospital personnel asked questions and took notes while I drifted in and out of consciousness. Soon, the puzzle of my life and what had happened revealed more than I would have conveyed to anyone. I had no control or memory of what was asked or what I said. My mind to this day is a complete void of those thirty-six hours and the hours prior to being taken to the hospital. Several times during the "sleep period", I exhibited strange behaviors to the doctors and hospital staff adding to the suspense as to what happened to me and why. I would sit up in the bed, check measurements of my leg to the edge of the bed, glancing frantically up and down and around the hospital bed, checking my position and the position of my pillow and covers.

My dreams were nightmares only resulting in my waking up screaming and crying out in fear. If I was semi-awake, I verbalized incoherently flashbacks of abuse. At times I was able to answer the hospital staff's questions about the abuse, other times I was too fearful and would withdraw, to the point of staring blankly at the gray hospital walls, non-responsive to their existence.

The details revealed during those 36-hours forced the hospital to isolate and protect me in the psychiatric unit to prevent Daniel from access to me. Daniel was calling and came by the hospital several times demanding to see me. DSS was contacted for the protection of Evan and to obtain information from the current ongoing case file, records from Family Services, and other records from counselors were obtained. Constantly I asked about the safety of Evan and Mitzi. I was consoled with they were both safe with Amber.

Dr. Jones predicted the symptoms of PTSD had begun approximately two months prior. I couldn't sleep, yet wanted to sleep in order to cope with Daniel's abuse, but my mind wouldn't let me go completely into sleep because of Daniel's anger and control with the way I slept. I was literally exhausted both physically and emotionally. The severity of the PTSD was diagnosed due to the severity of Daniel's abuse and prolong exposure I had to it. The symptoms revealed during those hours were of mental, emotional and physical violence. Most of the time I was tearful, frightened, and afraid to be left alone, resulting in the hospital having a difficult time assuring me I was safe.

What happened the night before I was taken to the hospital revealed that I was scheduled for surgery on sinus cysts and infection the next day. Daniel went into a violent rage over lack of money and no paid sick time for himself, making me feel guilty he was having to take a day off work. Daniel had raged for days about the inconvenience my surgery was causing him. I was exhausted from days of abuse. The Zantacs I took were prescribed by my doctor to be taken the night before the surgery, the next day prior to the surgery and afterwards. The more Daniel raged, the more stress I felt and continued taking the pills, trying to relax and sleep, but the pills didn't work. That evening, Daniel raged all night and into the wee hours of the morning. He followed me into the garage, the closet; everywhere I tried to escape to avoid his raging temper.

Amber confirmed all I revealed in my semi-conscious state when she received a call from DSS and the local Domestic Violence Agency. She gave statement Daniel seldom would allow me out of his sight, and she perceived him as very abusive and argumentative. He was jealous of Mitzi and controlled when I could see my children or any other members of my family. If I tried to leave, Daniel would threaten to kill himself.

On my third day in the hospital, I was able to get up, eat a little and walk, but Amber and the hospital staff had to be my memory. Each day Daniel tried to obtain information and the entry code to the unit, but was denied by hospital staff and security. He was demanding answers as to what information I had disclosed with regards to our relationship and what happened. The hospital staff stated he was difficult to deal with.

Each day that passed, I began to feel a little safer, protected, and able to answer questions regarding Daniel's abuses.

The day prior to my release, Domestic Violence, the hospital counselor and the Department of Social Services arranged a group family conference to discuss Daniel's behavior and the violence within our home. I was anxious and fearful of the meeting. Those at the meeting were Amber, my brother, Randy, Daniel's sister, Penny, her husband the minister, Shelia and her husband, Jim.

"The information we are about to discuss must be left within these walls. Understood?," The Domestic Violence counselor asked. All present agreed.

"It's imperative that details not be shared with Daniel or anyone else, ever," the hospital counselor reconfirmed.

For the next hour, the hospital counselor and representative from Domestic Violence gave the group a general overview of my diagnosis of PTSD and limited information regarding Daniel's abuse. At times Daniel's family were receptive to the information with comparison and reminiscing by Daniel's family regarding the abusive nature of their father. Daniel's behavior held many similarities of their father's anger and temperament.

At other times, Daniel's family members were insensitive and in denial, stating this was the first time they had heard of Daniel's abuse. This left the hospital counselor and representative from Domestic Violence confronting them with facts from Janelle's statements to Family Services and DSS. At that point, Daniel's family became deviant, refusing to admit any knowledge of our stay in the shelter.

Daniel's family repeatedly asked for specific examples of Daniel's abuse.

"What types of things would set Daniel off?," Daniel's sister Penny asked. "What did you do to make him angry?"

I sat motionless, being instructed prior to the meeting to allow the counselors to monitor and control what was revealed to the group. The counselor told me they would try to avoid referencing specific abusive details for Evan's sake and mine.

Finally, at one point, Daniel's family became angry, demanding to know what I revealed to the hospital regarding Daniel's abuse, stating they never personally witnessed Daniel being abusive.

"The common profile of an abusive person, which Daniel portrays, is to have the violence be covert, meaning his abusive side primarily happens when no one is around. In Kathy's case, if the children were home or someone else was in the home, Daniel would take Kathy into the bathroom, basement, garage or their bedroom to administer the abuse. At times he would place his hand over her mouth, forcing her to be quiet," the hospital counselor explained.

By this time, I was feeling frightened and hopeless. Just being in the same room with Daniel's family, feeling and witnessing the tension and anger they displayed, left me tense as I held back a cascade of tears threatening to flow at any moment.

Quietly I continued to listen as the hospital counselor struggled to rationalize with Daniel's family, and the Domestic Violence counselor attempted to educate the family about the various forms of domestic violence abuse. Nevertheless, demands continued by Daniel's family members for specific examples of the domestic violence.

Finally, the hospital counselor gave examples of my bruises and treatments by my medical doctor, the control of sleep by not allowing me to turn over away from Daniel in my sleep or allow me to hold a pillow or covers, depriving me of sleep for fear of abuse.

"This is one of the most extreme cases of control and domestic violence I have ever seen," the Domestic Violence counselor interrupted the hospital counselor. "Except for Kathy breathing, Daniel pretty much controlled every aspect of her life,"

The atmosphere in the small room was tense. The effect of watching Daniel's family denial and support of Daniel held my brother, Randy, and Amber in complete shock, as they watched and listened.

"I just want to ask one question," finally, after over an hour, my brother spoke. "What is the validity or truth of the information given by my sister during her thirty-six hours of semi-consciousness?"

"100%,"the hospital counselor and Domestic Violence counselor both responded simultaneously.

"All the information gathered in this medical state of mind is valid due to semi-comatose, no self-control or fear of retribution for Kathy's answers," the hospital counselor elaborated. "She wasn't aware of what she was saying, and if she came even partially awake or aware, she would 'clam-up' almost instantly."

At that point, seeing the hurt expression on Randy and Amber's face, I felt scared and overwhelmed with defeat as I stood up, no longer able to contain the rush of tears and frustration I was feeling and bolted out of the room. Back in the safety of my room, I was relieved from the tense, nauseating atmosphere Daniel's family created within the small confines of the hospital conference room. It was clear to me that no one in Daniel's family was going to make any effort to confront or accept Daniel's behavior or lifestyle of domestic violence. Not for me or for his own daughter's safety.

The next day, Daniel was called in to meet with the hospital counselor, a representative from DSS and me. Daniel arrived with a big-stuffed rabbit, a card and chocolates. He was sympathetic and seemed more than grateful to have "his wife" back. His display of affection, overly exaggerated for the benefit of the two counselors. For a moment, I felt like gathering all my things and running as far from the hospital and Daniel as I could. But where would I go?

Daniel was told of the diagnosis and the family session, but I could tell by the look on his face, Daniel already knew the diagnosis and details of the meeting. He was too controlled, too "charming," he carefully chose each word in response to their questions. Both counselors informed him that it was not a bashing against him but it was an opportunity to make both sides of the family aware of the domestic violence. This in turn was in hopes of a support system for me once I was released. They strongly recommended Daniel continue in anger treatment and informed him that Dr. Bryant had been notified.

"The safety for Evan, Janelle and Kathy is our number one priority," the Domestic Violence counselor concluded with Daniel. "We will be in touch more frequently than before."

The next evening I was released from the hospital into the care of Daniel. My discharge papers stated a diagnosis of "Post-traumatic Stress Disorder due to extreme domestic violence and severe exhaustion,"

"You're one of the worse cases of domestic violence I've ever seen here at the medical center," the nurse reviewing my discharge papers stated.

We had no more than made it to the car when Daniel began questioning me about what I said while I was unconscious. The information revealed in the family session, the information that the family was asked to "leave within the walls of the hospital conference room," hit the family telephone circuit immediately, exaggerating stories of abuse, Daniel was quite knowledgeable of everything discussed in the "family session" and for years, the family never let it die, only adding more fuel to Daniel's moments of abuse.

Chapter Fifteen: Beneath Them

"Are you hungry?," Cindy asked from the front seat. Jarring me awake from the memories. Driving had been slow due to the weather and I was sure Gary was weary from the downpour of rain that didn't seem to let up causing vision and driving difficulties.

Glancing down at the seat beside me was the soda and snacks we had bought earlier before we arrived at the cabin. I hadn't touched it. To be honest, I hadn't eaten at all that day. All the stress had taken away my appetite or any thought of eating.

"We can stop at the next town," Gary didn't wait for my response. I guess sensing I really needed to eat something and he was starving. "Do you know of any place, Kathy?"

"I can't think of anything. All I remember is a very small town with a few gas stations that may have inside grills," It was hard for me to remember much about the route to the cabin. Daniel and I had only made the trip three times. One was to look at it, the second was after we bought it for measurements and the third was the abusive one before Thanksgiving.

I leaned back and closed my eyes, feeling useless to Gary and Cindy. I hated to be this vulnerable and having to lean on other people. I use to be the "rock" of my family and friends. I was the one who carried others' burdens. Now, I was being forced to be dependent on others and I hated it.

Yet, I was so tired. Rest had been far from me the past week. My nights were interrupted with nightmares. My thoughts and worries for what lied ahead constantly nagged at me. Rest, solitude, peace of mind, was what I longed for.

Dr. Bryant dropped Daniel as a patient soon after my hospital stay. In less than a year, we had already lost three counselors, Dr. Bryant, Dr. Westlake and Dr. Leighman. Daniel was in a frantic search for a replacement due to the orders from DSS. Soon he found a psychiatrist by the name of Dr. Mayers.

Janelle reluctantly returned to us at the end of the school year in May. DSS needed to move forward with their goal of "re-uniting the family unit" and we were all in some sort of counseling ordered by DSS. Janelle was to seek private counseling. Evan and I were still seeing Elizabeth. Things slowly went back to the "norm" only this time things were different between Daniel and Janelle. Daniel seemed in fear of Janelle.

Within days of Janelle's return, Daniel began daily or nightly meetings in Janelle's bedroom with the door closed. Shutting Evan and I completely out. I never knew the reason or contents of what went on between the two of them behind Janelle's closed door, but it seemed to give Janelle the upper hand in her rule over Daniel and our household. Whatever "pack" or "alliance" the two of them formed remained consistently in place for the duration of our marriage. Daniel and Janelle were allies building a fortress of dominance over me. The relationship Janelle and I had prior to her leaving for Boone no longer existed.

Janelle's lying, stealing and manipulation soon came back in full force. Each time Janelle did something wrong or someone else did something to her, Daniel became violent towards me. Beating me down emotionally and physically, allowing Janelle to witness and use the abuse to her advantage.

As ordered from DSS, Daniel sought out counseling for Janelle but as soon as facts from DSS, Dr. Westlake and Janelle's other counselor in Boone, were revealed, problems with discipline would quickly be diagnosed as an issue with the normal routine of her lying, stealing and sexual behaviors. We went through so many counselors that I remember counting eight counselors in five years, just for Janelle, not including Daniel's.

Janelle's counseling mostly involved Daniel and Janelle, unless I was asked to participate, which I always dreaded. What little times I was asked to be a part of, if I revealed too much information, I was punished severely. But then again, most of the time, Daniel and Janelle did a good job of revealing the abuse on me, placing a noose around both their necks.

During the first summer after Janelle's return, I began to dread going home at lunch. No matter whether it was 12, 1 or 2, in the afternoon, Janelle would still be in the bed asleep. When I would arrive home from work that evening, she had been up only a short period, complaining of a migraine and crying of depression. I can only imagine how difficult this must have been for Evan living in the same house with her during the summer. Soon Evan and I began to find things Evan could do to get him outside the house and escape the difficult environment he was living in with Janelle. Utilizing my lunch hour, I was soon running Evan to summer camps, soccer practices, movies or friends' houses.

Yet, for Janelle, summer days would go by where she wouldn't bathe, brush her hair or teeth and you would see her wear the same outfit for days, which was usually the same outfit she slept in. She smelled of body odor and was literally gross. Janelle had no friends; no social life except for the youth group at church and that wasn't going well for her either. Her counselor at the moment tried to get her to get up in the mornings, encouraging her do things, making suggestions Janelle try exercising, cleaning her room, finding something to read or put on some music and dance. We lost that counselor after two months and a new counselor was found named, Sarah. Sarah was young and a little timid, but she tried hard. After Daniel and Janelle's first session with Sarah, they came home with the suggestion that I take Janelle with Evan to the mall or movies when I would go home at lunch.

Maybe that would help motivate Janelle to get up in the mornings and change her moods. I was willing to try it and so was Evan. However, Sarah's suggestion ended up as a bad idea.

The first day I went home to pick up Evan and Janelle, Janelle came out of the house loaded with make-up, dressed totally inappropriate and not only was Evan embarrassed, so was I. She was on a mission and not a nice one by the looks of her attire. Back in the house I sent her, telling her we weren't going anywhere with her looking like that. Janelle popped a major attitude, stormed back into the house, changed clothes and came back out looking somewhat decent, only to shed the outer layer and reveal much more than was necessary once I dropped her off at the mall.

On our next outing to the mall, Janelle saw a boy she knew from daycare and school. Evan described the boy as being "a little on the wild, different side," always dressed in black, a difficult youth with many problems. "Not the kind I'd want to hang out with," Evan stated, shaking his head.

That evening Janelle began searching through the telephone book, calling phone numbers with the same last name until she finally made a connection with the young man. Janelle literally harassed the boy by excessively calling him, trying to force him to talk to her, attempting to set up meetings with him at the mall, movies, or anywhere. Janelle was desperate and the boy wasn't interested. Finally, Janelle became so aggressive the boy called Evan begging him to make her stop calling. That ended the trips to the mall. Evan and I stayed involved with events that involved church youth participation, soccer and his friends.

The domestic violence abuse grew worse as Daniel's frustration with Janelle's behavior escalated. When Daniel was aggravated with Janelle's depression, mood swings, deviance, messy room, weight control, etc., he would have a conversation with Janelle privately in her room, and then abuse the living daylights out of me. Constantly I heard I was a failure as a mother because I couldn't make Janelle better, I wasn't a Christian and needed to pray more. Daniel would call me every despicable name he could think of, with continuous threats of having divorce papers served on me at work. I was Daniel's venting outlet; his "punching bag" for Janelle's problems and Janelle knew it. Always leaving the counselors and me wondering what threat Janelle held over his head. Daniel was fearful to discipline Janelle and it was becoming more and more apparent. I was powerless when it came to defending myself against the two of them. It was hard enough when it was just Daniel, twice as hard now with Janelle. Janelle would be just as verbally abusive towards me as her father was. What made Janelle's abuse towards me worse was the manipulation to gain sympathy, attention or whatever else she needed from Daniel. As it was before we were married, Evan and I once again became the target of

Janelle's misbehaviors and there was nothing we could do.

By now, I was doing whatever necessary to keep the bruises, evidence of Daniel's temper and abuse, hidden from Daniel and everyone else. If Daniel saw the bruises, he would start arguing again about how I deserved them or "oh, you just bruise easy," My back, arms, legs were the easiest parts of my body to cover inconspicuously.   It was my neck and Daniel's fingerprints that were the hardest to keep hidden, especially in the summer when a turtleneck shirt would draw attention.

Within months, we lost Sarah as a counselor. After that, counselor after counselor for Janelle continued to fail and we were in constant search for another one. If Daniel and Janelle felt like this counselor wasn't working, they would seek out another one. Excuses were always the same, Janelle didn't like the new counselor or Daniel didn't like him or her; they were too young or inexperienced, or once we signed release papers from DSS and Janelle's other counselors, the picture of our life with Janelle was "laid out" for the new counselor to work with and we were questioned about her deviance, family plans for consequences, why there were no punishments and improvements, her sexual misbehaviors, etc. If we made it to the fourth or fifth session with a counselor and it seemed the counselor was getting too deep, or trying to make home and family life improvements through suggestions, Daniel and Janelle would claim this counselor wasn't working either and the journey to seek out another would once again begin.

One of the things Janelle learned while living in Boone, was the world of Internet. What a nightmare. I soon found out we had a 14-year-old girl out on the Internet with numerous websites. She was "selling herself" as "18, driving a jeep, working at Victoria Secret" and "Daddy's Little Girl, Not!!!," She had at least three solicitation sites. If she went to visit or spend the night with family, the next day we would receive a phone call informing us Janelle had been visiting "inappropriate sites," contaminating their computer. Daniel punished us all by disconnecting the computer. That didn't stop Janelle. Where there was a will, Janelle found a way to stay connected to the internet and there was no way I was going to tell Daniel.

Janelle enrolled back into dance that summer, but her weight was a hindrance and she was struggling with health problems. Her medical doctor diagnosed her with borderline diabetes and depression. Evan and I hung tough with Janelle's behavior, but she was miserable and made sure the rest of us were too. Meanwhile, Daniel was getting deeper and deeper into debt. Between his hobby of collecting western films and memorabilia, attending western film conventions three times a year and Janelle's expenses, Daniel's credit card debt continue to rise as well as the home equity loans.

That fall, Evan and Janelle entered into the ninth grade at the local high school. I had hopes of a better year for Janelle, but immediately it became obvious Janelle had other plans. Unbeknownst to us, Janelle registered to be on the all-boys wrestling team with the first day of school ending in disaster. Janelle was desperate to get attention from boys and this was just another futile effort. At 5 ft. 2 inches and over 225lbs., Janelle's constant desperation and desire for a boyfriend was unquenchable. A phone call from the school administrators and wrestling team coach that afternoon resulted in a meeting with Daniel the next day. Janelle wasn't going to give up her plans of being touched and fondled by the boys on the wrestling team and she fought desperately to be on the team. It was a struggle of determination by Janelle and a very, very uncomfortable meeting between school officials and Daniel. I think if Janelle were athletic, into any kind of sports, it may have been helpful with her fight, but Janelle was so overweight, and any kind of strenuous activity from simple walking, riding a bike or lifting an object left her out of breath. The jokes and rumors Evan endured around high school once details of Janelle's enrollment on the wrestling team, were cruel. Evan struggled with the embarrassment of his stepsister's desperate attempts. Daniel wasn't able to win Janelle's fight to be on the all-boys wrestling team, and the last thing Daniel wanted was to lose and have Janelle mad at him. Therefore, I endured a long weekend of abuse with bruises, no food, and in the closet.

Then came the next abuse. Our cable went out and Daniel had arranged to have someone come and check it. When the cable man arrived, he needed to find the switch box, which just happened to be located in Janelle's room, under her window. We entered Janelle's room, finding her lying on her bed, listening to music, appearing to being happy, reading a teen magazine. I left the cable man in her room and went into the kitchen to pack Daniel's lunch for the next day.

"Can you come with me for a minute?," The cable man interrupted me.

"Sure," I said and followed him back into Janelle's room.

Janelle's entertainment center had been pulled out from the wall and he pointed to the switch box, showing me where the switch box was barely inserted into the wall socket.

"That's your problem," he stated as he turned to Janelle. "When you're moving things around in this area, you may want to pay attention to not knocking this loose from the wall. If you do, it disconnects the cable for the entire house, which is what it did."

"I didn't disconnect the cable or mess with the box," Janelle immediately became defensive and argumentative with the cable man. "This couldn't possibly be my fault. I only re-arranged my furniture and entertainment center one time last weekend," her rudeness embarrassing. The poor cable man got the full blow of Janelle's temper and disrespect. I abruptly left the room with the poor cable man hot on my heels in retreat.

"I wasn't trying to argue or get her in trouble; I was just trying to explain what happened," Reluctant to go back in there, the cable man apologized.

"It's not your fault," I apologized. "Her father will be home shortly and maybe he can help you," thinking we could stall for at least a little time for Daniel to handle Janelle's mood.

"Is it okay if I check the rest of the house, just in case there may be some other possible problem?," he asked. I got the feeling he wanted to wait for Daniel as a protective guard before entering in the "danger zone" of Janelle's temper.

A few minutes later, the cable man came meekly back into the kitchen. "The lines are still not working," he sheepishly said. "I've got to go back into her room," his eyes pleading for my help.

"Okay," I couldn't hide my disappointment. "I'll go with you," we were both greeted by a sulking, angry Janelle glaring up at us from her bed.

We removed a few items from the entertainment center, making it lighter for me to assist him in moving it further out to check the cable box. Both of us avoiding looking at Janelle, speaking softly back and forth to each other.

"There," relieved, the cable man found the source. "It's the input/output cable to her VCR. She's plugged the input/output cable in the switcher backwards," he explained in a low voice to me.

"I'll have to replace the box and switcher," he concluded as Janelle glared at him with the same mean, ugly attitude. Swiftly he left to go to his truck for supplies.

"Janelle, why do you have to be so mean and rude to him?," I pleaded with her. "He's only trying to help us."

Janelle looked at me with such hatred, that if her looks could kill, I would have dropped dead on the spot. Realizing it was useless to try reasoning with her, I turned to walk out of the room.

"Don't you dare turn your back on me and leave this room! You get back in here!," Janelle ordered me as she slammed her fist onto the doorframe. Refusing to stop, I continued on my way into the kitchen where I sat down at the kitchen table, my head down in my hands, realizing Janelle had just confirmed my place of order within the house, under the control of both her and Daniel. Daniel and Janelle were the parents; I was the child. I was held at a lower level, much lower, always beneath them.

When Daniel arrived home from work, the cable man and I had already moved the furniture back into place. The new box and switch installed. We were now working on the outside box. Daniel asked what the problem was and the cable man told him about the switch box in Janelle's room.

"I think I upset your daughter," he apologized, informed Daniel of his findings and the repairs, then left.

"What was that all about?," Daniel asked as we walked up to the house.

"I don't know," I began. "Janelle was in good spirits when I got home. But when the cable man tried to explain the problem she had created with switch box and cable hook-up, she was rude and ugly." That was all I could say, knowing there most likely would be consequences towards me, especially if Janelle played her cards right.

Daniel dropped his coffee cup into the kitchen sink and went straight to Janelle's room for his routine private time alone with her.

"She's upset," Daniel came into the bedroom an hour later where I was getting my clothes ready for work the next day. "She hates her life, she hates everybody and everything. She says no one likes her and she has no friends. She's so depressed, she's threatening suicide," Daniel sat down on the side of the bed. "But I wouldn't expect you to understand. You're so perfect. You wouldn't know what it feels like to be depressed. We both have thoughts of suicide," Daniel was sarcastic, turning his anger towards me. Powerless when it came to defending myself, I remained quiet. Seeing no response from me, Daniel retreated into Janelle's room where he remained until it was time for him to go to bed.

Meetings between Daniel and Janelle in her bedroom continued throughout the years. I often could hear their muffled voices or complete silence with the occasional noise from Janelle's TV. Maybe it was denial on my part, maybe it was fear of more ammunition for abuse, but I learned to accept those meetings, never questioning them, appreciating those moments Daniel's focus was on Janelle and off me.

Chapter Sixteen: On The Edge

I was right about the types of restaurants. There really wasn't anything Gary, Cindy or I could find except for a small grill inside a gas station. A very basic menu of hot dogs, hamburgers, and sandwiches. By the conversations within, it was mostly "regulars" from the town. My appetite still at a minimum from all the stress, I could barely eat half of the hamburger and fries.

I rode in the front seat with Cindy while Gary settled in the backseat. Soon soft snoring came from his exhaustion. Our next stop would be the motel to pick up my car. Cindy and I would follow Gary to my new home.

By October, Janelle was seeing her sixth counselor, Diane. Diane was an older woman whom I had a lot in common with and really liked. She was a Christian. Her voice was soft and kind, yet firm. She had experience in all the areas, abuse, weight difficulty, a deviant stepdaughter, second marriage blending, all the ingredients for the recipe of my life with Daniel and Janelle. The only thing bad about her sessions was the deeper Diane dug, the more frequent Daniel's domestic abuse was towards me.

Diane quickly picked up on the domestic violence based upon info provided by Daniel and Janelle. It was on rare occasions that I attended the counseling sessions once Diane realized I would be abused if she suggested consequences or behavioral modifications for Janelle. Diane tried everything imaginable to help not only Janelle but me.

"How does it make you feel seeing the way your dad treats Kathy?," Diane asked Janelle in front of me at a session Daniel was unable to attend.

"Dad isn't yelling at me, he's yelling at Kathy," Janelle retorted. No guilt, just pure, sarcastic, honesty.

"You realize that Kathy takes the abuse for your actions?," Diane seemed to be seeking out some kind of remorse or misunderstanding on Janelle's part. There was none.

"What about our last meeting, when you called me because your dad was angry, threatening and cursing at Kathy on the way home, blaming her for things you said?," Diane searched for a response from Janelle. Keeping to my silence, I found myself holding my breath, waiting for Janelle's reply.

How could I forget that evening? When we arrived home, Janelle called Diane and told her Daniel was furious in the car all the way home, cursing and yelling at me. Janelle held the phone into the hallway, allowing Diane to hear Daniel's abuse.

"He's really pissed off," Janelle had whispered into the handset to Diane. "He's been this way ever since we left your office," Diane asked Janelle to hand me the phone. "Kathy, you don't deserve this," Diane frantically pleaded. "I can't help you. Call the police department before it gets worse."

A few days later, I met with Diane privately. Diane seized the opportunity to question me about Janelle and her relationship with Daniel. It was blatantly obvious to Diane, as it had been with the other counselors, Janelle's control over Daniel. Once again, I wasn't much help. I never understood why Janelle held so much power over Daniel.

"You realize Janelle is following in her father's footsteps," Diane stated. "She's manipulative, abusive, and attempts to control you. There's no difference in the two when it comes to their behavior towards you. Janelle knows what buttons to push with her dad and uses it to her advantage and power."

Humiliating and embarrassing Daniel and I, Janelle thrived on. She would talk back and argue with such anger and determination that not only would leave Daniel afraid and angry. Janelle was in charge of our family the day she walked back into our home. She manipulated every parental or authority decision and refused to follow or acknowledge any rules. I never saw Daniel win a single argument or decision with her. He was completely terrified of her and the advantage she held over him made our household a constant battlefield. If Janelle did something wrong, she would correct it this week, but it would be a repeat performance, a lesson never learned. She had no boundaries, demanding her way. If Janelle didn't get it, she resorted to rudeness, isolation, gossip, abusive behavior or pouting.

For self-protection, I limited future conversations with Diane. I was struggling all too frequently just to keep myself from being abused. At times Diane would call me at work the day following a session with Daniel and Janelle, warning me another storm might be coming or just to talk and encourage me. On those occasions, Diane was a source of strength at a time when I had no one I could confide in.

At times, Daniel would attempt to punish Janelle for the benefit of either Diane, his insecurity to Diane's suspicions or just out of principal to make a point. However, those punishments were seldom, always leaving Daniel abusing me out of guilt, fear, or whatever.

On one occasion I remember Daniel telling Janelle, "I know you think I'm being mean, but just think of it this way, your mother is up in heaven smiling down and saying, 'Good! He's finally doing something about her.'"

Diane was truly the best of all the counselors. Her counseling sessions dug deeper than any counselor. Daniel and Janelle both hung in with Diane longer than any other counselor was only by the grace of God. Meanwhile, I was learning to make the most of my times in the basement closet. Soon that tiny space next to the hot water heater began to look similar to the camp outs Lyla and I had in my youth on Mr. Draper's farm. There was a blanket, pillow, flashlight, bottled water and packs of nabs, all hidden in what was camouflaged under my children's snow clothing.

Long before I came into the life of Janelle and, Daniel, Cheryl use to threaten to send Janelle to Harmon Military Academy out of frustration for her behavior. With Diane, if you make a threat, you need to follow through. It was also at this point that Shelia brought to our attention Janelle was suffering from bulimia. After a November weekend visit with Janelle, while Daniel and I attended a film convention in Asheville, Shelia noticed Janelle binge eating, then immediately going to the bathroom to force throwing up.

Diane didn't like the bulimia or Janelle's escalating deviance. Diane appeared to be out of suggestions or options with Janelle "completely out of control," Diane encouraged Daniel to follow through with his and Cheryl's threat to send Janelle to military school. Janelle was also failing the ninth grade in public school. "Good, I want to go to Harmon Military School. Then I can say and do whatever I please without getting into trouble," Janelle hatefully retorted back at Diane and Daniel once she realized military school was to become a reality.

In early January of 2003, Daniel, Janelle and I met with the Head Sergeant of Harmon Military School. Janelle fell in love with the campus and the idea of attending military school. Harmon was a small campus, located approximately 45 minutes from our home, with dormitories housing grades 9-12. The administration building was a white, southern- antebellum-style building that smelled of rustic, old, mahogany and cedar, big, heavy entry doors, tile floors and large fireplaces. It reminded me of the plantation style house in "Gone with the Wind," balcony and all. The original beginnings of the academy was a private, Quaker school. The classrooms were housed in more modernized, brick buildings located next to the administration building.

The dormitories were across the main road which was lined with big, old oak trees. The campus had the look of the early 1900's.

There were three dormitories, one for girls and two for boys. Each cadet shared a room with one other cadet. There was a common television and study room. Located next to the dormitories was a very old, small building, labeled "Post Office."

Tuition cost for just the 2nd semester was over $18,000.00.

I cried all the way home the day we left Janelle at Harmon, thinking it would be a horrible experience for her. For weeks, every time a family member would ask how she was doing I would cry. All the while thinking as young as she was, no matter how mean she had been to Evan and me, no one, not even Janelle deserved to be separated from their family and thrown into a military school for punishment. Visions of the cruelty of getting up at 4:00 a.m. for roll call in the cold winter air, push-ups, running, cruel sergeants yelling in her face, all plagued my thoughts. Yet, little did Daniel, Diane or I realize Harmon Military School was nothing like that and was one of the biggest mistakes of our lives. The label "military school" was a joke. Janelle had more freedom, more exposure and experimentation with smoking, drinking, drugs and sex than she had ever been exposed to before. There was limited monitoring and supervision on the campus before, during and after school, nights and weekends. Students were free to walk to the service station off base and get whatever drug of preference; blunts, cigarettes, alcohol, anything they had enough money to buy. They were allowed to wonder the grounds all hours of the night and early morning. Sex was open and with the ratio of approximately 150 boys to only 15-20 girls, the boys were desperate and the girls were few in number to satisfy the average teenage male hormones. Harmon was the answer in satisfying Janelle's desperation for male attention.

During the school semester, Daniel never received a progress report. When Daniel would call inquiring about Janelle's grades, the answer he received from the head sergeant was always, "She's doing great." To me, something didn't seem right, but Janelle was happy, it was not my place to question.

To make things worse, Harmon had no monitoring whatsoever on Janelle's Internet activities and she continued to expand her sexual advertising on multiple websites.

With Janelle out of the house, Daniel reconnected the computer for e-bay purchases of his collection of western films and memorabilia. When Janelle came home on break at Valentine's I found she had been on the computer and accidentally left information on the screen. Her new site, "Good Girl by Day, Bad Girl at Night!," In addition, Janelle had an ongoing relationship with an older man who lived in Norfolk, Virginia. He worked as a custodian in a local hospital. Janelle had given him all her personal contact information including directions on how to meet her at school. When Daniel arrived home from work that evening, I left the information and e-mails visible on the computer screen, knowing Daniel would never believe me if told him. I watched Daniel's facial expressions as he read Janelle's written communications with the man. I could see his face slowly turn beet red with anger. Daniel was more scared of the man than of what Janelle had done. He was afraid of losing his daughter to a possible maniac; therefore, little was said as Daniel left to confront Janelle.

"It's too much of a temptation for Janelle, and she can't control herself," was all Daniel said as disconnected the computer.

By the end of May, we were questionable as to whether or not Harmon Military was the right decision for Janelle. In mid-June, we received Janelle's grades. She failed the ninth grade. Not only that, but we had another problem. Janelle learned another thing at Harmon, which was to undress and display her naked body in front of her bedroom windows. Windows that faced the road.

The first week Janelle was home, I noticed when I arrived home from work, Janelle's blinds were pulled up, and the windows open in her bedroom while the air conditioning was on.

"Janelle, what's up?," I asked pointing to the windows. "The air conditioning's on and you know your dad doesn't like the windows open or the blinds up."

"Oh, I needed the fresh air. We always left our blinds up and windows open at Harmon," she defiantly told me. I bet she did with all 150 boys outside looking in. Of course, there was no way I was going to approach the subject with Daniel, so I just dropped it. For several days, I arrived home to the same situation, but Janelle was always careful to close the windows and blinds before her dad arrived home.

A few weeks later, on a Saturday afternoon, while Daniel and I were outside mowing and working in the yard, a movement from Janelle's window caught my attention. I watched as Janelle opened her bedroom blinds and windows and began to undress. Janelle then turned to go shower. I guess she thought her dad was inside the house instead of outside. Minutes later, I watched as she came back into her room parading around her bedroom completely naked, in full view of all who could see. Unsure of how to approach the subject with Daniel, I hesitantly went to the backyard and asked Daniel if he could help me move the timbers from the edge of the flowerbed. As we walked around the house, Daniel looked up and I watched the expression on his face change into awareness as he witnessed Janelle parading around her room naked. A flaming glow of red rose in his cheeks.

"God dammit!," Daniel shot out as he dropped his rake onto the ground. Storming across the front yard, Daniel yanked the front storm door open so hard, I thought he would tear the door off its hinges. The door echoed shut in the still summer.

I dug the trowel deep into the hard, red clay.

Of course, there was no rationalizing with Janelle as I watched Daniel come storming out of the house screaming at me, "I'm going fuckin' crazy!," he kicked the weeds I had just pulled out of the flowerbed, scattering them across the yard.

The hot sun had begun to exhaust me. I was hungry and thirsty. It was late in the afternoon. I had tried to drag out my work in the front yard flowerbed as long as possible, hoping and praying Daniel wouldn't take Janelle's latest escapade out on me. As I stepped into the house, Daniel followed me in as if he were finished too.

"You knew about Janelle's window and blinds, didn't you?," Daniel started as he reached for a glass of water. "You knew what I would see if I had looked up today," I said nothing knowing long hours in the sun, probably added fuel to Daniel's tank of rage.

"Janelle said you knew about it weeks ago," he dropped the empty glass into the sink. Too exhausted to play games, I took my punishment as Daniel dished out the usual physical and verbal abuse. I was a failure, not a Christian, needed to pray more, on and on. Then to the basement closet, I went willingly, tired and hot. The cement floor was cool to my body. In the dark silence, I slept.

Later that evening I awoke to the sound of laughter as Daniel and Janelle returned from Janelle's reward trip to Ann's. The smell of French fries and fast food drifting down the staircase and into the basement closet below. My stomach growled at its emptiness. I could hear them both talking and laughing as they sat together eating at the kitchen bar.

In the darkness, I drank my bottled water, ate a pack of nabs then laid and waited for the house to quiet. Hours later, I climbed the stairs, crept down the hallway and slowly opened the bedroom door. Daniel's snoring, gave me permission to take a shower and climb into bed.

Later the following week Janelle got her own punishment from having the windows open and parading naked, God sent a loose bat in her room. Janelle called me at work, screaming hysterically. Two nights before Janelle woke me up screaming saying she felt something soft fly across her face, but a search of her bedroom, revealed nothing. All along, the bat had camped out in her room. How long it had been there, we didn't know, but it was terrifying for Janelle. Her frantic phone call sent me racing home on an early lunch hour to remove the bat and set it free, back into the woods overlooking Janelle's windows. The only creature at our house interested in viewing Janelle's naked body through the open blinds and windows was an old bat.

Janelle's smoking blunts, cigarettes and marijuana increased at Harmon. Being away from Harmon and her easy source supply, sent her in search of a another resource. It only took a month before a member of Daniel's family began supplying Janelle with cigarettes. The sad part was it was an adult with children of her own. When I asked Janelle if she realized this was contributing to the delinquency of a minor, Janelle became outraged that I might threaten her source. Of course, I was punished the next two days for making the comment after Janelle called the family member, who then called Daniel threatening and asking, why he allowed Janelle to come over to their house in the first place knowing they smoked. Everyone knew Janelle had been smoking since the age of nine. My thoughts were what kind of family treated a young girl of age nine with vaginal crèmes to hide infections and freely supplied her with cigarettes. However, that was only my thoughts, not allowed to be spoken aloud, only retained in my heart and mind.

During July and August, Janelle and Daniel worked with Diane on what Janelle's next option for school. Daniel was completely out of money and then some. He had a large equity loan against the house and there were "additional expenses" for Janelle throughout each month, running up his credit card debt. Janelle was definitely a "high maintenance" child.

"An all-girls school," was Diane's next suggestion. "Janelle's too 'obsessed' with boys. That may never change, but maybe this will force her to focus on academics with no boys around to distract and encourage her misbehavior."

A search began for an all girls' school and in early August, Diane, Daniel and Janelle settled on St. Mary's All Girls' School in Raleigh, North Carolina, over an hour away. St. Mary's had a beautiful campus and their program provided everything a girl could dream of, swimming pool, tennis courts, beautiful dorm rooms. It was a college-prep school rated one of the top academic schools in the state. Daniel and I talked about how different our lives would have been if we had had the opportunity of St. Mary's when we were children. Janelle was lucky. The cost of St. Mary's was over $32,000.00 per school year. Another trip to the bank as Daniel increased his equity line loan.

Janelle loved St. Mary's. It was a great school with a lot of potential of helping Janelle in every aspect. The school was strict with academics and more communicative concerning her progress and performance. The first semester was a challenge for Janelle. She struggled socially and academically, coming up with every excuse under the sun as to why she couldn't study and do well. She complained her room had too many things on the wall to distract her, she didn't like being monitored while she was studying or doing her homework, the room was too quiet, there was too much noise, nobody liked her, on and on she complained. At the end of her first six weeks, right before we were to receive her academic progress report, Janelle began to work her magic to "block" us from receiving the report revealing her bad grades.

"I'm convinced Janelle has numerous learning disabilities," the school counselor called and told Daniel. Janelle knew better and was up to her tricks of manipulation once again. The year before Cheryl died, she had Janelle tested for learning disabilities, due to Janelle's bad grades and Janelle's insistence she had learning disabilities. The results revealed there were no learning disabilities and Janelle was up to her grade level learning potential.

Once again, Daniel went to the bank to borrow another $1500.00 for a test to be done by a psychiatrist in Raleigh. Two weeks later Daniel and I met with the psychiatrist.

"Janelle's good at manipulating people," he began. "She's at her learning grade level potential. The problem with Janelle is she doesn't want to attend school and learn. She's lazy and all she wants to do is sleep and play." The psychiatrist wasn't fooled at all by Janelle's antics and now the school counselor had "egg" on her face.

"Never before has any student 'tricked' me as badly as Janelle has," our follow-up meeting with the school counselor was extremely difficult as the counselor explained how humiliating and embarrassed she felt. I would have to admit, it was another magnificent performance by Janelle and just as she had lied and fooled all the counselors in the past, Janelle lost out again.

Christmas of that year was a disaster. Janelle was home from St. Mary's and in a bad mood. For days she walked around depressed, wearing the same clothes, she had slept in the night before for two or three days. The same behavior we experienced in the summer. On Christmas Eve, Daniel had had enough of her behavior and went into an abusive rage around 9 p.m. that evening.

"Just look at her," Daniel started after Janelle left the kitchen. "Her room is a mess. She hasn't showered in days, changed clothes or brushed her hair. What's her problem?" A trip two days before to the dentist revealed Janelle had four cavities, adding even more financial stress and frustration.

Directing his anger at me, Daniel flew into his usual abuse, "Cheryl was an angel compared to you!," He stated as he slammed the cabinet door. "No wonder Richard left you. He couldn't live with you and neither can I!," turning he stormed into the living room where he threw himself down into his recliner and grabbed the TV remote. "And why in the hell does your family have to come tomorrow for Christmas? This is my house. I don't want them here. They need to stay home with their own damn families!"

There was nothing I could say. Daniel was right, it was his house. My family was always good to Daniel and especially to Janelle. Even though all were aware of the abusive environment Evan and I lived in, they continued to be generous and thoughtful with gifts to both Daniel and Janelle, taking special pains to make sure they called me to get ideas of what Daniel and Janelle wanted or needed.

My silence didn't seem to work. The foot of the recliner slammed shut as Daniel came back into the kitchen.

"Call them!," he ordered his mouth tight as his frustration with Janelle turned into rage directed at my family and me. "Call them and tell them it's off! I don't want them here tomorrow! To hell with all of you!," He came over to the stove, grabbed my arm and jerked me around to face him. "And make sure you call Amber and Matt too! I don't want anyone here!"

Defeated once again, I tried to collect my thoughts, tried to respond, but could only stand facing Daniel with my usual speechless silence, tears spilling down my cheeks, a huge lump in my throat.

Christmas Day with my family had to be cancelled and there was no hope of changing Daniel's mind. I was shattered.

Why was I walking with the Lord and suffering so? Wasn't there supposed to be triumphs and victories if I relied on Him. Lately there seemed to be more trials and tribulations. I could feel the burden of resentment towards God weighing down on my shoulders and anger entering my heart. Why was God allowing this to happen? Why? Was God even on my side? Does He even know I exist? I questioned as I looked up at the evil in Daniel's eyes, then quickly looked down at the floor. I felt hopeless. All those years of yearning, learning and establishing family memories, adventures and traditions, Daniel was taking away from me. This was our family tradition, the one I had worked so hard at creating since the birth of Amber. The "tradition" I always shared with not just my family, but with anyone else who needed a place to call home at Christmas.

The first Christmas I shared with Daniel and Janelle while we were dating was great. Daniel seemed to fit in and liked the tradition of having brunch in the morning because the rest of the afternoon and evening was quiet with just us. The first year we were married, even though we were living separate, we still celebrated as a family at Daniel's house. Daniel seemed proud of the Christmas tradition I created.

Yet now, Christmas three years later, at 9 p.m. in the evening, Daniel wanted it to cease. Another attempt to take me even further away from my family. As Daniel continued to rage, I felt I was losing my entire life and identity.

"This is my house," Daniel jerked my arms with the purpose of bringing my eyes back to focus on his face. "No one is going to control what I do in my house!," He was so far gone that rationalizing with him was impossible.

"It's okay," I softly said, making a futile attempt to get the abuse over with. "I'll take the gifts to Randy's, Amber and Matt's tonight and leave them on their front porch with a note stating I was sick and needed to cancel Christmas Day brunch."

"If you do," Daniel screamed at me, "I'll take a gun and blow my head off! What are you trying to do? Make me look crazy in front of your family? They already think that! Your family doesn't like me anyway! Look at me, I'm fuckin crazy!"

I absolutely didn't know what I was supposed to say or do. "Maybe you could call them in the morning," I pleaded. "You can tell them I'm sick, and we need to cancel. We could get the gifts to them some other time."

"And then what? What do you think they will say, 'It's probably Daniel! He's a raging, cussing, crazy man?' You need to get the hell out of here!," he dropped my arm and pointed to the door, "Get out!"

Quickly I ran down the hall, into the bedroom, grabbing my pocketbook and jacket. Evan was at Richard's for the night and was to come with Matt tomorrow. Escaping down the stairs and out the door, by then it was after 10:00. Driving around the city, traffic was light, with families gathered for traditional Christmas Eve celebrations. Houses where parents were preparing for Santa's visit. After over an hour of driving I found myself back at the little cabin Evan and I had stayed in two years prior when we had left Daniel's and Janelle was living in Boone. The elderly couple was in Florida visiting their children for the holidays. Alone, curled up tightly in a blanket I had stowed away in the trunk of my car, I laid on the hard bench underneath the front porch, crying and praying.

"What am I going to do?," I prayed up to God, looking at the stars twinkling in the clear, winter night sky.

"Cheryl was the lucky one," I said to the heavenly sky. "She escaped all this pain and suffering. God had opened the gates of paradise where He relieved the troubles lying deep within her heart and her sufferings are no more. Oh, Lord, I'm still here. Please, help me!," I cried out. Exhausted, sleep finally overcame me.

The morning sounds of daylight awoke me and I looked down at my watch. It was 7:30, Christmas Day. Sore from sleeping on the hard bench, shivering from the cold, I made my way back to my car, dreading what the day would hold.

Daniel was sitting in his recliner, eating his usual bowl of mixed Cheerios and Raisin Bran, watching an old western movie on TV, as if it was just a normal morning, not Christmas.

With no words exchanged, I left for the bedroom and bathroom to shower and change clothes.

"Did you call everyone and cancel?," Moments later, I sat on the couch and asked Daniel, afraid of his answer.

"No," he stormed at me, his empty cereal bowl in one hand as he jumped up out of his recliner. "Have it your way, you always do, but I will not be controlled anymore by you or anyone else!," Throwing his empty cereal bowl into the sink, Daniel retreated to his theatre. Hearing the door slam, I went into the kitchen and hurriedly began finishing our traditional brunch meal.

The day was tense with Daniel mostly quiet, only speaking when spoken to. Janelle was completely anti-social, coming out when it was time to eat and for the presents, not acknowledging anyone with a "thank you," Then retreated to her room. My nieces tried unsuccessfully to visit with Janelle in her room, but she was flat out rude to the both of them, resulting in them quickly returning to safety.

Daniel finally came out of his mood around 3:00 that afternoon, after everyone had left. Pulling me into the bedroom, he sat on the edge of the bed, and took my hand in his.

"Brenda's still asking 'why and what was said to the counselors,'" he started. "My entire family is angry with me. Every time they call or I see them, they're asking questions. I feel like I'm losing my family," Daniel began to cry. "Janelle's failing school, again, she's depressed all the time and the school is complaining about her grades and behavior. I feel like nobody can help Janelle or me. I don't know what to do," he looked up and pleaded for answers. I had no answers and could only sit beside him on the bed and listen.

Our gifts and stockings laid unopened under the Christmas tree as the day drew to a close. A day, which should have been a celebration of the birth of Christ. Instead, it was a day, full of pain and despair.

In January 2004, Janelle began her 2nd semester at St. Mary's. Daniel and I began marriage counseling with a new counselor, Dr. Martin. Dr. Leighman had long since been history and Diane questioned why we were not in marriage counseling or some kind of family counseling. Daniel was starting to feel "threatened" by Diane's involvement and her openness about the domestic violence in our home. I knew that soon, very soon, Diane would be history especially with the knowledge of abuse. I followed Diane's advice and whenever possible met with the domestic violence counselor assigned to me from the hospital. We met at different locations, such as the women's shelter, park or public library.

Daniel was still in anger management counseling with Dr. Mayers, Three counselors analyzing and trying to mend our broken family.

Our current "crisis" to discuss with Dr. Martin, while Janelle was at Harmon Military School and now at St. Mary's her stealing had escalated. Janelle would steal things from our bedroom, Evan's room and throughout the house, taking the items back with her to school, hidden in her backpack.

Daniel was beginning to be more open over his own frustration with Janelle's stealing of his breakfast foods, snack cakes, and sodas. If Janelle saw it and wanted it, it would "disappear" to St. Mary's or her bedroom.

Dr. Martin quickly recognized what all the other counselors had, Janelle's control over Daniel and his refusal to implement any kind of punishment, enforce rules or consequences. Because of her control, Dr. Martin stated he felt Daniel had allowed Janelle's behavior to escalate to the point it was now, totally out of control.

The first attempt Dr. Martin made to address Janelle's stealing was his recommendation for me to voluntarily leave the house for two hours and for Daniel to let Janelle go through every room in the house, our bedroom, Evan's, into the attic, everywhere, allowing Janelle to take whatever she wanted. This would include my jewelry, clothes, anything and everything she wanted. Dr. Martin felt by allowing Janelle to get "all the loot" she wanted, maybe it would stop her stealing.

"Daniel, Evan and Kathy are being victimized by Janelle's behavior, more so than you. It has to be a horrible feeling for the both of them," Dr. Martin sympathized. However, his idea didn't work and Janelle's stealing continued. Evan and I lived in constant fear of Janelle thefts.

Dr. Martin's next plan of action was to order us to install key locks on Evan's and our bedroom doors as well on the cabinets that contained food and the food pantry door. For the remaining years of our marriage, Evan and I lived like prisoners in our home. If I left my bedroom only briefly to go downstairs to the basement, kitchen or even out to start my car in the mornings, I worried Janelle was lying in wait to steal from me. I locked the bedroom door when I took a shower and Evan's bedroom door was locked when he wasn't there. The food pantry and all food cabinets were locked at all times.

The "lock down" made me resentful of the fact Evan and I were the ones being victimized by a robber yet we were forced to live like prisoners in a high security prison. At all times, Evan, Daniel and I carried around a set of keys, with a couple of sets hidden throughout the house.

After a few weeks of the new "lock down" orders, we all realized the door locks didn't work either. Janelle continued to find ways to steal from the living room, bathrooms, den, everywhere to the extent Dr.

Martin instructed Daniel he would have to search Janelle's book bag before she left to go back to school from her weekend stays. Each time Daniel searched Janelle's book bag it was like watching the police search a shoplifter. I hated it. It didn't seem to be the right thing to do to resolve Janelle's stealing. I couldn't find fault with Dr. Martin's suggestions and counseling. He was just as frustrated as all the other counselors were. Somehow, someway there needed to be discipline and direction from Daniel, but it never came and Janelle continued to steal, finding ways to hide things on her person or in her coat or clothing pockets.

Dr. Martin suggested meetings with Daniel and I separately, then combined the last ten minutes. By now, I assumed Dr. Martin had Diane's records as well as all the other records Daniel signed releases for him to obtain. Dr. Martin began to address the abuse I was suffering.

"Kathy, how do you feel about Daniel's threats and abuse?," he gently asked.

Shrugging my shoulders, I avoided looking at the file or him, knowing the "door" he was attempting to open and I wasn't going all the way through it.

"I hate the threats of Daniel 'blowing his head off' and his wishes 'of getting cancer,'" I started, guessing this was pretty much knowledge now to Dr. Martin considering the thickness of our file sitting in front of him on his desk. "But the worst for me is when he threatens divorce papers to be served on me at work. I never know what to do with his threats, how or if I should plan for Evan and me to move elsewhere. Where would we go? The threats come so often, I never know how serious they really are," I paused to mentally evaluate the safety of what I had just said. Satisfied that it wouldn't cause retaliation by Daniel if Dr. Martin revealed what I had just disclosed, I continued. "Sometimes Daniel makes me wait for days with the threat that divorce papers would be coming any day. Every time I see a police officer walk through my building or in the parking lot, my heart surges with fear. Where would I go, what would I tell Evan?," I stopped, hoping that would be enough to satisfy Dr. Martin. This was the first time I had ever discussed this with anyone.

In our combined session after that, Dr. Martin was very firm with Daniel, ordering the abuse and threats to the marriage to stop. Words that fell on deaf ears. No one was going to tell Daniel how to treat his wife.

On Valentine's Day weekend, Janelle came home from St. Mary's for an extended break. Her plans for her time off were to focus primarily on calling guys at Harmon Military School in an attempt to arrange meetings with them at St. Mary's. We were forced to endure phone calls from guys begging us to make her stop calling and harassing them. Daniel was scared of Janelle's aggression and obsession with boys and that seemed to be the only thing Daniel would "sit up and listen to," forcing Daniel to remove the private phone line in Janelle's room. Janelle pouted the remaining time she was on holiday, while Daniel lived in fear and guilt over his punishment, making it a tense and abusive Valentine's for me.

The following week, Janelle was back on the Internet at St. Mary's with another website. This one worse than the ones before. Administrators at St. Mary's found Janelle's websites based upon her usage in their computer center. Once again, an embarrassing meeting was scheduled with the school administrators, Daniel, and I along with Janelle. We were all reminded about the school's Code of Conduct, as the school felt their reputation had been compromised. With us all in agreement, Janelle was reprimanded and her computer usage was closely monitored.

Chapter Seventeen: Quaker Lake

      Quaker Lake is a conference center for Quakers centrally located in North Carolina. It is owned and operated by the North Carolina Yearly Meeting. Members of Quaker meetings are permitted usage.

      Entrance into the conference center is a narrow, gravel drive leading down to a secluded retreat. The lodge is a log building that houses a spacious room with a rock fireplace at one end, a commercial kitchen that separates the open room from lodging rooms and bathrooms and a recreational room consisting of a ping pong table and various board games.

      Large windows frame the view of scattered, bunk-style cabins and two small lakes. Walking paths wind amongst tranquil pine trees.

      Tranquility best describes Quaker Lake, a place of beauty, a place of calm.

      Two lakes are separated by a channel. Still waters surrender reflective mirrors of peaceful surroundings of nature amongst crisp, blue skies. A small, wooden bridge offers a choice of views, one side of the lake or the other. It matters not. Each side gives solitude in which someone could stand and gaze for hours at the magnificent beauty of this sacred haven. Cool, refreshing breezes blow from across the two small lakes. Music of God's creations, fish and frogs delight, gently play a soft medley that echoes throughout acres. I have seen all seasons at Quaker Lake. Each one holds its own special beauty.

The Quaker faith for me represents spiritual guidance from within, a peaceful, individual relationship with God. Quaker Lake is my special, inspirational place, where I can walk, talk and spend time with God. A place I feel the presence of God and at times, run to seek peace and healing.

Quaker Lake and I go far back. From my childhood, we use to bale hay there for our horses and cattle. In my teen years, we had weekend church and youth retreats. My children attended summer camp programs. As a family, we attended yearly, camp weekends for our church congregation. An entire weekend full of family activities, square dancing, hay rides, board games, football and other outdoor games, canoeing and kayak, campfires, fishing, swimming, trail walks. Connecting with God and church family, away from the "world" and focusing on what was most important, our relationship with God and the nurturing of our families and church.

One year we reserved a weekend in December. The men in the church took the children in search of the "perfect Christmas tree". When they returned with a huge cedar, the women and children strung popcorn and made homemade ornaments. That evening, by the fireplace, we sang Christmas carols and read the Christmas story, concluding with our favorite Christmas memories.

Then was the year we held a traditional Quaker wedding for a couple in front of the old rock fireplace. After the nuptials, church members serenaded the bride and groom as we followed them to their honeymoon cabin, (which we secretly decorated during the ceremony with candles, flowers and fresh greenery). We encircled the cabin, holding hands, singing praises, and best wishes for a happy, prosperous life for the newlyweds.

I am "rich" from my experiences at Quaker Lake. I am "rich" that it is a part of who I am and a gift given to me by being a Quaker. Countless times Quaker Lake is the place I go to have my problems solved, my fears put to rest, my strength regained and my troubled heart mended. A place where I go to "be still and commune with God,"

Fortunately, for me, Quaker Lake is located approximately fifteen miles from Daniel's house. If I could sneak away during daylight hours without being trapped inside the basement closet, to Quaker Lake I would run. There I would take a humbling walk with God, as a broken woman in submission to God. Staying for as long as was needed for renewal of my spirit and strength to continue my journey on the path before me in my dysfunctional marriage.

Daniel never took me to the gravesite where Cheryl was buried, but I made my own special memorial place for her at Quaker Lake. Back in the woods, between the summer cabins was a small clearing. There I made a small cross out of twigs tied together with string. Around the base of the cross were stones I gathered on the walking trail, each revealing its own significant beauty, just like Cheryl. At times I would place wildflowers or pinecones on the small grave only to find them scattered by the wind on my next visit. Sitting beside Cheryl's tiny memorial, I would unload my pain and feelings of failure.

"You are now a part of my life," I told Cheryl, "Every moment I live, both good and bad you and God are at the bottom holding and steadying each step I take climbing up the ladder."

What defeat and discouragement up until her death Cheryl must have felt to be denied even a glass of water from Janelle, her only child. To me God was merciful to have spared her life from these difficult years. He chose to take Cheryl home to be with Him, giving her final peace.

"Please dear God have mercy on me and give me strength," I prayed. At times, I longed to be in heaven with Cheryl and God.

Sometimes my prayers were angry, "Why in the world did God choose me and think I could make changes in twelve-year-olds life? I need you God! Show me the way!"

It was the end of February, remnants of unmelted, white snow was still visible in the shaded areas and in the woods. The cold, winter air biting, as I walked the lonely trails. Finding a door unlocked to one of the rustic summer cabins, I wrapped up in the blanket I had stashed in the trunk of my car for emergency escapes. On a small child's, bunk bed mattress, too exhausted to even cry or pray anymore, I lay defeated. There God was too, once again, His arms of love and protection wrapped around the blanket and me. I was His chosen child. He loved me. I knew the pain Daniel and Janelle inflicted on me hurt God just as much as it was hurting me. Sleep finally came.

A rustle in the leaves outside the door, startled me awake. Leaving the cabin, just as I had found it, pulling my coat and blanket tighter around me, the moon was just appearing in the clear sky above, giving dim, grayish light on the path. Trying to collect my thoughts and the courage to go on.

"I am with you," I heard God say.

"But how much more?," I asked.

With a heart filled with dread, two feet heavy from burdens, I walked along the dimly lit path of carpeted pine needles to my car.

Leaning against my arm on steering wheel, one last plea, "Please God, help me."

Chapter Eighteen: Begging for Another Chance

The rain had let up to a light drizzle as we pulled around back of the motel to pick up my car.

"Is there a restroom inside?," Cindy turned to ask.

"Yes, in the lobby area," I responded.

Removing my belongings from the backseat, we transferred my things into my car then went inside the motel.

"Gary says we'll have to swing around the main road and take the back roads to avoid the possibility of Daniel spotting your car," Cindy explained as we washed our hands. "It'll take a little longer, but we can't take any chances,"

"Can you and Gary write down directions for me on how to get to work?," I asked.

"Sure.   That route won't be as long and complicated as tonight," Cindy turned and gave me a hug, then looked down into my face. "You'll be fine. A new beginning. Remember?"

A new beginning, yet daily, nightly reminders of the past. We left the bathroom, meeting up with Gary in the parking lot.

"Goodbye," I softly said to the family owned Christmas tree lot beside the motel as I looked out the passenger side window. One evening, after dark, Amber, little Stephanie and I walked out of the motel and over to the lot. Looking at the Christmas lights and decorations, walking through a maze of various shapes and sizes of beautiful different types of Christmas trees. "Ironic," I thought that evening as I laid my head down on the soft pillow after Amber and Stephanie had left, "I guess God just provided another place after Thanksgiving for us to search for that one "perfect tree" once again, keeping with our family tradition that was lost during my marriage to Daniel.

Come the end of May 2004, we found out St. Mary's didn't work for Janelle either; she caused just about as much chaos there as she did at Harmon Military Academy and once again, Janelle failed the ninth grade. Debts of over \$60,000.00 invested in counseling and private schools for Janelle resulting in grief and exasperation. By now Janelle would be twenty-one years old when she graduated from high school, if she graduated. It seemed as if Janelle had made up her mind, no high school diploma, no college, just failing.

"What the hell is going on?," Daniel slammed the letter from St. Mary's. "Is this never going to end?," he questioned me, his words seethed through his clinched teeth as he pressed his body up against me. My back creased in pain as the edge of the island bar dug deep. Daniel grabbed my wrist and jerked me around, pulling me down the stairs into the basement area where Evan and wouldn't hear the abuse.

"I'm broke and I've had enough," Daniel said as I tried to scramble out of his reach. Daniel's force was strengthening by his anger, yet I continued to resist as he pulled me down the stairs. Halfway down, squirming out from under Daniel's vise-like grip, my leg slipped on the carpeted stairs. Pain shot up my right leg and side.

"Get up!," Daniel ordered as he kicked me in the back. "Bitch!," he growled as he reached down to grab my arm once again. Scrambling from his reach, I somehow turned in an attempt to crawl back to the top of the stairs. With success, I stood up and made my way down the hallway into the master bathroom, with Daniel hot on my heals. Slamming the bedroom door, thanking Dr. Martin quietly for the door locks, buying me time as Daniel fumbled for his keys. Quickly I escaped into the master bathroom, another locked door in an attempt to protect me from Daniel's abuse.

"Open the God damn door!," Daniel yelled as his fist and feet banged against the door.

"Oh, God," I cried. "When is this ever going to end? Why, why is this happening?," I slid down the door, onto the floor.

A pause and silence. Then numbers were being dialed on the phone beside our bed.

"This is Daniel Thomas, I live at ### Road in Greensboro, NC. I need to turn myself in for domestic violence abuse. I just pushed my wife down the stairs," I heard Daniel say.

"Yes, yes, she's in the bathroom. I'm a bastard and I need you to come and lock me up," a moment of silence.

"Yeah, okay, yes, I'll be here waiting," another pause. "That's right, I'll be here. Come get me and lock me up."

A sound of the phone being slammed in the cradle. Then Daniel's footsteps storming out of the bedroom.

Turning to face the mirror, I lifted up my shirt to look at the damage to my right side; it was beginning to show signs of swelling and bruising. Slipping my pants down, I could see the carpet burns on the side of my leg.

I rested on the bathroom floor with nothing to do but wait for the police.

I awoke to stiffness.   Glancing at my watch, it was after 4 p.m. "Where are they? What's taking them so long?" Three hours had passed.

Pulling myself up with the assistance of the bathroom sink, I made cold compresses out of washcloths in an attempt to soothe the stinging pain on my leg.

Peering out of the bathroom doorway, I glanced around the bedroom room. No Daniel. The house was quiet. Softly I opened the bedroom door and made my way down the hallway. Looking in the living room and kitchen, no sign of Daniel. No noise from downstairs as I descended the staircase. Slowly I opened the door to Daniel's theatre and peered into the darkness. There, on the back row was Daniel, his arms crossed, engrossed in one of his western films.

"When are the police coming?," my voice was cracked and dry.

A sick grin appeared across Daniel's face, "What police?," his tone sarcastic.

"I....," I couldn't finish. There was no way I could believe my husband was that cruel, that sick as to fake something as mean as a phone call to the police.

Before I could finish asking the unthinkable, Daniel interjected, "I didn't really call the police; I just wanted you to think I did? Isn't that what you wanted? To have me locked up? Bitch!"

Defeated, I retreated to the living room couch where I stayed until Daniel went to bed for the night. Reality sinking in of just how mentally sick and evil my husband really was.

Once again we began visiting private school after private school, local ones that were less expensive. Public school was not an option as we knew from the academic testing Janelle received at some of the private schools. Public school would end up setting her back possibly lower than eighth grade. Each private school would test, and each one came out with the same results, academically she was 8th grade level or less. Finally, we found a small Christian school that was not "highly regarded academically" by state standards. Their studies were very basic, an academic level so easy, both Janelle and Daniel felt it would enable her to at least obtain her high school diploma. A minister and his family ran the school.

Daniel once again went to the bank, to "max out" what little amount of equity on the house he had left.

"Can you come by and see me, alone," The day I was to sign papers for another loan extension, Daniel's banker called me at work.

"Sure," her stress of the word 'alone' had me curious.   "Can it be done on my lunch hour this afternoon?"

"Yes, it won't take long," was all she said.

That afternoon I sat in the small bank office, a large window viewed the parking lot, behind a petite woman who had been Daniel and Cheryl's personal banker for years.

"I've known Daniel a long time and I knew Cheryl before she passed away," she began. "There's no easy way to say this, Mrs. Thomas, not really knowing you or your financial situation," she paused then continued. "All these loans for Janelle that Daniel's taking out...well... he's overextending himself," she hesitated again.   "He's in deep financial debt," she took off her glasses and laid them aside, "I've got serious concerns."

"What do you recommend I do?," Not sure why she had called the meeting, when usually, I just came in with Daniel and signed the papers.

"Don't sign any more papers," she bluntly stated, looking across the mahogany desk. A desk so cluttered I didn't see how in the world she could be even remotely organized much less find anything.

"The loan is a mortgage against Daniel's home and your name isn't on the deed if anything happens to you in regards to your marriage," she continued, "You will be held co-responsible for these loans if you sign."

Embarrassed, I left the bank without signing the papers, in agreement that the bank would re-writing the loan, leaving my name off.

With more loan money in hand, we went to the minister of the small Christian school with our decision to enroll Janelle. Nevertheless, even as small as the school was, and their desperation for our money, the tiny church school board looked over Janelle's grade history and performance from public schools to private schools and were not impressed. In fact, they were hesitant to accept Janelle. They voiced their concerns to Daniel and me. We literally begged for Janelle's acceptance in their school, knowing other the schools we visited were not exactly impressed and willing to accept her either. We assured them we would do a better job as parents if they would give us a chance, lowering ourselves to begging them to take her, stating we had learned a lot from Janelle's experiences with Harmon and St. Mary's and promised to make Janelle follow strict study guidelines and as her parents would stress to her the importance of her academics. With our persuasive "sales pitch" to the board, they agreed to enroll Janelle for a probationary period of six months. Janelle would have to prove herself academically to the school board. Once again, for the third time, Janelle entered into the ninth grade. The entire school had less than 100 students. The first graduating class we witnessed was five seniors. The school enforced dress code and students had to attend religious worship daily for religion credit.

Janelle found a part-time job working at a local bowling alley. The environment for Janelle would not have been my first choice, but Daniel saw nothing wrong with it. I was uncomfortable with the alcohol, age group and overall atmosphere, but knew I could say nothing. Janelle loved working at the bowling alley as she quickly gravitated to the "wrong crowd,"

Within her first month, Janelle struck up a romantic relationship with a man named Adam. Adam was twenty-eight. Janelle was seventeen.   I found out about it through a student enrolled at the college who worked in the bar. He knew of Janelle from seeing her with me at work. He warned me Janelle was involved with this man and a single mom in her mid-thirties, named Sharon.

The relationship between Janelle and the "older man" was kept secret from Daniel. I couldn't tell Daniel for fear of what would happen to me, knowing he would never believe me. Plans were that as soon as Janelle turned eighteen, she and Adam were running off together. "Adam and Janelle forever" written various ways in her teenage love handwriting on homework and test papers, scattered on the kitchen table one evening. "I hope he waits for me to turn 18," she confided in the student one evening, while sitting at the bar.

Janelle soon began to spend the night on numerous occasions with Sharon. This enabled Janelle to meet Adam secretly and Sharon was her ticket into karaoke bars, and various nightclubs. Daniel was aware of the bars and nightclub escapades as Janelle bragged about "clubbing" with Sharon. Soon it was a weekly event. Daniel saw no harm in it stating, "At least Janelle has a friend to do things with." Which was pretty much the truth. Friendships with Janelle were few. There was nothing I could say and refused to say out of fear. By now, Janelle was smoking heavily getting cigarettes by cashing her paychecks at local gas stations and convenient stores, or having Sharon buy them for her. Janelle was learning a lot from her newfound friends in Adam and Sharon.

"Janelle's spending the night at Sharon's again this evening," Daniel played the message on the machine. Janelle never asked permission, she told. Both of us were involved in the garage all day and evening, working on Daniel's truck.

It was close to Adam's twenty-ninth birthday. Secret plans were being made from the notes I had found beside Janelle's homework papers.

"Are you sure that's a good idea?," be gentle, I thought. Go slow. "Maybe she should come home tonight, Daniel, she's been gone for over two nights," I was scared of Adam and scared of what Janelle would do.

Daniel threw the grease towel he used to wipe his hands onto the concrete floor as he turned to face me.

"I know where my daughter is," Daniel snarled, "You're the one that doesn't trust her."

"It's not that," I tried, "It's just that it's been a long time since we've spent time with Janelle. Besides, don't you think we should get to know Sharon a little better? We don't know what their plans are for tonight."

"I know everything I need to know about Sharon. Janelle and I talk. I trust my daughter," Daniel was defensive and getting angrier and angrier by the minute.

"Back off Kathy," I could hear that still small voice saying. "But I'm scared. I know we'll lose her if we don't stop her," I thought, "What if she gets hurt or runs away? How could I live with myself knowing I knew this all along? "Dear God," I breathed in softly. "I'm scared, and I don't know what to do. Somehow I have to let Daniel know, I can't let you down," I closed my eyes. "God, please, show me the way without too much abuse afterwards."

"Do you know where Janelle's going tonight?," my long pause had forced Daniel to ask me accusingly, looking deep into my eyes.

"No," I stumbled, "I was just asking, 'Do you really know where she is and all there is to know about Sharon?,'" I started slowly.

"You know something, don't you?," Daniel threw the wrench down. "Answer me, damn it! What is it you're not telling me! Tell me!," He yelled into my face.

"Janelle's been seeing a man by the name of Adam. He's almost twenty-nine and the relationship has been going on for over six months," there, I said it. "Now, duck," I thought.

Daniel's expression was one of disbelief. I watched anger and redness begin to creep from his neck all the way across his face up and across his forehead.

"You damn liar. All you're trying to do is steal any chance of happiness for Janelle," Daniel harshly accused. "There is no way Janelle would go behind my back to see a man who was twelve years older than her. You're sick and you're crazy."

Daniel wasn't going to believe me or anyone else who had anything negative to say about Janelle. I retreated into silence and continued to help Daniel work on his truck. Daniel meanwhile cursed and raged as he threw and kicked his tools around.

Janelle called again, leaving a another message to confirm with Daniel she was spending night once again with Sharon.

"Have Sharon bring you home," I could hear Daniel when he returned her call. He refused to give her an explanation over the phone, just kept repeating, "No, you need to come home."

Less than an hour later, the slam of the front door and angry footsteps on the stairs announced Janelle's arrival. Straight into the basement garage, where Daniel and I were, her face flushed, immediately I knew Janelle was ready for "war," How dare Daniel refuse to let her spend the night with Sharon? Janelle was furious, demanding answers.

"Let me ask you a question?," was Daniel's response. "Who is Adam? " Janelle's facial expression went pale, then quickly blank. An 'innocent' face, revealing not even the slightest hint of knowing of whom Daniel was talking about.

"I don't know an Adam," she calmly lied. Bringing quickly back to my mind Dr. Westlake's words a few years earlier, "She's good. The best liar I've ever encountered in all my years of counseling."

"See, I told you so! Liar!," Daniel was quick to believe Janelle and not me as he triumphantly smiled into my face.

Janelle assumed she had won, but I pursued, knowing I would be abused afterwards. To me, Janelle's future was at stake and I was afraid she would run away with Adam at least that was the plan.

"Are you sure you don't know an Adam, Janelle?," I asked, looking straight in her eyes.

"Oh," she replied. "You must mean Adam Smith?"

"No, Janelle, not Adam Smith," Janelle's lies were as smooth as silk, as she held onto her poker face, no emotion or tale, tale signs of a lie.

The conversation went on and on with lies and denial by Janelle for the next thirty minutes until Janelle became trapped within her own lies. The moment she tripped with a slip up, realizing what she had done, she started screaming at Daniel and I, "Oh, my God! Leave me alone!"

Janelle was busted and furious, but then, so was Daniel. His daughter had been seeing a grown man for over six months with everyone, including his wife, knowing about it. Everyone but him. This was one rare occasion, that Daniel actually punished Janelle. Without thinking about what he was about to say nor the consequences, Daniel told Janelle she would have to quit the bowling alley.

"It's quite obvious the bowling alley is a bad environment and influence on you," stated Daniel as he wiped his greasy hands on the dirty towel. Daniel was in fear of Janelle seeing Adam. This was the only way he felt he could stop her.

Daniel questioned Janelle more about Adam, his age, how many times they had secretly met all the details that only fed into Daniel's fear and jealousy. Janelle told Daniel that Adam didn't work and had a criminal background. It scared the living daylights out of Daniel and me. Janelle always had a way of "spilling the beans" to counselors and now to us, information better left unsaid which made her defense worse. A moment where she would give out what my children labeled "TMI" (too much information.) Janelle argued, begged and cried to the bitter end; but Daniel wouldn't budge, not on this one. This was just as bad if not worse than the custodian she met in Virginia on her Internet website. This was the second time Janelle had tried to have a relationship with a grown, adult man.

For me, the same abusive routine. All of this was entirely my fault because I kept the relationship a secret. This was rated in the top ten of my domestic violence abuses. From that night on, I was ordered never to discuss or mention Adam's name in our home or to anyone. No one in the family or anyone else could know, it was to be another "Brenda" secret.

Daniel held a tremendous amount of guilt and fear over his punishment of forcing Janelle to quit the bowling alley. Over the next few weeks, Daniel hugged and loved over Janelle constantly. He knew he couldn't take back his words and each night he continued his nightly routine of visits with Janelle behind her closed bedroom door, shutting me and the world out, as he comforted her.

To make matters worse, the next week one of Janelle's teachers called leaving a message for us to call her. Janelle was failing science.

"I hate school and I hate living in this house!," Janelle yelled as she stormed out of the kitchen, down the hall and into her bedroom.

"You damn bitch!," Daniel turned his anger towards me. "If you were a better mother to her, none of this would happen!," quickly he left to comfort his daughter.

Janelle continued to lay guilt on Daniel, fighting hard not to quit the bowling alley. Daniel's guilt of punishing Janelle tormented him constantly and the abuse towards me by both of them was so intense, it seemed as if it would never let up. I was everything from a bad mother to the devil incarnate, words I heard on a weekly basis. Every weekend from that evening until the end of February I was punished. No food, isolation in the basement closet and constant abuse with cursing, yelling, and threats of the imminent divorce papers to be served. Though I spent a lot of time isolated in the closet under the stairwell or in the basement those months, I was never alone. I suffered with the abuse physically and emotionally, but God was a good listener and comforter.

A brief break from the abuse came the first of March. Matt called and asked if he could move in with us for a month while he awaited completion of a rental house his roommate and he were renting. At first I was hesitant, knowing Daniel's strict orders that after the children reach age of eighteen, they could not live with us. Things were still tense with Janelle since she had quit the bowling alley and hadn't found a job. Matt had no other place to go. Daniel agreed to a short-term stay of one month and gave Matt a key to the outside entrance down in the garage. Daniel instructed Matt, to use the downstairs den as his bedroom, so he would have privacy and would not bother us with his work second shift work schedule of 12:00-10:00pm. Daniel also gave Matt a key to the pantry and cabinets instructing him on the "lockdown" situation with Janelle and her stealing problems. Daniel warned Matt that he may want to lock his room as well.

"You need to talk to Matt," Daniel began one evening after work. "He's eating my Nutty Bars," Daniel started. "Didn't I make it clear that he couldn't eat my Nutty Bars?"

"No," I remembered. "You told him to help himself to anything he wanted in the food pantry and cabinets."

"Help yourself to whatever you want," Daniel was gracious on Matt's first day. "We just have to keep the food locked up because of Janelle," he concluded.

I remained silent.

"He's also leaving the basement door unlocked," Daniel commented.

"I'll talk to him," was all I could say as Janelle walked into the room.

The next morning, before leaving for work, I spoke with Matt about the basement door.

"Mom, I'm sure I've been locking it," he replied. "In fact, it's a little awkward to lock. The lock is out of line and you have to pull the door hard."

"I know," I explained, "Just try and make sure," I said as I walked out the door to leave for work.

I was too embarrassed to bring up the Nutty bars and decided to buy Matt food and replace Daniel's Nutty Bars.

Arriving home from work before Daniel, I checked the basement door. It was locked. I checked on Janelle who was in her bedroom watching TV. Quickly I changed clothes, glancing at the clock beside the bed.

"Good, an hour before Daniel would arrive home from work," I thought, as I grabbed my car keys and ran down the stairs.

Both Daniel and Matt were home when I arrived. Matt had the night off and was meeting his Dad and Evan later. Escaping first down the stairs, before Daniel could see the stash of food I had purchased, I opened the basement door to see Matt looking at me with a strange look on his face.

"Mom, I know I locked the door," he started.

"What?," I responded. I knew he locked the door too.

"Daniel said he found the door unlocked when he came home," Matt explained.

"I'll take care of it, Matt," I told him. "I checked it before I went to the store to get you some food. It was locked."

Matt followed me up the stairs to the kitchen where Daniel was talking to Janelle.

"The door was unlocked, again," Daniel turned to me and emphasized the word "AGAIN,"

"It couldn't have been," I replied, "It was locked when I came home an hour ago," Of course, Daniel didn't believe me and for the first time, Matt witnessed the full extent of Daniel's rage.

"What about the Nutty Bars?," Daniel accused Matt. "Did you ask Matt about the Nutty Bars? Didn't I tell you not to eat my Nutty Bars?" I could tell from Matt's face he was dumbfounded. Matt searched my face for answers. A face that could only speak silently, "I'm sorry" with my eyes.

"I've a hidden camera in the basement," Daniel proceeded to tell us. "I haven't watched the tape, but it'll tell me what's going on," there was no way I could tell Daniel that the only person left in the house was Janelle and the only logical explanation was that she was sneaking out the basement door to smoke. The cigarette butts were the accusing evidence, which I saw when I left earlier. They were all over the back stoop. Interrogation and accusations by Daniel went on for over thirty minutes. All for the love of Nutty Bars and an unlocked basement door.

"Kathy, how are things? Do you need me to do anything for the meeting Saturday?," The phone rang in the midst of Daniel's tyrant. It was Ann from the C.E. committee. Daniel was still yelling in the background. Oblivious to the phone call.

"I'll have to call you back," I quickly said. Knowing Ann could hear Daniel's raging.

"Kathy are you alright?," Ann's reaction was sharp.

"I'm sorry, Ann. I really need to call you back," Quickly I hung up the phone, knowing if Daniel saw me on the phone it would only make things worse, especially if he thought someone could hear him.

"Mom, I'm out of here!," Matt angrily said as he turned to leave. "Watch the damn video tape," Matt shot his last words over his shoulder at Daniel, taking the steps down the stairs two at a time as he slammed the door behind him.

Matt's exit only infuriated Daniel more.

"God dammit!," Daniel yelled as he slammed fist into the doorframe. "You can all go to hell!"

The unresolved mystery made me even more of a failure and the abuse was once again brutal. Daniel spoke vulgar things of Matt and Evan, as the violence continued for hours until eventually I was able to escape to the parking lots of Holiday Inn and K-Mart. At times, I would retreat and wait out time in parking lots, especially when the abuse was at night and Quaker Lake was closed. Besides, the basement closet allowed Daniel to yell and curse at me in the doorway throughout the night until he left for work the next morning.

The following day, I arranged for Matt to move in with Amber. By now, Mitzi was living with Amber as well and had been for over a year. Matt's stay in Daniel's house lasted less than two weeks.

I was looking forward to the C.E. Meeting in Goldsboro on Saturday. I was holding my breath that Daniel wouldn't go with me or change his mind about allowing me to go. A day of freedom from abuse. Daniel got up early that Saturday morning to work on his truck. As I walked down the stairs, I could hear him cursing and slamming things around in the garage. Still afraid Daniel would not allow me to go or insist on going with me.

"I'm leaving," I told him.

Daniel looked up from working under the hood of his truck. His eyes glared at me as he turned to face me, wiping the grease slowly from his hands on a rag. Then he walked to the garage door and firmly closed it behind me. Evan and Janelle who were still asleep upstairs.

Looking down at the concrete floor, I knew what was to come. Daniel needed to make sure he put me in my "right place" before I left.

"I guess you're happy to go," he began. His breath smelled of his morning cup of coffee that was still sitting under the hood of the truck. His hands reached me out to grab me before I could run.

"You better not tell anyone about any of this! Do you hear me?," his hands then moved up to my neck, as his thumbs pressed deeper and deeper into my throat, cutting off my air supply, choking me.

"He's going to kill me," was my instinctive thought. I couldn't respond, my mind, or what was left of it, telling me repeatedly that the best thing was for me to relax enough, to go limp, then maybe, just maybe, I could slip out of Daniel's hold.

"Do you hear me?," Daniel tried to force me to speak and look at him, all the while he was shaking me with his hold on my neck. I couldn't speak, he was choking me.

"Relax, relax," my mind repeated in my head. "If you relax, you can slide out from under his grip. Relax before you lose oxygen and faint," Slipping slowly into relaxation, I was able to feel Daniel's hold on me relax, and at that split second, I slid out from under his hold sinking down onto the floor, catching Daniel completely off guard. To be honest, I think his first thought was that I had fainted.

Quickly I ducked at Daniel's attempt to grab me again, and managed to escape, running up the stairs and out the front door. My heart pounding, my throat throbbing with pain from the pressure of Daniel's hands and fingers on my neck. Safely to my car, locked the doors and sped out of the driveway. Leaving Daniel standing at the edge of the yard.

For the next two hours, I drove to the meeting crying and praying. I developed a plan to gather my things and head straight to the bathroom, hopefully avoiding anyone once I arrived. Knowing the last thing I wanted was for anyone to see me. But Ann drove in and parked right beside me as I was lifting my things out from the back seat.

"Oh, Dear God," my head fell down in defeat. "Not Ann," Knowing there was no polite way to escape her.

"Kathy! Hey! How are you?," Her cheerful voice, excited to see me, as she bounced out of her car towards me.

"If only I could have washed my face," I thought with doom and gloom.

It was too late. Ann's eyes saw my tear-stained face, then I watched as her eyes traveled from my face to my neck. Her eyes stopping and focusing on my neck.

"Oh, my God," she gasped. "What happened?"

It was too late; her cheerfulness quickly disappeared at the sight of Daniel's fingerprints, revealing red on my neck. Suddenly, I realized I could hardly speak when I opened my mouth to reply. My voice was raspy, barely audible. My throat hurt terribly and my shoulders ached. Gently Ann reached up to pull my shirt collar back for a closer inspection of the marks.

I fearfully backed away from her hand, either afraid of the possible pain if she touched my neck, or fear she may see too much. It was too late; someone else now was witness to Daniel's temper. There was nothing I could say or do to hide or deny it. A powerful rush of tears quickly began to pour out of my eyes as the burst of emotions streamed down my cheeks. My voice raspy and hoarse, I confessed, as best I could of Daniel's earlier rage while we sat hidden on the parking lot curb between our two cars. Ann held me, rocking me gently in her arms. Her voice poured out soothing words of comfort. For the next few minutes, time stood still, our purpose and mission for the day put on hold, while we prayed and cried together. A peaceful, warmth of relief to finally confide in someone came over me.

Ann carried my things into the church, while I hurried to the bathroom to freshen up as the time approached for our meeting. It was the first chance I was able to really see the damage Daniel had done to my neck. The bruising by now was bright and brilliant. My neck ached as I tried to move it from side to side to look closer. Pulling my collar up and closer around my neck, I made a note in my mind not to move my neck too much to the right or left. Straight ahead, was the best position to hide the marks in an attempt for no one else to notice.

During the meeting, I spoke very little, trying to appear intent and absorbed in listing. As the hours went by, with the more water I drank, my voice became better. Tylenol kicked in to relieve some of the soreness.

Daniel was in a better mood when I arrived home eight hours later. He had cleaned up and wanted to go out to dinner. No reference to the abuse earlier that morning and I took care to keep the bruises covered, hidden from Daniel's sight for fear of further abuse.

After numerous applications and several months, Janelle finally got a job working at a local supermarket. She started out working the cash register then requested a transfer to the deli. To me it was like putting an alcoholic in a bar serving drinks. Janelle had an eating disorder. In the deli, she got all the free food she wanted as pocketbooks full of food were brought home each day. She hated the job and some of the people she worked with but she loved the free food. All the while, her weight plummeted out of control as her headaches and her moods of depression grew more frequent.

Chapter Nineteen: Things Unchangeable

There was a man who came into the hardware store where Daniel worked part-time who Daniel said married a "mail order bride from the Philippines,"

"She gives him back rubs, massages his feet every night, and works like a slave," Daniel informed me. "She even gives him any type of sex the man wants, whenever, wherever," his details were explicit. "The best thing that ever happened to him was ordering a Pilipino wife," Daniel would conclude.

The more Daniel repeated this story to me, the more I began to wonder if Daniel regretted marrying me because I wasn't more of a servant to him than the mail order wife.

The last meeting I personally had with Daniel's second anger treatment counselor, Dr. Mayers, left Daniel in a bad mood for days. I didn't know why I was called into the session, but you can rest assured, I was never permitted nor asked to attend another session with Dr. Mayers.

"She never says "no,"" Daniel bragged to Dr. Mayers. "We have a terrific sex life," he boosted. "Cheryl didn't like sex and when we were dating I made Kathy promise to never say 'no.'" Daniel triumphantly concluded.

I watched Dr. Mayers, as he looked up from taking notes. His eyebrows raised gave a keen look of question and wonder.

"How many times a week do you have sex?," he asked.

"Oh, at least eight, nine times a week," without missing a beat, Daniel boasted with exuberate male ego pride.

"You've got to be kidding," Dr. Mayers looked questioningly at me for confirmation. Embarrassed at Daniel's boasting, all I could do was shake my lowered head in a "yes" response, avoiding eye-to-eye contact with Dr. Mayers.

Silence filled the room, as Dr. Mayers appeared to be trying to process the "TMI."

For what seemed liked several minutes, I watched as Dr. Mayers made notes in Daniel's file. Finally, he looked up, his eyes, even with the edge of his silver-rimmed glasses.

"You're a very lucky man, Daniel. Spoiled too. I hope you realize that," was all he said.

At that moment, Daniel hadn't realized what sort of man he was making himself out to look like, or the depth of information he had just given to Dr. Mayers. It certainly wasn't my wish to have sex that often, but I was forced to and now, Dr. Mayers was realizing the sexual control Daniel held over me in our marriage. The information Daniel revealed at that meeting would in the near future give validity to the sexual abuse within our marriage. During the drive home, Daniel was solemn. I sensed he was reflecting on all the information he willingly offered to Dr. Mayers, realizing the mistake he had made.

"You need to make an appointment with Dr. Smith," Daniel said as he went into the bathroom to wash up after having sex that evening. "You've got another infection," he continued, "It looks green, not like a normal yeast infection Cheryl had all the time."

Over the past several weeks, Daniel had seemed obsessed within his mind that I was unclean and he was doing extensive, rough cleaning of the vaginal area prior to intercourse and oral sex. The cleansing ritual was painful as Daniel would use numerous objects such as his fingers (which were rough, cracked and dry), paper towels, a towel, washcloth, his undershorts, whatever was handy before proceeding. The "cleansing ritual" made me feel dirty and unclean even though I practiced good hygiene, not to mention how embarrassing and humiliating it was.

I had begun spotting blood after intercourse, feeling torn, sore and swollen. It seemed as if the area never had time to heal from both the cleansing rituals and excessive sex. If I flinched or made any movement indicating pain while Daniel did the cleaning, he would snap with anger.

"Oh, my," Dr. Smith gasped out as she took a visual examination. My head was turned towards the wall, as I attempted to hide my red, embarrassed face.

Dr. Smith was barely able to touch me, without me flinching or jumping in an instinctive attempt to withdraw from the pain. I was so sore and tender, even the heat radiating from the examining light hurt. Ever so gently, Dr. Smith tried her best to examine me, but there was no way possible for me to escape from the obvious pain as tears began rolling down my cheeks.

Quietly, Dr. Smith pushed back her chair and turned off the examining light, then slowly began removing her gloves.

"We need to talk," she stated softly as she gently padded the paper coverlet over my knees and with her outstretched hand, she proceeded to help me up.

"Meet me in my office," Dr. Smith was controlled, but obviously upset.

Dr. Smith was focused on note writing in my folder as I entered her office. For as long as I had known Dr. Smith, she always wore her straight black hair pulled back in a ponytail. She looked more like a cheerleader than a doctor. She never wore makeup, her skin was golden brown without a blemish.

My eyes avoided her writings as I glanced at the pictures of her children that lined the top of the shiny maple finish credenza. Her college credentials hung above. A happy family, a successful woman. Dr. Smith seemed to have it all. Dr. Smith and I knew each other well. We were more than doctor/patient, we were friends. I knew about her husband and two children. Our last visit we joked about her children's pressure on her and her husband to adopt a puppy. Dr. Smith was worried about the time and mess of raising a puppy as well as who would be the one actually tending to it. The thought of our last visit brought a brief smile to my face.

"Kathy, there is no so-called green infection," she broke through my thoughts. Looking up into her green eyes, I could sense an underlining anger.

"I'm really pissed right now," she said. "Not at you, but at Daniel. What is he? An idiot? No man treats a woman this way. He definitely has some issues. Is he still in anger treatment?" There was more than plenty of underlying emotion and tension that filled her small office as she questioned me.

"I think it's short lived," I told her. "Daniel's revealing too much information and Dr. Mayers seems frustrated. I think Dr. Mayers on his way out soon, just like the others."

"You're ripped, torn, red, swollen and it's quite obvious your vaginal area has suffered significant trauma," I was right as the edge of anger in her voice began to surface. "What's going on with him?," she demanded an explanation.

For about a minute, I strongly considered bolting out the office door behind me. I was too frightened to speak the truth. Too embarrassed to reveal the humiliating details of what Daniel was doing to me. Then, once again, a gush of tears literally broke lose as my feet felt as if they were glued to the beige-toned carpet.

Dr. Smith waited patiently for the sobbing to somewhat subsided.

"I can't," I stuttered through the tears. "I just can't," shaking my head violently.

Dr. Smith set her pen down on top of my folder, pushed back her chair and slowly made her way around the desk to the chair beside of me. Softly she took both of my hands into hers. "It's going to be okay," her voice soothing, laced with tears of her own. "We've been through a lot together, Kathy. You can tell me. Nothing, absolutely nothing is going to change how I feel about you or shock me. I'm your friend and doctor, remember?," her voice pleaded for answers. "What's Daniel doing to you?"

"He thinks I'm dirty and he has this horrible cleansing ritual," was all I say.

"It's okay, Kathy. You're not dirty. Tell, me, you've got to tell me, Kathy, what is he doing to you?," Dr. Smith prodded gently.

"I can't say no. He'll get angry and things will get worse," I mumbled softly. "You don't understand. He's just got problems; he won't let me say 'no' and he thinks I'm dirty," There, it was out. It may have sounded simple, but it was the only way I could describe what Daniel was doing to me. It was too embarrassing to talk to anyone about, including Dr. Smith.

"It's his problem, not yours," Dr. Smith sternly said. "You can't go on like this, Kathy. He's forcing you into sexual behavior that you don't want and you can't say 'no.' You're afraid of him and afraid to say 'no.' Kathy, look at me," she gently lifted my chin up to look at her. "Listen to me, you're being raped. This isn't lovemaking. It's rape. Talk to me."

For the next several minutes, Dr. Smith gently coerced me through questions.

"Daniel just has certain sexual preferences; some are very painful with his latest obsession with cleanliness. The ritual is painful, both before the act and afterwards. He's rough, his pressure is forceful. It's almost as if he's mad at me, his performance of sex, it's like he's taking his frustrations out on me and I don't know why," confused I concluded. A brief moment of relief swept over me. No longer was it a secret that only I shared. Leaning back in the leather chair, I let out a deep breath as I closed my eyes.

"No woman deserves this type of abuse and humiliation," Dr. Smith stated as she leaned forward. "Kathy," she gently shook at my hands. "You're young; you're a beautiful, intelligent woman. No matter what Daniel's mental problems are, you don't deserve to be treated this way," We continued to sit for what seemed like an eternity talking about Daniel's anger issues and the events of the last few years. At this point, I was feeling surer of myself, talking to my friend, not my physician. The whole environment had changed, as the words seemed to flow easier, even though at times they caused me to blush with embarrassment and humiliation.

Dr. Smith returned to her desk. Resting her chin in her hand as she silently read over the notes she had written earlier. Picking up her pen, she wrote more and then reached across her desk to pick up the prescription pad.

"This is an antibiotic to ward off any possible infection and I'm pretty sure you've got one, it just wasn't easy to exam you with the swelling and discomfort," she stated as she was writing. "I didn't see anything 'green' as Daniel admitted to," she stated with sarcasm. "What I did see is sexual abuse and domestic violence. It's highly possible you have a bacterial infection, especially based upon Daniel's so-called 'cleansing ritual.'" Tearing off the top prescription, she wrote out another prescription. "Take this one as needed for the discomfort. A hot bath might help too. You can also use a rinsing bottle of warm water after you use the bathroom. It might be more comfortable than wiping the area. Then just gently blot it dry," she continued. "I'm not sure how you are going to be able to explain this to Daniel, but if it helps," she tore that prescription off and began writing another one.

"This one is stating no sexual activity for two weeks," she ripped the last prescription off. "Maybe he'll follow my instructions," she said, and then shrugged her shoulders. "Then, maybe he won't. All we can hope is that he will."

Leaning across her desk, Dr. Smith handed me the prescriptions.

"Kathy, you're one of my favorite patients," I shook my head in a "no" response. I felt like an idiot and a nuisance.

"No, I mean it," she continued. "I'm afraid for you. I don't want to see anything happen to you," her hands gently padded mine before releasing the prescriptions. "Please, be safe. I never, ever want to see you in my office again with this type of abuse, or any other type of abuse," then she stood up and came around to me, her arms engulfed me in a much needed, comforting hug.

We walked together to the front check out and she hugged me once again. "Be safe," she whispered in my ear.

"You're both God-damn liars!," was Daniel's response as he threw the prescriptions onto the kitchen floor. I was afraid to bend down and pick them up for fear of him kicking me across the kitchen.

"Cheryl had these infections the entire time we were married! Janelle has these infections!," his voice getting louder and louder. "It's just a fuckin' yeast infection. All women have them. You're both stupid!"

"Daniel, please if you could just limit the sex for a while and maybe the cleaning, it'll clear up," I pleaded.

"No one, I mean no one," Daniel spit out at me. His eyes bulging with rage as he began shaking me. The red glare in his eyes revealed the look of the devil. "You, Dr. Smith, Cheryl, no one, no one is going to control my sex life! Do you hear me?," his shaking was sending me into a dizzy frenzy, the room was spinning and it was hard for my eyes to focus or my legs to hold me up.

"There will be no restrictions on sex and I mean it!," he yelled his spit into my face. "I've lived that way with Cheryl," he stated. "I'll never, ever live that way again," he warned me.

"You look at me!," Daniel ordered my eyes to look directly into his face. "Ever since I was ten years old, I dreamed of performing sexual acts on women, I read magazines on how to please a woman, and I'm damn good at it. Do you hear me! I'm damn good at it and no one is going to tell me how to run my own sex life!," violently pushing me away from him, I stumbled back against the kitchen counter, reaching out behind me, grabbing hold for balance. Daniel turned and stormed down the stairs, slamming the front door as he left the house.

That night and throughout the weekend, I spent inside the basement closet while Daniel continuously raged.

On Friday, Daniel had an appointment with Dr. Mayers.

"Seems to me that Dr. Smith doesn't have a damn clue what she's talking about," Daniel started the moment our car turned onto the main road heading home. "She must have been a lousy med student," Daniel stated with confidence. "Dr. Mayers said she was wrong about her diagnosis of a bacterial infection; the only thing you suffer from is a yeast infection, just like Cheryl, just like Janelle," the atmosphere within the small confines of the truck was tense. "Best thing for you to do is stop seeing Dr. Smith," Daniel concluded.

Knowing I would only be dooming myself into another violent hit of Daniel's cruel verbiage and physical abuse I sat in silence thinking another weekend in the closet wasn't appealing. Knowing that Daniel would even discuss any of this with Dr. Mayers made me feel even more humiliated and embarrassed. To hear of Dr. Mayer's statement to Daniel, was like a direct hit into my stomach. I felt nauseous from knowing only a tiny inkling of what dialogue went on between Dr. Mayers and Daniel. All I could do was look straight out the truck window, seeing nothing, deep in my thoughts.

"I never want to have this discussion with you again. No more Dr. Smith and no more sexual complaints. You understand?," Daniel made it clear as we pulled into the driveway. All I could do was nod in agreement as I opened the truck door.

"I guess it's time to get up," Daniel ordered as he swung his leg over the side of the bed and sat up. Two weeks had passed since Daniel's meeting with Dr. Mayers. It was Sunday morning. It was earlier than usual for Daniel and immediately I sensed something was wrong. After I showered and dressed, I went into Daniel's theatre where I found him sitting on the back row, staring at the blank silver screen.

"Is there something wrong?," I asked.

"I don't know," Daniel snapped. "You tell me,"

For the life of me, I had no clue what Daniel was angry about. I searched his face, and then looked around the dark theatre room. "You either don't love me or want me anymore, or there's something physically wrong with you," he started as he stood up to go into his projection booth. Daniel had his usual sex twice the day before and I was at a loss as to what was wrong with me now.

"Daniel, I don't know what you're talking about. I thought everything was fine,"

For once, Daniel must have believed me by his next statement.

"I think you're suffering from menopause," he started. "I'm certain there is something wrong with you and I spoke to Dr. Mayers about it. We both think you over-reacted about the infection with Dr. Smith and Dr. Mayers thinks you might be going through menopause. That would explain a lot of things," Daniel continued, "our sex life has decreased to six or seven times a week and Dr. Mayers said it was normal for a woman to lose interest in sex if she's going through menopause. We think you should be checked."

"Not another doctor, not another exam," I screamed inside of me. I was afraid to see Dr. Fischer, my gynecologist, again. He already suspected domestic violence just from the last time I went in for my annual exam.

"How am I going to request another menopause exam this time?," was my thought.

"Daniel please," I pleaded. "Yesterday morning, last night, things were fine. Wasn't it?," my stomach beginning to feel queasy again. Daniel went into his projection booth and sat down at the film rewind table with his back to me.

"You'll call Dr. Fisher tomorrow," It wasn't a question but a firm statement. Subject ended, as he place the rewind reel onto the machine.

"Are we still going to church?," I meekly asked.

"No," he stated. "When I spoke with Dr. Mayers this morning he advised us not to go to church and "put on a happy face when there wasn't one and the feelings of 'happiness' were fake,"

"When in the world did he call Dr. Mayers?," was my first thought. "Maybe while I was getting dressed," I pondered. Yet, I couldn't imagine Daniel calling Dr. Mayers at home on a Sunday morning and discussing our sex life and menopause. I couldn't imagine Dr. Mayers even allowing him to.

Slowly I retreated up the stairs, down the hallway and into Evan's bedroom where I told him once again we would not be going to church. Evan grumbled something unrecognizable as he rolled over and went back to sleep.

Two hours later, I heard the noise of Daniel's film ending. I was hanging up the last of Daniel's blue work pants in the bedroom closet. Daniel came into the room.

"I just called Dr. Mayers again and he said we had two choices to make for the moment. One, we could be apart for the rest of the day until I see him tomorrow, or we could have sex."

I was confused as I pretended to focus slowly on re-arranging Daniel's pants and shirts in the closet, avoiding to look at Daniel while thinking, "When in the world did he call Dr. Mayers again?," I wondered. "There's no phone downstairs, unless he called him on his cell phone."

Turning to face Daniel, I guess I didn't have the same poker face as Janelle.

"You don't want me, admit it. Say it!," Daniel exploded as his fingers grabbed my chin, forcing my face directly into his. His face red with anger, his eyes flashing thunderously as he began yelling and cursing, declaring I needed to take responsibility for the way he was feeling, it was my fault he felt this way. Trapped within the confines of the bedroom, for the moment I was unable to escape. My eyes focused on how to get to the bathroom. I looked and saw the folded towels and washcloths still on the bed from the laundry.

"Daniel, please," I softly said. "Let's just talk about this," his hands dropped from my face. Composed, as casually as I could manage, I walked over to the bed and picked up the towels and washcloths. I could feel Daniel's eyes staring a hole into my back.

"Slowly, slowly," I said to myself as I walked over to the bathroom.   Making it safely to the door, I quickly slammed it shut and locked it.

"Goddamn you!   Open the fuckin' door!," Daniel raged as he began beating on the door. Then he stopped, realizing Evan and Janelle could hear him. I listened as he stormed out of the bedroom.

Banging my head and fist against the window seal until exhaustion, I stepped into the corner of the small shower stall and waited for what was next to come.

Hours later, I heard the sound of Daniel picking the door lock.

"Get up!," he ordered. Impatient at my slow movement, Daniel grabbed my hand and pulled me out of the bathroom.

"Take off your clothes," he demanded once we were in the bedroom. I glanced over at the bedroom door, it was closed.

"We're going to have sex," Daniel began removing his clothes. "I think we should take Dr. Mayers' second suggestion."

"Don't forget to call Dr. Fisher when you arrive at work," Daniel reminded me before he left for work the next morning.

"I will," I responded quietly.

I was able to see Dr. Fischer on Wednesday, due to a cancellation.

"Daniel and his doctor think there's something wrong with me again, either physical or maybe menopause. Can you check me again?," I quietly asked as I sat on the edge of the examining table.

"Do you think there's something wrong?," Dr. Fischer searched my face. "It's still a little early for menopause," he began looking through my chart. "It's only been a little over a year since you were tested last. How do you feel? Anything changed?"

"No," I started. "No hot flashes and my cycles are regular. They just think I need to be checked," I glanced away from Dr. Fischer's face, looking down at the floor.

"Well, let's see," Dr. Fischer began the examination.

"Everything's normal, Kathy," Dr. Fischer said as he turned off the lamp and rolled his chair back from the examining table. Reaching for my hand, he helped me sit up. "Get dressed and meet me in my office," Dr. Fisher's normal, bubbly personality didn't seem to come through this time.

"He's frustrated with me," I thought. "How am I going to explain all of this? I don't want to explain all of this. I just want it all to go away," I began to scream in my head.

"Kathy, what's going on?," Dr. Fischer wasted no time asking before I was even seated.

"Daniel and Dr. Mayers think I'm going through menopause," I meekly responded, looking down at the floor.

"Why is Daniel questioning menopause this time?," he asked.

"He's questioning it because the amount of our weekly sex has decreased," I replied.

"How many times a week is Daniel demanding sex?," Dr. Fisher bluntly asked.

"It's down to six, seven times a week," I answered. I could hear the desperation in my voice, desperate for answers, desperate for help.

Dr. Fischer leaned back in his leather chair, folding his arms across his chest, as he looked me straight in the face as if to be searching for more understanding. Once again, embarrassed, I looked down at my pink and white New Balance tennis shoes.

"I think I'm beginning to see the picture," Dr. Fischer broke the awkward silence as he leaned forward to write notes in my file. After what seemed like an eternity, he closed the file and walked over to where I was seated. Reaching for my hand, he helped me up and with his arm around my shoulders, his well over 6ft. tall, lanky frame, gently led me to his office door.

"You're going to be okay, Kathy," his blue eyes kind and gentle as his hand refused yet to open the door. "Daniel's got some 'issues' I would say. 'Issues' you can't help him with. Be safe and hang tough. I'm here if you need to talk," With that, Dr. Fisher gave me a gentle pat as he opened the door. "Take care," he smiled and patted me on the shoulder once again.

"How stupid!," I thought as I drove back to work. "Hang tough? How can you 'hang tough' when you've got a husband and his doctor dictating your life? This is crazy!, " my words angry and loud within the confines of the car. "Thank God, it will be at least another year before I have to see Dr. Fisher again for my annual pap smear. Maybe I can postpone it a little past a year in hopes he'll forget all this crap!"

"Dr. Fisher said I was 'pre-menopausal,'" was the lie I told Daniel. "God, please forgive me," I prayed silently to myself. "You of all people know the consequences if I don't tell this lie.

Daniel bought the 'pre-menopausal theory' and I was safe for the time being. "Boy, do I dread when I actually do go through menopause. I can't imagine the abuse I'll endure then," I thought afterwards.

Three months later, I incurred another vaginal infection with spotting of blood as once again, Daniel had become aggressive with his 'cleansing ritual.' There was no doubt in my mind I was torn again. The pain so severe, I couldn't even insert the over-the-counter medication without it stinging, burning horribly. There was no way possible I could hide it from Daniel. Since Dr. Mayers and Daniel controlled and had better knowledge of my body, all I could do was ask Daniel if Dr. Mayers could help me. Daniel met with Dr. Mayers that week and explained my symptoms and that the over-the-counter medication wasn't working. Dr. Mayers and Daniel gave me permission to call Dr. Smith.

"Daniel and Dr. Mayers feel it just another bacterial infection and I should call you," it was difficult to persuade Dr. Smith over the phone that I needed the medication. I could hear the hesitation in her voice.

"I promise, if it's not any better in a week, I'll come in," I tried to sound confident and cheerful.

"Kathy, this is the last time," Dr. Smith gave in. "One more refill. You'll have to come in if this persists," she warned me.

The ten-day antibiotic treatment was a definite nuisance for Daniel, one he made known he was not happy with. Once again, after his usual Friday visit with Dr. Mayers, Daniel told me Dr. Mayers instructed him to masturbate during the time of the treatment if I was not able to succumb to Daniel's sexual appetite. Other sexual acts I should perform as well.

"There was a time during my marriage to Cheryl that I read a magazine article that stated a lack of sex could cause prostate cancer," Daniel proceeded to tell me. "I had to result to masturbation a lot when Cheryl refused me sex," he continued. "Dr. Mayers says prostate cancer is very prominent in men and with cancer a reality in my family...," Daniel left the sentence unfinished as if to make sure the decision was left to me as to whether he got cancer or not.

From that moment on, Daniel did as he pleased with me sexually. Whenever an infection occurred, I kept it secret from Daniel and treated it the best I could with over-the-counter medications in the early morning hours while he was asleep so the residue would be gone by that evening. However, the infections never completely healed and at times, I was so sore I would sneak quietly into the bathroom after Daniel went to sleep and placed hot towels against my vagina. Drops of blood were not uncommon for me to see, as well as being swollen and sore. Emotionally I became paranoid and obsessed with making sure the area was clean out of fear of being subjected to his "cleansing ritual," Yet, most of the time it didn't matter, Daniel did it anyway.

Chapter Twenty: Dinnertime

Gary's bright red turn light signaled a turn into the Wal-Mart shopping center.

"Why are we stopping?," I asked Cindy.

"I'm not sure," she said as we pulled into a parking space beside Gary.

"I thought we would pick you up some food supplies for you to take to the cottage," I wasn't sure if it was a question or a statement from Gary. None of us were sure of what appliances or supplies I would need. My guess was Gary was practicing his old Boy Scout survival skills.

Cindy looked over at me for a response.

"Sure, I guess I could maybe get a few things that'll last at least a couple of days," my appetite was minimal, yet I wanted to let Gary and Cindy know I appreciated their thoughtfulness and concern.

As we walked, I glanced around the shopping center at women shopping alone. Women who had freedom to come and go as they please. For five years of my life, there had been no freedom. I may have been broken inside, but I was free. My life belonged to me now and neither Daniel nor Janelle would ever take that freedom away from me again.

It was strange listening to suggestions from Gary and Cindy about what I would need for three meals a day, breakfast, lunch and dinner. I hadn't been allowed that in years. When Cindy and Gary asked if I was hungry during our drive to and from the cabin, I didn't know how to answer. The question felt as if a ball had hit my stomach. I was scared to answer. Was I hungry? I really didn't know. Someone else, Daniel, controlled a simple routine of my eating over the last five years.

Soon after my hospitalization, Daniel ordered me to stop cooking family meals in the evenings, stating we didn't need to eat supper and the lunches I cooked for us on Sundays were to end as well. I felt this was coming during the first month Evan and I were back in Daniel's home. I would have a meal cooked in the evening when Daniel came in from work only to have him say he wasn't going to eat or it wouldn't hurt for us to skip a meal.

Daniel would buy food for Evan, but Evan had to cook for himself. The same held true for Janelle when she returned from Boone. Daniel removed our Sunday lunches after church as well. It hurt me to see "dinner times" as a family removed by Daniel. Sometimes I tried to sneak and eat a half a sandwich before Daniel arrived home from work. Only to have Daniel question me if I had eaten anything. If I said "yes" he would get angry stating, "We were going out for ice cream, but since you've already eaten, I guess we won't get any ice cream," Making me feel guilty. Therefore, I never knew if I would get to eat or not. I missed cooking family meals and the time we spent together around the table. Sometimes Daniel would stop and get ice cream at Dairy Queen just for himself on his way home from work. Those were nights I didn't get anything to eat at all. My entire life controlled, even down to what I ate and when I ate.

The irony of all of this was the first year Daniel and I were dating, I was Director for the North Carolina Yearly Meeting and our theme that year was "A Family of Faith." All week we studied the importance of the family unit. That was the first time Daniel had ever seen or heard my lessons for children. He was there for my speech at the adult session when I spoke specifically about family dinnertime, the importance of spending quality time together over a meal. Emphasizing the impact moments at the dinner table contributed to a child's emotional and spiritual growth.

"At that special time, you're all together sharing the details of your day and bonding is taking place. Dinnertime is a great time to wind down, reconnect, communicate, grow closer and have fun as a family. That special time of sharing a meal together is an investment in your children and their lives," was part of the speech I delivered at the adult session.

"Our definition of a family is: 'A group of related individuals whose hearts are filled with Christ's love. Who make a home not known or recognized by its size, its style, or its amount of furnishings, but a warm home made up of treasures and memories of love, joy, peace, patience, kindness, goodness, gentleness, and faithfulness. A haven of welcome, comfort, and rest. This haven wraps those who enter into it in a warm blanket of love and acceptance. Laughter and singing are heard from the walls within while a sense of peace abides in its surroundings. Kind words are spoken and good deeds give love action. Meaningful hugs and kisses, along with tender touches and forgiving spirits show compassion to those receiving.' A family of faith gives a feeling of being loved and accepted."

I never realized, Daniel would take all of that away from me. I wanted so much to share those special moments and continue those dinner times with Evan,

Janelle and Daniel. However, that was not to be. Daniel had to control every aspect of my life, even dinnertime.

Dr. Mayers expressed concern and confusion as to why Daniel took away our family evening dinner privileges. Daniel's explanation was we didn't need the extra calories and at times he didn't want or feel like eating. Dr. Mayers asked about Evan and Janelle. Daniel explained that he bought meals for them to prepare on their own. It was obvious Dr. Mayers didn't understand the control Daniel had over dinners and whether we ate or not, yet he suggested maybe I could cook a light meal one or two nights a week for us as a family. Daniel refused to budge.

Janelle struggled with this rule far worse than Evan and I. In fact, Janelle suffered the most and I have no doubt it escalated her to a compulsive eating disorder. Both children would make a list of what they wanted and Daniel would buy it on a weekly basis. Janelle's list was always significantly larger than anyone else's was, yet it never seemed to be enough food for her. Janelle would grab handfuls of cereal, chips, cookies, pecans, cherries, and jelly, whatever she could "sneak" with hopes of it not being missed by her dad, Evan or me. In a one-week period, Janelle ate two five lb. of bags of raw sugar, straight from the bag. That was of course, before the lockdown was implemented.

After the lockdown, Janelle began taking containers of frozen soup, chili, whatever she could find and gradually chop off pieces of the food, until there was nothing left in the freezer but a tiny ball of whatever it originally was. Daniel never figured out a way to "lockdown" the refrigerator.

The more desperate Janelle became for food other than which was on her grocery list, the worse her stealing got and Janelle's weight climbed higher into the "red" zone.

The waste of money and throwing away of rotten food by Janelle was tremendous. Daniel spent two to three times more money a week on Janelle than he did on Evan, himself or me, sometimes more than he spent on all three of us combined.

Janelle would play games with Daniel by picking out certain foods in the grocery store in hopes of pleasing her dad, making him think she was dieting. Only to supplement his store bought foods with foods she really wanted that she took from her part-time job at the grocery store or stealing from family, friends, church or wherever she could find what she desired. The problem was the food Janelle chose to please her dad would sit and rot inside the refrigerator.

After over three years of rotting and stealing of food, Daniel became so frustrated with Janelle that he sought help from Diane. Diane, suggested an "action/consequence" contract signed by Daniel, Janelle and herself. If Daniel bought the food and Janelle let it rot, then Janelle would have to buy her own groceries for a month.

"Janelle is working and can afford it," Diane stated. The contract never worked and became "null and void" almost immediately. Daniel was not going to punish Janelle, and Janelle wasn't going to allow him to.

Daniel refused to pay for local garbage pick-up. He transported our trash in his truck to work, placing it in their dumpster. It was a 45-minute ride with a rotten smell that would linger in his truck for days. With the power struggle of wills between Daniel and Janelle, the frustration of smelly, rotten food began eating away at Daniel and the abuse on me grew with each incident.

"Damnit!," Were the first words I heard as I entered the doorway late one evening after attending a Jamaica Missions meeting. Slowly I climbed the stairs, all the while wishing I could go back out the door.

Once again, Daniel had come home to the smell of rotten food. "She'll never learn!," Daniel pointed to the mess in the refrigerator. Slamming the refrigerator door, Daniel grabbed my arm and began pulling me down the hallway and into our bedroom.

"Daniel, please, let's just talk to Janelle about it," I pleaded. "Can't we at least try Diane's suggestion with the contract?," I tried to show Daniel the contract lying on the dresser signed by the three of them, Daniel snatched the contract out of my hands, tore it up and threw it in the trash. Little did Daniel or Janelle know that while Daniel was paying the bill at Diane's office the week before, Diane handed me several copies of the contract, whispering to me, "We may need these," it was no use. Daniel was way past rationalizing.

"No!," Daniel exploded. "There will be no punishing or contracts with Janelle! To hell with you! To hell with Diane! Fuckin' damn you all!," He raged. "I don't need you or anyone else trying to tell me how to raise my own damn daughter! Go to hell! All of you!," At that exact moment, only inches from my face, in the midst of Daniel's cursing statement, an upper plate of false teeth came loose and flew completely out of his mouth!

"Oh, my God!," I questioned myself, "What was that? Did I just see what I think I just saw? No, it couldn't be!" Yet, it was real, I really saw it. Daniel wore false teeth! I never knew. I was in total shock. "Did I really see that?," I questioned myself once again.

For a brief moment, I almost lost it. I could feel the laughter bubbling within me, yet I knew couldn't laugh or say anything, only continue to endure Daniel's abuse. The physical pain would only be worse if I acknowledged what I had just seen, what I now knew. I watched in shock, and self-controlled amusement as Daniel's neck stretched forward like an ostrich, and he "sucked" his false teeth from out of the air, back into his mouth. What seemed to last minutes had only lasted a few seconds as Daniel's pursed lips and suction positioned the false teeth back into their rightful place.

Giving into no indication that I had just witnessed the funniest thing of my life, I continued to let Daniel rage to the point where I was able to escape without being hurt, I slowly slid across the bedroom wall, around the dresser, managing to edge my way to the doorframe of the bathroom. Then quickly, before Daniel could realize what I was doing I turned into the bathroom quickly closing and locking the door behind me.

Within the walls of our small bathroom, Daniel all the while thought I was crying. That he had succeeded in his punishment towards me because of Janelle. But instead, I was laughing hysterically at the sight of Daniel's false teeth flying out of his mouth and him sucking them back in. It was just too funny.

Once I gained control over my hysterical laughing, I was to process more clearly about the false teeth, I was confused over why Daniel withheld the knowledge of him having false teeth. Why it was such a secret. I knew about his artificial leg and other "difficulties", but not this. Now I was beginning to feel that trust within our marriage, was certainly an issue, as well as vanity.

It took several days after that for Daniel to calm down enough for me to ask him why he never told me about his false teeth. Daniel said he was too ashamed and embarrassed. Cheryl, Janelle, family members, as well as people he worked with all knew, but he didn't want me to know. When I questioned him about his surgeries, he said he always made sure the operating room nurse put his teeth back in before I could go back to the recovery area. Never once did I see him without his teeth the entire time we were married. If his teeth broke or needed an adjustment, he had an extra pair that made him look like Jim Carey in "The Mask," filling his entire mouth with "all teeth." He hated wearing the "Jim Carey" pair, so at times, Daniel would spend over an hour locked in the bathroom making the glue, adjusting and repairing his old pair.

After the revealing of false teeth, in an attempt to avoid future domestic violence abuse, regarding Janelle's spoiling food, I began sneaking the rotten food out of the refrigerator, throwing it deep into the woods beside our house after Daniel left for work early in the morning. For me, it was a faith-walk with God and I prayed each time I wouldn't be caught. I was desperate to find ways to minimize and escape any possible reason Daniel would use to physically or emotionally abuse me, also rationalizing that throwing the food into the woods was to the benefit of starving wildlife in our area, especially to Janelle's bat friend.

A few months later, I wasn't so lucky.

"Shit!," I heard Daniel yell.

"Not again," I thought walked into the kitchen. "Dear God, will this ever end?"

Daniel was standing in front of the refrigerator with the door open. The rotten odor once again fumigating the room. "That same God damn smell is back again," Daniel looked at me accusingly. "It's been stinking for a couple of weeks now. It was there while you were in Jamaica!,"

I walked over to the refrigerator to stand beside Daniel, reaching down, I opened Janelle's designated bottom food drawer. The odor swiftly drifted out like a smoke bomb.

"What the fuck!," Daniel yelled as he jumped back. There lying in Janelle's drawer were two packs of broccoli, lettuce and a bag of grapes, all rotten, slimy and gross.

"What in hell!," he began. "When in God's name is this going to stop? I'm wasting my fucking money every week for this! Diet my ass! Janelle's not fooling me or anyone else! I've had it!"   At this point, I realized it wasn't just the smell that was getting to Daniel; it was the waste of money. Daniel's finances were continuing to plummet.

"Leave it be!," Daniel ordered as he stopped my hand from pulling the bottom drawer out. "I'll handle this," he slammed the refrigerator door shut, turned and retreated to his theatre.

"Thank you dear God," I whispered a prayer as I walked down the hallway and into our bedroom. Sitting on the side of the bed, suddenly overwhelmed with exhaustion. "Thank you for at least a little precious time of peace." I knew once Janelle came home from her job at the grocery store, Daniel's abuse would be brutal. Quietly I lay back across the bed and closed my eyes.

The slamming of the front door awoke me. Looking over at the alarm clock revealed it was 9:15 p.m. Daniel must have remained in his theatre until he left to pick Janelle up from work. Turning my head towards the doorway, I watched the two of them go into Janelle's bedroom and close the door behind them. Their voices muffled low.

I went into the kitchen and packed Daniel's lunch, then back into the bedroom to set out my clothes for work the next day. I had just undressed for bed when Daniel came into the bedroom.

"I want to see you in the kitchen, now!," he ordered. He didn't wait for my reply, nor do I think I would have spoken one, I obediently followed.

When we entered the kitchen, standing in front of the refrigerator with the door open was Janelle.

"Clean it out," calmly and sarcastically, Daniel told Janelle.

"Bitch!," I jumped as Daniel yelled in my face. "You could try and do a better job of helping her with her diet and weight," Daniel began berating me front of Janelle. "But then, Janelle's not as good as your children, is she? That's her problem, you know. It's you. You're her fuckin' problem. You're good with your children, but you don't give a damn about her. You're a lousy mother when it comes to Janelle! Let's just all face it. You're the reason for all of her problems!," Daniel couldn't have been any meaner or uglier.

"Kathy's the one that found the mess," Daniel sarcastically turned to tell Janelle, as if he hadn't already told her making me look like a tattletale when all I was doing was solving the mystery of the smell he was complaining about. Daniel was in search of the smell, I became the victim.

Janelle's eyes glowed red with contempt and hatred as she looked up at me. A look that stated "Drop Dead! I hate you!," she bent down to remove the bottom drawer from the refrigerator.

There was nothing I could say; only stand there for the next twenty minutes and endure the words of abuse and humiliation Daniel hurled at me in front of Janelle.

"Janelle said you've been throwing out her rotten food for her to keep from getting into trouble. Is that true?," Daniel demanded an answer. "Answer me damn it! Is that true?"

All I could do was nod my head in agreement, saying nothing.

"What happened this time? Did you forget?," Daniel was mean and sarcastic.

Janelle's back was to us as she dumped the rotten food into the trashcan and walked over to the sink to clean the drawer.

"I'm sorry, Janelle," Daniel walked over and put his arm around her shoulders as she continued to clean out the drawer.

"I guess to please Kathy and Diane I'll have to make you buy your own food for a month," Daniel gently hugged her, leaning his head against hers, planting a light kiss on the top of her head. By Janelle's non-reaction, it was obvious to me that they had already had this conversation in her bedroom and an agreement had been reached. Janelle was way too calm with the announcement as she continued to rinse out the drawer.

"As far as you," Daniel stepped away from Janelle and came towards me, his tone dangerously threatening. "We'll discuss your behavior with Dr. Martin and Diane," he continued. "They're going to think you're crazy. Hell, I think you're crazy!," Lashing out with so much anger, Daniel slammed his fist into the hallway wall, a hole the size and shape of his fist implanted in the wallpaper and plaster.   He stormed down the hallway and into the bedroom, slamming the door behind him.

Janelle's next session with Diane was the following week.

"Do you need another copy?," Diane asked of Daniel after she heard the details of the rotten food. Daniel admitted to tearing up the contract when Diane referenced the contract in front of Janelle.

"No," Daniel sarcastically replied. "Janelle understands the rules. I've punished for a month and she's buying her own food,"

"Daniel, I don't think you realize the long-term effect of Janelle's outbursts and misbehavior. The basis for the contract was an understanding between you, Janelle and me. Janelle needs discipline, she needs boundaries. This is serious business," Diane read a copy of the contract she maintained in her file. The 20-minute ride home from Diane's was quiet and tense.

On Friday, we met with Dr. Martin. Dr. Martin sided with Diane and asked Daniel to follow the rules of the contract, confirming Janelle needed boundaries and discipline.

"Kathy's internalizing her feelings by taking self-defense actions to prevent abuse," was Dr. Mayer's explanation to Daniel's complaint and Janelle's revelation regarding me hiding the evidence of rotten food by throwing it into the woods.

Daniel's "no dinner time" and separating out our groceries never budged and Janelle's desperation for and dependency on food escalated. She was miserable and continued to prepare meals that looked like healthy choices for the sake of both counselors and Daniel, all the while supplementing the meals with candy bars, cookies, chips and sodas, whatever she could sneak into her room from her job and school canteen.

A line of ants soon found a source of food and made a trail on the carpet from the hallway into Janelle's bedroom. Trash, crumbs and empty wrappers hidden in various areas throughout Janelle's room gave the tell-tale sign of her actions. I watched the invasion of ants for over a week, trying to kill them the best I could without using a smelly pesticide that would serve only to alert Daniel of the situation. Finally, with no possible solution in site, I decided to ask Janelle if she could help me with the housecleaning and maybe bring all the dirty glasses and dishes from her room, as well as her trash. When Janelle brought me the dirty items, I thanked her and gently commented, "Maybe this will help us with the ant population." Unbeknownst, did I realize Daniel was listening from the hallway. It was against Daniel's rules for me to confront Janelle on anything that might resemble a complaint or punishment.

"What ants?," Daniel demandingly questioned. I didn't want to answer and quickly Janelle retreated down the hallway back into to her bedroom.

"Show me the ants!," Daniel ordered as he cornered me in the kitchen.

Solemnly I walked and watched as Daniel's eyes followed the ants as they marched in a straight line from the hallway, under Janelle's door. Daniel opened her bedroom door and his eyes continued to follow the ants to beneath Janelle's bed where her "stash" was hidden.

Janelle was lying across her bed, pretending to be absorbed in a show on TV. Daniel firmly took hold of my arm and led me out of Janelle's room, closing her door behind us.

"You need to learn to shut the fuck up!," Daniel's abuse started. "I heard how you spoke to Janelle. Yeah, you sounded so nice, but your tone wasn't gentle and nice enough towards her," his grip tightening on my arm. "That's what I've been telling you all along. You're her problem. You could have done something about the ants and you could do something about her diet!," There was nothing I could say in my defense.

"You need to get the hell back in there and apologize to her!," he ordered as he forcibly pulled me out of our bedroom, and literally shoved me back into Janelle's bedroom.

"Janelle, I believe Kathy has something to say to you," Daniel addressed Janelle then turned and threateningly glared at me with his angry glowing red eyes.

"I'm sorry if I sounded too strong in my voice tone, Janelle," the face and voice of a scolded child, not a woman or mother. "I'm sorry," I softly repeated.

Janelle glanced up at me revealing no sign of "apology acceptance", just a cold, hard glance, then she turned her eyes back to watching TV.

Daniel remained in Janelle's bedroom after I left to retreat into the bathroom where I closed the door and huddled in the corner of the shower. My arms folded across my knees, my head buried in my arms a rush of emotions and tears flowed uncontrollably. The humiliation and embarrassment Daniel put me through at that moment left me powerless over the way both of them treated me.

A short three months later, Janelle was serving another month of grounding due to rotten food in the refrigerator. Diane made a decision and implemented the punishment personally to Janelle in front of Daniel. Diane suggested Daniel and I shop with Janelle and help her pick out foods we knew she wouldn't waste. By now, Diane's insistence for action/consequences was placing her closer and closer to dismissal. Daniel was growing more and more afraid of Janelle while Janelle grew stronger in her control over Daniel. Words of Diane's inabilities and qualifications as a counselor were now frequent in our household only to confirm her time was limited.

The first Saturday we were to implement this latest grocery shopping rule, Daniel picked Janelle up from work and she had already purchased her groceries. Daniel held off our own grocery shopping in order to accommodate Janelle and her work schedule. But then again, nobody, not Daniel nor any counselor could tell Janelle what to do. On the way home, Daniel reminded Janelle about the agreement.

"This is so stupid," Janelle punched out a major attitude. "I'm perfectly capable of picking out my own groceries."

Daniel's expression and reckless driving confirmed there was a temper storm brewing. Once we arrived home, I tried to escape down the hallway and into the bedroom, but Daniel stopped me midway down the hall telling me we were going to go through the groceries Janelle had purchased. I didn't want to. This was another decision between Daniel, Janelle, and Diane. I stayed in enough trouble as it was, but sensing Daniel's tone, I knew not to press my luck or be disobedient to his orders.

As Daniel looked through her bags of groceries, Janelle leaned against the counter with her arms crossed, glaring at the process. Her only communication was an occasional impatient "huff" under her breath, as tension loomed over the room. All of this reminded me of Daniel searching Janelle's book bag, coat pockets and bags before she left for St. Mary's after a weekend visit two years prior. Once Janelle's groceries passed Daniel's approval, he reminded her again to wait next time. Janelle abruptly turned to leave the room, muttering a sarcastic "yeah, right" in response to Daniel's orders. Quickly I exited the kitchen, scurrying down the hallway, into our bedroom before all war broke out.

"What?," I heard Daniel yell at Janelle.

"I said 'okay.'" She sternly replied to Daniel.

A brief silence. I could envision them glaring at each other in a standoff. Then the sound of Daniel slamming his fist into the doorframe, cursing as he stormed down the stairs. These two people were identical in temperament and nature. Janelle had learned a lot from Daniel and this argument was a power struggle of wills and control.

Thirty minutes later Daniel came back upstairs. I was in the midst of folding laundry, hoping to weather this latest storm without too much damage. While fixing a cup of ice, Daniel slammed his cup into the refrigerator door.

"You all think I'm a monster! Don't you!?," He began to approach me. Physical abuse would soon follow the verbal.

"Please, Daniel, don't yell and cuss. It'll work out. Give it some time," I tried for a futile attempt to defuse him before things got worse.

"I'm not gay. Gay men have soft voices and don't yell," Daniel hatefully retorted, his voice soft at first, then rising to a yell. "Real men yell and cuss!," He stormed down the hallway and into the bedroom.

On our way to church the next day, Daniel informed Janelle and I, we were going to talk after church. Throughout the church service, I prayed that God would somehow soften Daniel's heart. Somehow make him forget or skip the meeting. It was to no avail. Once we arrived home, Daniel called us into the living room and started addressing the tension of Janelle not speaking since the night before.

"I told you this grocery shopping and spying on what I buy is stupid," Janelle angrily stated. "It's my money and I should be allowed to buy what I want, when I want."

Daniel, feeling threatened by Janelle's straightforward tone, backed down in fear and quickly compromised Diane's orders by telling Janelle we would not walk with her through the grocery store, but would wait and go through what she purchased when we got home.

"I think it would be best if I also got to look over the receipt," Daniel requested.

"You don't trust me," Janelle flew into an arguing fit, throwing accusations and statements at Daniel. Janelle wanted more money, more clothes, more dance classes, more social money, laying a guilt trip on Daniel as a father, accusing him of being an incompetent parental provider.

"You're the worse parent I've ever heard of. Jim wasn't like that. He was a great father to me and Stephanie," she compared Daniel to Jim in Boone and other parents, Janelle succeeded in making Daniel feel like a failure.

Janelle, satisfied she had put her father in his rightful place, turn to release her fury on me. Everything she had learned and heard Daniel say to me, she flung out in ditto.

"She's right," Daniel responded periodically from his "amen corner," Giving Janelle the fuel she needed for the next thirty minutes, verbally attacking.

If I tried to defend myself, Janelle would interject with, "That's not because you love me, that's so dad won't yell at you!," It was useless. In her opinion, and with Daniel by her side confirming, I wasn't a good enough mother to her.

Sitting there, allowing Janelle to follow in Daniel's footstep with her treatment of me, I realized there were things I can change and things I cannot change. I can change me, but I cannot change this seventeen-year old, how she feels, the lost opportunities of her first years of parental guidance and her apparent hatred of me. Janelle would never accept me as her stepmother. I could only choose to be the best I could be and lay my burdens at the foot of the cross. Trusting in God. Janelle wasn't just angry with me, she was angry at the world.

I honestly believe part of Janelle's desperation for food would never have existed if Daniel hadn't taken away our "family dinner time," We would have had that time to spend together as a family, blending, bonding, sharing, and communicating at the dinner table. Even the cost of groceries would not have been such a huge expense. There would have been no separate meals for Evan and Janelle, no issue of rotting food, no punishments and one less reason for Daniel's domestic abuse. At least that moment of time we would have had a small portion of a healthy, functional family environment, which would have forced communication, sharing and a time of unity. Meals could have been more nutrition for all of us, not just Janelle.

This was the last of Diane's futile attempt to enforce "actions and consequences" for Janelle. Daniel "fired" Diane, and the search began once again for a new counselor. Dr. Mayers was dismissed shortly thereafter as well. Neither counselor could enforce behavior adjustments for Janelle, or get too close to the relationship between Daniel and Janelle.

Chapter Twenty-One: Waiting for God

It was Sunday, and it had been over a month since we had been to church. I woke up hopeful we would get to go. The morning started great with us making plans to go until Janelle came out of her room looking horrible. She had taken a short blue jean skirt and slit it up one side, added a piece of material and leather lace, fringed the hemline with strings hanging out of the bottom. She had tied pieces of fabric in an attempt to "corset" her stomach, hips and thighs. She wore two shirts over all of that which only accomplished an outfit that looked gross and "trashy," I refused to say anything for fear of jeopardizing us going to church.

Janelle's appearance didn't escape Daniel's eyes. He was furious, softly fuming and cursing under his breath all the way to church. Once inside, Daniel whispered his complaints to me about how much weight Janelle had gained and how her atrocious outfit only emphasized her obesity.

"She isn't fooling anyone," Daniel's voice low, filled with disgust. "She's porked up. Did you hear her wheezing walking to the car? She's not fooling anyone trying to hide all the weight she's gained. She's too damn fat!"

"Why isn't he discussing this with her?," I thought as I listened to his complaining.

"She says she doesn't have any clothes that fit," Daniel was on a roll. "The only damn thing left big enough for her would be a garbage bag," he grumbled.

Daniel continued to fume softly under his breath during the ride home.

"We need to stop by K-mart," Janelle spoke from the backseat. "I need new kneepads for gym class tomorrow." In the store, Janelle bought the biggest adult size they sold. When she tried them on in the car, they were too tight. She was wheezing from working up a sweat trying to pull them over the calves of her leg. Janelle then flew into a tyrant similar to her dad's usual tyrants and when Janelle ain't happy, nobody's happy, especially Daniel. The minute we walked into the house, both Janelle and Daniel went into her bedroom, closing the door behind the two of them. An hour later, Daniel came out, retreating into his theatre. Later that afternoon, we dropped Janelle off at work. The minute she stepped out of the car Daniel exploded from hours of built-up anger, regarding Janelle's weight and the outfit she wore to church.

"When she gets off from work, we're going to have to take the damn kneepads back to K-mart. We need to try and find her some bigger clothes," Daniel was disgusted.

That evening, after buying new clothes for Janelle, Daniel informed me he would have to skip his credit card payment. Daniel and I had separate bank account and credit cards. I had no idea how much he owed. A few months back, Daniel took out another loan for Janelle's schooling and an extra $10,000 he said he need to pay off his credit card.

"Do you have any money?," he asked.

"Money I set aside to pay for taxes," I responded. "They have to be paid by the end of the month,"

"Hold off on the taxes and go by my bank and make my credit card payment tomorrow on your lunch," Daniel stated. "You can pay the late penalty on the taxes,"

The next morning, Daniel left his credit card statement on the dresser for me to make the payment. He owed over $16,000.00. The week prior, Daniel had purchased two more films on e-bay to add to his collection, which was reflected on the statement. I knew he had been over spending on models, films, projectors, conventions, his truck, Janelle's counselors and school. I had no idea he had spent that much money within a year. Janelle's second semester tuition was due in two weeks, adding to the credit card debt.

After lunch, Daniel called and asked if I had made the credit card payment.

"Yes."

"Good," he stated. "That will cover the reservations I just made for the film convention in Asheville in November."

Financially we were at Daniel making a payment then charging against the payment. Never bringing the credit balance down. How in the world were we going to be able to pay for all of this, I didn't know.

"Do you have any money for groceries this week?," Daniel asked on Thursday. We had just been to the grocery store on Sunday. Janelle was out of food.

I gave Daniel all I had and I left for work not knowing what we were going to do. While at work, Daniel called twice. He wanted to go to the Williamsburg Film Festival in March, and even though that was over six months away, he heard they were running out of reservations and he was at his limit on his credit card.

"I need you to call and make the reservation on your credit card," against my better judgment, I made the call.

The next day, Daniel won a bid on another film projector. Two new films arrived at the house. Deeper into debt we went.

On Saturday, Daniel wanted to go to a drive-in movie in a town over an hour away. A drive-in movie ends up being an all night and early morning event, as they show three movies starting at 8:00 pm and even though I don't mind supporting Daniel's hobby, I hate seeing three movies in a row into the wee hours of the morning. We're are not able to go to church the next morning because we don't get home until after 3:00 in the morning. I really hated sacrificing church for drive-in movies. Daniel would sleep late into the day on Sunday, and I wasn't allowed to get out of bed until Daniel did.

"You're not ready to get out of bed are you?," it was after 11:00 the following morning. Daniel must have felt my movement and thought I was getting out of bed without his permission.

"No," I whispered softly. "Just going to the bathroom." Sunbeams brightly slipped in between the closed slats of the window blinds.

"Fuck you!," Daniel's favorite words hurled into the air, startling me as he slammed the covers with his fist. "You make me feel fuckin' guilty if I want to sleep in! Hell!," he jerked the covers off and sat up on the edge of the bed.

"It would have been nice to sleep late," he was sarcastic. "But you had to wake me!," Daniel hopped into the bathroom without his prosthesis, slamming the door behind him. I could hear him slamming the medicine cabinet door two or three times. When he came back into the room, he dropped angrily back down onto his side of the bed. "I'm tired of the hell you make me live in!," jerking on his prosthesis, Daniel dressed and retreated downstairs into his movie theater.

"Daniel?," two hours later, I went down to where he was splicing one of his films. The last thing I wanted was another day of no food and abuse.

Daniel stood up, glared at me as he walked past me into the garage. I watched as he kicked whatever appeared in his way to the side. Anything and everything that wasn't what he was looking for was brutally thrown or kicked aside.

"Daniel, please, I'm sorry," I pleaded.

Walking over to me, Daniel roughly grabbed my chin in his right hand, his fingers piercing into my chin. My eyes began to water from the pain.

"Sorry? Nobody should have to live in this hell! You stay the fuck away from me," he snarled into my face as he threw his hand down. "You and your damn kids. Your stupid, fat daughter and your fagot sons. All of you get the fuck out of my life!," once again, I ran into the staircase closet.

The next day Daniel called me at work still angry. My apologies were useless. We were never going to the drive-in again. Three days Daniel raged. In addition, the threats of suicide were back. Daniel would quietly glare at me through hateful eyes and sarcastically and deliberately pronounce each word with emphasis, as he would give me a visual of his suicide threat. "I'm going to go and get my gun, hold it to my head and blow my brains out!,"

Daniel worked late on Wednesday evening. I went home and raked the grass from where we mowed the evening before. I did everything I was supposed to do. I stopped raking when I heard Daniel's truck drive up and went inside the house to say "hello," Daniel was still angry, ignoring me and retreating once again to his film room. I went outside and started raking again.

"Where in the hell have you been?," I jumped at Daniel's explosive temper behind me.

"Right here," I responded.

"No you haven't," Daniel, yelling loud enough for the neighbors to hear as I spotted Mrs. Kennedy peer out of her kitchen window. "I looked for you earlier and you weren't out here. I yelled for you in the house and you weren't there. Where in the hell have you been and why didn't you tell me you were going somewhere?"

"Daniel, I promise I've been right out here working in the yard," it was useless. Daniel was convinced I had left without his permission.

"I know fuckin' well you haven't been here working in the yard all this time," a statement as he stormed across the yard, slamming the door of his truck. His tires screeched out of the driveway and down the road.

The next day was Thursday, hardware store day. Daniel's over-the-counter sleeping pill didn't kick in as quickly as normal the night before and he was up a numerous times during the night. Before I left for work, Daniel was nasty and verbally abusive, once again bringing up how I should not have gone outside the night before without telling him or asking his permission. Backing further away from Daniel towards the staircase, trying escape to work before it got too bad, Daniel stopped me grabbed me, forcing my back up against the wall. Afraid of losing my balance, or falling down the stairs, I sank down onto the step.

"I'm a man, do you hear me?," Daniel roared into my face. "I'm getting older and this is the way men are when they're my age. We're different from women. We get mad easier. And when we get mad, we yell, we cuss and we throw things," Shaking uncontrollably from his force, I quickly nodded my head in agreement.

"When things don't go right, you push me into a rage and that's the way it's going to be. Do you understand?," he ordered me as he jerked my arm, forcing me to look up at him. "Do you hear me?"

"Yes Daniel, please," pain shot up my arm. Abruptly Daniel threw my arm down and stormed back into the living room to finish his cereal.

On Saturday, Daniel spent the entire day and late into the night working on the projector he ordered. On Sunday, Daniel gave me permission to go to church alone which rarely happened. In fact, I could only remember twice in our marriage that it was permitted. Daniel wanted to continue working on the projector. He couldn't get it to operate right and was upset. The sermon Eric preached on was 1st Corinthians 13 (the love chapter.)

"It's nothing but a damn piece of junk!," the moment I walked into the house from church, I witnessed Daniel throwing the projector down the first flight of stairs, stomping down the stairs after it. It stopped short of my feet on the landing. Daniel continued to kick the projector down the second flight of stair towards the basement and garage. "Best place for this is in the dumpster at work!"

In December, Daniel placed an ad in the Big Reel, trying to sell enough films to make money to pay our taxes and insurance due the end of the month. Janelle was playing games with the response phone calls by either not answering the phone, not taking messages of inquiries, or she would give Daniel only partial messages. The phone calls from the ad were irritating to Janelle and Daniel was getting agitated that he couldn't force Janelle to answer the phone or write down the messages. What messages Janelle did take were scribbled down to the point we couldn't decipher them or she would write down the wrong telephone number. By now, Daniel was in desperate need of money which increased his frustration with Janelle.

The day after Christmas, we were busy in preparation to leave for an after Christmas trip, which was planned back in October. We were going to New Hampshire. Arrangements for a babysitter for Janelle were arranged.

I had just gotten out of the shower and was drying my hair when I heard the phone ring. Due to the noise of the hairdryer, I didn't know how many times it rang because of the noise and I was unable to catch it in time. There was no message, just a hang-up. When I went into Janelle's room, she was standing by her phone at the bed folding her clothes.

"Janelle, why didn't you answer the phone," I asked.

"I was busy!," she snapped at me. As I turned to leave her room, I practically bumped right into Daniel.

"Who was that on the phone?," Daniel anxiously asked, hoping it was someone regarding one of his films.

"I'm not sure," I stammered, knowing the potential danger this would place me in. "I was drying my hair and heard the phone the moment I turned the hair dryer off. I'm not sure how many times it rang."

"Janelle, why didn't you answer the phone?," Daniel asked.

"I told Kathy, I was busy," she retorted sarcastically to Daniel.

"Here we go," I thought as I watched Daniel's face turn different shades of red and blue. Days of pent-up anger and stress. Days of Janelle's misbehavior and telephone games, all bottled up inside Daniel spewed out as he grabbed my arm and forced me into the bedroom.

"Oh, dear God. Not me. Please don't let him take it out on me. Let him take it out on her. Please," I silently prayed.

"This damn telephone game with Janelle is your fault," Daniel began. "She's depressed and doesn't feel like answering the phone. Can't you see that?," his face was now a complete shade of dark red, his eyes big and angry. "I can't believe you didn't hear the phone," to voice any defense would have been useless as I succumbed to taking Janelle's punishment.

"If you think I want to get on a plane and spend a few days with you in New Hampshire, you're dead wrong," Daniel stated. "You're the last person on the face of this earth I want to be with, Bitch! Get out!," Daniel pointed to the door. "Get out!"

Quickly I grabbed my pocket book and keys. The day after Christmas, in the church parking lot I laid in the backseat and wept until well after midnight. We were supposed to be at the airport at 5:00am.

"Janelle is still going to the babysitter's," when I returned home, Daniel still angry, informed me. "She wants to and it'll lift her spirits since she likes Ashley. Besides, they have plans," Janelle would be rewarded with Daniel letting her go with Ashley. "All of this is your own goddamn fault. There's no way we're going to New Hampshire,"

Solemnly, I unpacked my suitcases, placing clothes back into their respective drawers and closet, unable to escape Daniel's continued abuse as he followed each step I took, yelling and cursing at me until finally I was able to retreat into the basement closet.

An hour later, I heard Daniel's footsteps on the stairs. I braced myself for another round of abuse.

"If you behave yourself, I guess we can still go," Daniel's words came through the darkness. I crawled out of the closet, and followed him up the stairs.

"You're still a failure," Daniel state as we walked down the hallway. "You've ruined any hopes of a descent trip, but it's already paid for and we can't get a refund."

The flight to New Hampshire was difficult for me physically. I don't know if it was the stress of the night before or an upper respiratory infection I had been suffering from, but during the flight, I suffered an acute asthmatic attack.   I had suffered numerous asthma attacks throughout my life, a condition occasionally hindered by stress or health issues. Some severe, some minor. A condition that warranted me to carry around a rescue inhaler and a standard daily use inhaler. Though I seldom had to use them. Leaning my head back against the airline seat, gazing out the window, seeing the big, white fluffy clouds, I knew I was beginning to struggle asthmatically, loosing oxygen quickly as breathing became a difficulty.

"I'm ready Lord," I closed my eyes and quietly prayed. "I don't 'fit in' in this world. I'm ready to die. I want to be with You," I didn't want to fight the asthma attack. Without saying a word in an attempt to hide my difficulty with oxygen, I sat quietly next to Daniel, hoping and praying to peacefully drift into death. Daniel was still angry and had hardly spoken since we left home. In the airport he walked ahead of me, as if I didn't exist.

Upon landing in Manchester, New Hampshire, I was in a distressed state from lack of oxygen, yet at complete peace. Most of the passengers had unloaded, as we were in the back of the plane. I struggled to make it down the aisle only to collapse mid-way onto the floor in the narrow aisle.   Daniel was behind me as I lost consciousness.   The warmth of peace and comfort I experienced in those brief moments I have never felt before. Clouds, big white fluffy clouds. I floated into them.

"She's coming out of it, look at that beautiful smile," I saw lips moving as I looked up into blue eyes.

"No, no," I remember thinking, drifting in and out, up and down in mid-air it seemed. "I want to go to heaven and be in God's protective, safe arms. I want to see His face," I was weary and ready. "No, please, don't bring me back," my mind refusing, while my lips attempted to form the words audibly. Yet, nothing came out as I continued to float in and out of consciousness. "Please, don't help me. I almost touched the hand of God. Don't you understand? I'm at peace with the thought of going 'home.' I'm ready, please, I'm ready," then I drifted back into those big, fluffy, white clouds. Above the clouds was bright and warm. Fits of coughing woke me up numerous times, as I pulled at the oxygen mask. Then struggled to go back to that place of brightness and warmth.

Daniel said the paramedics worked with me on the plane, and throughout the airport lobby, stopping frequently to replace the mask I kept trying to pull away from my face, pumping oxygen and administering injections, forcing me to inhale from my inhalers they retrieved from my purse.

We were in the hospital most of the day, before the attack was stabilized. Never had I experienced an asthma attack to this extreme. I was so close to heaven and more than willing to escape my world of abuse.

Chapter Twenty-Two: Janelle Vents

It was dark when Gary, Cindy and I left Wal-Mart.   Twenty minutes later, I recognized the sign revealed the town I was to begin my new life. Gary knew the town well from working for Pepsi in his earlier years and growing up too not far. Except for a "Get 'n Go" gas station, a small Post Office and a volunteer fire department, that was all I could see of the little town. Gary turned right at the one and only traffic light. Cindy and I continued to follow Gary into the country.

My "new home," A broken, victim of domestic violence that had to be hidden. I couldn't even go back to live in the three-bedroom brick ranch I had once been so proud of purchasing on my own just six years prior.

"This the most dangerous time," the domestic violence counselor warned me. "The time most abused women are hunted down and suffer the most abuse, sometimes killed."

I had to disappear, to live at a place I had no idea where. It seemed as if I was being punished for what Daniel had done to me.

Long, winding curves, along rural, back roads. Lights softly aglow from farmhouse windows. Homes brightly decorated in anticipation of Christmas.

Janelle was on her own now yet, I couldn't help but worry what impact my leaving would have one her.

"Would Daniel vent his anger out on her like he did before he met me?," I wondered.

"You can't go there, Kathy," I shook my head, trying to knock the entire thought out of my mind. "You can't jeopardize your life anymore trying to 'fix' Daniel and Janelle."

Daniel, Janelle and I continued into the year of 2006 with the same struggles and at times, I felt powerless to make a difference in the challenges. I wanted so much to be an instrument of God's grace, but repeatedly Daniel and Janelle kept reminding of what a failure I was. We were in our fifth year of marriage and I realized despair, guilt, and depression was a way of life for both Daniel and Janelle.

Janelle had now turned eighteen. She was finally able to obtain her driver's license regardless of her school grades. A significant milestone in Janelle's life that made little difference in her moods of depression. This rite of passage, the age of eighteen, into adulthood, Janelle spent pretty much like always, secluded in her bedroom with few friends, depressed, lying across her bed in front of her TV, nourishing her pain with food stashed throughout her room, grossly overweight and unhappy.

There will be no curfews, was Janelle's first "adult" decision.

Daniel's response, "We can't control her now she's eighteen,"

Yet, when a behavior warranted parental attention, Daniel would forego Janelle being eighteen stating, "Oh, she's just a teenager. She doesn't know any better."

It was midnight on a Monday evening, the night of Janelle's eighteenth birthday. Daniel was asleep and Janelle was still up. Up and down the hallway, in and out of the bathroom and kitchen, Janelle noisily roamed throughout the house, rummaging and moving things around in her room, opening and closing doors. Janelle's bedroom was directly across from ours and we shared a common wall. I laid there for 2½ hours scared to death, she was going to wake Daniel. Finally, I quietly snuck out of bed and went into her room.

"Janelle, could you please be a little quieter?," I asked.

A nasty look of "Who do you think you are telling me what to do?," was Janelle's look of a non-verbal response.

"Janelle, please, it's after midnight," I pleaded.

"So?," Janelle questioned.

"Your curfew's 10:00 p.m. Your dad and I have to go to work in the morning," I tried.

"I don't have a curfew," Janelle smarted at me. "I'm eighteen now and I'm an adult. Adults don't have curfews," she turned to continue organizing her entertainment center.

"Janelle, I'm tired, I have to go to work and if you wake your dad, I'm going to pay for it," Janelle was unresponsive. I closed the door. Defeated, once again.

Lying in bed, I slept little that night. Daniel had been depressed for several days. On Saturday, he received notice he had bounced another check. This was the second one in two months. His credit card bill was getting higher and higher and his spending was getting worse.

The next evening, after midnight, Janelle was at it again. This time she was cleaning out her closet, banging around, going up and down the hallway, in the bathroom, out of the bathroom.

"What the hell!," Daniel sat up straight in bed.

"It's okay," I tried to calm him. "I'll go talk with her," quickly I jumped out of bed, went out the bedroom door, almost colliding head on with Janelle. Following her into her room, my hand stopped her from shutting the door in my face.

"Janelle, please," I pleaded. "Your dad's trying to sleep and he's angry you woke him up,"

"So?," was her smirky reply with a slight grin coming from the corners of her mouth.

"Janelle, please, I'm tired. Your dad's mad and you have a curfew," I tried reasoning with her.

"I'm eighteen and I told you, I have no curfew," she defiantly stated. "I'm an adult now. I do whatever I want, whenever I please,"

I stood in the doorway paralyzed at Janelle's remark. "We'll discuss this tomorrow with your dad. But for now, out of some respect and decency for your dad and me, we have to work tomorrow Janelle," Not waiting for another smart reply, I turned and softly closed the door. Daniel was still fuming when I returned to the bedroom.

"What did you say to her?," Daniel asked.

"I asked her if maybe she could be quiet so you could sleep,"

"Yeah, sure. Whatever you said, it better not have depressed her more than she already is. Damn!," he slammed the covers with both hands, and then punched his fist into his pillow. "Fuck you! Fuck you and your damn life!

"Shit!," Daniel threw the covers off him. "So much for the sleep tonight! I have to be at work in two hours. Another hell of an evening!," Jerking on his work clothes Daniel dressed and stormed out of the house.

Daniel was still angry when he called me at work.

"Daniel," I slowly started, "Janelle doesn't feel like she needs a curfew since she turned eighteen. She considers herself an adult."

"You're real shitty when it comes to Janelle. You know that?," Daniel yelled at me then slammed the phone in my ear.

We were now down to only one counselor, Dr. Martin. Daniel couldn't afford another counselor for Janelle and since we were no longer under the supervision of DSS, Daniel decided to utilize Dr. Martin in "family counseling."

Dr. Martin met with Janelle first, then Daniel and I, with a brief ten-minute follow-up at the end. Similar to the set-up five years prior with Dr. Westlake.

"Janelle's still living under your roof," our twenty minutes with Dr. Martin was very tense as he addressed Janelle's behavior, curfew and weight gain.

"She's still in high school and she needs discipline and boundaries, regardless of her age," Dr. Martin continued, "And stop threatening the marriage," Dr. Martin instructed Daniel once again. "Janelle's very much aware of your abusing Kathy and she uses it to her advantage."

"I'm sick and tired of counselors telling me how to raise my own damn daughter. I know how to be a parent. I'm not stupid," as we walked out to the parking lot, Daniel was furious.

"Try giving Janelle the opportunity to voice her anger. What I call 'venting'," in a futile attempt to sort out Janelle's problems, Dr. Martin made a suggestion at our next session after he met with Janelle. "Set some boundaries as to permissible behavior during the "venting," Dr. Martin instructed Daniel. "Don't use the word "punishment" but focus more on "actions/consequences". She's use to hearing those words," Dr. Martin stressed. "I feel Janelle's playing a game with threatening suicide and depression in an attempt to get sympathy and escape a consequence for her behavior. She's very angry and manipulative. She knows her threats of suicide are scary to you," Dr. Martin continued. "Just as your threats of suicide to Kathy and Janelle in the past were scary to the two of them, Daniel," Dr. Martin threw out, then strategically changed back to Janelle to avoid a confrontation or response from Daniel.

"This is Janelle's way of controlling the consequences of her actions and getting her way. It's been going on for years, long before her mother passed away. She aware you're both afraid of her," Dr. Martin turned to face Daniel directly. "Suicide threats and depression are just tools Janelle uses to control everyone, you, her friends and people at school. She wants everyone to live in constant fear of her committing suicide so they won't do anything that might cause her to get upset or depressed," the session ended with very little said by either Daniel or me. It seemed Dr. Martin had spent a lot of time pondering over our lives since our last visit.

That evening Daniel called Janelle and me into the living room. "We're going to have a family meeting," Daniel ordered with Dr. Martin's lecture fresh in his mind.

Janelle and I sat on the two separate couches while Daniel sat in his recliner. He leaned forward to look at us both.

"So, Janelle," Daniel began. "Dr. Martin, Kathy and I have some concerns about your behavior," he paused. "I guess, to make it clearer, Dr. Martin thinks you're playing games with us pretending depression and threatening suicide when you don't get your way. Is that true?," Daniel's tone was on the brink of sarcasm. Janelle was sitting with her legs curled up under her, her head down, picking at her fingernails. For a moment, I thought she hadn't heard a single word Daniel had said.

"Well?," Daniel's voice was beginning to rise in anger at Janelle's non-response. "What's going on Janelle?," Daniel demanded an answer.

Janelle looked up, shrugged her shoulders and rolling her eyes retorted, "This is so stupid."

"Stupid?," Daniel yelled, almost jumping out of his seat. "You call thousands of dollars wasted on private schools, counselors, and 'so-called' diets stupid?," Daniel was on the edge of his seat like a lion ready to pounce his prey. "Do you even know what you're doing? You're the stupid one!"

"Thank, God I'm out of this, for now," I thought. Knowing, eventually it would turn to me, but for the moment, I was watching for the first time Daniel and Janelle going at each other head to head. Two flaming, identical, abusive personalities.

"Yes it's stupid," Janelle boldly stated as she aimed her anger at Daniel. "Things are different living here than they were at Shelia's. Shelia didn't nag and yell at me about a diet or how I ate. We ate as a family, Shelia cooked meals and I got to eat," Janelle shot worded bullets straight from the hip.

"Maybe Dr. Martin finally hit on something here," I thought to myself. "Maybe this is exactly what Janelle needs, to vent all her anger and frustration over the past eighteen years of her life."

"Shelia and Jim didn't lock cabinets and doors to keep me away from food. I could eat whatever I wanted, whenever and however much I wanted," Janelle's face was beginning to turn a shade of pink anger.

"Yeah?," Daniel responded. "And all that weight you lost that Kathy worked with you on before we were married was packed right back on," Daniel was sarcastic. "You gained over 60 pounds the year you lived with Shelia. As far as the locked cabinets and doors, remember the two five-pound bags of sugar you ate in one week. Freezer meals Kathy prepared that you chiseled off portions, leaving little balls that wasn't enough for even one serving," Daniel's face was red with anger. "You stole my snack cakes, cereal, chips, sodas and lunch food. What else was I supposed to do?," Daniel asked. "Answer me, Janelle! What else was I supposed to do since you're the one with all the answers."

"Leave me alone!," Janelle yelled back. "You're always on me about my weight! Always! Even when mommy was alive and after she died. That's when you started hiding and putting food up high in the top cabinets so I couldn't reach them. Mommy never did that."

"And you stole those too," Daniel retorted. "Climbing on the cabinets to steal my food. Nothing ever worked. It was counselors who suggested locking the food up. I was sick and tired of your stealing. Look at you, just look at you. You're way over 225 lbs. for Christ sake! "You binge on food; your counselors thought you were suffering from bulimia. Hell! Even Shelia called me when you stayed with them because you were binging and throwing up. Don't talk to me about things being different there! You had the same eating problems there as you do here. At least here, I'm trying to help you and you're too damn stubborn to see it," Daniel shouted as his fist hit the armrest of his recliner.

"I don't see locked cabinets and doors as help," Janelle quietly retorted back at him, then looked back down and began once again picking at her fingernails.

Things were quiet between the two of them for a few minutes. It was Daniel who broke the silence, "Well, what else is bothering you? It's your time, Janelle. Spit out what else make you so miserable that you make these threats and are so called depressed."

"That's just who I am," Janelle looked up, her cheeks wet with tears, her face matching Daniel's, red with anger. "That's just who I am and you won't let me be me. The rules here are too strict. I want to go live with Shelia!"

"Well that's not going to happen again," Daniel shot back at her. "You're my daughter; you live with me and by my rules."

"That's just it," Janelle threw back at him. "Your rules. The food, the phone, curfews. I didn't have a phone curfew with Shelia. My friends should be able to call anytime, as late as they want. They don't have curfews. Why do I have to have curfews?"

"I have to sleep, damnit!," Daniel yelled. "Your friends are calling at all hours of the night and waking me up from my sleep. You call and tell them to call you back. You are always calling boys and harassing them. Why can't you let them call you?"

"Because they never will," Janelle screamed back at him. "Boys don't like me. Look at me. Nobody likes me."

"What else?," Daniel seem to want to avoid this particular 'vent.'

"What else is your problem? I'm sure there's more," Daniel glared at Janelle.

"I can't change who I am," Janelle began again. "I trash people when they make me mad. That's just the way I am and you try to control who I speak to in the family or what I talk about. Leave me alone. Let me be me," here we are I thought, finally Janelle's being honest about who she really is.

"Yeah, and you end up telling too damn much," Daniel defended himself. "Your mom and I both had problems with you tattle telling to family members. It needs to stop. What happens and is discussed in this family needs to stay here and you need to learn to keep your mouth shut!"

"That's just the way it is and you can't change the way I feel about people and things, what I say and way I do. You can't control what I am and what is normal for me," Janelle retorted back, aiming directly at Daniel. To me it felt like a threat. I couldn't read Daniel's face to see how he took it. His face flaming red.

"Your mouth, trashing people and giving out too much has gone on way too long. It will stop!," Daniel ordered.

"I lie. I steal. I trash people and all the other bad things you say I do. Do you know why?," Janelle darted back. "Because you never punished for me for my behavior in the past. Remember, that's what I told the Dr. Westlake and that's what the counselors told you. I did it to get attention from you! I never, ever got punished until Kathy came into the picture!," Driving in her point home, Janelle turned to glare at me.

"The first time I remember ever getting punished by you was in the 7th grade year when you took the door off my bedroom. Remember?," She chided. "Then there were no showers, just baths. You said it was Kathy and Dr. Westlake that punished me when you visited me in Boone. Then DSS said it was Dr. Westlake. I told the counselors I deliberately misbehaved and hurt people to get attention. I never learned anything because you never punished me. You were too busy and full of yourself!," Janelle's voice was at a yell now.

"Okay," I thought. "I've never seen a boxing match but these two are definitely going to need boxing gloves soon. Very soon," remaining quiet, I watched the show.

"Dr. Westlake ordered all of that," Daniel fired back. "You were being a real bitch! Remember?" Daniel mimicked her.   Yet, I realized that the truth of that "private" meeting in Boone was finally out five years later. Elizabeth was right and so was the Lead Investigator's instinct, Daniel tried to manipulate the charges off him and onto me.

Silence filled the room as the two of them faced off.

"If I don't feel well, leave me alone!," Janelle ordered. "I'll treat people the way I want to because that's just who I am. If I'm in a bad mood, I have a right to be rude and disrespectful to anyone I please!," Janelle was deviant towards Daniel. "This is the way I am and I will always mistreat, trash, and abuse anyone I please and I dare you to try and stop me!"

I watched as Daniel just sat there speechless, glaring at Janelle. I could see the tension in his face, his hands gripping the armrest on his recliner, yet, for the moment, Daniel appeared at a loss for words. For over seventeen years, Daniel had given Janelle learning by example. Now, they were acting as equals in temperament.

"Then I suggest you stay in your room if we have family or friends over and you're in one of your moods," Daniel's tone was low and threatening, "as Dr. Martin suggested, 'you either be nice, or don't come out.' No one wants to deal with you when you are that mean and nasty."

"Fine by me. It's my life and I'll treat people the way I want to treat people," Janelle fired back.

"That's your choice. Even if it's a holiday or any other family gathering we'll do it without you," It was as if the two of them were at a standoff. Once again, the two of them sat there for what seemed like an eternity in silence.

"Anything else?," Daniel asked Janelle.

"It's not my fault you get punished for things I do," Janelle turned to glare at me. "I told Dr. Martin and Diane and all the other hundreds of counselors I've been forced to see that dad punishes you for my behavior and they all said that was your problem."

"Be still," I silently told myself as I looked at Daniel who was now glaring at me.   "Keep your mouth shut. Let the two of them hash this out."

Janelle eyes seemed to be searching her memory for every shred of anger she had bottled up inside. "I wish you wouldn't speak to anyone, including the counselors about anything I say or do. I'm tired of counselors and I'm tired of you talking about my problems with family and other people," Janelle was direct. "I don't like it when you talk about how little Stephanie or anyone else is. It makes me unhappy and depressed. I know I'm fat and ugly. You don't have to remind me of that."

"And you," Janelle looked directly at me with hatred in her eyes, throwing out a statement that took me completely off guard. "You promised to never tell Brenda what dad and I told the counselors. You promised. I need to know for sure you'll never repeat it to anyone,"

After all these years Janelle was still afraid I would repeat what her and Daniel had said about Brenda. Wow! I could only imagine how heavy that was weighing on her mind both day and night.

"Promise   her,   Kathy,"   Daniel   ordered, interrupting my thoughts.

"I promise," I said to them both. I remembered learning in psychology class in college that "you're only as sick as your secrets" and thought at that moment of how true this was of Janelle and Daniel.   They lived in constant fear I would reveal knowledge of Brenda's "juicy past."

"You're so afraid of me and dad, its outright funny," Janelle laughed sarcastically at my obedience to her and Daniel. "You're still sneaking out my rotten food and throwing it in the woods so dad won't get mad at you," Janelle threw her head back in a laugh. "I see you mopping up the floor when I overload the washing machine and it floods," she continued, "You're so scared of dad, you act stupid.   You're the one who needs counseling, not Dad and I. You're scared out of your wits all the time," By now, Janelle was mocking me. "Dad's right, maybe if you would be a better mother to me, I'd feel better about myself," that was Janelle's stopping point. Ammunition to turn the table on me, and it worked. Daniel was now glaring at me, his focus completely off Janelle.

"Useless. Goddamn useless!," Daniel stood up and yelled as he slammed his fist into the doorframe then went storming into the kitchen, pacing back and forth.

Sitting there waiting, I realized no issues were going to be resolved, from Janelle's "venting,"

Janelle retreated victoriously to her bedroom, leaving me to face Daniel's wrath.

"Don't you ever learn?," Daniel shouted at me over his shoulder as he stormed down the stairs and into his theatre.

Taking my cue from Daniel and Janelle, I quickly escaped down the hallway and into the bedroom, grabbing my coat and car keys. I drove to the back parking lot of the church. When I returned home to the bedroom, his verbal abuse began once again within the small confines of the hallway.

"Bitch!," his breath hot and inches from my face. I quickly turned to run back down the stairs only to have Daniel grab my arm and forcibly pull me back up the stairs and into the bedroom, slamming the door behind us. "You think you're so good! You might be a good mother to your own damn kids, but you're a lousy mother to Janelle. Her problems are your fault, damnit! You heard her, your entire fault. Not mine!"

"You can expect divorce papers to be served on you tomorrow," he threatened as he pushed my body against the wall. "I'm tired of this shit!," He banged his fist into the wall, and then he abruptly turned and stormed back down the hallway. Once again, fear of more abuse, I returned to the church, parking near the cemetery.

It was late when I took another chance. Daniel was already in the bed but still awake. He laid glaring at me, from the bed, his hands folded behind his head. I undressed and crawled into bed, measured to the right position, turning off the lamp beside the bed, I threw Daniel's anger and my fear into the pitch-black darkness. Through the sound of Daniel's breathing, I could still tell he was seething with anger, barely able to contain himself from lashing out at me once again.

Daniel's soft snoring gave me my opportunity to quietly slip out of bed and go lie on the couch. The street light shown bright against the off-white living room wall. I snuggled down deep into the couch, wrapping the afghan that hung across the back tightly against me as I positioned the hard throw pillows beneath my head. Two pillows under my head and one to hold onto for comfort. The couch and afghan felt like God's arms wrapped around me. I stayed awake all night, with my head buried in the couch and pillows crying and praying. Around 2:00 a.m., before Daniel's alarm went off, I snuck back into bed, measuring to the right position next to him.

At noon, Daniel called me at work to continue his argument and threats, "You're to blame," Were his first words. "She's going to commit suicide because of you! I just know it. I'm seeing my lawyer this afternoon after work and divorce papers will be served on you this week. Neither you nor any damn counselor on the face of this earth is going to tell me how to raise my daughter!," The only words Daniel may or may have heard spoken on my end was "hello," Daniel never gave me a chance to respond as he hung up.

That evening, Daniel came in and went straight to Janelle's bedroom for his evening time alone with her. I was in the kitchen packing his lunch when he came out over an hour later.

"Janelle's depressed," Daniel's bad mood magnified by his visit alone with Janelle. "She's threatening suicide again."

"Well?," Daniel's voice began to rise. "What do you have to say for yourself? You know this is all your fault."

I knew the more I stayed quiet, the more Daniel's temper would grow, yet I didn't know what to say, all I wanted was to learn how to minimize my abuse.

While wiping down the counter, Daniel stopped me by grabbing my arm, forcing me to turn and face him. With his finger inches from my face, Daniel forced me backwards, cornering me in between the refrigerator and microwave.

"What can I say or do Daniel?," I pleaded, but it was no use, as usual, everything was my fault, Janelle's depression and suicide threats, Daniel feeling hopeless and stressed with bills, my kids were perfect, I loved them more than him, the same old arguments and accusations came out of the depth of his temperament. His usual angry words flew for the next thirty minutes. Words that verbally tore me apart emotionally, making me feel ugly, stupid and unworthy of God's love or his.

Turning, I reached for Daniel's empty glass on the bar nest to the microwave to take it to the sink. Daniel grabbed my shirt, his fingernails clawing deep into my back. I flinched and squirmed in pain trying to escape from under his hold and confinement.

"I didn't hurt you and you know it! What are you doing, where do you think you're going? What were you going to do with that glass? Throw it at me?," Daniel was quick to respond.

"I was going to take it to the sink to wash it," I told him.

"No you weren't," he yelled at me. "You were going to throw it at me. Admit it!"

"No, Daniel. I would never do that," I pleaded

with him. My skin burning from Daniel's nails that had dug deep into my back. Somehow, I managed to squirm out from Daniel's vice-like grip on my arms and escaped into the hallway bathroom, locking the door behind me. The rest of the evening, I spent in the bathroom. My arms aching, my back throbbing with pain.

The next morning I was still in pain. My night was spent positioning and re-positioning, curled up around the toilet or lying in a fetal position in the bathtub, trying to find comfort and relief from the pain. Hearing the front door close as Daniel left for work the next morning, I stood up and looking into the bathroom mirror, I removed my shirt and pulled at the skin on my sides in an attempt to see the damage Daniel had done to my back. It was a useless attempt, all I could feel was pain.

The pressure of my bra straps and hooks, my shirt, having my back touch the seat while driving to work was uncomfortable. Arriving at work, I called Amber and asked her to come to my office.

"Oh, Mom!," she gasped as we stood in the back handicap stall of the women's restroom.

"What are you going to do?," her eyes moist with tears, she asked as slowly she helped me pull my bra straps up and pull my shirt back onto my shoulders. Any kind of movement made my back sting.

Several minutes later, I succumbed to Amber's pleadings and went with her to campus police. We met with Officer Karen Richards. Karen was a mutual friend to both Amber and I. She was at my wedding.

"Kathy, I need to take pictures and write up a report," Karen spoke as she looked at the damage. "As a police officer, I can't just see and know these facts without documenting them."

"Karen, I can't file charges. I just can't. I don't want you or the school involved," I pleaded. "I should have never come here. I wish I had never let Amber convince me to see you."

"Mom, it'll be alright," Amber tried to comfort me.

"I can't force you to do anything," Karen stated. "But I have to do my job," Karen positioned me facing the wall as she took several different pictures with a Polaroid instant picture camera. "Any more damage?," she asked as she waited for the pictures to develop.

"Look at her arms," Amber stated before I could respond.

Unwillingly, feeling forced, I pulled up my sleeves and Karen looked over the bruises.

For the next several minutes, Karen wrote out the report.

"Karen, please, promise me you won't tell anyone. Please," terrified of what Daniel would do if he found out, I begged.

"I won't say a word," Karen promised as she handed me the report.

"Assault Against a Female," was the statement Karen had me sign. I watched as she took out a green file folder and labeled it with my full name, college id number and date. The photos were stapled on the back of the report. Karen then filed the folder alphabetically with all the others.

"There," she stated as she slammed the file drawer shut. "I don't like any of this, Kathy. But, it's here if we ever need it and I hope we never do,"

Amber and I went back to our perspective jobs on campus and finished out our day of work as if nothing had happened.

On Friday, Janelle met with Dr. Martin first. Then Daniel reviewed with Dr. Martin our allowing Janelle to "vent" and his anger at her response.

"Why did you take it out on Kathy?," Dr. Martin confronted Daniel who had deliberately left that part out.

"You want to really know what set me off?," Daniel was defensive. "It's Kathy. She continues to sneak Janelle's rotten food out the refrigerator, throwing the food into the woods. She secretly mops up the water on the floor when Janelle overloads the washing machine causing a flood all over the kitchen floor and down into my film room. The water is ruining the floor and ceiling tile," turning to face me, Daniel looked at me accusingly. "That's what set me off."

"I understand all of that. Janelle told me," Dr. Martin continued, "But your abusive reaction towards Kathy in front of Janelle or any other time because of Janelle's misbehavior is totally inappropriate," Dr. Martin's response was sharp. "Janelle and you are forcing Kathy to internalize her feelings. She's hiding things out of fear of abuse and Janelle is using that to her advantage. She enjoys seeing Kathy punished and is learning to punish Kathy the same as you. Janelle's abusive, just as you are," Dr. Martin stated.

It was quite apparent Janelle was revealing a lot of information about our family life in her private sessions with Dr. Martin, things I was too afraid to discuss.

"Stop threatening the marriage," he asked of Daniel. "If you want the marriage to end, Daniel, end it. Don't just threaten to end it, especially in front of Janelle,"

At the next session, Dr. Martin admitted Janelle's problems were too much for him.

"Janelle needs extensive counseling and I can't give that to her," Daniel was silent as Dr. Martin explained. "I, we, need to focus on you and Kathy and the issues within the marriage."

Chapter Twenty-Three: Jamaica – Doing God's Work

Throughout our marriage, I was able to continue going to Jamaica to do vacation bible schools in spite of Daniel and Janelle's criticism and beating down of my spirit as a Christian.

From January until July I spent time in preparation, studying bible material, creating crafts, picking out songs, putting together hundreds of gift bags and shipping boxes with hopes the boxes would make it to port and through customs in time. Jamaica gave me strength, something to look forward to, an escape from the abuse, even though it was only a temporary escape.

"You call yourself a Christian, you should pray more, just look at yourself, how can you live with yourself? You can't even be a good mother to Janelle, how can you help children in Jamaica," Daniel often berated me before my trips, making sure I boarded the airplane knowing I wasn't anything special or worthy. Putting me in my rightful place as far as he was concerned, both mentally and emotionally. Several times, I left under a threat of Daniel telling me while I was gone, he would be contacting his attorney and divorce papers would be waiting for me once I returned. Daniel's threats and abuse only hours or sometimes just a few short moments before I boarded the plane.

Jamaica gave meaning and purpose to my life, a sense of fulfillment and joy. I was a different person in there. It was freedom. Freedom from locked doors and cabinets, free to be what I wanted to be more than anything, God's servant, not Daniel and Janelle's. At night, I would lay in bed with lizards dropping onto the bed from the ceiling (or already on and in the bed.) Crawling microscopic insects made me aware of their existence not by site but by bite. Some nights I wept from a feeling of unworthiness to do God's work. During the day, staying focused on doing God's work sometimes was a challenge as Daniel and Janelle's voices played in my head.

One year a young boy wrote me a note, passing it to me with a boyish grin on his face during one of our days of vacation bible school. With the days being hot and long, it was only when I returned home a few days later, and was going through my papers did I find the note. It read, "Your visits make everything that's sad seem good again," the little boy's innocent, simple words made me realize how much I needed God to make "everything that's sad seem good again" in my own life. I needed a "missionary" visit; I needed hope, something to cling to.

I loved the children and people of Jamaica. They were hungry for a touch of kindness and love, receptive to God's word and me. I was able to live out the real me, teaching God's word, singing, playing and doing activities with the children. It was the only time during those years of my marriage to Daniel that I can truly remember laughing and enjoying life.

Two days before leaving for Jamaica in 2006, driving home from work that evening felt as if I was driving to my own funeral. Daniel called me at work in a bad mood. "It's like I've killed somebody in this place, and nobody is speaking to me," he complained.

"I'm not going to put up with this shit much longer. That damn George. He's nothing but a sorry, lazy, nigger and if he doesn't straighten up and stay out of my way he's going to get it," I hated hearing Daniel call George that name. No human being deserved to be talked down like that yet, Daniel could be the most prejudice person on the face of the earth. "George has bugged me all day, and I'm not going to put up with it," With Daniel in this frame of mind, there was little doubt what life would be like when I got home.

The garage door was open from the outside and I could see Daniel inside, throwing things around while talking to himself.

"Please dear God. Please. Not tonight," I prayed with my head lowered over the steering wheel of the car. Taking in a deep breath for strength, I exited the car.

"Janelle's depressed again. I called her after lunch and she was crying, said she didn't want to live anymore," Daniel threw a wrench he had picked up off the floor across the garage, it landing with a loud "bang" on the workbench. "Hell! Why you can't be a decent mother to Janelle, I'll never know! A sorry excuse of a mother and a damn hypocrite," Daniel's words were brutal as he came closer, shortening the distance between us. I was now cornered against the second garage door which was pulled down and locked. There was no room for me to move or escape to the outside. Fear overwhelmed me as I turned my face and body away from the evilness of Daniel's presence and words. Turning away from his anger, seeking shelter and an escape route from his physical and verbal abuse. Banging my head and fist on the door, as if someone could help me, I began to panic. I was trapped, with Daniel behind me, no way to escape.

"Why don't you take your fucking ass out of here and leave us the hell alone!," Daniel's hands on each side of me, resting above the panes of glass.

"Please Daniel, I'm sorry," I cried out in panic. With my fist balled up tightly I hit the panel glass, my hand back went through the glass. Blood quickly b began to pour from my hand, but Daniel didn't care; he was too far-gone in rage.

"Now look at what you've done," Daniel snorted as he looked down at the blood dripping from my hand onto the cement floor. "I guess you're going to blame that on me,"

Taking advantage of the small breathing space Daniel had given, I managed to escape up the stairs. The more pressure I applied and the more I tried to stop the bleeding, it just wouldn't stop. Wrapping my hand in a towel and securing it with a shoe lace from my tennis shoes, I grabbed my purse and went out the front door. Daniel still raging and throwing tools around the garage.

Once out of the driveway I called Evan. Evan was living at the fire department where he worked part-time as a volunteer fireman and paramedic, while attending college. He and his girlfriend, Katherine, met me halfway. With his paramedic kit, from, Evan picked out the glass and bandaged up my fingers.

"Mom, please leave him. This isn't worth it," Evan pleaded.

"I can't Evan. I'm leaving Friday for Jamaica,"

"We'll take you to the airport," Evan tried his best.

"You can stay until then with my parents and me," Katherine pleaded.

"What about Janelle?," I tried to explain. "If I leave, Daniel will take his anger out on her just like he did before I came into the picture," I continued. " You know what Janelle told the counselors in the shelter Evan. I can't leave her," I felt hopeless, not knowing what to do.

"Just be safe, Mom," Evan conceded reluctantly. It was dark and getting late.

"We love you. Call us tomorrow," Katherine and Evan hugged me as we parted ways.

The next day Evan came by to check on me at work, removing more pieces of glass and re-wrapping my fingers.

"Katherine's offer still stands, Mom," Evan tried. "You can stay with her and her parents and we'll make arrangements to take you to the airport tomorrow morning,"

"It's just for one more night, Evan. I'll be okay," I tried to reassure him. "After I return from Jamaica, Daniel will have forgotten all about this latest rage."

"You're not going to Jamaica," Daniel spat-out in anger when I returned home that evening. "I'm not taking you to the airport. If you can't help Janelle, how do you expect to help the people and children of Jamaica? Damn hypocrite. You to stay here and spend your time praying and reading the bible," Gripped by fear at what Daniel said and escaping more pain, I spent the night in the basement closet. For hours, I wept in the cool, damp darkness, not just for me, but for the children and people I had grown to love in Jamaica. My heart was breaking. My bags still packed in hopes Daniel would change his mind, lying in wait of the early morning flight a few hours away.

An hour before we were to leave for the airport, light spilled into the closet.

"Get up and get your stuff," Daniel ordered. "I'm taking you to the airport, but you can be damn sure this time I will have divorce papers ready and waiting for you when you return," Our hour and a half drive to the Charlotte airport Daniel's abuse continued, Daniel made sure he put me in my "proper place" of what a useless nobody I was, undeserving of God's love or anyone else's love.

Arriving at the airport, Daniel helped me unload my bags from the trunk and without a "goodbye". He slammed the trunk and drove away. Leaving me standing underneath the departure sign, with my luggage.

Two hours later, I boarded the plane praying to God I would never return. I was empty and exhausted.

"Divorce papers will be waiting for you when you get back," throughout the week, Daniel's words nagged at me. "I really mean it this time."

Would Daniel be waiting for me with divorce papers in his hands? How would I get home, if he wasn't there? Who could I call to drive an hour and a half to the Charlotte airport to pick me up?

Ann and I were assigned a new site that year where there were two orphanages, a Boys Home and a Girls Home. We stayed at the Girls Home. Our numbers topped out over 250 children, which included both orphanages and community children. On Saturday, our first day in Jamaica, we walked into town and passed out flyers to shops and homes announcing our Vacation Bible School the upcoming week. After two hours in the exhausting heat, we began our walk back to the orphanage. As we were walking through town, all at once I felt Ann fearfully grab my arm and she was pointing ahead of us. Looking in the direction of her point, I spotted a "derelict" on the sidewalk. People were gathered around him laughing as he stumbled. His speech was slurred as he communicated with the crowd.

"What are we going to do?," Ann frantically whispered in my ear. We were heading straight towards him. My first instinct was to cross over to the other side of the street in a non-discrete attempt to avoid the scene, but something inside of me made me think otherwise.

"We'll be fine," I placed my hand over hers, which was still gripping my arm in fear. "We'll deal with it the best way we can," I said. "Just smile."

As we approached the man, his frantic blue eyes were shifting quickly from side to side, up and down, apparently not aware of the spectacle he was making of himself, stumbling, rambling incoherent amongst the laughing crowd. He wore shabby, dirty clothes, and carried an old suitcase with its contents spilled out all over the sidewalk and half in the street. Ann continued to hold tightly onto my arm, as we approached the man. Once we were close enough for him to see us, I forced myself to look directly into the man's face, gazing into his green eyes.

"Good afternoon, sir," I acknowledged his presence with a nod of my head as I softly and directly mustered up a courageous greeting.

With a slight head movement of receipt of my words, the man smiled back only briefly, and then turned back to the crowd. Ann and I stepped down off the curb, to making room to walk around him and continued on our way. I could feel his eyes burning into my back as we continued our walk back to the orphanage. Realizing we were in his view for a quite a distance. Ann was close to tears once we made it safely back to the orphanage compound. Dropping to my knees beside the bed, I lifted up thanks to God for our safety and the courage to acknowledge the derelict's presence with grace.

Our training sessions prior to our trips to Jamaica were intense. "Stick to the lesson plans, do role play, make the Jamaican's take lead. We're training them to do Vacation Bible School on their own." It was always the same strict, regimented training.

On Monday, Ann and I stood in front of over 250 children who were staring questioningly into our faces, all in wonder of what the week would hold. The loud noise that filled the small room revealed their excitement at being there. As I gazed across the room at each face, I saw an image of myself at their age. It was the boys and girls from the orphanages that stood out in my mind the most. They were separated from the community children as if they didn't belong, grouping themselves in their own space on broken and termite infested pews.

"If it weren't for me, you'd be in an orphanage," My father's threats came into my mind. A thought tucked away deep in my secret childhood past. On occasion, my father would drive us past an orphanage in Thomasville slowing down to deliberately point it out. "See, that's where you'd be," he threatened. There were times his abuse made me wish he had placed me there, thinking life surely would have been better. For a brief moment, those abusive childhood years came crashing in on me from out of nowhere.

Rarely is it out of character for me to go against the instructions and routine of our training, but this time I allowed the Holy Spirit to direct me.

"Hello," I began. "My name is Kathy Thomas and I'm from North Carolina," From that point, normally I would have introduced to the children our weekly VBS lesson theme, but something inside me kept tugging at my heart, moving me in a different direction.

"Tell them!," the voice spoke strongly within me. "Tell them you're no different from them. Tell them," Words loud, clear and firm. Words so strong, silence overcame me, and for a moment I stood there speechless. Not knowing what to say or do. Ann and the children, staring at me, waiting.

Ever since I began working in Jamaica, I had heard from numerous people that Jamaicans saw all Americans as rich and happy, far better off than the Jamaicans who mostly lived in unbelievable impoverished conditions. The need to "set the story straight" overwhelmed me. I had a bond, a connection with these children. These children's lives mirrored mine.

"For such a time as this," I lowered my head in thoughtful prayer. "Thy will be done, Lord."

Quietly and softly, I turned and placed the lesson materials and my bible on the makeshift table made out of weathered, broken boards and concrete blocks. The table wobbled under the weight of the materials. I grabbed the edges to stable it. Turning back to face the children, I walked down closer to the children, standing in between the rows of pews.

"When I was your ages, my life wasn't much different than yours," The room grew still with all 250 brown faces staring at me. Somewhere behind me, I heard Ann move as she walked towards the front right pew. The look on her face was priceless. "My mother was not a very nice woman and throughout my childhood years, my father was an abusive man. At times, his verbal temper was just as bad as his beatings," At that moment, the room was so quiet, quieter than I had ever heard in my years of Jamaica VBS. A brief moment, fear struck deep down inside me as I stumbled in my thoughts, questioning if this was really God's will. I had never exposed that secret, ugly side of my childhood. Nevertheless, the need to connect to these children was strong and powerful within me. A desperate need to let them know I survived and so would they. I swallowed down deep the moment of anxiety and panic.

"I never remember hearing the words "I love you," from my step-mother or father. I don't remember the feel of a kiss on the forehead or cheek, or the warmth of a mother or father tucking me in bed at night. My childhood was difficult and abusive, just like yours," a glance at Ann showed tears streaming down her face.

"When I was seventeen I met my husband, Richard. For the first time in my life, I felt the warmth of a hug and the feeling of being loved," I continued, my eyes moving across the faces of the children. "It was the most beautiful feeling in the world. I felt loved for the first time in my life and I prayed that God would never let me forget or take for granted the warmth of a hug, softness of a kiss and those beautiful three words, 'I love you.' To this day, a hug from a friend or a loved one makes me realize how lucky I am, just a small sample of what God's love is really like."

The children were focused, grasping onto to each word as I opened up my heart and soul to reveal the deep dark secrets of my dysfunctional childhood.

"Don't look at me as different from you, for in reality, I've come from a childhood very much like yours," I reiterated. "Look at me as someone who has been in some of the same situations you are living in this very moment. With God's love and through the salvation He sent through His Son, Jesus Christ, you will survive just as I. It is my hope and prayers that you will overcome all the bad things that have happened to you. In the future if you become sad, remember me. Once upon a time, my life was just like yours and I survived. I survived because God was there. He gave me hope. Hope in Jesus Christ,"

"Now, Ann, let's talk about our week," By now, my face was wet with tears as I mustered up the courage to move on. Ann quickly jumped up at that point, and with her own tear-stained face, we began our first week of VBS in Highgate, Jamaica.

Throughout the week, orphans came up to me and questioned, "Did you really have a bad childhood, or did you just tell us that?"

"It was real and I survived. You will too," I would confirm as I touched them, knowing how important just a comforting touch and a voice of understanding would have meant to me when I was their age. Occasionally I would get a spontaneous hug, a hug goodbye or a greeting hug. A hug that snuck up from behind me or a hug from a little one on my leg. Every hug from a child I smiled and laughed with glee, "Wow! That feels so good!," I would respond as I hugged them back. Then I would receive precious gifts of a childish grin from ear to ear. It almost became a competition. I had more hugs and gave more hugs that week than I have ever experienced in my life. The warmth of a hug or touch, how amazing it felt to both them and me.

On Friday evening, we held our VBS concert. The children did beautifully. We had over 400 people packed inside the small church. After the children's performance, we did an open session where everyone was invited to share an "item," the sharing of an "item" meant the floor was open to anyone who wished to share a song, poem, story, dance, whatever. After several performances that were awesome, a man, dressed in a nice, gray suit, white shirt and blue tie, came forward with six empty beer bottles. Strategically the man placed the bottles on the makeshift table and blew into the bottles the most beautiful melody of "Amazing Grace" I had ever heard. Groups of people, including myself were mesmerized by his performance. Incredible. When the man finished I walked over to him to shake his hand and thank him. Warmly and graciously, he took both of my hands in his, smiling.

"We've met before," looking closely into his green eyes, my knees went weak, as I tried to hide my surprise. He was the derelict on the street the week before. The "drunk" who staggered, dirty, with slurring speech, living out of a worn out suitcase.

"You didn't turn away," he continued. "You greeted me with love and acceptance. I had to come tonight just to let you know."

I smiled. Not at his words, but in pure gratefulness to God that I had not turned away from him that day, even though Ann and I wanted to. What if I had deliberately avoided him by crossing the street? What statement would I have made?

God knows our future and holds it in His hands. It was God's strength and power that enabled me to go forward and bravely greet this man in love and kindness that day. Each year at Vacation Bible School, he attends our concert.

Our flight out of Kingston was late leaving and we didn't arrive home until after 10:00p.m. on Sunday evening. I knew if Daniel was there, he would be angry because that meant he would be very late going to bed with only a few hours of sleep before leaving for work at 3:15 in the morning.

The entire Jamaica team was exhausted with most everyone looking forward to going home. Everyone except for me, I had to go home to. I missed the days when it was a "family event" when I returned home. Amber, Matt, Roland and Evan all waiting with flowers, hugs and a joyous welcome. Amber and the boys have mentioned how they miss it as well, but Daniel seemed to think that should be held in the past.

"They have their own lives now," Daniel would say, and they were not invited. Matt and Roland running towards me in the airport, late as usual, with roses and a big smile on their faces. Two teenagers, totally out of place. Long, lanky and true "rednecks", but what a greeting. Memories of once upon a time came crashing through my mind, memories so overwhelming, I was forced to escape into the airport bathroom and let the tears of hurt and pain come pouring through.

"Did I serve you well God? Why can't things be the way they should be? Why is there so much pain and suffering in our home? Why am I such a failure with Daniel and Janelle?," I let the feelings flow. God somehow must have a purpose for these things unchangeable in my life.

Daniel's angry expression that greeted me wasn't due to my delayed flight or the conditions I left under. Instead, I quickly learned in the car, Daniel and Janelle had gone to Boone to settle up Cheryl's mother's estate.

"Everyone's arguing with each other on how to distribute her personal and real property," Daniel said disgusted. There was no mention of his threat of divorce papers before I left.

"What the hell?," a week later, Daniel received the phone bill, it was over $120.00. Sixty-six was for the two phones call he made to me in Jamaica. "We're going to have to do something about Jamaica next year," He ordered. "That's a ridiculous amount of money to be charged for two phone calls," For the next twenty-four hours, Daniel continued to fume over the bill, making me feel guilty of the expense.

"Daniel, please, let me pay the bill," I begged when he called me at work complaining.

"You think I'm not man enough to support my own damn family?," he yelled into the phone. Pushing back from my desk, I went into the last bathroom stall at work, and sat crying. Since my return from Jamaica, moments just like this overwhelmed me. At times, too exhausted and overwhelmed to fight the urge, I gave into the emotions, dissolving into tears sometimes for no reason at all.

On Saturday, almost two weeks since my return from Jamaica, we finally got to go out and eat a real meal.

"We can grab something for lunch," Daniel stated. "Janelle needs school supplies,"

While sitting in the restaurant, waiting for our order, Daniel brought up the expense of the phone bill again. At that moment, I started to feel sick, dizzy, with a knot forming in the back of my throat. Desperately I fought to hold back the nausea as well as the tears. All I could think about was if only I could pay the bill without him knowing, yet knowing there was no way and it would only make matters worse. Our food arrived, but I wasn't able to eat, as the phone bill continued as the sole source of conversation the entire time.

The next morning I woke up to the same sick feeling again and for no reason I began to cry. Daniel was in the shower getting ready to work on his truck. Quietly I buried my face into my pillow so Daniel wouldn't hear. My tears flooded the bed sheets and pillow. I cried until I was completely exhausted. Hearing the sound of Daniel's shower stop, I got up, removed the bed linens, raced down the hallway, and threw them in the wash. Taking pains to make sure I stopped in the hallway bathroom, to wash away any evidence of my outburst of tears.

After getting dressed and making up the bed with fresh linens, I went down to the garage to get the vacuum and mop bucket. The moment Daniel saw me, he started up again about the Jamaica long distance bill, stating it was $66.00 for only eleven minutes and he was going to call around and see if there was something else, we could do next year. Quietly I told him I was sorry and left the garage.

There was very little expense for me. I never asked for much when we went to grocery store, knowing the cost of Janelle's food was astronomical and what personal items Evan or I needed I bought from my own money.   I cried most of the way through cleaning the house. In our bedroom, I saw the phone bill lying on the dresser. The long distance calls, the minutes and cost, Daniel was right, the phone call to Jamaica added up to $66.00, yet Daniel hadn't mentioned the remaining bill that was from him and Janelle's personal long distance calls. "I'm not worth $66.00," I said to myself as I began to cry again. Feeling stupid and childish for my thoughts along with the outburst of tears, it reminded me of "nobody loves me, I'm gonna eat a can of worms," I knew if I didn't stop crying, I would end up in the closet, no food, and Daniel's abuse. All I seemed to do was clean house, mow the grass, do the laundry, pack Daniel's lunch, fix his coffee while being trapped in a locked prison cell. Now all I could do was cry. I even cried cleaning the toilets.

While finishing my chores, Daniel came up from the garage slamming things around on the bar.

"Damn it!," he started. "I slammed the son of a bitch garage door on the bumper of my truck. The damn thing is scratched. I can't get ahead on that damn truck no matter how hard I work," Daniel hit the island bar with his fist.

Before I realized it, the tears started pouring down my face. I tried to turn quickly towards the sink, hoping Daniel wouldn't see them, but it was too late.

"What in the hell is wrong with you?," Daniel was livid. All I could do was quickly take Daniel's shock for the moment and slip past him, down into the basement closet, away from Daniel, and cry until the feeling subsided. Then slowly I went up the stairs where Daniel was sitting in his recliner.

"I called both drive-in movie theatres in Mt. Airy and Eden," he complained. "I don't know why in the world both of them have to show the exact same movies, neither one worth seeing," he grumbled as he stood up. "Let's go out for ice cream."

Closing the front door, Daniel spilt a little of his drink onto his pants. He snapped. Yelling and cursing, he threw his remaining plastic cup and drink out across the yard. A look of rage glared in his eyes. I knew what that look meant and terrified I ran to the back of the house, hiding behind the storage building in hopes Daniel wouldn't find me. A few hours later, after dark, Daniel left in his truck, giving me the opportunity to slip into the house and into the closet.

The front door closing and footsteps on the stairs, jarred me from a restless sleep. I waited for Daniel to drift off to sleep. The bedroom was dark as I quietly opened the door, I paused while my eyes to adjust to the darkness.

"Fuck You!," were the words that greeted me when I took my first step, quickly I retreated back down the hallway and stairs and into the basement closet where I stayed until morning.

The next day was Sunday. The clicking on and off of the hot water heater beside me in the basement closet indicated Daniel was up and taking his morning shower. I woke up several times during the night sick, weakly climbing the stairs and into the bathroom throwing up what little food was on my stomach, mostly experiencing dry heaves. I was weak and dizzy. I waited for Daniel to settle in his recliner with his cereal and coffee.

After a shower, I sat down at the kitchen island bar and tried to eat a small bowl of cereal for breakfast. A wave of nausea hit me so quickly, I didn't make it to the commode and ended up throwing up all over the bathroom floor. Daniel stood in the entrance of the bathroom, his arms crossed over his chest, glaring at me as I weakly cleaned up the bathroom, and then struggled to bed. As I drifted off to sleep, I remembered the wicked, hateful look on his face and thinking no one has ever hated me as much as he does.

"Do you want something to eat?," the closed window blinds reflected a rosy, dusk color.

"I must have slept through the entire day," was my first thought.

"I'll try," I was so weak.

"You're the reason for my temper and problems. All these years of counseling have done me no good. You're the cause of my misery," Once inside the truck, driving towards Wendy's, Daniel argued, beating his fist on the steering wheel, driving like a crazy man, jerking the truck back and forth, refusing to let off the gas as he sped around sharp curves. I was too afraid to speak, holding onto the door handle, terrified we were going to wreck. I wanted to get out of the truck, feeling trapped within the front cab. There was no place for me to hide. No place for me to run.

"Daniel, I'll try to do whatever you want me to," I pleaded.

"Shut the hell up!," He looked over at me and grabbed my arm, steering recklessly with the one hand. "You think you and your kids are so perfect. God doesn't love you or me!," He stated. "We need to do something about this!"

"Can we wait and talk with Dr. Martin on Friday?," I pleaded, frightfully watching the road.

"Shut the fuck up!," he raged. "We don't need counselors to talk to. They're all stupid! Janelle and I are the only people who know who you really are!," his eyes were menacing. "We 're the only people you should talk to. Do you hear me?," he swerved the truck right, into the library parking lot, squalling tires as he circled around, turning us to drive back towards home.

Daniel walked ahead of me into the house, once entering, Daniel went up the into the kitchen and I retreated quickly down the stairs into the basement closet. Two hours later, I heard Daniel leave to pick Janelle up. Quickly I went upstairs, used the bathroom, drank a glass of water and retreated down the stairs, into the closet before Daniel and Janelle returned.

Things must not have gone right with Daniel and Janelle during their drive home. I could hear Daniel's angry footsteps on the stairs as he came to the closet door. Light from the hallway spilled part ways into the closet as Daniel peered in an attempt to see me tucked away in the back corner.

"I know you hate me," Daniel aimed his words into the darkness. A brief moment of silence. "You know something," he began. "My anger and temper is just like a story a preacher once told me about "cat shit," he laughed. "The more you stir it, the stinkier it gets," he exhaled. "You know you need help; admit it. You're the source of Janelle's problems and you're the source of my problems. You're a fuckin' failure."

Rolling back to sit on his heels, I could see Daniel's face, it was as if he was pondering his thoughts.

"You're the one who makes me feel like blowing my head off. Yep," he took his right hand and formed it into the shape of a gun as he played out his suicide threat. "I'm going to take a gun, like this," he stuck his finger into his temple. "And blow my goddamn brains out," he slammed the closet door, throwing me back into the pitch-black darkness.

Storming up the stairs, I heard him yelling down towards the closet. "Tomorrow you'll hear from my attorney."

An hour later, it became apparent that Daniel had no plans to sleep, his plans were to continue coming up and down the stairs into the closet doorway cursing and yelling at me the entire night.

Finally, I snuck up the stairs and out of the house. I drove to work with hopes of sleeping in my office. Walking around the building, pulling on the doors, all were locked. Knocking, banging on the doors was to no avail.

"Cindy must still be working on the second floor," I thought. It was a cold walk up the darkened sidewalk across campus to the closest outside campus phone.

"Campus police," was the male response I got from the number I dialed.

"Hello, this is Kathy Thomas. Is there any way I can get into my building to do some work?," trying to keep my voice upbeat and level.

"I'm sorry," The third shift officer apologized. "We don't have authorization from your supervisor."

"When do you officially open the buildings?," I tried not to sound too panicky.

"We usually open them around 7:00 a.m.," was his reply.

"Okay, thanks," defeated I returned to my car. Exhausted from lack of sleep, I drove just a short distance down the road to the Harris Teeter supermarket parking lot and crawled into the backseat of the car. It wasn't a restful sleep. I was afraid of being seen or oversleeping. In and out of short naps, I waited for the first the sun to rise and kept tabs of the time on my watch. At 6:45 a.m. I drove back to the campus and waited for campus police to unlock the doors. Once he was out of sight, I went into the building. Taking the back stairs to avoid being seen by Cindy, I slipped into the bathroom and washed up the best I could realizing I would have to wear the same clothes I had worn the day before.

That was the first of many early morning escapes and sleeping in the parking lot at Harris Teeter. I purchased a battery operated alarm clock and would set it for 6:45. My car was becoming my second home, self-contained for survival with a pillow, blanket, alarm clock, flashlight, toothbrush, toothpaste, change of clothing, all the essentials I needed to escape from the abuse.

It had been two weeks since my return from Jamaica. Two weeks of abuse, all starting with a $66.00 phone bill. Jamaica was worth the abuse. Jamaica gave me hope and strength. The work was fulfilling both spiritually and emotionally. In some instances, a week of intense God-therapy. That one time a year, I was allowed to be myself, the real Kathy. A place where there was no criticism of me as a person, just unconditional love. A brief ten days that gave me strength to endure my abusive life for the next 355 days until my next return to Jamaica.

Chapter Twenty-Four: No One to Guide Me

In September, 2006, Janelle entered into the tenth grade. The realization she had two more years of high school caused her a lot of grief which created even more abuse and turmoil in our home. Daniel refused to accept Dr. Martin's suggestion for another counselor for Janelle and continued to take her with us to our sessions. Dr. Martin avoided taking Janelle back to his office, he greeted her in the waiting room when he came to retrieve Daniel and I, but that was the extent of any interaction with her.

"Nobody can help her," Daniel's answer was sarcastic when Dr. Martin asked if Janelle was in counseling. Daniel was out of money and hope of anyone ever helping Janelle.

At our next "couple's only" marriage counseling session with Dr. Martin, he requested we meet with him separately, asking me to go first.

"How are you holding up?," Dr. Martin wasted no time expressing his concern.

Immediately, without warning, I began to tear up. "I don't know what's wrong with me. I cry for no reason, I'm exhausted all the time and I'm having difficulty sleeping. I've been this way since my return from Jamaica three months ago," the referenced tears of evidence began to spill down my cheeks.

"Kathy, that's a normal response to the abusive environment you're being forced to live in. Janelle needs extensive therapy and so does Daniel," Dr. Martin paused to write in the file.

"How about Janelle? How is she doing?," he looked up.

"Worse," I told him. "Daniel's out of money, therefore, he can't afford for her to see a counselor. Even if there was money, Daniel's given up hope. He's frustrated and angry most of the time."

"I'm sorry Kathy. That's kind of why I wanted to meet with you alone," he hesitated. "I'm going to recommend an extensive six-week Anger Management program for Daniel. He will be institutionalized, but will be able to leave daily for work. It's a good program, if Daniel is willing to receive the therapy," Dr. Martin leaned forward over his desk. "Daniel has some very serious violence issues and I'm afraid for you," he leaned back in his winged-back swivel office chair. "I can't give Daniel the extensive therapy he needs and insure that you are safe."

"I don't think Daniel will go for this," was my initial response.

"I've got some ideas and some real-life experiences I think I can share with Daniel when I meet with him," Dr. Martin seemed more confident than I was.

"Do you have a safe place to go if things don't work out well in my sessions with Daniel?," he asked.

"Yes," was Dr. Martin's final attempt and I knew it. If this didn't work, Dr. Martin was quitting just as others had in the past.

"How do you feel about a separation?," Dr. Martin asked.

At that precise moment, I realized "I" was ready to give up too. Maybe it was Dr. Martin's demeanor of defeat that gave me the strength or maybe it was just the right timing. Whichever, I knew I was ready to start over, no matter what it took.

"In my mind I'm ready to leave Daniel," I told Dr. Martin. "But physically doing it is a different story and there's Janelle. I'm scared of what Daniel will do her if I'm not around."

"Kathy," Dr. Martin leaned forward once again. "At this moment, you're the one in imminent danger. Not Janelle. Janelle is an adult. She can make decision on her own and she knows her father a lot better than you think. You are the one both Daniel and Janelle are abusing now. You are their target for releasing their own mental illnesses. You have to be prepared to leave if Daniel doesn't agree to treatment. Are you ready?"

"Yes," I felt stronger now. "Yes. I'm willing to do whatever you suggest," I missed my life and identity. I missed my children. I knew the situation with Daniel and Janelle was volatile towards me. The abuse needed to end, before it was too late for me.

"Like father, like daughter," Dr. Martin stated as he stood up to walk me to the door. With his arm around my shoulder, Dr. Martin gave me a quick hug before opening the door. "Be safe," he said. " I'll be in touch. Can I call you to follow-up with how things go with Daniel at your work?," he asked.

"Yes, that'll be fine," I appreciated his concern and willingness to help.

I walked and prayed around the parking lot outside Dr. Martin's office, asking God for direction. Thirty minutes later, Daniel came out of the building. As we walked to the car. I glanced sideways at Daniel's face for some kind of reading. There was nothing. The forty-five minute ride home was quiet as Daniel appeared deep in thought.

Once we arrived home, Daniel went into the kitchen to rinse out his coffee cup and I went to the bedroom to drop off my pocketbook and sweater. Daniel came in just as I was leaving the room.

"We need to talk," he walked over and sat at the foot of the bed. I sat down beside him. I could see both of our reflections in the dresser mirror.

"Dr. Martin said you need to attend some extensive Anger Management classes," Daniel began.

The statement was clear and matter of fact. I was dumbfounded.

Looking at Daniel's reflection in the mirror revealed absolutely nothing. My reflection, I went pale, a shocked look appeared on my face. No words would come.

"No way," I thought as I turned for a closer search into Daniel's face. "This is the exact opposite of what Dr. Martin had told me. Is it possible they were both plotting against me? Do I really need it and Dr. Martin was just playing along with Daniel?," I didn't understand, as thoughts began to race erratically through my mind. I was completely speechless.

"I'll attend them with you," Daniel stated. "That is, if you want me too?," he asked. "Dr. Martin thought we could both benefit from the treatment."

All I could do was shake my head in a "yes" motion.

"Good," Daniel jumped up from the bed. "I'll call Dr. Martin on Monday and make the arrangements for both of us to attend," Daniel said. "I'll let you know when and where," Daniel left the room to go down and watch a film.

I must have sat on the bed for over an hour, completely confused. "Could Dr. Martin have lied to me?," I thought. "None of this made any sense. I can't call Dr. Martin and ask, especially if it's true, he'll think I'm even crazier," my mind chaotic and jumbled. Not knowing what was going on, what was true, what was a lie.

Daniel was in a good mood that evening and the next day. Meanwhile, I walked around in a daze. Waiting anxiously for Monday. Hoping Dr. Martin would call and I would know what was real.

On Sunday, Evan and his girlfriend, Katherine, showed up at church. They were attendees of another church, but chose to surprise me. It was great to see them. However, Daniel didn't think so, as he cruelly whispered in my ear, "they only came for the free lunch the youth are serving after the service." Evan and Katherine had no idea of the free lunch, nor did they stay, they already had plans immediately following the service. Daniel treated Evan and Katherine rude and cold. Daniel's hatred and jealousy of my three children was no secret to them. What Daniel never knew was that all the efforts he made to keep the children and I apart, only made us stronger in our love for each other. Each through their own individual experiences knew how abusive Daniel was. Nevertheless, we survived in secret as a family.

Monday morning I reminded Daniel about calling Dr. Martin as he was leaving for work. "No problem," Daniel replied as he closed the front door. Monday came and went, I never heard from Dr. Martin, nor did Daniel mention calling him. I was too afraid to keep asking. Like the other counselors in our past, we never saw Dr. Martin again.

In late October, Daniel and I found a "unique fixer-upper" cabin in the mountains of Virginia. I took out my first equity loan from the three bedroom brick house I purchased months before our marriage. I was hoping that the project of the cabin would make things better in our marriage, keeping our minds and hands busy. The view from the cabin was breathtaking!

The loan and purchase was complete on October 30th. The imminent need for the cabin was to put on a metal roof before winter set in. But that would have to wait until after the film convention in Asheville in two weeks.

The week before our trip to Asheville, Daniel lost out on purchasing a mint, original western film on e-bay to another bidder. At the convention, Daniel and I arrived early as he was anxious to get the first opportunity to preview and purchase films before anyone else had the advantage. One of Daniel's friends, Bill, had purchased the film Daniel asked me to bid on that he lost out on the week before.

"Daniel, you should see it. It's in mint condition," Bill bragged about the bid. Daniel always set the limit to what I could bid on eBay and Bill had no idea he was bidding against Daniel. Daniel had me use a false name on eBay so no one would know it was him. I watched Daniel's face as Bill's bragging got the best of him. Daniel left the dealer's room almost immediately after inspection of Bill's new purchase. With his hand firmly on my arm, he roughly guided me through the lobby, into the elevator and down the hallway. I felt like a child who had done something terribly wrong taken to be punished. Daniel held me tightly as he guided me sternly down the hall and into our motel room.

"I told you I wanted that film!," Daniel began to yell as soon as the door closed behind us.

"Daniel, you're the one who told me what to put as the cutoff limit on the bid," I tried to rationalize with him.

"We're leaving," he yelled in my face. "Get all your shit together. We're leaving!," He flung my arm down and started kicking his film boxes.

"What about the movie stars? I'm supposed to take them out in less than thirty minutes," I asked.

"I don't give a damn about the stars! You've ruined this entire convention for me! Get the fuck out of here!," he pointed to the motel door. "Get out!"

Quickly, I turned and scurried out of the motel room.

My eyes blurred with tears, somehow I made my way downstairs into the lobby bathroom. Standing in the last bathroom stall, I shook and cried in fear of what the remainder of the day held in store. Terrified of what the ride home would be like. There would be no escape from the abuse and I knew it. I stayed there crying until the very last minute before I was to leave with the stars then did my best to pull myself together. Greeting them all in the lobby as I was given the keys to the van.

"The hell with you!," The room was dark when I returned later that afternoon from my day with the stars. "What are you trying to do? Ruin my life! That was a beautiful mint original! You've ruined this entire convention!," He raged. "I told you before, pack your damn bags! We're leaving!," he ordered. Quickly I packed my bags and ran out the door.

"Shirley, we're leaving," was all I could muster up to say as tears streamed down my cheeks.

"Kathy? What's wrong? What's happened?," Bill's wife answered my frantic knock on their room door. She looked up and down the hallway then quickly pulled me inside and closed the door. "Tell me. What happened?"

Briefly I explained about the film Bill outbidded Daniel on and Daniel's rage.

"You'll have to find someone else to drive the van to take the wives shopping tomorrow. Daniel says we're leaving," I sobbed in my hands as I sat down on the edge of their bed.

"Oh, Kathy, I'm so sorry. Is there anything I can do?," she asked.

"Short of asking Bill to sell the film to Daniel, that's all I can think of," I turned and pleaded with her. "Do you think Bill will sell it to Daniel?"

"I don't know, but I can ask," she replied.

I left Shirley soon after and spent the next six hours curled up in the back seat of our car. The mountain air was bitter cold both inside and outside the car. Gathering up my coats and the blanket Daniel used to cover his films, I wrapped myself up tightly in an attempt to stay warm. My face underneath the layered pile, allowing my breath to warm me. My body was completely hidden so no one who might pass between the two cars in the parking lot would see me. I waited for Daniel to come and drive us home.

A hard rain began to fall on the metal car roof. A soothing, erythematic, natural, sound that comforted me as it lulled me into sleep.

"Get out," Daniel ordered as he threw the blanket and coats off me. The doom light shone brightly into my eyes, blinding me. It was still dark yet appeared to be in the wee hours of the following morning.

"Are we leaving?," I asked, still blinking from the interior light, groggy from sleep.

"Get out I said," Daniel reached into the backseat and began pulling me out of the car, closing and locking the door, leaving my luggage inside.

The hallways were empty and still with sleeping guests in their rooms. No words were spoken between us until we were inside the motel room. A glance at the tableside clock radio showed it was 3:00 a.m.

"We're staying," Daniel said once the door was closed. He undressed and crawled into bed. Without undressing, I laid down beside him, worried and scared of what the day would hold, yet too tired to even care.

"Maybe I'll wake up in the morning and realize this was all just a bad dream," I thought as I soon drifted back off to sleep.

Daniel left out early the next morning to have breakfast with some of his film buddies. I went out and brought my luggage back in from the car, showered, changed and went downstairs to take the wives and movie stars shopping. Not looking or attempting to answer Shirley's questioning expression, looking forward to an entire day away from Daniel's abuse, only if it was for a day.

"How can you love me? Why do you love me?," When I returned, Daniel was sitting on the side of the bed in the motel room crying. For the next hour, Daniel cried and talked about what a mean and hateful person he was. "I wish I was dead," he begged as he reached his arms and hands upwards towards the sky. "Why, why can't I just die?"

Wanting more than anything to just make it through the convention, I sat beside him, my hands folded in my lap, not knowing what to do as I listened to him cried in anguish and despair. Daniel was definitely a man tormented inside and there was nothing anyone, including myself could do.

Chapter Twenty-Five: Four Bounced Checks, Seven More a Pending

No this isn't a redneck version of the Christmas song "A Partridge in a Pear Tree," It is the week before Thanksgiving. Daniel and I had just returned on Sunday from the film convention.

Monday, November 13, 2006

Janelle was depressed, again, sitting at the table doing her homework; crying and telling Daniel, she was financially broke and confessing to a spending problem with her money. Janelle had a high spending lifestyle and it was finally catching up with her. Every Friday night she went out to eat at expensive restaurants, then shopping, the movies, whatever she wanted to do, wherever she wanted to go. Within a brief 24-hour period, Janelle had usually spent most of her paycheck.

"Janelle deserves to go out and have a good time," Daniel would shrug off Janelle's excessive spending each time she would come to one of us to borrow money to cover her bad checks.

Moments of Janelle's "bankruptcy crisis" were becoming more and more frequent, but this time seemed different. Janelle appeared overly upset to the point I was sensing there was much more to this than she was telling. It was almost as if she was setting us up, leaving me feeling something bad was soon to come.

Tuesday, November 14, 2006

The next day we went straight from work to the rental house to complete a repair job on the plumbing. Daniel and I got home around 9:00 and Janelle was in another panic. She needed to go to the bank immediately and check her account balance; she thought she bounced her car insurance check.

"Wait," Daniel asked with agitation edging his tone, "I thought your insurance was due on the 1st of the month?"

"No," Janelle replied. "I called and asked for an extension and they told me I could have until November 10th."

Today was the 14th.

"When did you mail it?," Daniel asked.

"On the 10th," Janelle was getting grumpy with Daniel's questions and need for details. This was getting bad, and confusing.

"I'll take her to the bank," I interjected out of self-defense, noticing Daniel was starting to lose his temper, Thinking Daniel could go on to bed, I would loan Janelle the money to deposit and all would be well.

Janelle's bank balance revealed $13.99 in her account.

"Don't let that be the gospel truth," I warned her. "You still don't know which checks have cleared. Are there any more outstanding checks other than the insurance check."

"No," Janelle was adamant.

Calling out to Janelle from our bedroom, Daniel was lying in bed waiting for us.

"There's a $13.99 balance," Janelle stated. "But I'm not sure which checks have cleared."

"Well you better call the bank first chance you get tomorrow. Even if you have to ask to use the school phone," Daniel stated. "Are there anymore checks other than your insurance check that might not have cleared yet?"

"No," Janelle agitated that both Daniel and I had asked the same question.

"Might not be a bad idea to call the insurance company too," Daniel told her as she turned to leave.

Wednesday, November 15, 2006

Janelle had a field trip with her class to tour Bill Jones University in South Carolina. They were to be there until Friday.

"Did you call the bank and insurance company?," I heard Daniel ask when she called that evening.

Not able to hear Janelle's response, I could only assume she hadn't since Daniel asked "Don't you think you should?"

Fearing the worse, I left Daniel alone in the living room and went to the bedroom to take out clothes for work the next day. Daniel was upset when he came into the bedroom and prepared for bed.

"Damn it!," He punched at his pillow, then flipped it over, crawling into the bed and jerking the covers over him. "I'm sick and tired of this shit!," I retreated into the bathroom to shower and brush my teeth. Dragging out each task, waiting until I heard Daniel's snore, then laid in my respective, measured space beside him.

Thursday, November 16, 2006

The following evening we arrived home from work to a frantic phone message from Janelle for Daniel to call her on a friend's cell phone. Janelle had tried to get money out of her account and it showed a negative balance of over $100.

Daniel went through the mail. A bank statement had arrived for Janelle and it revealed she had bounced three checks written to Union Cross School for cash. Janelle was livid. I could hear her voice in high pitch, making out she didn't know how she was going to pay for them.

"The bank has frozen your account," Daniel read the statement info to Janelle. "They've charged you $30 per check, plus the amount of the check."

I decided to let the two of them handle it and I proceeded into the kitchen to pack Daniel's lunch.

"Are there anymore checks?," I heard Daniel ask from the living room. "Good," Daniel seemed satisfied there were no more.

"Have you called the insurance company?," He asked again for the third day in a row. "Don't you think you should?," Was his sarcastic response. "Call them tomorrow, you hear me?," Daniel ordered.

Friday, November 17, 2006
Daniel and I went up to the cabin and began work on the roof as soon as I got off work at noon. Janelle called while we were working.

"Janelle said she called the insurance company and left a message. She still hasn't heard back from them as to whether the check has cleared the bank yet," Daniel stated. "I don't know why it's taking so damn long for that check to clear," Daniel was aggravated as he slammed the box of roofing nails onto the deck beside the ladder.

A few minutes later, the phone rang again. It was Janelle and I could tell by Daniel's conversation, Janelle was asking permission to go out with her friends that night. It surprised me to hear Daniel say "yes," But then, Janelle deserved to go out every Friday night.

"Where was the money coming from for her to go out with her friends?," I questioned within myself.

I didn't say a word; abuse would only follow if I did not remain quiet. Daniel was struggling and stressed out with his own bills and excessive spending, on top of that, was Janelle's expenses. She still had years of private school. Taxes and insurances were due on Daniel's house and my house. His credit card balance continued increasing. I received a phone call at work from the homeowner's insurance company that Daniel was late on the payment. "Lord, it is in your hands," I prayed up to the mountains.

Later that evening, Daniel spoke to Janelle again about her checking account. She stated with her account frozen, with this week's paycheck she wouldn't have enough money for gas to work and school. Once again, he asked her to call the insurance company Monday as soon as she got home from school.

Saturday, November 18, 2006

Daniel wanted to get an early start for our trip to the cabin. The roof was leaking badly. Next week was Thanksgiving so the possibility of working next weekend was not an option. I wasn't looking forward to the trip. It was bitterly cold and Daniel was still in a foul mood from Janelle's past week of bad checks.

"Lift the damn metal higher," Daniel yelled down at me from his position of leaning over the edge of the roof, losing his patience with me. I was doing well to lift the 3ft x 16ft sheets of metal roofing up to his reach on the roof. However, I wasn't quick enough or good enough.

Daniel's constant, "Damn bitch! What do you think you're doing?," was a continuous reminder of what a failure I was to him. Finally, I managed a system. I would slide the metal roofing sheets on their sides out of the cabin and onto the deck. Then place one end of the sheet on the deck rail, walk under the sheet, lifting the length of the sheet to the maximum length of my arms and legs, stand on my tiptoes, until I had lifted the 16 ft. sheet of metal reached to the edge of the roof. The lift was as high as my body could stretch for Daniel to grab the end of the sheet metal and pull it up onto the roof. The sheets weighed more than I and the entire pulling and lifting was painful for me, yet it was a system that seemed to work, at least to the satisfaction of Daniel, until Daniel shifted the position of the lifting.   That one movement change made the system I had accomplished, awkward for me. Soon I realized my body was unable to lift the weight of the metal sheet. When I tried to lift in this different position, I immediately buckled under the weight of the sheet metal, unable to get a good hold to lift the metal sheet up to the roof. As hard as I tried to stand under the sheet metal and lift it, the sheet metal would collapse in the middle or slide sideways out of my grip.

"Shit! What is your problem?," Daniel yelled down as he watched me struggle.

"I'm sorry," meekly I called up. "I had a system but when you shifted I couldn't grasp hold of the metal sheet to lift it high enough to reach you," I continued to struggle in an attempt to find a way to make it work, only to have it drop to the deck. I ran inside the cabin to get a chair to wedge under the metal sheet at an angle on the deck rail. Hoping, praying that would give me enough support to lift.

"Bitch! Shit! You're useless!," Daniel yelled down as he threw a piece of roofing furring strips down onto the deck, barely missing me.

"I didn't know we had specific instructions on how to hand up a damn sheet of metal roofing. Excuse me for not following instructions!," his sarcasm hurled down at me.

With the chair wedged under the sheet metal mid-way across the deck, I struggled with the piece of metal, my muscles stretched painfully as sweat rolled down my back. My arms, shoulder and back aching unbearably. I stood as tall as I could on my tiptoes, and finally it was enough to get the sheet within Daniel's reach. Full of rage, he yanked the sheet out from my hands as I felt the metal edge cut into the palms of my hand.

"Damn! It's about time," he yelled down as he threw the sheet metal onto the roof and it landed with a loud "bang," "

"Why in the hell did I ever marry you?," He mumbled under his breath as he began to hammer in the roofing nails. "Sorry bitch!"

Retreating into the cabin, I grabbed a bottle water I had brought and used what was left of it to rinse the blood gushing from my palms. A Kleenex from my coat pocket, I used as a gauze and wrapped an old towel found under the sink firmly around my hand, tucking in the loose pieces tightly. The bulky bandage made carrying and lifting the metal sheets even more difficult but mind over pain, I continued to lift and slide piece after piece, balancing them onto the rail and chair, lifting them up to Daniel as I listened to what a sorry excuse of a human being I was.

The air was crisp. The view from the deck was of bare trees with mountains hovering in the distance. The trickling sound of the flowing creek below. It smelled like snow. "I bet this place is absolutely beautiful when it's covered in snow," I thought as I did my best to "tune out" Daniel's temper tantrum, focusing on the beauty of the mountains, trees and nature, anything to take my ears far away from his abusive words. Even the small sparrows weren't interested in Daniel's cussing and temper. They twittered far into the woods, flipping from tree to tree while the squirrels scurried around gathering their harvest for the long winter months ahead. Deer tracks below showed evidence of the activity around the cabin at night or when we weren't there invading their privacy and freedom. Wild turkeys called one to another in the distance. Very few cars came down the road. Neighboring cabins were sparse.

Finally, dusk was beginning to fall upon us and with no electricity in the cabin, Daniel was forced to quit for the day. We were able to only get about one-fourth of the roofing on.

"I guess we can expect more leaks since it'll be at least two weeks before we can get back up here," Daniel cuttingly said, angry at how slow the roofing process had gone. It was obvious whose fault the incomplete job it was.

Sunday, November 19, 2006
Daniel didn't allow us to go to church because of the long day and late night at the cabin. He wanted to sleep in. There continued to be a lot of tension because of Janelle's bank situation and the anticipation of Monday when we could find out the status of her insurance check. When Janelle arrived home from work, Daniel reminded her to call as soon as she got home from school the next day about the insurance check.

Monday, November 20, 2006
The next morning I called Union Cross to apologize for the bounced checks and found out things were a lot worse. Janelle had been writing bad checks and post-dated checks since May. She would call and ask Mrs. Caudle, the school secretary/treasurer to hold her checks longer than the posted date, because she didn't have the money. Mrs. Caudle informed me it had been an ongoing problem since Janelle first opened her checking account and the school told her they would not allow her to post-date checks anymore because of the delay in school deposits and bookkeeping. I asked Mrs. Caudle what the checks were for and she said mostly

food, sometimes Janelle told her it was for gas money. I didn't understand. Each week Daniel bought food Janelle packed for her lunches.   Plus, Janelle was bringing quite a bit of food from the deli where she was working.

When school started back in August, Janelle began once again writing post-dated and bad checks to Union Cross. When Mrs. Caudle tried to deny the checks, Janelle always had various, compelling reasons for needing the money, promising to make good on the checks once she got paid. Mrs. Caudle said Janelle called her from the bookstore of Bill Jones University the previous Thursday and told her to hold the remaining seven post-dated checks she had cashed at the school until she could let her know when it would be safe to deposit them.

For the past week we had asked Janelle if there were any more outstanding checks, and her response was always "no,"   Realistically, there were seven more. Janelle had lied to us.

"Janelle asked me a few weeks ago not to tell you or her dad. I told her I wouldn't if she came up with cash money to make them right by the end of the month," Mrs. Caudle explained.

Union Cross knew more about Janelle's bad checks and credit than we did as her parents.

" Why doesn't her dad take away her checking account? Does he know?," Mrs. Caudle questioned me.

"It's difficult to control her, especially now that she's eighteen," I felt safe in saying, leaving Daniel's name out of it as much as possible for fear of punishment. "We didn't know about her bad checks to Union Cross. The ones we have just recently learned of," I paused. "I guess we hoped she would learn her lesson after she pays all the bank charges for the bounced checks,"

"But her credit," Mrs. Caudle stated. "Are either one of your names on Janelle's account?"

"Daniel's name is on it," embarrassed at revealing our personal lives to a stranger.

"You realize that this affects your credit too?," I could hear the concern in Mrs. Caudle's voice.

"Oh no," I quickly stated. "Not according to Daniel and Janelle. They said it wouldn't affect me at all. The bank doesn't even know I exist. Both Janelle and Daniel bank at the same bank. I bank elsewhere," was more info than I wanted to give her. With North Carolina's marital interest rights could Daniel and Janelle's credit rating affect mine? I had maintained separate accounts on my credit card and banking, never realizing up until that moment what a crucial decision that may have been five years ago.

"Maybe you should check with your bank," Mrs. Caudle concluded. "I really don't know, but think you might need an opinion from someone more familiar with the state marital laws. Possibly someone where you bank could advise you."

"If it would help," she offered a suggestion. "I could schedule both of you an appointment to speak with Reverend Gallimore. He's talk with Janelle about this on numerous occasions and could maybe give you some guidance?"

"Daniel wouldn't hear of it," knowing Daniel would be furious if he knew I had spoken to Mrs. Caudle about this. All I wanted to do was call and apologize for the bad checks and maybe pay them off. Now, with seven checks, there was no way I would be able to pay for all Janelle owed. At least not until the end of the month.

"At least let Reverend Gallimore suggest to you both someone for family counseling," her voice was gentle with concern.

"Please don't tell Daniel or Janelle I called," I asked. Frightened now by all of this, I wasn't sure I could trust Mrs. Caudle or Reverend Gallimore. No one knew what I was living with.

"We won't discuss with either of them," Mrs. Caudle promised. "Do the best you can to help Janelle and we'll not accept any checks from her."

"Thank you," Was all I could muster up through my fear.

"Have a good Thanksgiving," was Mrs. Caudle's final words as we hung up.

Around 2:30 p.m., Reverend Gallimore left a message for me at work to call him. When I returned his call, he had already talked with Mrs. Caudle and was fully aware of the problems.

"I've spoken with Mrs. Caudle and a few of Janelle's teachers. Janelle's got some serious problems and we as a school have made a final decision not to accept any more checks from Janelle," he was direct and to the point.

"I know," was all I could say.

"Do you think Mr. Thomas would be receptive to me counseling both of you as a family concerning Janelle."

"No! Please don't tell either Janelle or Daniel we've spoken about any of this," I begged.

"It's okay, Mrs. Thomas. I promise," Reverend Gallimore said hesitantly. "I'll discuss this discreetly with Janelle. She and I have had conversations about her checks numerous times. It stops this moment as far as Union Cross is concerned."

The house was quiet when I entered the front door. Daniel was in Janelle's bedroom. I sat down on the side of the bed.

"Please God," I prayed. "Not another bad evening. Please. Let it all be taken care of."

"We need to talk," Daniel interrupted my much-needed moment of silence. Without a word, I stood up and followed him into the kitchen. Janelle was sitting at the table, staring at an envelope with her checkbook in her hand.

"Janelle's check bounced from the insurance company," Daniel began.

"Janelle, I'm sorry," the room filled with silence. "Are there any more than the other three you told us about?"

If looks could kill, that was one that just shot me down, aimed from Daniel and Janelle.

"No, Janelle said only three and now four with the insurance check," Daniel's temper was beginning to rise.

"Janelle, are you sure?," I avoided Daniel's face and looked directly into Janelle's eyes.

Shrugging her shoulders, pretending to flip through the pages of her checkbook, without looking up, Janelle responded, "I don't know."

Slamming his fist against the table, Daniel yelled out, "Hell Janelle, how many are there?," Daniel realizing there was a possibility of more.

Janelle sarcastically replied. "I bounced three checks written out to Union Cross and one to the insurance company," another lie and cover up by Janelle.

"Oh, I guess I misunderstood. I thought you meant there was more," Daniel meekly and cowardly backed down from fear of Janelle's wrath.

At that point, I lost all hope and respect for Daniel.

"Could there now be more than four Janelle? Maybe around seven?," I gently prodded Janelle. Knowing I was going into a very dangerous area that would only produce abuse. Yet, also knowing that I needed to know the truth if I was going to be the one going to the bank or school to make good on the checks.

Janelle face went white, then red, a rainbow of colors flashing around her shocked expression of revelation. "How do you know?," Janelle snapped angrily as both her and Daniel glared straight at me.

Now the truth was out. Now there was no way to take it back. How did I know? With hopes of saving Janelle's sinful spirit and a feeble attempt to clean up this mess, I told them both I had called Mrs. Caudle to apologize for the bad checks in an attempt to go by the school and pay off the debt.

"Janelle, I'm willing to do what I can to help, but I'm not sure even I have enough money to pay off your debts to Union Cross," I looked at them both. "I called my bank, and was told this could affect my credit, even though Daniel's name is on your account. Especially if the payments become "uncollectible. North Carolina is a community property state and I have marital interest in whatever is in Daniel's name."

"You don't know a fuckin' thing," Daniel's fist came down hard on the butcher-block island top. "You're a fuckin' liar! All of you!," Daniel was seething with anger. Completely out of control. "How many times have I told you not to speak to anyone, I mean anyone, about our personal lives? How many times?," coming around the island he grabbed me.

"I was just trying to correct all of this," My defense statement to them both.

"It's my account and dad is the only name on it besides me! Dad's right, you're a liar. It doesn't affect you. It doesn't have anything to do with you!," By now, Janelle was on her feet yelling at me.

"You didn't believe Janelle or me," Daniel screamed into my face. "You have no faith or trust in what we tell you. Do you? Bitch! The only people you need to listen to is Janelle and me! You're a liar, your shitty banker is a liar, and I'm personally going to call him tomorrow. What is his name?," Daniel ordered.

"I don't know," was all I could say knowing good and well I didn't want Daniel to call my bank and make a scene. Too many people were already involved.

"Liar. You're nothing but a fuckin' liar! We see who you believe and trust. Don't we Janelle? Bitch! It has nothing to do with your fuckin' credit," Daniel continued to rage. "You're trying to ruin me and Janelle. You don't know what you're talking about!," With that, Daniel slammed my arm down and stormed down the hallway, slamming the door to the bedroom.

"Are you happy now?," Janelle glared angrily at me from the kitchen table.

"No, Janelle, I'm not happy now. Lying doesn't make me happy. It makes me sorry for you and your soul," I retorted back at her, and retreated to the couch in the living room to wait for Daniel to fall asleep.

Around midnight the house was quiet and I crept into our bedroom only to be greeted with, "Bitch! It's all about you isn't it? You've ruined another fuckin' day! Why don't you get the hell out of here and leave us alone!," Rolling over onto his side, he stared, seething at the wall.

Closing the door, I retreated into the living room and waited until Daniel began his shower the next morning for work, then I slipped into the bedroom, sliding into bed pretending to be asleep.

Tuesday, November 21, 2006
Daniel and Janelle were in a good mood when I arrived home from work. I could hear them laughing and talking behind her closed bedroom door. A few minutes later, Daniel and Janelle came into the bedroom, both of them smiling.

"Janelle called the insurance company this afternoon and they're going to hold her check until Monday," Relief shown on both their faces. "They said the only repercussion of her bounced checks would be that in the future she would have to go in person to the insurance company with cash to make payments. They are also going to waive their bad check fee since the bank has already charged one $30.00 fee as a penalty," Looking at the two of them smiling, it was as if Daniel and Janelle were best friends, smiling and slapping each other on the back. Best of friends, with Daniel saying, "Oh, don't worry about it, I bounced two checks a few months ago and when I was your age I bounced checks too," Not the normal parent/child relationship.

I envisioned Janelle going to school the next day telling her classmates, teachers and school staff, whomever might ask what her dad's response was to her bad checks, her reply would be, "Oh, nothing, he bounces checks too," Two good 'ol boys bouncing checks and making it through. Beating the system. No big deal.

Nothing was mentioned about the money owed to Union Cross nor when or how that money was going to be paid back. Something inside me just didn't feel it was right to write bad checks to a church or Christian-based school. But then, these things were all controlled and orchestrated by Daniel and Janelle. It was not my place to question or understand only to realize my life was being controlled in every aspect, including my credit by a father and daughter whose authority I was not to question, my place was to be submissive only to them.

Thanksgiving Eve, November 22, 2006

Daniel nor Janelle were speaking to me, which was a relief. I threw myself into making the traditional Thanksgiving brunch. Reliving the past with my children and all our Thanksgivings. Memories of them helping me with the rice Krispy treats and brownies. The conversations and laughter. It was almost as if they were there, sitting at the island bar, keeping me company.

Daniel and Janelle spent the most of the evening in Janelle's bedroom. I could hear their voices and laughter, happy as two peas in a pod. Occasionally coming into the kitchen to get a snack or something to drink. Never a word was spoken to me, I was the enemy.

It was late when I went to bed. Daniel was already asleep. Sliding wearily into bed, I measured my leg length from the edge of the bed, making sure I was positioned where I was supposed to be next to him, no touching or holding the pillow or covers. By now, after over five years of marriage I did everything mechanical and perfect, not thinking twice about what I had become.

Thanksgiving Day, November 23, 2006
Daniel was still not speaking. I continued with the preparation for brunch.

Running the vacuum in the living room, I glanced out the window and noticed Janelle's car was gone. I remembered hearing her earlier in the shower, but didn't realize she had left. Amber and little Stephanie were the first to arrive, followed by Daniel's cousin and her husband along with their two boys. After greeting them, I went back to the bedroom to let Daniel know they were here and to ask about Janelle. The moment I asked, I realized I had made a big mistake.

"She's at work!," Daniel shot a cold, dangerous stare at me. "Why the hell does it matter to you?"

" I'm sorry. I didn't realize she had to work. If I had known, I would have made a plate and sent it with her," meekly I apologized. "I'll make her a plate," Turning to avoid abuse, I attempted to leave.

"Well, I guess I've done something else wrong haven't I?," Daniel angrily retorted, as he stepped between me and the door, blocking my escape. Quickly I retreated into the bathroom, closing the door, sliding down onto the floor, and began to cry. All the ugliness and abuse of the past week, built up inside, came flooding out of me in a river of tears. I was tired of doing nothing right and the two of them defeating me. I was the child;

they were the parents, controlling me. Each tear, a heart-wrenching river of pain.   Meanwhile, family and friends were only a short distance down the hallway waiting for their traditional brunch.

"It's finished, God," I whispered up at the white, popcorn ceiling. "I can't live like this anymore. I've searched for you, but I can't find you in all of this. Please, please, God, help me!"

A few minutes passed, the bedroom was quiet. Slowly I opened the door, a hand clamped down on the edge, pulling the door wide. To my despair, Daniel waiting for me. I tried racing towards the door, but he grabbed me, slamming against the wall beside the dresser. His eyes glaring red in rage. Sliding around the dresser, I tried to escape the pending abuse. Daniel moved with me, one hand in a tight grip on my arm, a finger from his other hand pointed inches from my face. Each advance, forcing me backwards.   Further and further into the corner wall. All the while, Daniel spoke softly, almost at a whisper, so no one could hear him. He raged his nasty verbal torture and threats. I was trapped against a wrought iron table in the corner next to the closet. Holding on for balance to the table, fear engulfed me as I looked into Daniel's face, afraid of what he would do to me. His right hand reached out and shoved me, delivering a deep punch into my left shoulder. I stumbled backwards, my back hitting then bouncing off the iron table. Losing my grip on the table, I slipped sideways, the back of my head hitting the corner and door casing of the closet, forward I plunged, my forehead crashing into the closet door, while my left leg buckled underneath me and my knee went crashing down on the metal guide bracket of the bi-fold door.

I cried out in pain as I felt the sharp pain shoot up my left leg. My body crumbled as my legs turned from steady limbs to jelly flesh and I sunk deeper into the closet bifold doors that pushed open under the pressure of my fall.

"Get up!," Daniel ordered, losing all reality that his voice was louder now and could possibly be heard throughout the house. "You did that on purpose!"

"No, I, you pushed me," I stammered through pain and tears.

"You're a damn liar!," He yelled. "You're not hurt! Get up! I didn't push you!," Daniel refused to help as I struggled to get up.

"You're nothing but a damn liar," he seethed through clinched teeth, looking down at me.

"I'm sorry, I'm sorry," I begged, struggling to get up. Only to find my legs wouldn't work as I limped forward.

"You're not hurt, so stop acting like it!," Daniel ordered.

Limping, sore and scared, I felt like throwing up. Standing somewhat in an upright position, slowly I made my way into the bathroom as Daniel stormed out of the bedroom.

"I have to go on," I thought as I cleaned up my face. "I have to pretend nothing happened" Taking in a deep breath, combing my hair, replacing the tear stained make-up with fresh, I proceeded into the kitchen to finish preparing brunch.

From that moment on, is a fragmented memory of events. So fragmented, even to this day the pieces don't fit together to complete the puzzle. Pieces lost, that will never be found. I don't know how I made it through brunch. I don't remember who all was there, except for Amber and little Stephanie. Little Stephanie, clinging to Amber's leg as I entered the kitchen.

Amber knew I was in trouble, even though I made a futile attempt to hide the abuse with a nod and fake smile. Later I was to find out from Amber that little Stephanie tender three-year old ears had heard Poppee hurting her Meemaw.   Amber swore to never go back into Daniel's house again.

This is what we have managed to "pull together" from reports, pieces of my memory, various people and other resources of the next three days:

Sometime after Thanksgiving Brunch I left. Somehow, I drove myself to the cabin and collapsed onto the floor with just a blanket. The cabin was bare, except for the sheet metal roofing and tools left from the weekend before, and a kerosene heater. Sparse memories or dreams of walking outside to throw up numerous times, throughout the day and night, but mostly sleeping, curled up in a fetal position, on the cold, hard floor. No memory of the drive up to the cabin.

Friday, November 24, 2006
The next morning, I managed to call the Stokes County Sheriff's department. I don't know how I got their phone number or what I said. I don't know how I even knew the address of the cabin, but they found me. Arrangements were made for me to meet the Lieutenant on duty at the Guilford County Sheriff's Department. I was given this cell phone number and instructed to call him when I got near our town. I have no memory of how I got there either, just a piece of paper in my console with his name and number. It seemed like I was completely out of my mind and body and someone else was in control. Somewhere in Greensboro I met up with the lieutenant.   The lieutenant and two other officers followed me to Daniel's house. No one was there. The lieutenant had me call Daniel on his cell phone. I asked Daniel if he could come home. When Daniel arrived, there were three police cars in the driveway, I was in one. The other two officers spoke with Daniel about charges of

domestic violence and arrangements they had made for me to be placed in a women's shelter. The one thing the officer the following week which was planted deep into my mind was that I had been missing for over 24-hours, and my husband didn't even care. Daniel never tried to find me or call me nor did he file a missing persons report. The officers stayed with Daniel in the driveway while the other officer escorted me into the house so I could get a few things.

I was escorted by two of the officers to the women's shelter. It was there my memory comes to surface. Though I cannot remember where the shelter was located.   When the door opened, I found myself looking up at a large, middle-aged, African-American woman. "Come in," she smiled, "It's going to be okay," she continued, "You'll be fine, just fine."

I crossed the threshold, onto a carpet runner that ran down a narrow hallway with a flight of stairs to the left, leading to what I assumed were upstairs bedrooms. I followed the woman into a small room to the right. The old house smelled musty but was neat and clean with dark hardwood floors and rugs scattered. It took every effort I could muster to hold back the tears threatening once again to spill down my cheeks.

"Name?," The woman started as she began filling out the paperwork. The next few minutes were filled with questions, so many questions, I attempted to try to emerge from my own pain and grief to answer, yet everything seem to be an emotional, numbing blur.

The house seemed loud with people and children, running up and down the hallways, doors slamming and loud voices. I laid on the narrow, twin bed, curled up once again in a fetal position. Slowly I drifted off to sleep, only to wake up hours later startled and scared. It was dark, and sometime in the early morning.

"I've got to get out of here!," thoughts of Daniel finding me were pushing me into panic. I needed to keep running. Quickly I gathered my things and the few items the woman at check-in had given me, soap, washcloth, toothbrush, a small tube of toothpaste and a trial size of shampoo, and quietly shut the bedroom door behind me. The hallway was silent in sleep. Slowly, with shaky legs, I crept down the wooden staircase I made my way and out the front door.

The sky was dark, crisp and clear. Bright with stars. I could see my frantic breath in the cold air as I ran towards my car. Once again, I drove myself back to the cabin where once again I laid on the floor and slept. It was the only place I felt safe and far enough away from Daniel.

Saturday, November 25, 2006

"Wake-up," a small, quiet voice deep inside of me was trying to pull me awake. "You've got to get up!," Someone was speaking to me, but I never knew who. No one was there.   Throughout the day I struggled with exhaustion, wanting nothing more than to sleep, wrapped up in my coat and a blanket on the cold, hard floor.

"Choose life," Were the strong words I heard running through my head. "Choose life, choose your children," Slowly becoming aware of my surroundings, slowly I was waking up. I was one of God's creations. During the early years of my life, I had dedicated my life to God. I missed my life, the life God had given me before Daniel and Janelle. I missed my children.

"Oh God, how could this have happened?," I cried, "How could I have screwed up my life over the last five years?"

"Never again, life is good, life is a gift," I was determined to erase the bad memories I began to sing hymns, quote scripture and bible stories repeatedly over and over in my mind as I rocked myself, wrapped in a blanket, in front of the kerosene heater on the cold, hard bare cabin floor.

"I deserve my children. I deserve a life far better than this," Weakly I forced myself up off the floor. My entire body was sore, especially my left leg. I struggled over to the front door and walked out onto on the deck. The sun threw its rays of warmth on my cheeks as I glanced over the treetops and up at the tall mountains. The view was breathtaking. The cool, fresh mountain air, just enough to energize me to thinking a little more sensibly.

"The children," I thought. "I've got to get back to Amber, Matt and Evan," Looking around one last time, I went back inside the cabin and shut off the heater. Locking the door, I stiffly made my way down the steep steps to my car and left the cabin.

Without a plan of action, I drove towards home. My heart began to race as I drew closer and closer to Greensboro. Closer and closer to the possibility of seeing or being found by Daniel or Janelle.

"Rooms starting at $49.00 a night. Weekly stays discounted," The sign read on an extended stay motel on the outskirts of town.

I was exhausted and weak, the strong desire to sleep overwhelming me once again. With what little belongings I had, I walked up to the young man who reminded me of Matt. Small in frame, around twenty-four years of age with dark hair and dark brown eyes.

"Do you have a room for the week?," I asked. "I don't need much, just the cheapest you have."

"No problem," he searched the computer. "First or second floor?," I fumbled in my purse for a credit card and driver's license.

"Second," I spoke almost too quickly. It seemed as if the farthest I could get from the entrance and street the safer I would be from Daniel. Why? I didn't know. I just panicked and was glad the clerk didn't hear the panic in my voice. "You'll be okay. You're safe here. There's no way Daniel will find you here," I heard that same voice from the cabin say. I was at least twelve maybe fifteen miles from Daniel's. The motel wasn't directly on the main road, it sat behind a professional office park and the parking spaces were not visible from the road, My car would be hidden on the side of the building.

"Ma'am?," I'm not sure how long I had been lost in thought and fear of being found but it must have been enough for me to temporarily "check out mentally," not hearing desk clerk. A questioningly look on his face, his hand held out with my credit card, driver's license and pen to sign the bill.

"I'm sorry," I nervously apologized.

Glancing over the bill, $279.00 total for the week. "I can do that," I thought. "It'll hurt a little but I'll make it."

"Thank you, and let us know if you need anything," the young man kindly stated as I took the key and copy of the receipt.

It was a suite complete with a small kitchenette containing a small stove, refrigerator, microwave, and dishes, everything I needed to cook and eat my meals inside. A half wall separated the small kitchen from the queen-size bed and a floral sofa that matched the drapes perfectly on the opposite wall where the entrance to the bathroom was. The setting of the sun reflected through the white panel curtains.

Only briefly did I sum up my surroundings and living conditions for the next week. Exhausted, I collapsed crossways onto the bed, placing one pillow under my head and one to curl up to for comfort and security.

That was the first of many nightmares. Nightmares laced with my own screams that kept waking me. Disturbing memories, playing out in my sub-conscious mind. At times, I would jump up out of the sleep, shaking and crying, my heart pounding in fear, only to collapse back on the bed, back into a deep sleep.

Throughout the night, I struggled with flashbacks of horrible memories torturing me. A part of me running in my sleep, trying to escape from Daniel and Janelle in horrified fear. Waking up in the early morning darkness, curled up with the bedspread that I must have pulled off the bed wrapped around me, lying on the floor in a corner of the room. Half-asleep, half-awake, full of fear. I would fall back to sleep after rocking, crying and praying until sleep overtook me once again.

Chapter Twenty-Six: It Is Real

In my wildest dreams could never have imagined a more beautiful place. The driveway Gary, Cindy and I drove down was gravel and winding. A split rail fence outlined the front and ran down the right side of the driveway. By now it was dark, the sky was clear, sprinkled with bright, twinkling stars. The moon loomed directly in front of us as we approached the main house. Trees shadowed what Granny Sara called "lace against" the sky, a phrase I use to love to hear. You only saw the lace in the dead of winter, when all the leaves had fallen off the trees. The bare, naked branches, high up in the sky, created God's reflective pattern of gray lace against a dark sky. To the left of the drive was a forest of trees, to the right a pasture with silhouettes of horses and a small pond.

However, the first thing that really caught my eye at the top of the driveway as we began our descend down the long driveway was a very bright star. A star that stood out so brightly directly in front of us that I almost thought it was lights from an airplane, but soon realized it wasn't. One star, so bright it seemed to lead us to the cottage. The drive dipped up and down, we swerved to avoid deep potholes, yet the star stayed as a constant visible. It reminded me of the "Star of Bethlehem," the star that led the wise men to the newborn king. Even though my curiosity of the surrounding settings of my new home forced me to glance away from the star, my eyes would soon focus back on the bright star. When we arrived at the cottage, the star hovered over the rooftop of the cottage. The star had led me to my new life. A life safe and warm, cradled up securely within the arms of my Savior.

Since that first night of arrival, I have never seen that star again. I've been up and down that driveway many times at the exact same hour of night, yet no star such as that. I see the Big Dipper lined up directly to the right of the cottage and the sprinkle of various stars, but never that one star that shone so bright that one night.

The main house was a beautiful three-story brick house with huge white columns on the front porch. The first thing I realized was that my little cottage was separate from the main house, yet close enough for safety. Marla and Don, the owners, were waiting behind the full glass storm door of the main house and ran out to greet us, along with a black lab, named Jake and a collie mix named, Simon.

Gary and Cindy helped me from the car, while Marla and Don offered assistance with my menial belongings. I was embarrassed at what few items I had, but it didn't seem to faze them. We walked across the driveway, down a small path then stepped onto a covered walkway that led us to the entrance of my new home.

The cottage was small with beautiful, arched dormer windows. It was one bedroom, a combined kitchen/living room area and a full bath. The moment I stepped inside, I felt an immediate sense of comfort and safety. Marla and Don had decorated the cottage with all the comforts of home, a small kitchen table with two chairs, a big brown leather chair and coffee table, a few kitchen utensils, the double bed covered with a homemade quilt.

"I hope it's all right," Marla was apologetic. "I know it's not much, with such short notice, we weren't able to do all we really wanted to do to make it more suitable."

"It's perfect," I exclaimed with a real smile for the first time in a long time. I could feel the sense of freedom and delight. "It's beautiful," I walked in awe at the different angles of the ceilings carved out of the rooftop trestles. "I can't wait to see out the windows tomorrow. I bet the view is amazing," I turned and told them both. Cindy and Gary looming in the background.

"Fifty acres," Marla said. "You can walk them all," she said as she hugged me again. "You're safe now."

"We better go," Cindy spoke.

"You'll be fine," Gary reassured me with a hug goodbye. "We live not far from here,"

"Call us in the morning," Cindy looked into my eyes.

"She'll be fine," Marla assured Cindy and Gary, sensing their concern at leaving me.

"I'll be fine," I assured them both as we walked to the door. "I'll call you."

Sensing my exhaustion, Marla and Don walked with Cindy and Gary towards the door, then Marla stuck her head in one last time, "We keep the side door under the covered walkway unlocked to the main house if you need anything. I'll check on you in the morning. Around 10ish?," she asked questioningly.

"That'll be fine," I smiled as I watched them all walk away, leaving me alone to become acquainted with my new home. For a brief moment, closing and locking the door, I fought a brief moment of fear. "I'll be fine," I reassured myself.

Yet, safely tucked in my little cottage, for many nights to follow, I continued to wake up in the early morning hours, grab my pillow and bedspread, and curl up in a corner of the room, weeping and praying while rocking myself back to sleep. The bed giving me no comfort, only the shelter of the corner, waking up each morning on the floor in a fetal position, cramped and sore. I was like a widow or an orphan. I cried from the pain and memories. I cried from the withdrawals of abuse like the withdrawals of a drug addict. The weeks that followed found me slowly emerging into a brand new life.

On Wednesday, I had a follow-up visit with Dr. Smith. Quietly I waited and watched as she read over the hospital and doctor reports. Looking at her various emotions revealing themselves on her face, it was obvious Dr. Smith was in just as much pain as I.

"I have only a fragmented memory," I broke the silence apologetically.

"That's okay," Dr. Smith came over to comfort me as I sat on the edge of the examining table, my feet dangling down towards the floor. "There are just some things that are best for you not to remember," she explained. "It's God's way of healing your mind. Healing it by leaving out the bad and in anticipation of filling in the good that is yet to come."

"It looks like from the notes from the hospital that the moment you fell from Daniel's last abuse, you shut down in trauma and shock," Dr. Smith began to explain as she sat on the stool in front of me. "Your mind shut down. Your mind was protecting you, isolating you both mentally and physically from the abuse, fear and stress that was to follow."

"I guess that explains my feelings of numbness," I thoughtfully tried to take in all she was attempting to explain.

"It explains why you are unable to reveal full memories, only fragments of the three days after Thanksgiving, the fall, and the voids," no pressure, just her time, Dr. Smith sat as if no other patients were waiting and we had all the time in the world to sort through my questions and thoughts.

"The nightmares and the night walks," I tried to explain to her through my tears. "I'm exhausted in the mornings, I don't remember getting out of bed and crawling into a corner. What's happening to me? Will I be okay?," Secretly I was afraid I was losing my mind, seeking out some type of relief or reassurance from Dr. Smith.

"You're still in trauma; let it run its course," she gently replied as her hand reached out soothingly to stroke my arm. "You're reliving, I'm reliving the past five years of your life," she stated. "Kathy, you've endured sexual, emotional and physical abuse. This time it was only a severe contusion," she said. "Thank God it wasn't worse," she then smiled and stood up, pulling me to her as she hugged me. "I'm so proud of you, Kathy. So proud."

I left Dr. Smith's office with another diagnosis of Post-Traumatic Stress Disorder (PTSD). The contusion seemed to well on its way to healing while the bruises were fading, at least the visible bruises.

The following week was filled with many new starts of healing and a new life. Exploring my surroundings was truly an adventure. I think I must have walked all fifty acres over the course of the week. The farm was located in a very rural town twenty-one miles from where I worked. The three dormer windows greeted me every morning with bright sunlight from the east that completely filled the tiny cottage. No closed blinds and curtains. No locked prison cell doors or cabinets. Freedom. The farm animals consisted of three barn cats and three horses, a black pet rabbit, chickens and the usual possum, deer, jackrabbits and raccoons. Each morning I am greeted with waging tails and "meows" and when I come home from work in the evenings, they are there to greet me with unconditional love. What a change from the past five years.

"It Is Real" is what the sign read on the little white church. I pass a dozen or more churches on the way to work each day on my new route from my place of protection and shelter, but this morning that one small sign stuck into my mind "It Is Real." The sign was meant for the Christmas season. Those past five years of domestic violence happened. It is real. The facts of my life were hitting the feelings traumatic; the denial lessening.

A few days later, we had two very tragic cases causing death due to domestic violence in a nearby town. I do not know the details because every time someone would reference it I would leave the room or turn away. I did not want to hear or know. I received a phone call from a friend of mine who had heard of the case and she tearfully asked, "Did you hear about the domestic violence killing last night?," I replied, "no, and please don't tell me."

"Kathy, we're so thankful you're alive," she cried. Another friend from the police department comes by daily to check on me at work and asked me the same question "had I heard about the killing caused by domestic violence, he had been at one of the scenes," I replied as before, "no, I don't want to hear about it."

"It could have been you," he stated. "All I've thought about since that night was the face of that young mother, and it could have been you," It was too close to the timing and it affected my friends and family deeply. My children call every day, along with friends and family. The realization of what I had been through made everyone aware it was real, it happened and I survived.

On Friday, Daniel left a message at my work that I forgot to sign a check to the insurance company and I needed to call and take care of it immediately. At the end of his message, he said he hoped I was doing well and that he loved me. I didn't return his call. To me, hope was in short supply now, even though I knew the promises of God were still good, no matter what was happening to me. I was still fragile and scared of what the future would hold.

On Monday, Daniel called through a different line at my office and unfortunately, I was forced to talk with him.

"Didn't you get my message on Friday?," He asked. When I didn't respond, his tone quickly changed. "Do you need your clothes?"

"No, I'm fine," I stated.

"You've got mail here. What do you want me to do with it?" I could hear a hint of anger in his voice.

"You can take it to the hardware store on Thursday and Amber will pick it up," wanting the conversation to end quickly.

"That's right. I'm sure you don't want to see me," Daniel temper was rising. "What did you tell the hospital?," He questioned. "For the life of me, I don't know why you went. But I'm sure you told them what a monster I am. What was the diagnosis?," The same questions Daniel had asked a week prior when I hung up on him. Automatically I found myself falling back into that void labeled PTSD (post-traumatic stress disorder.) I was scared and unsure of myself. It had been two weeks since I left Daniel. Recovery, I realized at that moment, was going to take a very long time. Like so many times before, I was back where I had lived over the last five years. Was it real? Was it my imagination? Remembering Daniel and Janelle telling me it never happened, it was not real. Somewhere in that new, small healing part of me, a voice spoke up reminding me "It was real, it happened."

"Daniel, it was real, it did happen," I found my voice scared and shaking.

"Kathy, I don't see how you can live with yourself and call yourself a Christian!," Daniel yelled into the phone.

Once again, I bravely hung up the phone. No more.

Chapter Seven: Hope

The next week I visited a small Quaker meeting just a few miles from the cottage.   The minister's message was of "hope," "Where do you have hope?," was his opening question. Hope motivates. Hope, a steering mechanism that guides us back to where we belong. His scripture reading referenced **Psalm 18:2 "The Lord is my protector; He is my strong fortress. My God is my protection and with Him, I am safe. He protects me like a shield; He defends me and keeps me safe,"** He told a story about asking his wife if there had ever been a time in their marriage that she struggled the most with hope. Her response was when they were separated for three years. The minister never elaborated much about their separation except to say that during that time he just wanted to fly away, disappear and find himself. "I was foolish," he honestly admitted. Nevertheless, what stuck out the most in my mind was he said what drove him back to his wife was the thought of her in the arms of another man. True love.

"My wife never stopped praying for our marriage," he revealed. "It was her hope and prayers that persevered through my selfishness."

The symbol of hope in the Bible is the "anchor" **Hebrews 6:19 "Which hope we have as an anchor of the soul, both sure and steadfast."**

Hope. If I had been something like a film, Daniel's daughter, Janelle, a poster, an antique model or horror creature, any other material thing that he collects as his hobby and worships, the thought of losing our marriage and me would have sent him in a rage. For many years, I watched Daniel fight violently for his hobby to the point of losing his temper, making enemies and overextending himself financially to the point some weeks we only had enough money for food for Janelle. His collection had to be perfect, mint originals. I was not a "mint original," I was not perfect. To him I was a disappointment and a failure. Of myself, I'm embarrassed I allowed the abuse to go on for so long, hurting my family and friends.

I saw the abuse of Daniel and Janelle before I married Daniel but I was in love. I thought I could do anything through Christ who strengthens me. Nevertheless, I was wrong. My marriage to Daniel almost cost me the losing of my family, my children, my friends, my work in Jamaica and even my life. I have to own up to the responsibilities that were mine and leave the failures of my life at the feet of Jesus. I never deserved any of it, nobody does.

When I was going through the few things I managed to grab from my dresser drawer at home with the assistance of the police, I found tucked away in my clothes a prayer I had written one of those many times when I was in the basement closet under the stairwell. A prayer scribbled down with a crayon and a piece of paper I had found amongst the Jamaica Vacation Bible School "stuff" piled in the closet.

"Dear Lord, I wish I was silent and strong. You are my strength. I need you so desperately, Lord. I want to be more like Jesus and able to handle these difficulties with strength and your love as an apparent shield. Can I pray to be still and quiet? Could you change me to be untouched by the anger and ugly words

thrown at me? Please, oh Lord, shield me from these attacks. Please Lord, comfort me. Make me different and stronger. Show me your face through all of these moments. I need to see your face! Let me know you are there and let me not disappoint you. Oh Lord, how I love you! You are my life! You are my strength and hope. You are my future and I need your presence. "Nothing is secret, that shall not be made manifest; neither anything hid, that shall not be known and come abroad," That is your promise, Lord. Let this temper and anger be known in such a way to bring hope and acknowledgement. To bring support and confirmation. Please, oh Lord, let this be my prayer. Let it be known that which is hidden and secret. Thank you for always being there for me. How I love You and lean on You. You are my strength. Please protect me. Make clear what is real and happening to me. Thank you for hearing and answering my prayer. Amen"

That prayer was scribbled sometime in 2004. Revealing how difficult things were and how I was searching for hope somewhere in, that little hidden space of comfort in the tiny closet under the stairwell.

"One woman in five is battered by their male partners at least once. Many times these episodes are related to alcohol or drugs." I read this in the brochure given to me by the hospital. Daniel's abusive nature would have been somewhat understandable, possibly even more acceptable if Daniel's abuse was caused by alcohol or substance abuse. However, it wasn't. Daniel didn't drink alcohol or use illegal drugs. This person was who Daniel really was, a sober, mean, cruel, abusive and destructive human being. It was difficult for me to accept the fact that an individual such as he could be so vile. Daniel had the Dr. Jekyll and Mr. Hyde personality. Only rarely did Mr. Hyde appear in front of other people, only me within the walls of our home. I learned within the first year of our marriage from the DSS episode and hospitalization that others would never believe me if I spoke of this monstrous side of Daniel. Yet, we as domestic violent victims convince ourselves of a hundred and one reasons why we need to stay. "We deserve it, admittance of failure, the children, financial repercussions, our abusive husbands need us, we can help them, fix their pain, on and on I could list the reasons of why I stayed those five years. The worse part I believe was not the physical abuse but the emotional abuse. All the abuses were followed by a "honeymoon period" that could last anywhere from a couple of days to possibly a week, but never more than a week. During those times, Daniel was the model husband who convinced me that I was the "queen of his world." "How lucky he was to have someone like me," A glimmer of hope only to be extinguished by another abusive episode. An abusive roller coaster ride that is so difficult to get off because the roller coaster never really comes to a complete stop.

Domestic violence not only hurts the victim, but it also hurts their family and friends. Though it was the making of "bad" memories, the memories were made and I survived.

The week before Christmas. Gary, Cindy and I traveled once again back up to the cabin to finish the metal roof. What a difference three weeks had made. What a different person I was from the lost, abused woman who Cindy and Gary had taken to the cabin weeks before. What fun and laughter! The "making of a beautiful memory," Cindy and I dancing to the Drifter's cd "Under the Boardwalk" in the freezing cold as Gary was on the roof putting down the remaining tin. He thought we were crazy! Cindy terrified of ladders and heights, even though I told her "someone would hold the ladder." Gary's comical runs to the old "Johnny house" with its spiders and freezing cold wooden seat, while Cindy and I just used the woods. We laughed and I couldn't remember how long it had been since I had laughed and had so much fun. It had only been a month since I had left Daniel and Janelle, and I was slowly coming back to being me, the person Gary and Cindy remembered and the mom my children had missed.

The sky was amazingly blue with big, fluffy white clouds. From the deck, I could see the untouched beauty of God's world. The ground below was soaked from the previous evening rain. I felt a moment of sadness well up inside me as bad memories snuck in. Lifting my head up, trying to make the thoughts go away by taking a deep breathe in from the cool, gentle mountain breeze. My eyes began to cloud again with emotions. At that moment, I asked God to heal the painful memories of the past five years. "You are mine, I bought you and sealed you and no one can take you!," I could hear His response. God wanted to give me a new life, a new purpose, a different direction, holding onto Him and continuing on His journey.

Everybody is somebody for whom Christ came and died for.   I remember the day before my appointment with the attorney to begin the separation process. I was not angry, bitter or full of vengeance. I had spent most of the morning collecting all the appropriate documents from doctors, counselors, both hospitals, Department of Social Services, Police and Family Services; I just wanted it to be over and solely based upon facts and records. There were scars that had to be healed.

With God by my side and the pages of the past, I walked into the attorney's office simply stating, "Here is my life for the past five years, documented only by facts and records, not my words or feelings. I want my life back, I missed me and who I once was," I needed to end the life I had lived with Daniel and Janelle and this was just the beginning of the process. I almost lost me, my identity, who I use to be who I really am and if I had stayed, possibly my life. I almost lost my children, both biologically and those whom I shared my home with as "strays", as well as my friends and my family. Our memories and traditions were struggling.

Why did those years happen? I don't know. Only God can purify our memories. For over twenty-five years, I had fought against family violence and did my best to make sure my children and I were safe as I struggled to break the generational cycle of abuse within my own biological family as a child and I was successful. It gives me great joy and delight as my children reminisce of what a wonderful childhood they had. The family that God and I created is and was a family full of love, laughter, making memories and unique traditions.

Somehow, that dysfunctional, domestic violent behavior snuck into my life when my guard was down. As the Bible says "like a thief in the night," Maybe I overestimated myself; thinking was strong in my faith, good with children and had a kind enough heart to fix anything. Nevertheless, I failed. In God's book, I am now His "unique fixer-upper."

The only thing that Daniel and Janelle could never control or take away from me was my love and relationship with God even during those moments they were critical of God and my walk as a Christian. Those horrible moments over and over when they would say to me, "You're not a Christian; you're a failure, just look at you! How can you live with yourself?," God was there with his arms wrapped around me, loving me, protecting me and most of all crying with me. I didn't deserve those words because I never let Him down; I never let go of Him. I never stooped as low as them retaliating in an ungodly manner by cursing, yelling, physical violence or emotional abusive words. I cried a lot and hid a lot, but in my hiding places, God was always there.

Remember my fear of snakes? I loved Daniel yet I lived in fear of him, just as my fear of snakes. Every curse word, each physical abuse from Daniel slowly cut me into small pieces and each time I slowly grew back together with a piece of me missing. If I had continued to live with Daniel's abuse, it would have been virtually impossible for all the pieces of the real Kathy to grow back together into the whole person I once was. The only thing left of me would have been an empty, thin skin that only remotely resembled a human being. Daniel would eventually succeed in blowing away all the real, true pieces of me. Leaving virtually nothing left of me to grow back together into the person God had intended for me to be.

God is a God of second chances, we fall, we get up, we ask for forgiveness and strength to endure as we wait for those words we long to hear "Well done, thy good and faithful servant," I realized that final day with Daniel I had come to what the Bible and many ministers speak about, "that fork in the road," the road I was on, the road I chose, was not a spiritual walk, it was a tearing down of my spirit and soul, a criticism of God and religion within a home of bitterness, secrets, hatred and guilt. A home that chose to take me, God's precious daughter and beat her down by attacking her faith and questioning her as a child of God. I chose to go back and take the other direction, the one where God held my hand as we walked and filled my inner spirit with His love and joy. No longer a prisoner, being shamed and abused. Like Jesus, I cried out many times in weakness and desperation, "My God, My God, why hast thou forsaken me?" Adversity is a part of our lives and I accept it with humility. I chose the fork that took me be back to the joining of my spirit as one with God.

The separation and normal steps of grieving all occurred during the time of year when we celebrate the birth of our Lord and Savior Jesus Christ. I suffered greatly from the PTSD with 'bouts of sickness and nightmares that was partnered with the normal stress of the upcoming holidays. Yet even though I was broken from a failed marriage, God's amazing mercy, compassion, love and strength was wondrous!

My first trip to the grocery store alone in five years was one the most frightening experience of all. I remember on my follow-up visit to Dr. Smith telling her how I almost broke down in tears in the middle of the store, literally having a panic attack as I stood in fear, shaking, not knowing what to do, terrified at decision-making. The control over those years was overwhelming. I didn't know whether to buy Scott toilet paper or soft Charmin, which brand of paper towels, Brawny or Bounty, which toothpaste was better, Crest or Colgate, which brand of cheese, Kraft or Borden. My life had been controlled right down to the grocery shopping and product brands. Many times Daniel punished me if I picked up the wrong brand of product he and Janelle preferred. For months thereafter, grocery shopping was a challenge for me, as I struggled to get past the idea of punishment and learned decision-making skills all over again. As simple as it may sound – over and over in my mind I had to keep repeating, "It's okay Kathy, you can do this, and you can do this. You're free!"

The day before Christ's birthday, a day of rejoicing and a time of celebration, I was alive and well. I survived. Matt and I went to church together, ate lunch and finished our last minute Christmas shopping. Both Matt and Evan were a little more protective of their mother now and we were spending a lot more time together.

When I returned to my little cottage Evan and Amber were there, sitting on the back of Evan's pick-up truck watching little Stephanie running, screaming with laughter and fun as she chased the chickens around the yard.

Relaxing on the porch, rocking gently back and forth in the wooden rocking chair, I felt happy and safe at last. Completely satisfied at the way everything had fallen into place. Little Stephanie now jumping on the trampoline with my landlord's daughter while Jake and Simon barked at her delight. We were all home together and what a terrific feeling! A gift of peace and joy for the season!   It was a little over one month to date that I had left Daniel and Janelle and I could not imagine those five years ever existing.

Marla and Don came out to sit with us.

"What do you think of your Mom's new home?," Marla asked of Amber and Evan.

"We love it!," Amber's grin, huge and bright. "She's safe. That's all that matters. It's the happiest we have seen her in years!," Evan chimed in as he threw a stick at Jake.

How proud and happy I was as I rocked back and forth, listening as Amber and Evan shared stories with Marla and Don of their happy childhood, their adventurous mom and the way things use to be. I am back where I belong, happy, and alive with my family under the protective wings of my Lord and Savior. What a wonderful Christmas Eve. What love! All the simplicity of life, family, God's mercy and grace. The weather was bright and sunny.

The next day was Christmas. My little cottage felt festive and warm. Sparsely decorated with what few decorations the children and I could afford to buy along with greenery and pinecones I collected during my walks on the farm. As in times past, the children and I spent it together having brunch, carrying out our unique tradition.   The children spent time reminiscing and joking about the things they did when they were younger, and actually confessing to pranks and tales of adventures I was naïve to.

The day was cold and rainy outside but inside our hearts were warm and joyous. It's Jesus' birthday! Matt said a beautiful grace as we joined hands to bless our meal, thanking God we were together, rejoicing in the birth of Christ and a new beginning for us as a family. The thought of how they almost lost their mom and the traditions we created was transparent in each face and within our hearts and minds. Peace, joy and love filled our little cottage. Just the way God wanted it to be and the way we had once enjoyed many years ago as a family.

Once the children left, I knew my day was not complete without taking that journey to Quaker Lake. The place that once was my happiness, then became my hiding place, was now back where it belonged in its' proper order in my life, an inspirational place of peace and tranquility. No longer a place to run and hide. I made the walk around the secluded lake amongst the pine-needled road to Cheryl's makeshift grave. I placed a winter wild flower on her wooden cross and sat beside her, letting my thoughts drift back over the past five years. I thought of Cheryl and could only imagine what her life had been like. I asked God to take care of this special woman and the pain she suffered long before me. What an amazingly brave woman she must have been. Cheryl and God were my strength and encouragement through all our talks, prayers and tears. Cheryl is in heaven and I know she knows my heart and how hard I tried. I felt the touch of God's hand on my shoulder as I cried, while knowing deep down inside that Cheryl lived my life through her eyes from heaven as I felt the raindrops of her tears flowing down upon me.

Chapter Twenty-Eight: The Greatest Gift is Love

One year later, I am still in hiding, but God always provides a place for healing of the spirit. My home continues to be the beautiful little cottage on fifty acres. Thus far, I still have fears and have no desire to leave my comfort and safety zone.

Sleep comes a little easier at night now. No more foot bed measurements, no more sleep pattern abuse. I love jumping into bed, looking forward to snuggling down and falling into a peaceful night of sleep. On my bed are four pillows, two for my head, one that I snuggle to and one that I purposely bought that is actually a pet pillow. It is made of soft flannel and reminds me of Mitzi as I nuzzle down in it. Mitzi passed away in February 2006, nine months before I left Daniel. I wasn't there to hold her or say goodbye.

The little rural town and people have been accepting and friendly. My children visit me frequently and at times, we share evening meals together. All the dreams I once had for my family, the memories we lived once upon a time are back. Oh, how I had missed my children! Oh, how I missed me! I saw a bumper sticker the other day that said, "I was going to waste, but Jesus recycled me," described me at this moment of my life.

Occasionally little Stephanie and Amber come and spend the weekend with me and the "farm animals,"

What joy and pleasure. Recently on one such weekend, after her bath, all crisp and clean, innocently Stephanie took my face in her tiny hands and looked deep into my eyes. I knew the look and knew of the thoughts flashing through her mind; it had been over a year since I had left Daniel, yet she still thought of that day and occasionally, in moments such as this she questioned what happened. Wrapped in a blanket, snuggled down in the big brown leather chair with a book Stephanie asked, "Poppee hurt my Meemaw; he hurt her. Why Meemaw?," I hugged her tight as my voice choked back tears, "sometimes people do bad things," was all I could say. How confusing in her young life it must have been to see the prison of locked doors her Meemaw lived in every time she visited, watching as I unlocked the bedroom doors and cabinets. I wish Stephanie carried voids in her memory just as I carry so she would never remember those events. We allow Stephanie to talk to doctors and counselors about what she heard, and allow her to talk to close family members and daycare teachers if the need arises out of a moment or memory, realizing that you cannot tell a four-year old not reveal her feelings or questions. They are too honest at that age. A pure honesty, untouched from a questioning mind. A tragedy that one day we hope she will heal from and forget. In the meanwhile, we handle her questions with gentleness while I carry the scar and guilt that my precious grandchild was hurt and may never forget her early learning years of domestic violence.

One of the most amazing things shortly after I left Daniel and Janelle was the strong desire within me to write. I spoke with a friend of mine who is a grief counselor asking her what was going on? God had me up and down throughout the early morning hours, jolting me out of sleep, causing me to somewhat "wake up" and jot down notes of things I was remembering, some bad, some good. "God's literally exhausting me with these reminders and His writings" I confided in her. From a clinical standpoint, she explained that my body was not able to cope with the trauma of those five years, and God was slowly releasing the incidences of abuse from my memory as I became healthier.

"As the healing process continues, you become more capable of acceptance that the domestic abuse happened," she stated.

"Plus, when you feel the hand of God driving you to do something, He can be very persistent. He knows what's best," she reminded me.

Yet, I wasn't as confident and sure. But God continued over the next several months waking me up, placing me in front of the computer or with a notepad and pen at the foot of my bed, and writing. God revealing the deep scars within the depths of my post-traumatic stress.

Overcoming the pain of the abuse and walking away from domestic violence, I learned takes an amazing amount of strength. At times, I experienced deeply why 75% of the women stay and the remaining either walk away or are carried out on a stretcher. Many times, I would go to sleep at night weeping and wake up in the morning weeping. I was like the two young fawns I frequently see early in the morning outside my window, legs shaky and constantly looking around, making sure they are safe. This was the hardest thing that taxed my inner strength more than anything I had ever been through in my life. The process lasted for months as the normal process of healing from trauma followed its natural path.

Ruth Graham once replied when she was asked about her relationship with the Reverend Billy Graham, "It's my job to love Billy, its God's job to make him good," That summarizes my years and purpose with Daniel and Janelle. "It was my job to love them, and I did. It was God's job to make them good," In Daniel and Janelle's eyes, I may have been a failure, but I truly tried and suffered a lot of abuse at the hands of both of them. To Daniel, I was a good and faithful wife, submissive to the point of violence with scars that run deep both inside and out. To Janelle, I never wanted or attempted to take the place of her real mother. My purpose and place was to be a friend, to help guide and direct her and in some way protect her from her abusive father.

Fearful thoughts and sometimes-debilitating memories still creep into my mind while nightmares slip into my peaceful sleep leaving my heart pounding in terror. Yet ever so slowly, day after day, I continue to slowly climb the ladder of my life. God holding the sides tightly. His soothing, tender voice encouraging me towards the top as each day begins and each night's sleep awaits me.

So in answer to your question, Evan, as to "Who Will Hold the Ladder?," for a brief moment in time, our ladder was leaning up against an unstable wall, yet God never intended to let me or us fall from the ladder. God will hold the ladder for us, Evan, always.

Jude 24: "To Him who is able to keep you from falling and to bring you faultless and joyful before his glorious presence,"

(The rest is for you to fill in, Lord!)